In wonder, Daryn drew the sword. The blade was clean, new, and glistened wetly, red on gold. He touched the moisture cautiously, and his finger came away bloody. Not his own blood, but Orym's—a man dead one thousand years. Daryn knew that instantly. In the same instant came other knowledge in an overwhelming flood.

The sword sang to the duke of power, and his Sorcerer's Stone joined its own blue voice to Kingslayer's. *Dark king*! they wailed. Daryn felt a heaviness on his brow, the weight of a crown—a thing that was there, but not there. Behind his eyes visions flowed unendingly, alien and familiar, impossible and possible. Time streamed around him, the currents tugging him forward and back across great distances, showing him possibilities, probabilities.

Kingslayer sang to Daryn of power. His power! To use as he would, where he would. He saw Lucien dead, saw mighty kingdoms crumble, and godlike, witnessed the fall of a single leaf from an autumn oak.

A thin moaning sounded in the chamber, and the duke realized it was his own strangled voice.

"No," Daryn groaned.

Power! the sword cried.

"No."

Immortality! Kingslayer promised.

"No!" he answered as he fought to loose his fingers, to release the sword's hilt.

Other TSR Books Books

STARSONG
Dan Parkinson

ST. JOHN THE PURSUER: VAMPIRE IN MOSCOW
Richard Henrick

BIMBOS OF THE DEATH SUN
Sharyn McCrumb

ILLEGAL ALIENS
Nick Pollotta and Phil Foglio

THE JEWELS OF ELVISH
Nancy Varian Berberick

RED SANDS
Paul Thompson and Tonya Carter

THE EYES HAVE IT
Rose Estes

MONKEY STATION
Ardath Mayhar and Ron Fortier

TOO, TOO SOLID FLESH
Nick O'Donohoe

THE EARTH REMEMBERS
Susan Torian Olan

DARK HORSE
Mary H. Herbert

WARSPRITE
Jefferson P. Swycaffer

NIGHTWATCH
Robin Wayne Bailey

OUTBANKER
Timothy A. Madden

THE ROAD WEST
Gary Wright

THE ALIEN DARK
Diana G. Gallagher

WEB OF FUTURES
Jefferson P. Swycaffer

For my mother,

Emily Hamilton Oates Buckley

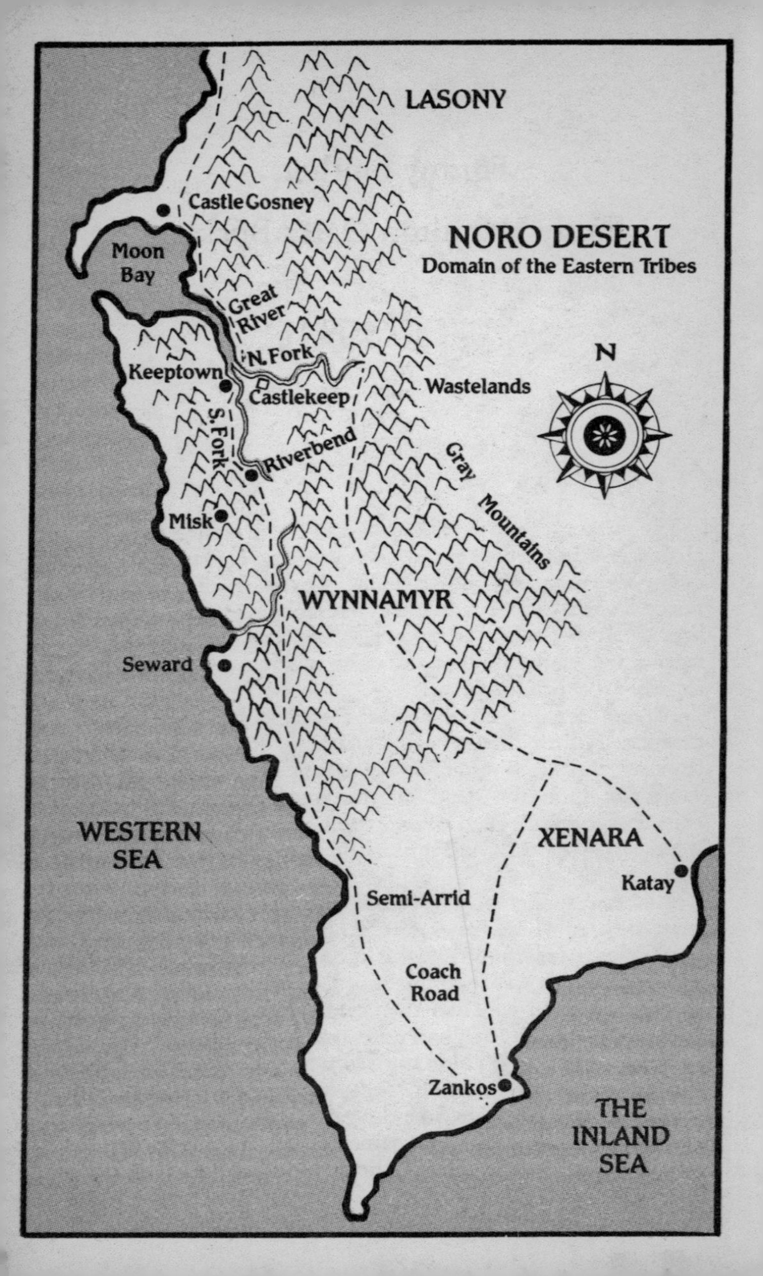
LASONY
Castle Gosney
Moon Bay
NORO DESERT
Domain of the Eastern Tribes
Great River
N. Fork
Keeptown
Castlekeep
Wastelands
N
S. Fork
Riverbend
Gray Mountains
Misk
WYNNAMYR
Seward
WESTERN SEA
XENARA
Katay
Semi-Arrid
Coach Road
Zankos
THE INLAND SEA

Prologue

The memories swirled about him in the darkened chamber. His ancient inhuman eyes saw cascading colors far above and below the range of human sight. Alone. Again. As it had been. As it should be. But the remembrances brought feelings, acute and with cutting edges. He, who could recall millennia, was haunted by the memory of a few moments strung together like precious pearls.

He had meant to kill the child, to destroy him out of hand, that scruffy little man-child—until he'd seen the ring and in the ring, the Stone. That Sorcerer's Stone had made him look more closely at the child. In the youngling he'd seen the thread of empathy that bound the boy to the Stone, an odd melding of earthly and unearthly energies, a certain rare magic.

Misk had spoken of this, but he had not believed her. Poor mad Misk, to whom time came in random spurts, temporality having lost its continuity. She said one would come who could find that which was lost, the sword and the night-black gem that empowered it. Then the child had appeared, Stone in hand, and the old man had dared to hope. More fool he.

So he'd kept the child to tutor him from the *Book of Stones*. Out of pity, he told himself. Self-pity, perhaps—a game with which to mark the time, like the game that had ended in this hideous exile. And like that game before, this one had ended just as badly. He had pushed the boy too fast and very nearly destroyed him after all. In that near-destruction he realized what he'd begun, what he had tried to create again.

It was too awful, too selfish and cruel, so he drove the boy off, sent him back to his own kind with his love and his childish laughter and his unique human tears.

Painfully the memories washed over him once more, and bitter, he knew the cost of his transgressions—to be alone, even more alone than he had ever been before.

One

❖

Sweet summer had fled and in her wake came promises of winter—brisk windy days and chill nights. The change of seasons came subtly to Wynnamyr in dusky greens and grays without the colors of flame to carpet forest floors. It was a deceptive beginning in a land that would soon face torrential rains and heavy snows. Winter often arrived early and tarried late, but so far this year Nature had stayed her boreal hand.

Daryn of Gosney laid a gentle finger on the reins, bringing his blood-bay mare to a momentary halt on the ridgetop. A stiff breeze rippled dark mane and dark hair alike. The mare was tired, sweaty, and salt-encrusted, the warm animal odor of her comforting to him. He gazed for a short time westward, savoring the scents brought on the wind, following the lines of the land with slate-gray eyes.

Ahead, the coastal mountains lay as small and rugged as the native pony that inhabited them. With the wild pony ran elk, mule deer, bear, and cougar, and below, cut deep in the forested valleys, the Great River coursed, harboring salmon and trout. Daryn stood in the stirrups, loosening stiff muscles, then turned the mare south again to travel the narrow ridges to the north fork of the river.

A young man dressed in heavy broadcloth, a dark leather jerkin, and riding breeches, Daryn appeared at a casual glance to be a man of indeterminate means. Of medium height and slender build, he moved with the unconscious grace of a swordsman, which he was and was not, depending upon the situation. A lute in velvet casing, tied behind the saddle, named him minstrel, which he was and was not, depending upon mood and financial necessity.

A closer look revealed the lute to be of exquisite southern hardwood, designed by a master, and the sword, though simple and unadorned, was of the finest tempered steel. A person might look again at the man and see the angle of cheek bone, the large wide-set eyes, and the fine long-fingered hands of a man noble born.

Daryn of Gosney was indeed all this and more, but he was also the third and youngest son of Emil Geofson and stood to inherit little or nothing of his father's wealth and property. He carried on his person the only inheritance that mattered to him—a thin gold ring that his mother had bequeathed him upon her death. He wore it now, his only jewelry, on the forefinger of his left hand. In it was set a homely gray stone, uncut and nondescript—a Sorcerer's Stone.

Few people in this age possessed a Sorcerer's Stone, and of those who did, few had mastered its magical power. Daryn didn't consider himself a master, and though the Stone's power was his, he used it rarely. Or so he led himself to believe. Even now, just a thought from him called to life the subtlest of magicks that set the mare onto the faint track along the ridge toward Castlekeep.

Daryn remembered how this journey had begun. He'd been far to the south in Katay when the missive arrived. Sketchy and succinct, it told of his father's death and requested his presence at the royal court. Irritated, he thought to ignore it. What use was his flying to Castlekeep? The letter was several weeks old, his father long interred. All else would be dealt with by his very capable half-brothers. Daryn felt no rancor; he'd never cared for title or wealth. Indeed, he felt rich as he was, prizing his freedom above all else. Except for his mother, Edonna, young Gosney had never been close to anyone in his family.

Unlike his warrior brothers, he'd had nothing in common with his father. Emil Geofson had been a heavy-handed and overly critical man where Daryn was concerned, finding nothing but fault with his youngest. No, when the message had come, Daryn threw it without a thought into the fireplace at the inn. He had no intention of returning to Castlekeep.

That night, Edonna had come to him in a dream, raven-haired and beautiful, unchanged in death. Daryn's mother had touched his face, a soft butterfly brush of his cheek.

"You must go home," she admonished.

When he made as if to protest the woman smiled tenderly, and her eyes radiated the love he so dearly missed, even now, after all the time that had passed.

"I would have flowers on my tomb, Daryn." And as she drifted away, her voice came back faintly, "Blood-red roses for my tomb."

He stood frozen, unable to follow, but the warmth of her eyes stayed with him long after he awoke. So Daryn had paid his bill at the inn and rode out, first east to the edge of the wastelands, then north along the foothills, cold and barren and dry. At a high break in the Gray Mountains, he had gone west through rugged Claw Pass and, finally, south again to arrive at last on this ridgetop.

Far overhead in a cloudless sky, a lone hawk voiced its high wheedling cry. Daryn shaded his eyes with a slender hand and watched the red tail circling upward in a thermal. On his finger the Stone awoke, pulsing with a soft blue inner light, and he felt a tug at his soul, remembering the unfettered joy and almost drunken freedom the wind could bring a sorcerer. The remembering also brought a prickle at the nape of his neck, a deep shiver. Daryn willed the Stone dark again.

All about him were the foothills he had hunted as a child. Unlike the dense forests of the coastal range, here were dry meadows only meagerly dotted with deciduous and live oak. Only the north-facing slopes, where the late summer springs still flowed, had patches of green.

Daryn spoke soft encouragement to Amber, and the mare struggled up one last incline to stand trembling at the top of another ridge. Far below, the north fork of the Great River ribboned, shrunken and shallow. But the steep banks and flotsam caught high in nearby brush revealed the river's true nature. In winter and spring, swollen with rain and melted snow, it was an awesome force.

Directly across the river, on a neighboring hilltop, sat Castlekeep, home to the royal court. From Daryn's high vantage it seemed near, but the distance was deceiving. Between the young man and his destination lay a league or more of rugged terrain. The sun stood well past the meridian, and, though he had made good time this day, young Gosney would have to push his mare if he was to make the keep before dark. Even now, the hillsides were colored by a golden, late daylight. Somewhere nearby, a meadowlark piped sweetly, and cocking his head, Daryn listened, charmed.

His eyes were on the ancient stones of Castlekeep. The place was as old as Wynnamyr itself. Like the kingdom, it was both rugged and beautiful at once, sitting alone above the spot where north and south forks of the Great River met. The keep was so strategically placed that it had never been taken by force—despite several long and bloody wars with Xenara, Wynnamyr's huge and wealthy neighbor to the south. At the castle's feet, on a small plateau above the rivers, sprawled Keeptown. Smoke from the town's many chimneys drifted upward in the afternoon light.

Even at this distance, Daryn saw the glint of light on the many fountains in the keep's stately grounds. He could see clearly the rose gardens in their last full bloom of the year and felt a sudden surge of homesickness. Eagerly the young man sent the mare in a zigzag pattern down the slope to the river's edge, where he let her drink lightly.

"Enough now," he murmured, urging her on. "Soon there'll be a good dinner and rest for us both."

Obediently Amber sloshed through the knee-deep water toward the small woods on the opposite side of the river. As man and horse gained the trees, Daryn leaned over to slap the mare's neck affectionately. That move saved him. The hair at the nape of his neck ruffled suddenly, and he heard the angry buzz of fletching. An arrow buried itself with a solid *thwack* in the oak bole next to his head.

In one fluid motion, Daryn kicked free of the stirrups and

landed on the ground, sword drawn. A smack from the flat of the blade sent the mare bolting into the trees, then the young nobleman dived behind the oak to stand wide-eyed and wondering.

There was a joyous shout, and a beautiful dapple-gray horse charged into the small clearing. The rider laughed breathlessly, his bow slung over one shoulder now while he fought his mount to a standstill using both hands.

Daryn stepped out to face the rider with a naked blade and a wry smile. "You missed, Lucien."

"A thousand pardons, Lord Gosney. I mistook you for a rabbit." There was no mistaking the insolence in his voice.

The young man wore fine gray leather, well matched to the horse that he sat astride with careless grace. Despite his fragile appearance, Lucien D'Sulang was a heavy-handed equestrian; his horsed pranced beneath him, sweated and foaming. Fair-haired and handsome, he bestowed a dazzling smile on Daryn, a smile that lit eyes of the palest blue with mischief.

"Tis sorry circumstances that bring you back to us, Daryn Emilson."

To hide his irritation, Daryn turned his back on Lucien, intent on locating Amber. Emil was his father's name, and only the titled son could take it upon his death. Daryn's eldest brother, Geof, would be Emilson now, but Lucien never missed a chance to taunt or belittle. Rabbit indeed!

He slid the sword back into its scabbard and cursed silently as he continued his search of the trees for some sign of the bay mare. It wasn't like her to go so far afield, but then it wasn't like *him* to strike her in such a manner. Behind Daryn the gray horse fidgeted, jangling bit and curb, and the young man felt Lucien's gaze on his back.

"Shall I give you a ride to the keep?" Lucien asked at last. "It would seem you're horseless."

So it would seem, thought Daryn ruefully. He turned and took Lucien's proffered arm, swinging up behind him. "You've missed more than one rabbit today," he observed, indicating the young lord's empty game bag.

"In truth," answered the man sweetly, "I was hunting larger

game. Hold tight!"

Reluctantly Daryn put an arm around Lucien's waist, and with obvious pleasure, Lucien put the spurs to his mount. The animal responded with a leap forward that nearly unseated them both, then took them crashing through the woods toward the keep. There was no time for Daryn to think of anything but dodging low branches and staying with the horse while Lucien played a deadly game of thread-the-needle among the trees, giving little if any thought to his animal's footing.

By the time they reached the castle stables the horse was wheezing and foam-flecked. The great-hearted beast was windbroken, its lungs virtually ruined. Daryn fought down an inner seething. He and Lucien had been bitter rivals for as long as they had known one another, but to destroy such a beautiful animal simply to harass his hapless passenger showed a new and even deeper cruelty in the young lord.

At the gate the wild ride ended with the gray rearing to gain relief from a sudden and vicious jerk on the reins. Two liveried stablemen dashed from the yard to help Lucien fight for the animal's head. Daryn simply slid off from behind and backed away to safety. Lucien gained quick and brutal control. He dismounted, smiling, amused by Daryn's obvious disapproval, then turned to speak with a groom.

From the shadowed courtyard a figure emerged, heading toward the stables, a small lean man with a shock of snow-white hair. He wore the neat blue livery of the household staff, and even without the telltale hair, Daryn would have recognized the fellow by his curious halting step, a constant reminder of his days as a soldier fighting beside the old king in the southern wars. Telo had been steward, irrefutable head of the royal staff, for nearly thirty years. He made straight for Lucien, drawing him aside to speak privately.

His eyes on Daryn, Lucien listened to the old servant.

"Well, there you have it," the fair young lord said brightly. "I must leave you here in Telo's competent hands. The king bids me attend him." Lucien laughed. "Too bad. I should have loved a nice long chat with you. There's so much that has happened in your absence."

Telo was obviously growing annoyed, but Lucien showed no inclination to go about his business. The young lord continued, "It appears your horse arrived before us. Gave everyone a bad moment. The whole court's fairly buzzing. Seems they thought perhaps we'd lost the—"

"Lord D'Sulang," Telo interrupted hastily.

"Ah, well," said Lucien with sincere regret. "I must go." With a flourish, he bowed. "Later, then." He headed away.

Telo stood back, looking Daryn up and down, his deeply lined face, as always, devoid of expression. One long moment passed with Daryn uncomfortable under that close scrutiny, then the old man nodded, somehow satisfied by what he saw.

"Welcome home, young sir," he offered, then smiled. It was a rare fleeting turn of the lips, gone in an instant.

"Thank you, Telo." Daryn glanced around. He had expected his brothers to greet him. There was no love lost between the siblings, but they had parted friends.

"Your apartments have been readied and your bags removed from your mount and placed there." Telo nodded, all business once more. "The king is most anxious to see you, but of course, you'll bathe first."

"Of course," Daryn agreed. He would have loved to walk the gardens before the light failed, but that luxury would have to wait until the morrow. Standing there, beside the white-haired little man in his spotless uniform, Daryn was acutely aware of his own travel-stained clothing and strong horsey smell.

They walked, crossing the courtyards in long shadows, passing common folk at the endless menial tasks involved in keeping a royal court at ease. The evening wind brought a hint of wood smoke and roasting meat from the fire pits behind the kitchens. Daryn's stomach rumbled loudly, and he remembered suddenly that he'd failed to stop for his midday meal. If Telo heard, he was too polite to acknowledge it and only continued to march purposefully through the inner courtyard in that rolling gait that best suited his bad leg.

At the door to Daryn's apartments, the young man paused

to thank Telo, thinking the servant would have more pressing duties elsewhere, but the man followed him inside and passed immediately into the bedchamber. Daryn could hear him fussing about quietly. In the large living area where Daryn stood, a fire already burned on the hearth and the lamps were lit. He looked about fondly.

The room seemed unchanged. All the things he'd left behind were here, and amongst them now were some of his father's possessions, mostly weapons and war mementoes stored in a large rack on the far wall—an odd inheritance for a scholarly son. Before the fire sat a favorite upholstered chair and on another wall, a tapestry that had been in his mother's dowry. On a table Daryn spied his lute, Candilass, safe in the protective velvet, but he checked it all the same, using the edge of the cloth to renew the wood's lustrous shine. Then, tuning the instrument idly, he wandered into the other room.

Telo poured steaming water from a kettle into a great copper bathtub on the floor. The scent of roses wafted upward on the warm moist air. The steward had laid fresh clothing from the wardrobe in precise, neat order on the bed: white silk shirt; nut brown velvet doublet with matching knee breeches; fine knit hose; and soft knee-high boots of darkly tanned elk hide, adorned with silver buckles. Daryn recognized the clothing as things that he'd left behind, but the boots were new.

"Milord?" Telo helped Daryn off with his dusty boots and clothes, then whisked the filthy apparel from the room. Daryn climbed into the tub and slipped down into the water with a groan of pleasure. Moments later Telo reappeared, armed with soap and scissors and razor.

"If I'm keeping you from other tasks, Telo, please say so."

"No, milord. I serve the king alone these days, and he has given me leave to help you until suitable servants have been found for you." Telo rolled up his sleeves and drew a stool to the tub.

"How is the king?" Daryn asked as the old man applied a stiff brush to his shoulders.

"In excellent health, milord, but terribly busy this late in the year, what with all the crops and taxes to be taken in."

"And Prince Gaylon?"

Here Daryn had struck a fond chord. The stoic servant smiled hugely. "Ah, the lad's grown so, I doubt you'll recognize him. He's just turned ten, you know."

Daryn nodded. "I remember. How is he doing with his weapons and schooling?"

"Forgive me, sir, but he's a young hellion, that one. He's certainly not forgotten all you taught him. And so full of questions he drives his tutors mad. As bright as a shiny gold coin, he is. And he's missed you terribly, milord."

A tiny thread of sorrow wound itself around Daryn's heart. To dispel it, he asked, "And the Princess Jessmyn?"

"The sweetest jewel ever imported from Xenara," Telo announced. "She's not forgotten you, either, sir."

"That can't be true. She was a baby when I left."

"Aye, but she's six now. Same birth date as the prince's, if you remember, milord."

"I do," Daryn murmured and let the memories flood back. Those were happy times spent with Gaylon in his infancy, and later as a toddler. Gaylon had been Daryn's special ward, always. There'd been an affinity the first time he'd seen the baby prince cradled to his nurse's breast.

The king had been away so much of the time, campaigning in the South, and Daryn, not much more than a boy himself, had become Prince Gaylon's surrogate father, teaching the tiny child to ride, to hunt, to play the mandolin, and to use weapons.

When the last war had finally ended, King Reys returned, bringing the infant, Jessmyn, home—an infant princess, betrothed to Gaylon to ensure a lasting peace and, eventually, bind Wynnamyr and Xenara together through royal marriage. Soon it was as if she had always been with them. After that, no one had dared belittle Daryn, the strange young son of the duke, who at eighteen played with little children rather than seeking out those of his own age, who sang them songs, told them tales, taught them rhythms. No one except Lucien—but that was to be expected.

Then Daryn had had the final confrontation with his father,

all the bitterness, the anger, and mutual disappointment pouring like oil on a flame. He'd fled the keep without a word, disappearing as he had when his mother died, only this time he'd meant never to return. But all that was changed now, though he intended to leave again as soon as his father's estate was settled. Only this time he must face the children and say goodbye properly—if Gaylon and Jessmyn would let him.

With effort, Daryn dragged himself from his reverie. He had been so careful not to dwell on this line of thought when he had first begun his journey, there was little sense in indulging it now. He turned his mind to other matters.

"Telo, do you know where Geof is? Or Garec? I expected them to be here when I arrived."

Telo, agile fingers working at the lather in Daryn's hair, was oddly silent. Then his hands stilled.

"Milord, the king asked me to attend you so that you would hear this first through him." He paused uncomfortably. "I am to tell you that you are now Daryn Emilson, duke of Gosney."

At first the words made little sense, but Telo rushed on through Daryn's confusion. "The king knows how little you care for court life. He feared you might not return if you knew the entire reason for which you were sent. Your brothers were killed in a skirmish with the Anlyn tribes on the eastern border only a year after you departed."

Of all the emotions that assailed Daryn, the most curious was a sudden overwhelming sadness for his father. How lonely he must have been in his final two years of life. The duke would never have admitted to that loneliness. He still had his king—always his king. Emil had been closest friend and advisor to the old king, and the present king, Reys, had inherited that fierce loyalty.

Daryn felt the loss of his brothers, but not nearly so keenly as some would expect. Geof and Garec were only half-brothers and had been grown men when Daryn was born. He'd seen less of them than his father. What a bitter thing that must have been for the old duke, to lose his sons, not in those long tortuous years of war in the South, but in a senseless skirmish with the barbarous tribes of the northeastern desert, to have them die at the hands of those ragged cannibalistic wildmen. He shuddered.

"Were they . . . ?" Daryn began, finding the words difficult.

Compassionately, Telo answered his thought. "Their bodies were recovered. They lie at peace with your father in the crypts at Castle Gosney."

The bath was finished in silence, Daryn gnawing at the knuckle of a thumb, trying to absorb this sudden turn of events. When at last he stood, the water streaming from his body, he turned to Telo.

"My father, Telo? How did he die?"

Again the old servant was slow in answering. He wrapped a great towel around the young duke's shoulders. "An accident. He was thrown from his horse while hunting. The fall broke his neck. He died right away . . . without suffering."

"Alone? Was he hunting alone?"

Telo returned from the bed with the shirt. "No, milord," he said gently. "He was with the younger Lord D'Sulang."

"Lucien," Daryn said. It was almost a hiss.

"It *was* an accident," Telo hastened to repeat.

"Of course," Daryn agreed, but kept his eyes lowered as he pulled on the breeches. Telo helped him into the doublet, while Daryn adjusted the collar of the shirt himself, his newly trimmed black hair curling damply at his neck. He pulled the brocade doublet, stiff and confining, straight. Well, the new duke decided, I can play the courtier again—for a time.

The boots were slipped on next, soft and pliant, cleverly stitched and wonderfully useless for travel, but they were quiet on the stone floor, as silent as the tread of a cat. Daryn loved them instantly. He donned the feathered cap that Telo produced and, setting it at a rakish angle on his hair, stepped over to the full-length polished mirror to admire himself.

"You look splendid, sir!" said Telo, nodding proudly.

Daryn Emilson, the duke of Gosney, turned to the old servant with a boyish grin. "I do, don't I?"

Two

Lucien D'Sulang left the king's presence with a carefully schooled expression on his handsome face, but as the doors of the throne room closed behind him, both body and face went rigid with anger. He very nearly backhanded the young page who got carelessly underfoot.

The boy managed a well-practiced dodge under Lucien's arm, then knocked softly, smoothing his hair and straightening his blue tunic before the great doors swung open. The servants of the keep treated Lord D'Sulang and his uncle, Feydir, as they did any other obstacle—they simply found a way around them and went about their business. The ambassador and his nephew were Southerners, which was all the excuse they needed for their churlishness.

Lucien dawdled in the hallway, loath to miss any chance to goad Daryn. So far he'd been an unsatisfactory target. Three years on the road had mellowed Gosney, but Lucien was certain that, with a little practice, he'd find a tender spot. He'd always managed before.

"Good gods!" he cried joyfully at Daryn's approach. "Is it truly the new duke of Gosney? I hardly recognized you without the stink of horse on you."

Daryn looked resigned, but couldn't resist a return exchange. "And you, Lord D'Sulang, have an unmistakable odor all your own."

Something flashed behind Lucien's eyes, the tiniest glint of hatred that quickly turned to triumph. He chortled in delight. "Oh, you're gorgeous, man, in your frills." And when Daryn made to go by, "What will you do tonight at dinner? Will you sing us a song or amuse us with your great magical powers?"

Daryn's smile tightened. "Excuse me, milord. The king awaits."

"Yes, yes, by all means, the king awaits his new duke." The sleek voice followed Daryn to the entrance. "I wonder though, can the man fill his father's boots?"

Daryn's hand paused a moment at the door, then he turned a last time to the golden-haired youth. "The man doesn't intend to try."

Now Lucien stood alone in the hall once more, with one pale eyebrow cocked.

The throne room was brightly lit, but very nearly empty, the long day's business finally at an end. King Reys leaned his red head close to his clark, and both of them spoke in low tones. As Daryn crossed the great room, the king turned toward him, and the warm smile of welcome faded for an instant.

Daryn had no chance to ponder that strange response as he dropped to one knee at the foot of the stairs leading to the throne. From somewhere behind the dais a small flurry of white lace and green silk hurled down the stone steps at him. He was caught around the neck by small arms and kissed full on the lips by a sticky face that immediately buried itself in his collar.

"Your Highness," he whispered into a tiny ear, "your pantaloons are showing."

"Oh, Daryn!" cried the child. But modesty prevailed, and she shook her skirts carefully straight before climbing back upon the duke's knee and resuming her fierce hug. A great sweet pain washed over Daryn as her arms entwined his neck once more.

Princess Jessmyn, betrothed of Prince Gaylon and young ward of Wynnamyr, peered intently into Daryn's face.

"Why are your eyes watering?" she demanded.

"Why is your face so sticky?" he countered.

"Honey," came the matter-of-fact reply, then the little girl blurted, "Gaylon won't come. He's mad at you. You've been gone ever so long, you know. He says you'll only go away again. I said you won't—you won't, will you?"

Daryn opened his mouth, then closed it again as the monologue continued.

"Will you sing me a song? Where's your lute? Do you still have Amber? May I ride her? Oh, Daryn." The princess hugged him close and sticky once more. "You must never, never, never go away again. Promise me you won't!"

The duke stroked Jessmyn's hair, unable to answer, but his silence made her angry. "I command you to stay!" she snapped, her voice sharp and undoubtedly royal.

Somewhere above the pair a throat was cleared. "Ahem."

"Sire, forgive me!" Daryn bowed his head.

Jessmyn hopped from the duke's knee and stormed up the steps to the throne. "Command him to stay, Uncle. Please!"

"Dearest heart," said the king, "go find Lady Gerra and ask her—kindly, mind you—to wash your face and hands." When the child hesitated, his voice deepened. "Now!"

With a dignity beyond her six years, the girl curtsied and fled the room.

"Please, Daryn, come stand by me. Here at my right." Reys motioned to the young duke. "You must forgive my earlier lapse. I'd forgotten how much you resemble your father, in the face and eyes especially. By the gods, lad, it feels good to have a Gosney beside me again."

"You look well, Your Majesty."

"I am well." The king set his square, thick right hand on the arm of his chair and ran the fingers of his left over closely trimmed red hair; the latter was a gesture Daryn well remembered.

Reys went on. "But we can defer the amenities until dinner. We have a bit of business to discuss first."

"Certainly, Sire."

"Your father was a careful businessman. He's left you a fairly wealthy young man. Now that you've come home you'll find much that needs your personal attention. And there's a lovely young woman come to court whose father is very interested in meeting you. As an only child, she'll bring a fine dowry. Beautiful girl and good bloodlines, as well."

Daryn stared, face blank. After Jessmyn's tirade, the king's rush of words was little better, even though they were spoken in a gentle, persuasive tone. The new duke of Gosney had no intention of being bound to a loveless marriage for the sake of bloodlines.

"Is there a problem, Lord Gosney?"

Daryn heard the formality that came into the king's voice.

"Sire," he said carefully, "I hadn't planned on staying."

Reys's fingers rubbed his short beard. "In some ways you're very like your father." He caught Daryn's gray eyes with his own intent blue ones. "If I asked you to stay?"

"Your Highness, please—"

Reys ignored the plea, slapping the arm of the chair hard. "And if I were to command you to stay, Daryn of Gosney, what will you then?"

"Then I should have to obey my king," said Daryn without enthusiasm.

"You think me unreasonable and totally unfair, but none of us can always have things as we please—not even a king. Come now, don't be the poor loser." He gripped Daryn's arm. "You have no idea how greatly I need you here. Lucien has nearly driven the prince beyond my control, and his uncle, Feydir, is about to drive me insane with his nagging and griping!" The king rose, standing a full head taller than his duke.

"Daryn," he said. "I'm not asking you to take your father's place. I know there were great differences between you. I ask only that you come back to us. Gaylon needs you. Jessmyn needs you." Reys started down the steps, drawing the duke with him. "Let me arrange this marriage for you. The girl is intelligent and witty, as well as rich. If you must feel a prisoner here, let me at least offer you soft prison walls, eh?"

At Daryn's stark expression, the king shook his head. "All right, all right, but at least have a good look at her. You must have an heir. Perhaps you have someone in mind already?" He motioned the clark toward his private offices. "No? Good! We'll see you at table then, sir."

"Yes, Your Highness," Daryn said and bowed, watching the two men disappear behind the high drapes.

Alone in the empty throne room, the young duke tried to let his anger dissipate. He felt suddenly trapped and helpless, caught up in things beyond his understanding or control. Somehow, there had to be a way out of this royal snare. Yet nothing came immediately to mind.

* * * * *

There came a scratch at the door. Feydir D'Sulang, ambassador from Xenara, closed the massive volume on his desk and slid it carefully into the hollow base of the black marble statue near the wardrobe. Then he reseated himself and settled his dark robes over his long, angular form.

"Enter," he said when the scratch came again.

His nephew, Lucien, sauntered in to lean carelessly against the door after closing it.

"Am I interrupting anything, Uncle?"

"So you would wish," Feydir grumbled.

"Fooling with your silly Stone again, no doubt." Lucien smiled a wicked little smile. The lad was an incorrigible tease.

"I've told you, you're not to speak of the Stone." Feydir eyed the boy with displeasure and watched his nephew run a delicate hand in idle insouciance over the fat and ugly statue of Emis, the Xenaran patron god of ambassadors. "Just what is it you want, Lucien?"

"Daryn's back." The hand paused on the marble.

"So I've heard. So we've all heard."

"What do you propose to do?"

"Nothing. I doubt very much he'll stay. He has little liking for court."

"Ah, but the king has commanded him to stay."

How Lucien took pleasure in bearing bad news. With a perversity of his own, Feydir refused to react. Instead, he shuffled the papers on his desk.

"Perhaps he'll be commanded to leave," the ambassador replied thoughtfully, dark eyes unfocused for the moment.

"How?" There was an eagerness in the youth's voice. "May I help? I want to help."

"No," said Feydir resolutely. "Now get out."

Ill-temperedly, Lucien yanked the door open. "You are such a bore, Uncle!"

The ambassador leaned to retrieve the book from its hiding place as the door slammed shut. "And you, dear Nephew," he muttered, turning pages brittle with age, "will one day overstep yourself."

* * * * *

"Jess! How could you!" Gaylon exclaimed in disgust.

"You *are* mad at him. You said so," replied the six-year-old princess with the still-dirty face. She had gone straight to Gaylon's chambers instead of returning to her nanny. Now the child thumped her heels on the front of the dressing table on which she perched.

"But you didn't have to tell him."

"Well, you mustn't be mad at him any longer. He's going to stay."

"Who says?"

"The king says."

Gaylon raked a sandy blond forelock out of his hazel eyes and wrinkled a freckled nose. He was subjecting his image in the mirror to a scrupulous inspection.

"You missed supper," Jessmyn stated.

"I'm dining with the court tonight."

"Oh," she said without rancor. "That's why you're all dressed up." She scrambled down and stood beside him in front of the mirror. "You're getting awful tall," she observed and was rewarded by the boy's look of pleasure.

At ten, Gaylon was beginning to worry if he would ever grow. Of course, to Jessmyn almost everyone was tall. He kissed her on the top of her head anyway, avoiding the sticky cheeks.

Satisfied with his own image, the prince took a washcloth and dampened it in the water basin. Jess submitted to his ablutions with a deference she would have shown none of her ladies. She was a bright child, willful and spoiled, but with an immense capacity for love, most of which was directed at Gaylon.

He was perhaps one of the biggest reasons she was so spoiled. Gaylon, on the other hand, had never been spoiled. It could be said of him that he was somewhat proud and a tiny bit arrogant, but that was to be expected of young royalty.

Elegant in deep blue velvet knee breeches and doublet, Gaylon left the chamber with his princess in tow. Lucien stood in the hall, waiting. The ambassador's nephew promptly grabbed Jessmyn, tossing her high in the air.

"Lucien!" she shrieked. "Put me down!"

"Don't you love me anymore, little one?" The pale eyes for once were guileless, the smile genuine. Setting her on the floor, the fair lord took her two tiny hands in his, while Gaylon watched, smiling indulgently.

"Don't be silly," the princess answered, annoyed. "I'm just too old for that sort of thing."

"Ah, then, are you too old for this?" And Lucien began tickling her mercilessly until the child squealed with delight.

Her laughter brought Lady Gerra, overweight and blustering, down the long passageway.

"I might have known you'd be here, Princess. It's past time for your bath and bed, dearie," she scolded.

"I'm clean. I had a bath." Jessmyn dodged the fat woman's outstretched arms.

"When?"

"Gaylon gave me one!"

"What?"

"I only washed her face," Gaylon said.

"That's clean enough!" wailed the child as she was herded away to the nursery.

Gaylon watched until the pair disappeared around a curve in the hall, then glanced up at Lucien. The lord was ten years his senior and far taller. "Shall we go?"

"If you will lead the way, my Prince." The young nobleman bowed neatly.

They walked in silence along the corridor. Lucien, dressed in fine rusted silk now, remained a careful pace behind Gaylon's left. It was a formality rarely used between them, and finally Gaylon paused.

"Lucien?" he queried. "Is something wrong?"

"Your Highness," the young man said, then trailed off.

"If you're worried that Lord Gosney's return will interfere with our friendship, don't be."

Lucien looked uncomfortable. "Your Highness, the new duke has had a royal command to stay with the court."

"So Jessmyn told me. But it'll make no difference between us. *I* do not take friendship so lightly that I desert my friends." Gaylon tossed the short, formal cape off one shoulder as if for emphasis. The satin lining shimmered royal blue in the candlelight.

Lucien smiled in gratitude, and they started out again, this time side by side as friends should.

* * * * *

Seated at the long trestle table, Daryn made a surreptitious survey of the dining hall. There had been many changes in his absence, some subtle, some not. The court had nearly doubled in size. The plates and eating utensils were silver now, the food more formally served, the diners more fashionably attired, but the bones were still tossed on the rush-strewn floor and many a silk sleeve was still employed as a napkin. There were many old and kindly remembered faces, far too many new ones.

As interested as Daryn was in his surroundings, he realized that several at this table were just as interested in the new duke of Gosney. Well, he was on display this night and must endure it. Daryn glanced at Lady Marcel, seated on his left. The king had certainly not failed in his description of the young woman he seemed so keen on Daryn marrying. Demurely the lady sipped her wine. She was lovely, barely fifteen, and though this was her first winter at court, she accepted it all with a seemingly calm reserve.

Daryn found himself staring at her more than once out of

the corner of his eye. Lady Marcel was as fair as he was dark, and behind eyes of periwinkle blue lay the spark of mystery that marks a genuine beauty. Daryn, usually reserved, tried in his own quiet way to be attentive and she, responding prettily, made polite conversation all through the meal.

Reys watched happily from the head of the table and tried hard not to congratulate himself too soon. Yes, yes, there was definitely something happening between them. He hadn't been entirely honest with Daryn, but not unlike the breaking of a fine colt, the structuring of a statesman from a reticent young lord required a firm but gentle hand. Because of his music, Daryn had never lacked for the attentions of pretty women, but Reys felt he knew the lad's tastes well enough. Lady Marcel was just what was needed to further the king's plans for them all.

Reys offered a silent toast to the old duke. Emil, my gruff old friend, for a time I thought we were lost, but now I dare to hope again. I promise you that he shall be as my own son. The king sipped a summer wine that flowered once again on his tongue.

Gaylon ignored Daryn during the meal—not obviously, for there were certain proprieties that had to be upheld by a prince and heir, and he loved his father far too much to hurt him with ill-behavior. But he talked little and ate little, again without being obvious, and was grateful to Daryn for this much: the man did not try to engage him in meaningless conversation.

The prince kept his attention on Lucien, who was as animated as always, thoroughly enjoying himself and the meal. His antics had Gaylon laughing outright, despite himself, and the ladies nearest, tittering. Feydir, sitting on the left of Lady Marcel, frowned his disapproval. But, then, thought Gaylon, when did the ambassador ever approve of his nephew?

Daryn ignored Lucien's performance, taking time to savor the food so far removed from the simple and ofttimes meager traveler's fare to which he'd become accustomed. Here were some of his favorite southern dishes, hot and spicy; traditional northern meat pies with their rich flaky crusts; a rosemary sherbet; fresh fruits; and trenchers of roast meat and salmon.

The day had been a long one even before Daryn had arrived at the keep, and now the wine and food and warm, stuffy air of the crowded room were beginning to take their toll. He yawned behind a hand and fought off drowsiness, letting himself drift with the music floating from the far end of the hall. A quartet of stringed instruments performed an almost perfect rendition of "The Queen's Repose." The lutenist was good, very good.

"Were you injured?" Lady Marcel asked shyly, turning the duke's way.

"Injured?" Daryn repeated, his mind on the music.

"When you were unhorsed today." At her companion's blank look, she added, "Lord D'Sulang said you were thrown today."

"Did he?"

Even in the midst of his own private conversation, Lucien's ear was bent toward Daryn, and he looked across the table expectantly. The duke seemed prepared to drop the subject of their meeting before it had been properly begun.

"Yes, tell us. Were you injured?" D'Sulang poured more wine into Daryn's cup, a sweet smile of concern on his lips.

With unnecessary care Daryn placed his fork on his plate and leaned forward. "Since I am not nearly the rider my father was, I suppose I'm lucky not to have broken my neck."

Daryn had spoken in a gentle but clear voice, and as Lucien's smile faded so did the conversation at the table.

"That was an accident."

"No doubt," said Daryn, but his tone suggested there was doubt. The young men's eyes locked.

Gaylon watched the exchange in embarrassed fascination. Most unseemly, this behavior at table, but there were many here who disliked Lucien enough to enjoy seeing his game turned back on him. If something wasn't done soon, this would become a matter of honor, and Lucien already had a finger near his knife.

"Lucien, I would have that plate of sweetmeats, if you please," Gaylon said loudly, and Lucien dragged his eyes from Daryn reluctantly to pass the candied fruit. The king shot his son a look of approval and a slight nod that said, "quick thinking."

Utensils rattled on plates again and conversation resumed, but Daryn still gripped his wine cup with a tense hand. He was angry with himself for losing his temper so quickly, so easily. Then came a gentle touch at his leg, and a hand was placed firmly on his knee. A quick glance to the left revealed Lady Marcel eating daintily beside him, both hands above the table. He felt shame at his first thought.

If not her, then who? Marcel's father, Baron Graystone, sat at the duke's right. Carefully Daryn let his napkin slip to the floor and leaned down to retrieve it, casually lifting the edge of the tablecloth.

"Princess!" he whispered. "What are you doing?"

Jessmyn had no time to answer.

"Lord Gosney," the king called, "is there a problem? Has one of the hounds gotten in? They're no longer allowed at table." He motioned to the servant at his elbow. "Cespar, remove it, please."

"Sire," said Daryn, "it's not a dog."

"Well, what then?" demanded Reys, dipping his head to sight down the underside of the table through skirts and boots. "Aha! Come out of there immediately, young lady!"

Daryn slid his chair back, and Jessmyn crawled free. Her night dress was filthy, her hair in disarray, and she ground dirty fists into tired eyes.

"Just what is the meaning of this?"

At the king's stern tone, Daryn saw Jessmyn's face contort and her eyes grow huge, filling with salty tears.

"Well?" snapped Reys.

"I—I—" she stammered. "I couldn't sleep. I wanted Daryn to come play me a sleeping song." Then the storm broke and tears flooded down her cheeks, great sobs racking her small body. The king looked at her, stunned.

"Now, now," he begged. "Come here, child."

Without hesitation the princess fled into the man's arms, and he hugged her close before lifting her into his lap.

"You'll have your song. Hush, now, hush." He blotted her tear-streaked face and motioned to Cespar. "Bring Lord

Gosney a lute."

An instrument was brought to Daryn. Taking it in hand, he arranged himself more comfortably in his chair, then smiled at Jessmyn, who smiled back timidly, laying her tousled head against the king's chest.

"I'll gladly sing you a song, milady," the duke said formally. "This is a lullaby that was taught me in the north country, about a fat little pony that once gave a princess a grand ride." He strummed a chord. The voice of the lute was sweet, but not so sweet as his own Candilass. "It's an old, old song, and the pony's name was Thistledown."

The great hall with all its worldly diners was still, and though he sang quietly to the child only, no one missed a word. Jessmyn, her fingers twisted in her hair, was asleep long before the song had finished.

As the last note faded in the hall, Gaylon shook himself free of the spell and glanced about him. The others seemed as bemused as himself, all of them suddenly tired and sleepy. The prince stared at the duke, wondering. Had the man's Stone glowed almost imperceptibly as he played? Perhaps the music alone was magic enough.

The king rose to his feet, the child nestled in his arms. "I think, good folk, that the evening is done. Safe sleep to you all, and sweet dreams."

There were soft murmurs of assent, and the finely dressed lords and ladies began to disperse. Daryn stood, bidding the Lady Marcel and her father good night. The king paused a moment to speak with Gaylon, then turned to Daryn.

"Lord Gosney, will you escort us to the nursery? I would have a word with you after."

"Of course, Sire." And setting the instrument carefully on his chair, Daryn followed the king from the hall.

* * * * *

The evening had not gone well for Lucien. His dinner sat in an angry knot in his belly now as he watched the exchange between the king and Gosney, watched them leave together. He turned his attention to Gaylon, who stood beside him. The prince was speaking, but the young lord had failed to listen.

"Lucien, did you hear me?"

"Pardon me, my Prince?"

"I said I'd forgotten how well Daryn sings. Did you see how he controlled his audience? I think I shall pay more attention to my music lessons."

"What a fine thought," said Lucien a bit shortly. He saw the brightness in the boy's eyes and knew him to be still slightly under the spell Daryn had woven with his song. The resentment welled up, threatening to drown him. Seething inwardly, Lucien bade the prince good night, thinking to go back to his room where he could vent his anger in private. But the evening was not done. Feydir materialized at his side, gaunt and spectral in his dark robes. His angular face showed no expression, but his displeasure was obvious.

"Come with me," he told Lucien tersely.

Well enough, thought Lucien. He had a few things to say to the old man himself.

They found a servant in Feydir's room on their arrival, turning down the bed clothing.

"Out!" the ambassador snapped, and the man scuttled for the threshold, looking neither left nor right. The door closed gently behind him.

Feydir took a seat at his desk. His throne, Lucien observed scornfully. There were no other chairs in the austere bedchamber, and the young man disdained to sit on the bed, so he stood, trying to look nonchalant. The old man ignored him, playing idly with a stylus, seemingly lost in thought. Drama. How his uncle loved drama. Well, he would give the man no satisfaction. Lucien affected a careless slouch and waited, bored. He had stood far longer than was comfortable before Feydir set the pen down and took notice of him.

"Did you enjoy your meal, Nephew?" he asked casually, and when no answer came, he added, "What game do you play now, boy?"

Lucien stood, stubbornly silent.

"You're up to something. I know you too well. You've been

cultivating this friendship with the prince for months now, and tonight I think you would have gladly forced Gosney into challenging you." Feydir smiled thoughtfully. "I wonder why?" He settled back in his seat. "You consider yourself quite a swordsman, don't you?"

Lucien flashed his uncle a contemptuous look, and Feydir shook his head, amused.

"You know," the man said quietly, "while Gosney was in the South, I received regular reports on him from my people in Katay. The new duke is more than a fair hand with a sword himself." He eyed his nephew speculatively. "Of course, you're taller and have a longer reach. But, no. He'd kill you in a thrice, and where would that leave me?"

Lucien glowered. "I could take him."

"Why, Lucien? Why should you want to? This is more than your usual venom. Does he present an obstacle to whatever little plan you have going?"

"I have no plan, Uncle." Lucien said the words a little too quickly and found himself fidgeting under that hard stare.

"Could it be that you *are* somehow responsible for the old duke's death?" Feydir watched the boy closely. "You think five years a long time to wait for a kingdom. Well, I tell you, you may wait another five years. Or more, if I deem it necessary." All along the ambassador had spoken in a deceptively soft voice, but now it formed a sharp edge. "You will stop your little personal intrigues now, and you will leave Daryn of Gosney in peace. I will deal with the man in my own way. Is that understood?"

It was finally too much for Lucien. His beautiful fair features twisted. "I'll take no more orders from you. I'll do as I please, and it pleases me to kill Gosney and anyone else who gets in my way!"

Feydir reared back in his chair, laughing. "The cub snarls."

"I'm warning you, Uncle."

The laughter ended abruptly. "*You* warn *me*? Watch your tongue, boy!" Feydir snatched a gold chain from under the neck of his robes. The Sorcerer's Stone that hung there pulsed softly.

Now Lucien laughed. "You may have frightened me with that nonsense when I was child, but no more. I've seen no evidence of this power of which you boast, not from you or from Gosney with his precious ring. At least he admits it has little power, while you continue to delude yourself, you ridiculous old goat."

There was something more Lucien wanted to say, but the words were suddenly lost. Instead of the rage he had expected from his uncle, there appeared a cold smile that matched the ice-blue glow of the Stone at his breast. Lucien took a step backward towards the door.

"Stay," Feydir commanded, putting his hand to the Stone, and Lucien found he couldn't disobey. "When you were a child, I beat you for insolence. It's been a long time since then. Perhaps too long." He came to his feet and stood very close to Lucien. "What we need now is a practical demonstration of power—*my* power over *you*. Something to make a lasting impression, don't you think?"

Feydir touched the young man's face with a gentle finger. "Perhaps a scar. Say, from here to here?" He drew a line with his nail from Lucien's temple to the corner of his mouth. Pain followed his touch, fiery and awful. Something hot flowed down Lucien's cheek. He endured silently, unable to do anything else.

"Or perhaps an eye, Nephew. What would the lovely ladies think of you then, an empty socket where your right eye should be? I shall pluck it out with my bare fingers and hand it to you. It's so easy, you see, for the sorcerer who masters a Stone. Put out your hand."

A nausea born of terror churned in Lucien's stomach, cold sweat beaded his upper lip, and his hand came up of its own accord to take the dreadful offering. This time the pain that stabbed the young man wrung a straggled shriek from him, and he collapsed to his knees, suddenly blind in the right eye.

Then, just as suddenly, vision returned, and the pain vanished. The memory of the agony still burned deep, engraved on his soul. He was free! With shaking hands he reached up to explore the angles of his face. Whole, unblemished.

"Next time, it will not be your imagination. Do you doubt me?"

From somewhere, Lucien found the strength to master his voice, to climb back to his feet. "No, Uncle."

Feydir watched the youth closely, saw a new respect in those perfect blue eyes and something more, something buried deep, carefully hidden. Hatred, perhaps?

For Lucien, the distance to the door was greater than he remembered. He gathered his ragged dignity about him and, praying his knees wouldn't betray him, approached the exit with a near-normal grace. Once outside, he paced the dimly lit passageway to his own room. There he found the wash basin and was completely and horribly sick.

Feydir sat a long time contemplating the closed door. It had been a nasty thing to do to the boy, but he'd deserved it. In fact, punishment had been long overdue. Still, there was a chance he'd read his nephew wrong. Instead of reformed behavior, he may have wrought something altogether different. It would be just like Lucien to take this as a challenge. Pity. Lucien was his key to the throne and must be kept alive at all cost. Feydir preferred not to damage him permanently either. After all, the boy was his dear sister's son.

The fire on the hearth was dying. With care the ambassador slipped the Stone back into his robes and, crossing the room, bent to stir up the embers. Well, if nothing else, he decided, Lucien will hereafter mind his manners.

Three

❖

The children were quartered at the very end of the southeast wing, well away from the great hall where the adults might gather late into the night. Daryn stretched to keep pace with the king's long-legged stride. A deep nocturnal chill had penetrated the keep, and they walked in passages musty and damp. On wall brackets, thick candles in smoky glass globes gave off a thin begrudging light.

The oaken door to the nursery swung inward on well-oiled hinges, and Daryn stepped back to let Reys, with Jessmyn tucked warmly in his arms, enter first. The large room slept some twenty children communally and was often a madhouse at bedtime. Now it was still. A single candle on a tall stand flickered in the draught from the door and dimly revealed a clutter of beds, cradles, and discarded toys. The only sound was Lady Gerra's raspy snores from her cot near the princess's empty bed. In Xenara, Jessmyn would have had a room all to herself, but in a small country court, the royal toddlers were raised together.

The king laid the child in the sheets and pulled the quilts up over her. For a long moment he stared down at the small oval face framed in ringlets of honey-colored hair. When finally Reys looked up, his expression was as peaceful as hers. He smiled faintly.

"Come," he said softly to Daryn. "There are things to be said and things to be seen."

* * * * *

It was less a king's bedchamber than a soldier's—except perhaps for the rugs that lay thick on the cold stone floors, the drapings that hung richly on the walls. The furnishings were spartan, a few wooden chairs, a chest, an armoire, and a huge bed covered with soft furs. It was obvious from the surprise on Telo's weathered face at seeing Daryn that this was also a very private place. The young duke felt suddenly intrusive.

Telo busied himself with laying out a heavy robe on the bed until the king's broad hand came to rest on his shoulder.

"Sire?"

"You may retire, Telo. Sleep well, my friend."

"Thank you, Sire," the old servant murmured, bowing. He frowned slightly as he passed Daryn and whispered, "The fire will need rebuilding," then closed the door behind him.

Reys went to a cabinet near the bed and rummaged through a compartment. "Daryn, sit there, before the fire. Be at ease."

One of the two chairs appeared well worn, and Daryn chose the other. He listened as the king continued. "Blasted cold tonight, but I've something here to warm us."

The tall man produced two heavy cut-crystal goblets and a matching decanter filled with an amber liquid. A goodly amount was poured into each glass. Daryn accepted one, sniffing at the contents cautiously. Thick fumes stung his nostrils, and he perceived a sweetish, nutlike scent.

"It's something new, to us at least—a twice-distilled wine," Reys said. "Not your ordinary tavern fare." He took the chair Daryn had left him. The leather bindings creaked as the king settled back and stretched his long legs out on the hearth, crossing his ankles. He raised his cup to his lips, taking three great swallows, then peered at Daryn over the rim. "Go on, taste it."

The liquid ran smoothly over the tongue and tasted of smoke and wood and something undefinable, then turned hot in the throat. Daryn nearly choked.

The king watched him intently. "Well?"

"Very good," the young duke managed.

"Good? It's marvelous! But it'll give you a big head in the morning, if you're not careful." Reys filled Daryn's cup again even as he spoke, then refilled his own and set the decanter with a *clink* on the stones beside him. The flames of the fireplace trapped the king's gaze as he sipped his drink.

Daryn followed suit. The heat in his throat grew pleasant, the warmth of the liquor flowing throughout his body, his mind.

"Your father's death was harder on me than my own father's," said Reys suddenly. "Odd, isn't it? I never realized how much I depended on Emil until . . . he was gone. If you'd ever taken the time to get to know him . . ." He turned bright blue eyes on Daryn, saw the young man's face harden slightly. "No, forgive me. I'm being unfair. It was as much his fault as yours. But you must accept some of the blame, Daryn."

The duke took a long swallow from his goblet, but remained silent. Reys sighed.

"We'll leave it be. I think I've learned how easy it is to expect a thing, even demand it of a son, however unreasonable. Gaylon and I don't argue, but we have so little to say to one another of late." The king's voice tightened. "That's Lucien's influence. Gaylon's been so lonely, but of all the friends he might have chosen. . . .

"Do you know what Lucien teaches my son, besides insolence and dissembly? I've seen them at it in the arms room when they thought no one about. He teaches Gaylon artful murder—trains him in the ways of the assassin. Can you believe it? My only son! A future king!" He turned his head away in disgust. "What else can I expect from a D'Sulang, raised as he was in the courts of Xenara, where a child cuts his teeth on the hilt of a dirk and finds lessons on poisons in his primer?"

The drink had finally loosened Daryn's tongue, and he looked at the king with eager, over-bright eyes. "Give me leave, Sire, and I'll gladly rid you of the problem. Let me challenge D'Sulang on some pretext, any pretext. Let me kill him."

Reys's face reddened almost to the color of his hair, and he bellowed, "Never! I forbid it!" He leaped to his feet.

"Sire—"

"Listen to me, Daryn." Reys lowered his voice. "Lucien D'Sulang is my brother."

Dumbfounded, the duke could only stare, and Reys came to sit on the edge of the hearth, his face close to Daryn's.

"What I tell you here, few men know, and it's best so," the king said. "In his last campaign along the southern border, my father got a child on a noblewoman of King Roffo's court. She was Feydir's sister. How she came to be with my father, I don't know, nor do I care. And I don't blame my father—my mother had been many years dead—but he suffered much guilt over it. You know how unlike old Roffo's lot we are. We're not so lusty a people, and content with one wife at a time. Roffo's misbegotten sons wear their bastardy with pride, and it seems every family in the South has some royal blood, some claim to the throne—hence the murderous bickering that follows that huge court." Reys paused to drink heavily and refill his goblet. "Dasser heads my council now, and he's privy to this information. I've told no others besides you."

"Lucien must know," Daryn said.

"I'm not certain. Feydir does. He's never said anything, but he takes liberties, makes demands—" Reys refilled Daryn's cup. "My father sent papers claiming the child. He begged the mother to come to him that he might marry her, but we were still at war. I can't help thinking that had she come to live with us, Lucien might have grown up a far different man. You see, don't you, why I can't allow violence against him? There are several of my lords who've wanted to challenge Lucien. They're most unhappy with my decisions in these matters. The boy's caused me no end of grief—and now he alienates my son! No, Daryn, you must win Gaylon away from Lucien by wit alone. That's the one thing from you I'm counting on.

"Enough of this!" The king drained his cup, climbing to his feet. When Daryn made to rise, he motioned him back. "No, wait here. I've something to show you."

Daryn leaned back in his chair and watched the man disappear into an adjoining chamber. The room had taken on an alcoholic haze, a misty glow. Tiredly, the duke mulled over the king's words. Gaylon had been coldly polite at dinner, but Daryn had sensed the resentment behind it. Lucien could be so charming when it pleased him—only ask the women of the court to know the truth of that. What Reys wanted would be no easy thing.

Daryn could hear the king moving about in the other room. There was a sound as of stone grinding on stone, then silence. Reys emerged a moment later, a long, cloth-covered object in his hands. He offered it to Daryn.

"What's this?" he asked as he took the object. It was heavy, and the duke laid the thing across his knees, pulling away the cloth to reveal an ancient, ugly two-edged sword. The leather of its scabbard was shrunken and split. The hilt was twine-wrapped and lacquered, the lacquer dark with age and webbed with tiny cracks. With his right hand, the duke drew the blade a short ways from the sheath. The metal was deeply pitted with rust. He glanced up and found Reys watching him.

"That is part of my son's heritage," said the king, smiling. "An odd part. Do you know of Orym's Legacy?"

"Not Kingslayer!" Daryn hissed, snatching his hand back from the hilt as if burned.

"The same. Behold it in all its evil glory." Reys laughed gently. "Hardly seems a thing of legend, but the Red Kings have held it in trust for nearly one thousand years. Your father gave the sword to me upon my father's death, and so you will give it to Gaylon when I die."

Daryn shifted uneasily. "Milord, if this is truly Kingslayer, why hasn't it been destroyed? It turned on Orym and killed him."

"Well, if ever a man needed killing, Orym was the one. Did your mother ever speak to you of the Dark Kings?"

"Never. No one speaks of Orym, except to use his name as a curse."

"Your mother was a descendant of Orym. His blood flows in your veins, Daryn, though I realize it's not something one willingly admits to. You're the first of the Gosney sons to ever wield a Stone. Did you never wonder why? I think your father feared that part of you—your sorcerer's powers."

"My powers are sadly lacking, Sire."

"You underrate yourself. You've always underrated yourself as a magician, a musician, a swordsman. It's one of your most endearing—and irritating—traits." Reys took his chair again. "Listen now, carefully, and I'll tell you the story of Orym's Legacy as your father told it to me—as you must one day tell it to Gaylon. Some of this is known to you, but bear with me."

The man shifted in his seat, and the bindings groaned. "The Dark Kings were the first to rule Wynnamyr. They were a jealous lot, clinging to their power fiercely. They inbred, marrying brother to sister, father to daughter, in order to keep their control of the throne, to keep their dark wizards' powers pure. By Orym's time, madness was prevalent in their family. But it was a cunning madness. When his father died, Orym poisoned his two eldest brothers and garroted a younger one before taking a sister to wife. He was not actually a bad ruler at first, but neither was he good. In all, he was a vain, greedy man who pleasured himself at the expense of others.

"Legend has it that one day in the eighteenth year of Orym's reign, a strange little man came to him desiring to strike a bargain."

"The wizard," Daryn interrupted.

"No. That's a common misbelief. His name is lost to us, but it's said he was a foreigner, hardly able to speak our tongue, and he had no mystical powers. What he did have was a jewel unlike anything ever seen, then or since—a gem with the fire of the stars trapped in it. He offered to forge a sword with the gem fixed in its hilt, to make a weapon with such fabulous power that Orym could subjugate his wealthy neighbors or any nation that might stand against him. In exchange this little man wanted a Sorcerer's Stone, and he wanted Orym to teach him the black arts." Reys took up the decanter, sloshing its contents. "More?" he asked. When Daryn shook his head, the man filled his own cup.

"Of course, Orym agreed. I suppose he had nothing to lose in humoring the odd little fellow. The sword was made and was as wondrous as promised. Orym fell on his neighbors with bloody glee, laying waste to whole cities, killing thousands upon thousands. But when he was asked to complete his end of the bargain, he refused. Perhaps he feared the little man. Who knows? Orym ordered him thrown into the dungeons. The fellow cursed the sword as he was dragged away, commanding that it kill whomever took it up.

"When next Orym tried to use it, the sword destroyed him in a most horrible way. They say his flesh melted from his bones like wax. By then, though, Orym had grown so evil and cruel that his own people had already turned against him. After his death a pogrom began—every blood relation of the Dark Kings that could be found was put to the sword. Next, every witch, every magician in the lands along the Western Sea was hunted down and killed. People so feared magic that for hundreds of years after, the mere possession of a Sorcerer's Stone meant instant death. There has never been a sorcerer-king since. My family, being of a distant royal line, was chosen to rule because we were plain, simple folk—as slow-witted and steady going as the cattle we raised, with not a whit of mystical blood in the lot." Reys smiled wryly. "No one knows what became of the sword's creator. And there you have it. As to how much is to be believed . . ."

Daryn leaned forward in his chair, the sword still heavy across his knees. "What of the jewel that powered Kingslayer? What happened to that?"

"Unknown. The sword is as it was when it was entrusted to us, but a riddle comes with it. Here." Reys passed a tiny bit of parchment to the duke. "It's in the ancient script. Read it aloud. I was never good with dead languages."

Daryn unrolled the brittle paper carefully, scanning the runelike letters. His tongue felt leaden, and he licked his lips.

"As royal blood is turned to rust,
So then does gold become as dust.
The king's bane is the sorcerer's lot.
What is not, is—what is, is not."

He glanced at Reys. "What does it mean?"

"My father's father's father might have been able to tell you, but I can't. Another part of the legend says that one day a Red King will rise to master Kingslayer and undo the evil

Orym perpetrated with it. Personally, I've never seen the legend as anything but an old wives' tale, but family tradition requires the passing of the sword from father to son through a Gosney. And you're the only Gosney I have." He regarded Daryn almost sadly now. "Twenty long years of war with Xenara has been hard on us. Never have the Gosneys or the descendants of the Red Kings been so few in numbers."

"But we won the war, finally," Daryn offered.

"Did we?" Reys lifted a shaggy red brow. "We've won an uneasy peace, that's all. Our country is so inhospitable, so poor of climate and rugged of terrain, that we were able to defend it, but Xenara will take what it wants in the end."

"How so?"

"With one tiny princess. What they couldn't take by force, they'll gain through Jessmyn. When she and Gaylon are wed, how can we deny our good relatives the water and trees they so badly need? Our water will make their arid land bloom, and lumber from our trees will build their ships. We're only a tiny, poverty-stricken nation beside a large and wealthy one. They will bleed us dry in the end. Surely you've seen the aqueducts Roffo's constructing already, so sure is he of the future?"

Daryn nodded slowly, suddenly aware of his exhaustion, aware that he was more than a little drunk. Despite Telo's warning, he'd let the fire die.

Reys, silent now, gazed into some far place. Daryn set the sword aside and kneeled at the hearth. A few coals winked in the ashes, and he used the fire iron to scrape them into a pile.

"No," said the king quietly. "It grows late, and I've kept you overlong. You must go to bed. Take the sword, find a safe place for it. I charge you with its keeping now." He smiled. "But, come, sit beside me a moment longer. I've one last thing to say to you before you go, something you probably don't wish to hear, but you'll listen all the same." The smile faded. "Between your father and I, there were no secrets, none. . . . What I say now is no less than truth. Emil Geofson of Gosney had three sons, and, of them all, the most beloved was his youngest."

Something inside Daryn gave a dreadful wrench.

"You don't believe me," the king accused. "I see it in your face. Hear me. Your mother was the most precious thing in Emil's life, and you were so like her, so different from your brothers. Your father's love for you made him feel vulnerable, so he treated you with indifference. He expected more of you, so he was more demanding, more critical.

"When he returned from the campaign in the South and found your mother had died and you had disappeared, he was like a madman. He rode the mountains alone for weeks, searching. But it was as if you had turned to vapor. No one had seen you, knew anything of you. Finally we believed you dead, and the life seemed to go out of Emil. He thought he had lost you both."

"So he beat me near to death when I returned," Daryn said bitterly.

"You refused to tell him where you had gone, or even why."

"I was about my mother's business," Daryn replied coldly, remembering that those very words, spoken so insolently by a twelve-year-old boy, had driven Emil into a murderous rage.

"You never told him, did you? You never told anyone. We surmised some of it. You had the Stone and knowledge of it. Somewhere you spent a year with a master being tutored in sorcery."

Daryn turned his face away to hide his distress. His fingers fumbled at the ring on his left hand. That was not a year he wished to remember. He'd tried so hard to learn to control the Stone's powers, tried so hard to please the old wizard—and failed. He had loved Sezran as he'd never been allowed to love his father, and it hadn't been enough. Sezran had sent him away, forbidding him to ever return.

"You're angry with me," Reys muttered.

"No, Sire," Daryn said quickly. "Never." He reached down to retrieve the sword from the foot of his chair.

"I shouldn't have burdened you with so much tonight." The king's eyes unfocused. "But, somehow . . . somehow it seems that time grows short. That . . ." Then the smile returned, warm and confident. "Go to bed, my young duke. Sleep well, sleep late. In three days I take my son on a hunting trip. I promised for his birthday that we would go to the lodge, but there's been no time in the last few weeks. It's all to our favor though, for you shall come with us. There'll be an entire week away from sweet Lucien." He gave Daryn's shoulder a squeeze. "Time enough to renew old friendships."

* * * * *

Somewhere, far away, a cock crowed. Daryn's bedchamber darkened as the candles, one by one, snuffed themselves in puddles of wax, and still he sat on the edge of the bed, unmoving. Of all the burdens placed on him this night, his father's love was the hardest to bear.

With effort, he finally roused himself and struggled to pull his boots free, then left them where they fell with a dull thud on the rug. Orym's Legacy lay on the blankets beside the duke, as stark and as ugly as before, and he wondered dimly where it might be safely hidden. He hated the thing for what it represented—another bit of tradition to bind him, to hold him with his duty as a Gosney.

Daryn reached out to the sword, this time with his left hand, and the Stone on his finger flickered. Eyes blurred with fatigue, he thought at first that it must be a trick of his tired mind, yet the glow brightened steadily. Curious now, he grasped the hilt.

A vibration ran tingling up his arm, and Kingslayer seemed to leap in his hand. Then a low hum began, building steadily, and with that came a burst of clarity, of energy unlike anything Daryn had ever felt.

In wonder, he drew the blade. It was clean, new, and glistened wetly, red on gold. He touched the moisture cautiously and his finger came away bloody. Not his own blood, but Orym's—he knew that instantly. In the same instant came other knowledge in an overwhelming flood.

The sword sang to him of power, and his Stone joined its own blue voice to Kingslayer's. *Dark king*! they wailed. The duke felt a heaviness on his brow, the weight of a crown—a thing that was there, but not there. Behind his eyes visions flowed unendingly, alien and familiar, impossible and possible. Time streamed around him, the currents tugging him forward and back, across great distances, showing him possibilities, probabilities.

He saw the fire of stars chained within a jewel as black as deepest night and knew their power was his. The sword offered omnipotence! A longing surged through him, threatening to drown him in its intensity. It was partly his own, partly another's. Orym's. Remembered madness and death came to Daryn next, then inexplicable joy and fierce hatred. Desire! He felt a stirring in his loins. All his base instincts were responding.

Kingslayer sang to him of power. His power! To use as he would, where he would. He saw Lucien dead, saw kingdoms fall, and saw a single leaf drifting from an autumn oak.

A thin moaning sounded in the chamber, and the duke realized it was his own strangled voice.

"No," Daryn groaned.

Power! the sword cried.

"No."

Immortality! Kingslayer promised.

"No!" he answered and found somewhere within himself the strength to loose his fingers, to release the sword's hilt.

The pale light of dawn filtered in from the high windows, outlining the furnishings of the room in dingy gray. Kingslayer was a dim, lifeless form on the bed beside him. His Sorcerer's Stone remained dark on his finger. Daryn almost believed that he'd dreamed it all, but he still shuddered uncontrollably. There was a foul taste in his mouth and a smell of ash in the air. So close! Too close. He'd nearly succumbed to Kingslayer's promises.

With loathing, the duke took up the sword in his right hand, keeping his Stone well clear of it. More by memory than by sight he carried the weapon to the far wall and racked it with his father's war mementos. There Kingslayer sat in ugly anonymity among the other rusted blades. He stumbled back to the bed and fell across it, fully clothed, to slip into a deep and dreamless sleep.

Four

Daryn leaned his head back gently on the sun-warmed pillar. The light glowed orange through his closed eyelids, dispelling the last of the hazy, discomfiting memories of the night. The wine had helped. He had awakened with a headache and a dry, foul mouth, unable to face the tray of fruit and cheese that had been left in his room. But he'd taken the wine gratefully. Now it lay a little uneasily on his stomach, though it lessened the throb in his skull.

He'd performed a modest toilet before wandering out onto the broad terrace off his rooms to find the day nearly spent. The afternoon sunlight now dappled his face through the honeysuckle that spiraled up the pillars and along the second floor balcony. The warmth of the day coupled with the sounds of the children playing on the lawns evoked remembrances of his own childhood, here and at Castle Gosney far to the north.

Daryn opened his eyes finally. Just below him, a young man worked in the flower beds that lined the terrace. Intent on his task, the lad didn't look up when Daryn took the stairs. Beneath a silver maple, turned deep purple by the autumn nights, a lone child played. The duke watched a while before realizing that the little girl in long homespun skirts was Jessmyn.

Her back to him, she dressed a small rag doll in a blue baby's gown and wrapped it carefully in a blanket before propping it upright on the stone bench. She served the doll imaginary tea and cakes, babbling incessantly. Daryn smiled. Across the sward, a group of young boys raced toward the princess, whooping and shouting. They paused momentarily to engage in mock battle, their wooden swords clacking and clattering in the still air, then whirled past Jessmyn. She paid them no mind until one bold youngster detached himself from the band and, with a barbaric cry, grabbed the doll by a dangling arm.

When Jessmyn turned around, the outrage was plain on her face. She caught the boy by the edge of his tunic and, using his own momentum to swing him around, put a small leg behind his knee and shoved him over it. He hit the ground hard, the air exploding from his lungs, and she had the doll and sword from him in an instant. The doll she clutched possessively in one arm, and the point of the wooden sword she pressed firmly to his throat.

The rest of the children circled back, and there were jeers of derision mixed with their laughter. Sheepishly the young warrior received his weapon from his princess and raced away with the others in search of easier prey. Jessmyn soothed the doll with matronly concern until she noticed Daryn watching, then the doll was heartlessly discarded, left to lie in a sad little heap on the grass.

"Daryn!"

He caught her up and swung her around, accepting and returning her hug and kiss.

The princess frowned. "You slept all day." At that he could only smile apologetically. Jessmyn ran her hand over his face, feeling the freshly shaven jaw, burying her fingers in the thick black hair at his neck. Daryn grinned at her.

"Put me down," she demanded, momentarily embarrassed. Then, "What would you like to do?"

"How about a walk?"

"Come on then." Jessmyn snatched up one of the duke's hands in both of hers and tugged him forward. "Gaylon's in the practice yard with Lucien. Hurry! I don't want Lady Gerra to see me." She glanced over her shoulder toward the keep. "It's almost time for my lessons, and she'll make me do something silly, like sewing or spinning. I want to learn sword fighting like Gaylon. Will you teach me?" She didn't wait for an answer.

Daryn let the child lead him where she would. The headache had gone, and the night's disturbing revelations were forgotten for a while. They meandered through the gardens while Jessmyn pointed out places of high interest. "That rock is where I fell last week and skinned my elbow," she noted, pulling back her sleeve so he could admire the healthy scab. "And here, Toshi, the gamekeeper's son, caught a gopher. Toshi's very clever!"

Without realizing it, they had found the roses. Jessmyn dropped the duke's hand and picked her way carefully in among the bushes.

"Where are you going now?" Daryn asked, following.

"Here." She stopped by a plant covered with close-petaled white blossoms. "Give me your knife." She pulled it from the sheath at his belt before he could protest.

"Be careful. That's sharp," Daryn cautioned.

She wrinkled her nose in disgust. "I'm *not* a baby," the little girl said and began whacking so indiscriminately that the duke plucked the knife gently from her fingers and cut the thick stems himself, avoiding the thorns.

"Why are we doing this?" he asked, handing the flowers to her one by one.

"For Lady Marcel, of course," she answered, which gave Daryn pause. "This is enough, don't you think? She'll love them. Come on. We'll go past the practice yard on the way." Jessmyn looked up when the duke hesitated. "Don't worry. Gaylon won't mind—really. And we won't stay long. Besides," she added cheerfully, "you don't want to take wilted flowers to the lady."

Daryn trailed behind the princess in wonder as she skipped and danced in high energy on the stone flags. The roses wrapped in a hanky and clutched in one hand, she periodically called, "Come on!" It wasn't long before they heard the sounds of metal on metal.

"Shhh." Jessmyn put a finger to her lips. "I know where we can watch without being seen." She led Daryn to the small gallery that lined the northern edge of the long arena, then into a shaded area where they could look down into the yard.

Gaylon and Lucien had shed their shirts and jerkins. Sweat glistened on sun-gold skin and dripped unnoticed from jaw and brow, and it was obvious to the duke that this was a regular sport for them. With fierce concentration the combatants beat each other back and forth across the hard clay. They fought with edged steel—the slender and gently curved blade that was growing popular in the South—not with dulled practice swords. They were careful of one another, but pulled no punches, and despite Lucien's maturity, strength, and length of arm, the prince at only ten held his own. But they were slowing and had been hard at it for a while by their looks.

With a sudden feint left, Gaylon dropped into the dust and dived under Lucien's guard as only a small boy might. The young Southerner's legs were rolled neatly out from under him, and the two of them landed in a tangled heap, laughing.

"Foul!" cried Lucien, choking on dust and mirth.

Daryn turned in time to see Jessmyn scrambling down the short steps into the yard. He reached for her too late and resignedly followed after.

"Hello," Gaylon hooted when he saw her, then noticed Daryn. The boy wiped at the dust on his face and only smeared it worse.

"Does the king know you're using real swords?" Jessmyn stalked around the man and boy where they still sat in the dirt.

"We know what we're doing, Jess," Gaylon snapped in sudden irritation.

She would not be shaken. "Does the king know?"

"This is a fine piece of workmanship," said Daryn, thinking to divert her. He lifted Gaylon's small weapon.

The prince leaped to his feet, and snatched the sword from Daryn's hands, then glanced at his fair-haired friend, who still sat cross-legged in the dirt. "Lucien had it made for me for my birthday." He turned on the little girl. "You're not going to tell, are you?"

The princess's lips formed a tight, straight line. "Maybe."

"Of course, you aren't," Daryn told her firmly.

She looked unhappy about that, but nodded. "Only, you'd better not do it again."

Daryn caught the glance Lucien and Gaylon exchanged.

"Well?" Jessmyn demanded, giving the prince a hard look.

"Sure, Jess, sure," the boy said halfheartedly.

"These are the new type, aren't they?" Daryn looked with just a little longing at the sword in Lucien's hand. "How do they balance?"

Lucien's blue eyes sparked. "Just a bit different. Care to try one out?"

Daryn frowned slightly as the young Southerner climbed easily to his feet. "No, thank you anyway."

"Please," Lucien said. "I've another here. I can't choose which I like best. You can help me to decide."

"You must be tired—"

"Not at all," argued Lucien, seeing the war that waged in the duke's eyes. "Here." He handed the blade to the dark-haired man, watched him test the temper and heft it with appreciation. "Let's go a bout, you and I." His smile was warm and friendly. "Just a short one."

"Lucien," Jessmyn warned, sensing something beneath this sudden amicability.

"Leave off, will you, Jess," Gaylon said shortly. Even the prince's hazel eyes had begun to glitter with anticipation. "I'd think twice if I were you, Daryn. Lucien's the finest swordsman in the realm."

"Now, now, my Prince," Lucien said with mock humility. "Don't say that. You'll frighten him away."

Jessmyn looked from Gaylon to Lucien, aware of the little game they played. She tugged at Daryn's sleeve. "Please, don't." But she could see the two friends' ploy had worked, for Daryn had taken the sword hilt in a firm grip before handing it back to Lucien. He pulled off his jerkin, shrugging it up over his head.

"A short bout," Daryn agreed, taking hold of the sword again.

"Splendid!" Lucien leaped across the yard to the wall where his clothing had been discarded. He lovingly unwrapped the oilcloth from his other blade.

"Let's go upstairs," said Gaylon, trying to capture Jessmyn's hand.

"No," she said petulantly, refusing his help.

"Well, you can't stay here. You'll be in the way. Listen, we'll get a good seat. This is going to be fun."

"Gaylon," Jessmyn argued as they climbed the steps, "they hate one another."

"I know," he agreed with such glee that she winced.

"You're awful!"

"Oh, what do you know?" the prince retorted. "You're just a little girl."

That callous remark silenced her. Jessmyn looked away to hide the hurt. Ever since Gaylon and Lucien had become such fast friends she'd been shunted aside for the most part. She didn't dislike Lucien—he was always kind to her—but Gaylon she loved unconditionally. Individually, the two friends were fine, but when together it seemed to her that they changed for the worse; the one becoming older than he ought, the other becoming almost childish.

They'd been so close, she and Gaylon, after Daryn had left, finding solace in one another's company, ease for the sudden emptiness in their lives. It was only recently that Lucien had begun to take such a keen interest in the prince. Jessmyn had hoped that with Daryn back things would return to the way they had been before. But Gaylon was ruining it all, and Daryn . . . well, Daryn had changed. She felt his love, but he was somehow different.

The princess watched the two young men in the yard approach one another, one bare to the waist, one shirted; one towheaded, the other dark. They touched pommels to chins in salute, and suddenly she was afraid. In the arena, in the warm afternoon sun, Daryn and Lucien circled warily, taking one another's measure. They were speaking, and she strained to listen.

"By the way," Lucien said, "this is the superior sword." He cocked his wrist so the blade flashed silver in the sunlight. He was still out of Daryn's reach, but the duke was not out of his.

"Really?" Daryn said, unimpressed. Lucien's pale eyes betrayed the next move, and the duke parried his quick probing thrust.

The fair Southerner disengaged. "Yes."

"Have you had the blade long?" They continued to circle out of range.

"Several months. Gaylon's right, you know. I'm quite good."

"I don't doubt that." Daryn smiled, dropping his guard almost imperceptibly. Even so, it was a blatant invitation.

"One other small thing," Lucien said, ignoring the bait for the moment.

"Yes?"

"I think I'll kill you with it."

Daryn's heart beat faster, though he truly believed Lucien to be joking. Still, the threat brought a surge of blood to his head and a giddy rush. That made the duke laugh and wonder briefly why it was that only at times like this he felt truly alive. "Come try!"

And they engaged again, Lucien once more on the offensive—a downward stroke to the left shoulder. Met. The right knee. Met. The sleek blade fell toward the duke's left knee, then at his right shoulder. Met, and met again. They were simply playing; neither man had yet to draw a heavy breath. Lucien backed away, smiling.

"Shall we give the children a show?" he asked.

"Why not?"

This time the two men tested one another seriously, searching for weaknesses. Despite his lack of experience with such a light sword, Daryn was no easy target. His gentler pursuits on the lute served him well in this, giving him better control. Still, Lucien found himself driving the man back across the yard. He halted, watching Daryn move once more out of range.

"This is fun, but not very exciting. I'm going to kill you, Gosney. At least fight back."

Daryn laughed again. "You're too easy."

"You think so?"

"I could have killed you half a dozen times."

"Then prove it," Lucien challenged.

"No. This has gone far enough. We're through."

"Hardly!" Lucien took a step forward, his expression gone cold. "Your death will be an accident. Such things happen often enough in the practice yard—an unfortunate slip of the blade. No one will dare gainsay me." He smiled, a deadly twist of his lips. "The Gosney bloodlines end with you. Lift your weapon."

"I think not."

"Oh, yes," said Lucien and drove at Daryn so hard and quick that the duke reflexively used the one real weakness he'd found.

The blond man had grown used to the lighter sword, and Daryn, having practiced with his heavier blade, had the stronger wrist. When Lucien came in straight, instead of parrying the thrust, Daryn snapped his weapon hard sideways. The blades met flat to flat with a resounding clang of steel. Lucien's sword was flung wide. The fair lord staggered back in shock, only just managing to keep his grip on the hilt.

Despite a numb and aching hand, Daryn held the neat point of the slender blade on Lucien's breast, resting over the heart. The color drained from the young lord's face, but he held his eyes steady on Daryn.

"You see?" The duke backed away, letting the blade drop until it pointed earthward.

From above in the gallery, for just a moment, Jessmyn thought that the match was over, her worst fears unrealized. But, no. Lucien flexed his wrist and took a step toward Daryn. The duke moved back again, refusing to raise his weapon. Another step. They were talking, but she still couldn't make out the words.

"Oh, Gaylon! Lucien's going to kill him."

"Nonsense," said the boy, but he had his own doubts. Despite his easy reply, the prince gripped the low railing with tense fingers.

Daryn said something more and turned away. As he came toward the children in the gallery, he smiled.

"Daryn!" Jessmyn screamed as Lucien lunged at the duke from behind.

Gaylon only watched in mute horror, unable to move, unable to think. But Daryn heard the crunch of boot on dirt, saw the swift shadow, and dodged away, turning and reluctantly bringing up his sword.

The contest was begun again, in earnest now—no time for idle chatter, time only to stay alive and barely that. Blind rage could be disastrous to a fighter, but Lucien's anger was cold and clear. And Daryn found himself with a serious handicap—he couldn't kill the young lord.

In moments they were sweating heavily. Lucien's hair was plastered in ringlets and nearly as dark as Daryn's. The fighters were too evenly matched now, and Daryn had already exploited his one chance. Lucien never once left him an opening. In fact the young lord left the duke little time to think, to breath, to react. Daryn backed in a zigzag pattern across the ground, trying to avoid being driven around so that the long slanting rays of the afternoon sun were in his eyes.

"He's cut!" Jessmyn gasped, having seen what no one else had—a tiny bit of white shirt sleeve fluttering loose.

"Who?" demanded Gaylon. "Who's been cut?" It was quickly evident. A bright red stain spread across Daryn's right cuff. The material grew quickly soaked, the blood running over the back of his hand toward the pommel. In a sudden blur, Daryn switched the sword to his other hand, leaving the blood to drip harmlessly in scarlet blotches on the dust.

"He's left-handed!" Gaylon cried, clutching Jessmyn's arm so tightly it hurt. "I'd forgotten, he's left-handed."

"But he fights with the other," the princess snapped.

"He'll be all right."

"He won't be all right! He's hurt, and Lucien will kill him, and it'll be all your fault!" She began to cry.

That was a sobering thought. True enough, Daryn was very nearly done. Twice he'd stumbled, narrowly avoiding death.

"What'll I do, Jess?" the boy pleaded, close to panic.

"Get the guards, quickly!"

"There's no time."

Gaylon looked down. The swordsmen were directly below the gallery now. The blows ringing in the dust-laden air were mingled with the sound of tortured lungs. Daryn found himself against the wall and rallied enough to push Lucien back, one small step, two.

On the third step back came a shower of white roses, raining down on Lucien from above. One thorny stem caught him along the cheek, another landed under his heel. The boot compressed the lovely petals, crushing them underfoot. The burst of perfume went unnoticed as Lucien slipped. Daryn's blade spiraled down the fair-haired man's, lifting it neatly out of hand. The sword hit the wall, and the stones snapped it a hand's breadth from the point.

In the gallery, Gaylon dragged Jessmyn back over the top of the wall where she had hung precariously to throw her bouquet.

Lucien looked down at his shattered sword, stupid with spent energy, with amazement. A fly buzzed idly by his ear, drawn to the sweat and the scent of blood.

"Well?" the young lord said, when he realized that Daryn still stood with poised steel. He drew a great ragged breath and spread his empty hands in a gesture of submission.

Daryn's breathing had slowed. He, too, had difficulty adjusting to this turn of fortune, having seen his own death all too clearly. He looked at the tall Southern lord and knew he faced a superior swordsman, no matter how much he despised the man. With a sigh he threw his sword in an arc toward the far end of the field. It hit the ground and skittered away. There was no sign of gratitude from Lucien for the gesture. Instead, a flicker of hatred flashed in the man's pale blue eyes, followed by profound disgust.

The children came slowly down the steps, and Lucien lifted his chin. Tiny beads of blood welled on his cheek in a thin line from the corner of his eye to the corner of his mouth, the mark of the falling rose. He glanced at Gaylon, then spun on his heel and strode away across the arena. The prince watched him go, feeling a strange pity, a strange empathy.

Jessmyn opened her mouth to speak, but Gaylon cut her off.

"You might as well have killed him," the prince said to Daryn, voice cold.

Jessmyn turned to Gaylon, stunned.

"You should have killed him," the boy repeated cruelly. "You've humiliated him, and he won't take that." Gaylon retrieved the pieces of the broken sword, mourning silently the beautiful weapon. Then he rounded on Daryn. "Why did you have to come back? No one wants you here. *I* don't want you here!"

The duke, his smoke-colored eyes revealing only the barest glint of anger, listened to the boy's tirade. When Gaylon finished, Daryn continued to stare at the prince with such intensity that Gaylon had to fight to keep from dropping his gaze. The boy took the offensive once more.

"Is there something you wish to say, Lord Gosney?" he demanded belligerently.

"No, my Prince."

"Then you are dismissed."

The duke bowed stiffly. "Milord. Milady."

Jessmyn had recovered one of the fallen roses from the dust, and she slipped it into Daryn's right hand—a peace offering. But the duke took no notice, only turned and headed across the grounds, away from the keep. She looked back and saw the self-satisfied smirk on the boy's face. With deadly accuracy, Gaylon's tiny bride-to-be aimed a kick at his shin, just below the knee, where his boot top ended.

"Ow!" he howled, doing a one-legged dance on the clay. "Why did you do that?"

Jessmyn opened her mouth, fully intending to tell him why, but she was too angry, too hurt. She fled back to the keep with only a wordless cry, leaving Gaylon tight-lipped and furious.

* * * * *

The headache had returned ten-fold, thought-obliterating in its intensity, and Daryn had no idea where he was going or why until he found himself at a break in the high whitethorn hedge that surrounded the parklike grounds of the keep. It was a secret, furtive little gateway, a shortcut to the wooded path that led down the hillsides to the royal cairns, ancient and crumbling—and the newer, stone mausoleums that housed the kings and queens of this age.

Edonna was here. It had been her wish. She didn't want to lie at Castle Gosney so far from kith and kin. Daryn hadn't once gone to visit his mother's tomb, though that had infuriated his father. Death had never held any fascination for him, and even now, he went toward its monuments unwillingly.

Quickly he began to walk and finally to run, a driving, punishing pace that caused the blood to thunder in his head. He reveled in the pain, welcomed it. He was deeply angry, an anger born of frustration, and so he turned it inward. Within the woods an uneasy twilight lay, and gray-green moss hung fingerlike from oak and evergreen. They were ancient trees and dying, but in the way of trees, they would be a long time about it. The duke wove his way among them, coming finally to the low rock wall that ringed the burial grounds.

Daryn went to Orym's cairn. All these years, he'd never questioned why his mother would wish to rest in the Dark Kings' family crypt. The duke paused on the slope before the entrance. The cairn was falling to ruin. Some of the chambers that ran deepest into the hill had caved in and never been dug out. Orym, himself, was lost among those tunnels.

Trembling and weak-kneed, Daryn leaned against the lichen-shrouded retaining wall that held the crypt's single portal. There was no sound but his own harsh breathing, and even that seemed to deaden and fall as if unwelcome. Dipping his left thumb into the tall urn of woodash that stood within, the duke drew a thick horizontal line across his sweating brow to honor the dead, then lifted a torch from the wall. He closed his eyes and tried to envision the rotting, pitch-soaked wood flaming, but his head only pounded the worse. Though the Stone in his ring brightened, he couldn't direct the energy.

"Serve me in this," he half-pleaded, half-demanded in a murmur and tried once more. To no avail. In frustration, he fumbled for the steel and flint that lay on a small shelf above the urn and painstakingly used them to light the torch.

Shadows leaped on the walls as Daryn took the narrow steps that led down into the main chamber. The pitch on the torch crackled, releasing a thick smoke that censed the clammy air. Eyes stinging from the smoke, the duke circled the room until the entrance he sought was found. The Gosney coat of arms—a shaggy brown bear with a coronet in its teeth, barred by crossed lances—was carved in the stone over the tiny doorway. Protector of kings, it proclaimed, a house nearly as old as Reys's and running parallel to the Red Kings for eight hundred years, always advising and protecting. Now the Gosneys were reduced to a solitary young man who wanted only to deny his heritage.

Daryn ducked into the tunnel, the torch sooting the low ceiling, and came into a small chamber that held a single sarcophagus. He found a bracket for the torch before approaching the stone coffin, slowly, almost fearfully. He realized now why he had never come here—for the same reason he hadn't been at his mother's side when she died—he'd been able to deny her death. Even now a small voice within repeated over and over, "She's not here. She's not here." But he could no longer support the lie. His fingers traced the fine script on the endstone.

Edonna. Beloved wife and mother. There was more, but Daryn jerked his hand back as he recognized the words. They were from a poem he'd written years before.

Where are you now, Dark Woman?
I stand alone with night
Cupped in these two hands.

Somehow, Emil had gleaned this one small verse from among the many Daryn had given his mother. It had been Edonna's favorite, though she had accepted each clumsy ode from her adolescent son with equal delight. Now that same son brought her a final offering. Gently he opened his fingers from around the white rose and set it on the lid of the coffin. The petals were crushed, and ragged, and smeared liberally with his own blood. The significance of that struck Daryn, and he was shocked into harsh laughter that sent the pain crashing once more in his skull. Against his will, the laughter turned to tears, a stifled, uncontrollable sobbing. He hadn't cried since the day he'd left her dying, not even when the old wizard, Sezran, had sent him away, not even when his father had beaten him so horribly. The thought of having left her to face death alone was agony now.

Daryn dropped to his knees beside the sarcophagus and leaned his forehead against the stone. The cold surface soothed him. He slid down farther, turning until he was sitting, his back supported by the coffin. A great weariness settled over the duke, and his eyelids grew heavy. Before him, the torch guttered suddenly on the wall, though the air was deathly still, and now, woven in the strong pine scent of smoke, a hint of violets came to him. Daryn's head came up, nostrils flaring, trying to catch that remembered essence. Again, the torch fluttered.

"Mother?" the duke cried hollowly. "Edonna?"

I am here. The words were in his mind, not his ear.

"I can't find you," he said. "See? I've brought you a rose."

Yes, my darling, she breathed, *but I must ask one other thing of you.*

"Anything, Mother." He searched the shadows. "Where are you?"

Bring me the sword, Daryn. Orym's Legacy must rest here with me.

"Yes, Mother. Tonight. I'll bring it tonight while everyone sleeps." His voice was a child's now, the tone begging approval. All around her sweet violet scent grew strong, a warmth against the chill of the room. He felt her near.

Daryn, I shall trouble your dreams no more, for you have done what was needed, will do what will be needed. I have no gifts to give in life now—know only that I love you. And know this, also. Be careful, my son. What you hold dearest will be broken and taken from you. To choose life will take great courage, to choose death will not bring dishonor. And when all is done, I shall come for you. The voice grew faint. *Fear not the dark, my darling, for in it you shall find me.*

Daryn, duke of Gosney, woke lying on the floor, his head resting on one out-flung arm. He remembered nothing; the headache was gone, replaced by a peacefulness he hadn't experienced in a very long while. Curiously refreshed, he rose and inspected for the first time the wound Lucien had given him. It was a shallow slice, just above the wrist. A little salve and a small dressing and it would heal without scarring. The shirt, unfortunately, had not fared so well. The one sleeve was blood-soaked and torn.

The torch had burned well down. Daryn took it from the wall and left the chamber. Full darkness greeted him at the top of the stair. A thin blue light poured into the clearing from a full moon with a halo about it. The weather changes soon, he told himself and smothered the torch in the ashes of the urn. His breath was visible on the cold air, but he felt pleasantly warm as he followed the path through the trees. What had seemed almost menacing in the daylight seemed conversely close and comforting in the dark. Overhead a night bird called once and was answered from another part of the wood. If anyone bothered to ask, he would say that he had walked to town. A thought occurred to him, then: he would bring Kingslayer to the cairn. How fitting that it should lie in secret so close to Orym's bones.

In two days, he would go with the king and Gaylon to the hunting lodge. The trip was not something he looked forward to, but perhaps without Lucien's interference, he might find a way to gain the prince's confidence again.

* * * * *

It had been easy enough to get in. The terrace door had been left wide open. Westerners were fools, all of them—so trusting in nature—and few doors in the keep were ever locked. In the heat of his anger, he had thought to stand in the shadows of the duke's room and murder him, but as the evening progressed and Daryn didn't return, another plan had begun to form, a plan both brilliant and promising a great deal more satisfaction than simple violence.

Carefully, so as not to disturb anything, he searched the chambers until he located what would serve him best—a small jeweled dirk. In one drawer another item was found, a curled bit of paper much like the pages of his uncle's hidden tome. He took that also, then slipped from the room only just in time. Daryn had returned. For one brief moment, he saw the duke clearly in the light of a window. The man was a mess—grimy and blood-stained with a thick band of soot across his forehead. Daryn must have gone into Keeptown to one of the taverns, then tumbled, drunken, into a gutter on his way back to the keep. Faintly amused, Lucien turned his mind to more important matters.

The young Southerner returned to his own rooms in a fever of thought. A message sent by post in the morning would bring him the necessary help. The court physician, Girkin, was very fond of wine and would go on at length on any subject if provided with an attentive audience. And Ketti, the fat woman in the kitchens, had a penchant for blond, blue-eyed boys.

Yes. With careful timing and the least bit of luck, there was a very good chance of gaining everything he desired in a single night's work. And he had two days in which to perfect the details. Of course Feydir might not . . .

The thought of his uncle caused Lucien's heart to hammer in his chest. But the fear brought anger, and the anger only made him all the more determined. He cared nothing for his uncle's long-term plans. The old fool would thank him in the end—had *better* thank him. After all, Lucien thought brightly, I will be his king.

After the initial excitement came a peace that settled gently over the young lord. He drifted easily into sleep and dreamed beautiful dreams.

Five

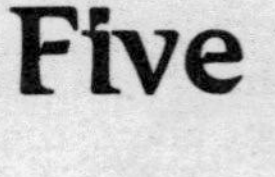

The royal party rode out at first light in a jangle of bit and spur. The morning dawned misty, cold, and gray, and the day promised no better. The clouds crowded low, obscuring the treetops and shrinking the scope of their world. In orderly pairs they descended into Keeptown at a smart trot, stirrup to stirrup, the king, Gaylon, Daryn, and three men at arms. Telo had gone the day before, in charge of the luggage, the servants, and supplies.

Amber acted playful, seemingly glad to be under Daryn's hand again. She danced on the cobblestones, rolling her eyes at a wheelbarrow, shying at a shaggy red dog that dashed from a doorway to yap at their heels. He scolded the mare halfheartedly, knowing it only a game. Time and again, Amber had proven her worth in dangerous situations.

The clatter of so many shod hooves on the cobbled street brought curious townsfolk, merchants and artisans alike, to their windows. Some waved and called hellos, some merely smiled and sat back to their breakfasts. Above, smoke drifted lazily from stone chimney tops over shingle and thatch roofs, and from all directions came an undercurrent of sound, the murmur of life and contentment. In front of the blacksmith's, a flock of speckled hens scattered, squawking.

Gaylon enjoyed the short ride through town. With his stomach full of hot barley, honey, and cream, the wet weather hardly mattered to him. He fought off the little frisson of excitement that rippled through him, tried to recapture the guilt he'd felt at leaving Lucien behind. His friend had been gracious enough about it, saying he had plenty to keep him occupied until Gaylon returned. When questioned, Lucien had been mysterious and a bit reserved. He'd been like that since the incident in the practice yard.

Jessmyn on the other hand had been very angry when Gaylon left. She'd kept silent about the trouble between Daryn and Lucien, and Gaylon convinced himself that she was only upset over not being invited to come along today. Last night, though, the prince had argued bitterly with his father over the fact that Daryn had been asked to the lodge. The thought infuriated the boy. This hunting trip was a belated birthday present, and he didn't want to share his father with anyone, especially Daryn.

Gaylon hunched deeper into his wet-weather clothing. This morning the entire party had donned colorless gray woolen capes and broad-brimmed caps impregnated with lamb's oil, which shed the water easily. And well they had, for as the light grew, the mist turned to a fine steady rain that beaded their clothes and ran in rivulets off the horses' flanks.

Below the town, they crossed the south fork of the river with a thunder of hooves on the heavy planked bridge. In Gaylon's short life the bridge had been rebuilt twice. It was a massive structure, strong and sturdily made, but the river was fickle and what she might leave standing unmolested for twenty years, she'd been known to tear down two years in a row. It would take heavier rains than this to murk her clear waters and fill her steep banks. For the time being she wound her way, docile still, to meet her sister from the north and join the Great River.

The main road west quickly turned to black muck, and the royal entourage slowed the horses to a walk. Gaylon rode Katy, a tiny bay mare with black points, neat and fine-boned from her head to her trim little hooves. Somewhere in her ancestry ran the blood of the hill ponies, and she was a miniature version of Amber. The prince had trained her himself and was extremely proud of her, but it had been more than a week since he'd ridden her last and now she proved a handful. Where the other horses covered the ground with a long-strided walk, she insisted on jogging and, more often, jigging. The little mare fought the curb, splattering Gaylon and everyone else with mud.

The prince had chosen Katy not long after Daryn had disappeared because she so resembled Amber. Each day as he worked her, using all the techniques Daryn had shown him, he thought of how pleased the man would be when he returned. But the days became weeks, the weeks months and finally years, and never a word or hint of Daryn came to the prince. Later, as Gaylon's friendship with Lucien developed, a resentment grew toward Daryn, and Lucien's subtle sophistry only served to feed the hurt, the anger.

Straight-backed and grim-lipped, Gaylon rode Katy now as she danced through the mire, exploding here and there. He saw Daryn giving him a studied look, though the young duke never strayed from the king's right hand, continuing to listen to an all but one-sided conversation.

After a time, Daryn slowed Amber, dropping back in line just as Katy, tucking her chin, jittered sideways across the road. She did a series of little half-rears, hitting the ground stiff-legged until Gaylon's teeth rattled in his head. He resisted jerking her down or putting the spurs to her. It would only make matters worse.

"Give her a little more rein," said Daryn, suddenly beside the prince. The duke's face was lost under the floppy brim of his cap, so Gaylon could only guess at his expression, but his words were low and gentle. "When she tries to surge forward, draw back, then give her back the rein. She'll soon understand what you want. She's got a fine set to her head, but holding her up so close is only serving to make her nervous. It can't be pleasant for either of you." Then Daryn slipped off again to the king's side.

Gaylon felt a flush spreading from the roots of his sandy hair and was grateful the rain and his cap hid it from the others. Anger quickly followed the embarrassment. Daryn had no word of praise, no appreciation for all Gaylon had accomplished, only notes on his shortcomings. Katy wagged her head violently and pulled, nagging the boy for more rein. Automatically he set about putting Daryn's advice to good use, momentarily forgetting his anger. It worked miraculously, for Katy was bright and eager to please.

When the group had traveled several leagues south of Keeptown they left the main road, taking a narrow path that led through the forest and, in a series of switchbacks, up a high mountain toward the lodge. Here they were forced into single file, but at least the mud was replaced by rich forest soil. By now Katy had settled and walked placidly behind the king's tall sorrel, Remy. She still mouthed the bit, but was content to keep her place in line.

Newly dropped oak and maple leaves littered the ground, and though the rain had ended a short while before, the trees and vines continued to drip. The air warmed, and the scent of old summer, moist now, became a heady perfume. The riders began to shed their cloaks. The first rain had waited until late into the fall—not unheard of, but it had made for a long dry season. The folk of Wynnamyr would be in high spirits today; the long months of dangerous fire weather, the time when a single uncontrolled blaze could bring devastation to a country predominantly mountainous and wooded, were ended. The horsemen moved up the slopes in a festive mood. Even Gaylon found himself smiling at some of the ribald japes being bandied about behind him, though one or two references were beyond him. He made a mental note to question his father about them when he could get him alone.

* * * * *

The king, Gaylon, and Daryn had gathered in the huge common room of the lodge to await dinner. Divested of mud-splattered wool and installed, clean and shining once more, in front of an immense wood-burning stove, they relaxed with cups of hot spiced cider. Gaylon wandered the room idly, feeling ignored by his elders. His father, with a favorite book in hand, was draped elbows akimbo on a crude leather and wood chair. Daryn rested, eyes closed, in a shadowed corner where the heat from the stove had driven him. With wide metal doors open, the stove served as a fireplace, causing shadow and flame to caper on the oiled wood paneling of the walls.

The lodge was a pine log structure, notched, stacked, and chinked, then nicely paneled inside with local softwoods—cedar, redwood, and yew. There were hunting trophies everywhere, from the undistinguished horns of a young elk buck on a wall to the unhandsome shape of a stuffed cougar in some fanciful stance of attack near the entrance. The latter was very old. His great-grandfather's, Gaylon believed. And either the taxidermy had been faulty or time was taking its natural toll,. for the poor creature was nearly bald. But it would be left for a later king to deal with and perhaps disturb his ancestor's shade by throwing the thing away. So the cougar snarled hopelessly, endlessly, hairlessly from its place among the rest of the trophies.

Gaylon was circling the room again, fingering this and that, enjoying the tactile sensations, when he noticed Daryn had moved to the round oak table centered in the room. From the hanging oil lamp overhead, light pooled on the table's surface. The duke began to set up the feirie board. The king glanced up once, only mildly interested, then disappeared into his pages again.

Some potentate of Jynlar, a country far to the south—a far wealthier place than Wynnamyr—had sent the dicing game as a gift to Reys's great-great-grandfather. The board was covered in fine felt. The discs of ivory were edged in gold. The case, carved of a dense black wood, was cleverly hinged and inlaid with other hardwoods ranging in color from blond to deep red and set in an intricate spiral design that could suddenly invert when stared at—either by magic or trickery of the eye. If it was magic, it was very old magic, indeed.

Daryn laid the game out, sliding the chips with a click into place, setting out the dice in their wooden blinds. Gaylon found himself watching the long fingers moving effortlessly in the lamp light. The duke looked up.

"Care for a game?"

The boy stood by the table, his young face carefully devoid of expression. At the question, Reys began to watch his son, saw him run a finger along the edge of the game board with just a hint of amusement in his hazel eyes. The slouch, the movement, the bland look were all in perfect imitation of Lucien. On Lucien it was irritating, but on ten-year-old Gaylon it was hateful.

"I think not," the prince answered finally.

Daryn fished in a leather pouch at his belt and, finding what he desired, slapped it to the tabletop with an extravagant gesture. "A wager then!" He took his hand away. On the table, the light struck a small oval stone and was trapped there, sparking sudden bursts of brilliant green and crimson, aquamarine and gold. Unable to resist, Gaylon reached for the gem and rolled it in his palm. The little stone flashed back at him, the colors caught impossibly deep within its crystalline body.

"What is it?"

Daryn grinned. "A fire opal from the great Noro Desert east of Xenara. Some say they grow up out of the sand like flowers waiting to be plucked. I got that one in Zankos. They're pretty, but not very valuable. The stone is soft and mars easily. Well?"

Gaylon could not take his eyes from the opal. "I'm afraid I haven't anything to wager," he said with genuine regret.

"A prince of the realm with nothing?" Daryn winked at Reys.

"Wait!" Gaylon began emptying his pockets onto the table and produced a motley assortment: the molar recovered from the jawbone of a deer found along the trail; a crumbled sweetcake clinging to raisins; lint; and a speckled feather, oddly enough intact.

Daryn picked up the feather. "This will do nicely. Is it a bet then?"

Gaylon balked again, knowing full well what other game was being played here. Still, he wanted the stone. Very much so. He slid into the chair opposite Daryn.

"Done."

They each rolled a die to see who would lead off. Gaylon won.

"I'm very lucky," he warned Daryn, choosing the black discs. "You can play the game perfectly and still lose if your opponent rolls enough double sixes."

"True," Daryn agreed.

"Do you ever use your magic?" Gaylon asked conversationally while he made his first move.

Daryn looked up. "To do what?"

"To cheat. To make the dice turn to your advantage."

"Well," the duke said carefully as he rattled the dice in the blind. "They say an honest man wears his Stone so all may see it. Watch mine if you like. If it begins to glow . . . well . . ." He tossed the dice onto the board, and fate, ever perverse, gave him double sixes. He grimaced at Gaylon, who in turn began to laugh.

It was the only double Daryn threw the entire game, and Gaylon won handily. The prince looked longingly at the prize.

"We could go two out of three games," the boy offered generously.

"There's not time, I'm afraid," said Telo from the doorway. "Dinner is served."

"And a good thing," grumbled Reys, unfolding his lanky form from the chair. "I'm half-starved."

Daryn pressed the gem into Gaylon's hand. "You've won it fairly."

Pleased, the boy carried the opal with him to the dining room. Daryn stood back to let the king pass, but the tall man paused beside him to squeeze his shoulder once, quickly.

Dinner was rabbit stew, a fitting meal for a hunting party, even when served on silver. Almost immediately though, Telo appeared carrying another steaming plate.

"Ketti sent this along," he said, setting the platter beside Daryn. "She knows the duke has a taste for hot southern dishes."

It was curried lamb, and the steam carried the pungent aroma around the table as Telo spooned a generous portion onto the duke's plate. Daryn took a bite, relishing the exotic flavors, and within moments his mouth was afire. He blinked back tears, smiling across the table.

"Delicious," he wheezed to his companions. "You must try some."

Reys shook his head. "Thank you, but I don't fancy a scorched tongue. I've never understood why a man would punish his mouth and stomach so."

"I'll try some," said Gaylon stoutly. It took no more than a taste for him to decide he wanted no more. He wiped his now-running nose and took several swallows of water, which seemed to help not at all.

"Eat some bread," Daryn told him kindly. "I can't imagine why you think this too hot. In the city of Katay, they make a dish with nut meats and chicken that can curl a man's toes. Now *that's* hot." But he had drained his wine cup twice already, and Telo refilled it again, smiling indulgently.

The conversation turned to hunting, and the trio made plans for the morrow. They would hunt mule deer first, on foot and close to the lodge. The rain had wetted the fallen leaves enough to make stalking silent, promising good results. There was no hurry, for the week was theirs to spend however they pleased. For a while they argued pleasantly over weaponry—which bows were best for what game, and the advantages and disadvantages of the new style of sword.

In the midst of the meal, Daryn grew quiet. He'd begun to feel light-headed. From the wine, he suspected, until the dizziness became an overall queasiness that grew steadily worse.

"Excuse me, Sire," he said finally, "but I think I'll retire. With your permission."

"Of course," said Reys, then with concern, "Are you all right, Daryn? You look pale."

"It may have been something I ate," Daryn muttered wryly.

Reys smiled. "Do you want Telo? I'm sure he can find something to settle your stomach."

"No. Thank you. A little fresh air is what I need."

"Go then, and rest well. We'll be going to bed ourselves shortly." The king patted Gaylon's arm. "It's an early day coming."

Daryn stood, managing a bow to them both before turning away.

"Good night," Gaylon called after him.

Outside, the weather had cleared, and a light frost covered the yard. The stars were spun in a thick band across the heavens, but Daryn hardly noticed. He stumbled twice before finding the midden and a post to cling to while he vomited helplessly, his stomach in utter revolt. The violence of it frightened him. He stood, waiting for the weakness to pass, his face clammy with perspiration. His mouth tasted of spent wine.

The illness seemed to pass, to be replaced by an incredible feeling of mental clarity and well-being. Daryn marveled at the beautiful curling vapor his breath created, and the cold air felt exquisite against his cheeks. He returned to the lodge, aware of the crisp scent of the firs and the crunch of frozen grass underfoot.

In the dark hallway, the door to his bedroom stood open, and he leaned against the jamb, exhausted. Across the wide chamber the fire danced in the woodstove. Daryn wanted to sit in the stuffed chair before it, but the effort seemed almost beyond him. He repelled from the doorway, staggering, only mildly curious as to why his legs had acquired joints in several new places. The floorboards seemed to sink beneath his feet, and he found the chair only just in time. The weakness came again, and he was distantly aware of another wave of sickness rolling in on him. This time there was nothing to lose, but the convulsions doubled him over, spasm after spasm racking him until his stomach muscles ached. It took some time to find the strength to right himself in the chair again. He longed to close his eyes, to sleep, but the flames of the open-fronted stove trapped his gaze.

A breath of cold air prowled the room, guttering the candle flames and coaxing the fire into a throaty roar. Daryn wondered dimly if the window had been left ajar, foolishly thinking he might attempt to close it, might attempt to navigate himself to the bed.

That notion was discarded when a shadow crossed the flames. A demon face, disembodied, floated into his watery vision, the fire framing it, burnishing pale hair. Candlelight caught the features and revealed a glint of teeth in a malicious, thin-lipped smile. Those lips began to form words, and the duke struggled for comprehension.

"Daryn." The sounds distorted, echoing hollowly. "Daryn, do try to follow what I'm saying." Lucien watched the duke's overbright eyes with their widely dilated pupils.

A furrow of concentration appeared between the dark brows, and Daryn's mouth worked soundlessly. Finally he managed a word, guttural, but thick with accusation. "You!"

"Don't waste your strength, Gosney." Lucien picked up Daryn's lax wrist and moved the man's hand into his lap so he could perch on the arm of the chair. "You've been poisoned." He waited for the statement to sink in. "There was one odd spice in your curry tonight. Oh, you won't die from it. At least not technically. Are you wondering why I would poison you?" He licked his lips, savoring the feel of power.

"I shall never have another like that sword, you know," the blond man murmured. "I named her Galimar. Do you know the word? It means, 'heart's own.' Oh, yes, I'd forgotten—you're quite fluent in the Xenaran tongue, aren't you?" Lucien leaned close. "Perhaps once in a lifetime a blade is created that fits the hand as Galimar fit mine. So fine a sword becomes an extension of a man."

Now the young lord stood and moved out of Daryn's line of vision. "But, then," he continued, "you have a feel for fine things, too." He returned carrying Daryn's lute. "There are some things on which a value cannot be placed." Lovingly Lucien stroked the beautiful golden wood, then carefully nestled the instrument in the coals of the fireplace.

The lacquer blackened and the wood caught. The gut strings flared, and the lute sighed, moaning a whisper of a tune as it died. Lucien settled again on the arm of the chair.

"As much as I enjoy your energetic and witty company, I really mustn't stay long. The moon will rise soon, and I've a long hard ride ahead of me." He refastened his cloak. "I just wanted you to know who was responsible. Everything's been arranged. The king and Gaylon will be dead soon, and the lodge set afire." Lucien's fingers fumbled at their task. A curious lethargy had overtaken him and with it, just a hint of danger. "You'll be blamed. That's been arranged also. Clever, don't . . . you . . . think?"

Lucien's tongue grew thick, and his words began to slur. An odd heaviness pulled at his limbs. Almost too late, he saw the blue glow from Daryn's ring. With an arm that seemed to move against some strong current, Lucien backhanded the man in the chair, a hard crack to the side of the duke's face to break his concentration. The lethargy vanished.

"For shame!" Lucien laughed exultantly. "Almost, almost." Where he'd struck Daryn the cheek purpled. "That's the first time I've ever seen you use your Stone. I'm impressed." He gathered his cloak around him and disappeared from Daryn's view once more. "Remember me." Icy air circled the room again. "When the flames are at your feet, remember me."

The lute was white ashes now. Daryn let his head drop forward, eyes finally closing. A bitter tear leaked from under his black lashes.

* * * * *

The knife was small, a straight-bladed dirk with a wicked point. The handle was weighted and molded to the hand, and a row of small emeralds ran the length of the guard. It had been the old duke's, and now was Daryn's. The dirk should have been in young Gosney's apartments at Castlekeep, but instead had been carried to the lodge, to the bedchamber of the prince by a rogue in Lucien's employ. The blade had always been kept sharp, but now was honed to bitter perfection, and it parted flesh like warm butter, quickly, deftly.

Something stung Reys on the back, below the left shoulder blade. An ant or a wasp, he thought. The king had only a moment for that fleeting thought before he realized something was most dreadfully wrong. A moment more, and he knew with cruel certainty that he was dying. Reys opened his mouth, but there was no time for more than a breath. His young son lay on the bed before him, eyes on the pages of a small book, reciting a verse. In that fleeting instant the words took on new meaning for the king.

"And if I say to thee,
Thy day is done.
At last the silken night
To thee is come . . ."

A tiny crimson droplet fell upon the page.

"Wouldst thou go with me?"

With that last line of the poem Gaylon stopped in confusion. His father's arms barred his view of the room, those immense hands, fingers spread, were resting on the covers at either side of the prince. Gaylon looked upward into Reys's face, and what he saw there turned him cold. A thin trickle of blood had appeared at the corner of the king's mouth. In horrid fascination the boy watched a string of expressions pass across the beloved face in only a moment's time—amazement, then anger, fear, and finally sorrow, all running, melting into one another like heated wax. The great arms quivered, the face gone white.

"Daryn," his father said almost inaudibly, then collapsed across Gaylon's lap, leaving the prince to face a stranger in muddy, ragged clothing, a craven man with pock-marked cheeks and rotting teeth, a bloody dirk in his grip. The boy's first thought was only that the man's breath stank.

A scuffle in the shadows near the dresser dragged the attention of both murderer and intended victim to its source. In the night gloom, Telo had jumped another man, one who had not slipped from behind the drapes as silently as the one who now stood before Gaylon. It happened quickly, without time for reason or comprehension. A single muffled cry and the accomplice was down. Telo whirled on the first man too late. The dirk took the old servant in the throat so that he staggered back, falling.

From where he lay, Telo watched the killer turn once more on the boy. The prince had struggled from the blankets and had drawn his father's sword as he stepped to the floor. The assassin discarded the knife and drew his own sword. Slowly, painfully, the blood bubbling in his lungs, Telo reached out and caught the boy's assailant in a dead man's grip.

All this was lost in the shadows at the edge of the lamplight. Gaylon saw nothing except the killer coming toward him. The boy had no time for fear, only barely enough time to calculate his chances. He raised the king's sword. Too heavy for him normally, the weapon felt feather-light. The pock-faced man grinned as he came, certain of the outcome. Then, somehow, he tripped, pitching forward onto the boy's blade. The sword slid easily between the ribs, passing through the heart. The fellow died without a sound, his lips forming a surprised O that shrieked silently in Gaylon's ear, on and on.

The blood slid in a glistening, viscous stream down the blade, running hotly over the prince's knuckles. The dead man toppled sideways, wrenching the sword from Gaylon's hands, and the boy sat abruptly on the floor, weak and sick with horror. A deep shudder racked him, and he began to cry, then thought better of it. The guards must be found immediately.

When he stood, the prince saw the bloody jeweled dirk on the blankets beside his father's body and remembered the knife—a Gosney heirloom. How did it come to be here? A rush of sudden anger replaced the horror, and clear thought became near impossible. The duke had spent several years in the South, where political assassination was commonplace. Perhaps the man had come back for only one reason. By all the gods, if Daryn were somehow responsible. . . .

Gaylon got to his feet, automatically found his clothing, and discarded the bloody nightshirt. He pulled on his boots and strapped on his own small sword, mindlessly stepping over the bodies, around the puddles of blood. He would not look at his father. There was no reality there. This was some horrible dream, the prince told himself. It could be nothing else.

The bedroom door opened on thick clouds of smoke. Gaylon slammed it closed, backing away and stumbling over Telo's still form. Panic began to clutch at him, clambering at the edges of his mind, and he ran for the window. It opened easily. Outside, quiet, undisturbed night greeted him. There were no shouts of alarm, no sign of the fire.

The moon was up, a fat gibbous lantern, paling the stars. By its light Gaylon found the men at arms, dead every one, in their small barracks off the stables. Their throats had been cut while they'd slept. He suspected, then, that no alarm had been sounded because there had been no one left alive to sound it.

A horse nickered softly from inside the stable, and Gaylon realized the fire would spread even there in time. One by one, he opened the stalls and turned the horses out. When he came upon Amber, he paused, considering, then let her go with the others. Katy he intended to use to ride for help, but when he tried bridling her, she charged past him and raced after the rest, her tail a dark plume streaming out behind her. Angrily Gaylon followed, calling to her, trying to coax her back, but she refused. The prince trailed the little mare down the mountainside, through its eerie, moonlit shadows.

* * * * *

Daryn had fallen asleep, or unconscious—he couldn't be certain which. When awareness finally returned, he found himself choking in a smoke-filled room. The candles had gone out, and in total darkness, he tried to orient himself, tried to force his thoughts into coherency.

The door to his chamber lay behind him and slightly to the left. Ten paces down the hallway to the right of that first door was another leading outside. He slid from the chair to the floor, fairly certain that he was capable of crawling the distance to safety. The air remained freshest near the floor, but not by much, and every few moments a fit of coughing brought him up short.

It was the faint orange glow of the fire that finally revealed the first doorway, and slowly Daryn dragged himself out and down the hall. The lodge was filled with a directionless crackling now, a rustle of flame behind walls. Several times he was convinced that he'd gotten turned around and was heading into the fire, not away. Each time, heart pounding, Daryn found new strength and determination.

In the smoky darkness, he found the second door and, fumbling, unbarred it. But it resisted the duke's feeble attempts to pull it open. The smoke was growing thicker and hot. Terrified, he renewed his efforts, and the door gave slightly, then came open with a small popping sound. The lodge seemed to inhale, a great ragged breath of icy air, a howling in its lungs.

First came the implosion, then, almost instantaneously, the explosion. It blew Daryn against the door and the door from its hinges.

* * * * *

Deep in the night, Jessmyn had a dream that woke her. She remembered only the Lady Gerra holding her close, rocking her gently, crooning softly, "There, there, love. There, there." Tired still, she let herself to be soothed back to sleep.

When the princess woke again at morning, she found herself oddly alone in another room, lost in the midst of a huge four-posted bed. The child knuckled her eyes and yawned, only mildly surprised. She'd slept in this room once before, when Gaylon's third cousin, Taddi, a robust, red-headed four-year-old, had shown the bad manners to catch the measles. After his fever had gone she envied his lovely red spots and soon had a marvelous collection of her own.

Jessmyn wondered vaguely who had caught what now and whether she might get it. Sometimes being sick was nice, everyone worrying about you, and other times it was not so nice, not at all. She shoved the quilts back with her feet and slid the short distance to the floor. Cold! Wriggling ten small pink toes, the child inspected them briefly before shoving them into the tiny red slippers left by the bed. There was no one about, no sounds from the passageway. This room, being upstairs, had a grand view of the stables, and she could never resist a chance to look at the horses. She climbed into the window seat.

This morning there was unusual activity. Lots of horses out, being readied. Even as the princess looked, a company of soldiers rode into the yard. Fascinated, she watched the bubbling rush of adults, behaving like so many ants in a threatened hill. Young Gandy's father, the stable master, gave the boy a leg up on a tall black gelding. Several of the lad's brothers, lithe and strong, were being tossed onto other horses—the swift ones, the post horses. Each had a letter pouch tied behind the saddle.

If she leaned against the thick glass pane Jessmyn could just see the steady influx of men coming through the bailey, too. Something exciting was happening, of this there could be no doubt. And she was missing it! Where was Lady Gerra, and where were her clothes? The princess marched out the door clad only in her thick flannel gown and slippers, determined to find the very center of the commotion and insinuate herself therein.

Down the hall, only minimally lit by the high-slotted windows, she traipsed, lifting the hem of her gown from the stone floor. The halls were empty, but she could hear a murmur of many voices in the distance. The sounds led her toward the galleries above the throne room. Jessmyn found herself skulking and thoroughly enjoying it. Children were never allowed upstairs, there were too many balconies to fall from.

The first gallery ran the length of the room, to the left of the throne. It was empty—almost. She knew him instantly by his pale hair and sweet-faced profile. Lucien, on his knees by the bannister, was using an upright post of carven stone to support one shoulder. He wasn't looking into the room below, but rather listening, his head gently cocked, attentive. Jessmyn moved so that she could better see his face. The young lord's hair was in slight disarray, and his eyes had a bruised, sleepless look about them. As always, though, his clothing was neat and fresh.

He saw her, and something passed behind the blue eyes, gone before she could decipher it. He put a finger to his lips and motioned her to him. Jessmyn came slowly, unsure, but the young lord wrapped a warm arm about her and drew her close, settling back on his heels so she might sit in his lap. Together they gazed into the throne room.

The chamber was jammed pillar to post with men—courtiers and townsfolk—with more pressing in all the time. The princess picked out Feydir's tall dark shape in his deep blue robes at the bottom step of the dais. The gaunt ambassador stood a full head taller than the rest. Only the king was taller, but Jessmyn could find him nowhere in the crowd. There was Baron Graystone and several more she knew. None of them looked happy. The drapes behind the throne stirred, and a figure came through from the council chambers—not the king, but Dasser, the head councilman, who was pale and visibly shaken. He waved his hands, calling for silence, but it had already fallen. Staring out at the quiet, expectant faces, the man cleared his throat to speak.

Someone in the crowd couldn't wait. "Dasser! Is it true?"

"Aye," said Dasser, voice quavering. The entire roomful of men groaned. "They've found the bodies in the ashes, badly burned, but we're certain enough that it was the royal party."

"And Gosney? Is it also true what's being said?"

"It would appear so. Papers were found in his rooms offering payment for the work, and quite a bit of Xenaran gold."

"Assassin! Too bloody long in the South!" someone snarled.

"What shall we do now?" another cried.

"There are search parties combing the mountains at this very moment. If Gosney shows his face anywhere he'll be taken, but we're convinced that he didn't work alone. This will not go unpunished." Dasser found the strength to carry his words. "As for the throne, we've sent for the king's first cousin, Chace of Greenwood. He should be here within three days."

"That half-wit!" came a mutter, instantly silenced.

Feydir raised his voice, steady and clear. "Dasser, I have something here of interest to you."

The councilman stiffened as if struck, but no one seemed to notice. They had all turned at the voice.

"This is no concern of yours, Feydir," Baron Graystone called above the noise. There was a chorus of agreement.

"If you know what's good for you," another called, "you'll leave Wynnamyr and take that demon-spawned nephew of yours with you!"

Feydir ignored them, passing a packet of documents tied up in a ribbon to Dasser. If the councilman appeared shaken before, now he quaked.

"What's happening?" Jessmyn whispered with a growing apprehension.

"Hush. Just listen," Lucien murmured.

"I'll need the council convened," said Dasser, the unopened packet tight in his hands.

"Then call the members," Feydir demanded.

An angry rumble from the crowd followed his words. Irritated, Dasser rounded on them.

"There's nothing more to be done. Go home, all of you! As soon as we know more, you shall all hear it." No one moved. "Get out!" he shouted, and finally the group flowed grumbling to the doors.

In a short while they were alone, the six council members and Feydir. The ambassador followed them to the drapes, but Dasser turned to him, braving a hand on the man's chest.

"You are not a member of this council," he said.

"Yet!" snapped Feydir and called after them, "I have the original papers safely put, Dasser." The door slammed shut on him.

Feydir strode for the exit, but paused in the center of the floor and looked up at the gallery. His eyes found the spot where the watchers sat hidden.

"Lucien!" he cried.

The young man shifted away from the railing, pulling Jessmyn with him. She saw a quick fear on his face.

"Lucien!" his uncle cried again in the great empty hall. "What have you done!" Then the sound of his footsteps faded in the distance.

When she knew the man had gone, Jessmyn turned on Lucien. "What's happened?"

The young lord gazed at her, face momentarily blank, then that odd look passed behind his eyes again, and she saw what it truly was—pity. There was pain there, too.

"How can I tell you, little one?"

"Tell me!"

"The king and Gaylon are dead."

She blinked once, twice.

"It was Daryn," Lucien added quickly. "He murdered them."

"No!" she cried and struck him hard on the chest when he reached out to comfort her.

"It's true, dear heart. I'm so sorry." But she was gone.

Down the hall Jessmyn raced, her slippers making a staccato pattering on the stones. She fled back to the room with the four-poster, desperate to return to the first waking moment, when she might start again. As the child neared the room, she heard sounds of weeping. From the doorway she saw Lady Gerra, her plump, disheveled form lying on the crumpled bedclothes. The woman sobbed so brokenly that the bed shook under her.

"Stop it!" Jessmyn screamed, covering her ears. She began to quiver like a trapped coney. "Stop it!"

Six

❖

The sun rose. To the east, sparse layers of clouds brightened from dark blue to pink to gold and finally to white. Deep in the narrow valleys a fog lay so thick that the mountaintops were dark islands anchored in a ghostly sea. Somewhere in the firs overhead, a bird fluttered, beginning its morning song.

It seemed wrong somehow that the sun should rise on such a day as this, for the deer to move on feather hooves through the woods as if all were as it should be. Gaylon's desolation was as tangible as the dried blood on his hands, and it seemed only fitting that desolation lay on the land as well.

Katy had refused the company of the other horses and had headed off alone, leading him all night south and east through the forest. Each time he'd thought he'd lost her, she had reappeared like a wraith in the trees, urging him on. Gaylon remembered clearly the explosion that had rocked the mountain. Far above him, the lodge had disintegrated, flames gouting skyward, shingles and other fiery debris cartwheeling in the sparks. For a while he'd watched in awe as the fire raged, taking the nearest trees with it. But the earlier rain prevented the flames from spreading. Then Katy had come again to clatter by him in some rocks, and he'd stumbled after her, blinded by the night and the tears he had no idea he was shedding.

Now Gaylon watched the sunrise set the frosty ground shimmering. He was lost. Below him the fog hid everything; around him, the trees crowded close; and nowhere was there a familiar landmark. Worse yet, Katy had disappeared, and he feared her gone for good. Exhausted and in despair, the prince settled on a boulder, thinking to wait for the fog to burn away. Eventually he dropped into a fitful doze, his head on his knees.

The snap of a branch upslope brought him awake with a start. This was not the timid approach of a curious deer, but the sound made by something two-legged and purposeful. For a moment he panicked, exposed and vulnerable there on his rock. Sliding from the mossy surface, the prince slipped behind a thick fir bole, loosening his sword and drawing it noiselessly from the scabbard.

There came a step close by, beside the very tree he used for cover. Breath held against any sound, Gaylon watched a man move past the tree—Daryn, limping badly, with a long bent stick employed as a clumsy staff. A sudden rage swept through the boy, overcoming the sorrow and misery. His father and all the others were dead, but this man lived. That could only mean treachery.

The prince stepped away from the tree. Daryn had just enough time to turn and fling up the stick to ward off the sword stroke. The blow staggered him, and the weight on the bad ankle sent him down, flailing. Gaylon was on the duke before he could recover. The boy stood with the sword clutched two-handed, poised over Daryn's heart. The prince's small arms quivered with effort, but something in Daryn's face gave him pause.

"I thought you dead," the duke said gently, without fear.

"I don't die so easily," the boy snapped. "Murderer!"

Daryn lay still under the blade, under the accusation. His voice bleak, he answered, "If you truly believe that, then kill me now."

The unreasoning moment had passed. Gaylon, with a wail of pain and frustration, plunged the sword point harmlessly into the dirt beside Daryn. His fury spent, he crumpled. Daryn caught the prince and held him tight while the boy sobbed out his story of horror and confusion.

It was almost more than Daryn could bear, to live the night

again through the eyes of a ten-year-old who had watched his father murdered. He held Gaylon close while the sobs racked him, and tried to piece together as best he could what had happened. The poison, though fading, still worked its foul way through the duke's body, and he found it was difficult to extract reality from the dreamlike thrall the drug created.

Laid over Gaylon's story were Daryn's own memories or imaginings. The explosion had blown him outward into the night. He vaguely remembered tumbling as a leaf before a gale, until lines of blue light had burst from the very center of his being. These lines had wrapped themselves weblike around trees and rocks to anchor him and break his fall. Perhaps his Sorcerer's Stone had glowed brilliantly for a time, but that too may have been a dream.

"Daryn?"

He looked down, trying to focus on Gaylon's tear-streaked face.

"How did you survive? I found the others. Their throats had been cut."

A vague smile touched Daryn's swollen lips. "I think Lucien planned a crueller death for me."

"Lucien?"

"Yes." Daryn tried to explain as well as possible his side of the tale.

Gaylon's confusion faded, and his expression grew hard as he listened. Unconsciously, the boy pulled free of Daryn to sit cross-legged before him on the rocky, cold ground. He studied the duke while the story unfolded. A strange tale and rambling, the prince concluded silently, but it rang of truth. Daryn was certainly a mess. He'd sustained a scalp wound and dried blood streaked the right side of his face. The right eye was nearly swollen shut, his hair was singed and sooty, and his clothing little more than rags. Yes, it all made an odd sense. Lucien D'Sulang was very capable of such revenge.

"Why us, Daryn? Why should he harm my father and me just to get at you?"

Daryn's good eye shifted away. "Lucien is blood heir to the throne if you should die."

"A Southerner? Impossible."

"He's a bastard half-brother of your father's. Someday I'll tell you more about that, but first I must somehow get us safely back to Castlekeep."

"Can you conjure us horses with that ring of yours?" Gaylon asked half in jest. "It's a long walk home."

"Amber's somewhere near. I've been following her all night."

Gaylon's eyes widened. "I've been following Katy."

As if on cue, a high whinny sounded on the slopes below, and there, disappearing into the fog, were both animals. Daryn reached for his staff and used it to pull himself awkwardly to his feet.

"With two of us now, perhaps we can corner them," the duke said, hobbling painfully forward.

Gaylon, recovering his sword, followed.

* * * * *

Armed only with insolence, Lucien went to his uncle's room. He'd slept first, knowing full well he needed his wits about him for the coming confrontation. He was both apprehensive and well pleased with himself—a curious mixture of fear and elation. The deed was done! Whatever the price, he'd willingly pay. If he played this final hand skillfully, though, payment might yet be deferred.

Feydir had not returned, and the room was locked. It took some time for Lucien to track down the chamberlain amidst the madness that still gripped the keep, and when the fellow was found, he acted sullen and uncooperative, only opening the door after dire threats to his person, threats Lucien had every intention of carrying out.

Afternoon light, diffuse and golden, found its way through the room's one tiny window. This was hardly a generous room, unworthy of a Southern nobleman, but that was about to change. Restless, the young lord stalked the chamber. He hated this place; it was permeated with past defeats, past humiliations. Lucien vowed that would change as well.

Finally he drew the high-backed chair out from the desk. It was as unattractive and angular as his uncle, and when he sat in it Lucien decided it was certainly as unaccommodating. He tried the drawers to the desk. Locked. He considered forcing them with his dirk and discarded the idea. Let the old man keep his petty secrets . . . for a while. Instead, he settled back as well as possible and propped his heels on the desktop.

Down the dark passageways of the northwest wing, a mind-weary Feydir swept like some nocturnal bird of prey. The council still bickered behind closed doors. Those fools. He knew what Dasser was about, but it would do the head councilman no good. The documents were legal, and his claim—Lucien's claim—to the throne could not be denied.

He pushed the iron key into the lock before realizing the door was already open. Furious, he flung it wide, and the door slammed against the wall with a bang. Lucien lounged in the chair at his desk, boots up. The boy sent his uncle a deprecatory smile, though Feydir was too angry to see that his nephew's eyes belied the whimsy of his lips.

"Well, well," the ambassador said through clenched teeth. "Dear nephew. I had thought it would be necessary to have you dragged here kicking and cawing. How kind of you to save me the trouble." He enjoyed the brief fear he saw in the young man's eyes. "Stand up!"

Lucien moved not a muscle.

"I said, stand up!" Feydir slapped the boots from his desk.

Lucien straightened in the chair, muttering.

"What was that?" Feydir demanded.

"I said, no."

With outraged disbelief, the older man's long thin fingers sought the Stone beneath his robes and pulled it forth. The Stone pulsed blue with the mage's fury, and Lucien went rigid. He remained seated, however. Feydir's fingertips caressed the rough surface of the Stone. He let the touch calm him momentarily, smiling benignly at the towheaded youth. He must not let anger guide his hand where the Stone was concerned. That would only prove disastrous.

"I shall be kind," he said, "and let you have your say before

I punish you."

Lucien cleared his throat. "I have nothing to say. I've done nothing wrong." He spread his hands, palms up. Surprisingly, they were steady. "There's no blood on my hands."

"Foolish child. You were never good at lies." But Feydir knew that to be untrue. Lucien had always been a master of dissembly.

"I swear I had nothing to do with this. It was Daryn. I spent the afternoon and night with sweet Kari in town. Ask her."

Feydir regarded the young man intently. His own careful plans, his years of work had been shattered in a single blow. With great good luck, he might be able to piece his scheme back together, but there was far more at stake here than the kingship of a minor realm like Wynnamyr. Lucien could have no idea of the scope of his uncle's plotting here and in Xenara. Or could he? His nephew was anything but simple, and as a pawn, he left much to be desired.

"I don't believe you," the older man said finally.

"Believe it!" snapped Lucien, growing bold.

"Why should our good duke do such a thing?"

"How should I know? If not for gold, then perhaps to gain favor . . . or out of fear. Who knows what goes on in the mind of that black wizard? He was always a queer one."

Feydir's Stone had lost its frighteningly intense blue glow and was a simple gray pebble again. Lucien used the moment to pull a bit of parchment from his jerkin. He offered the little roll of paper to his uncle.

"What's this?" Feydir asked, accepting it.

"I have no idea," Lucien lied. He'd had the keep physician, Girkin, translate it for him when he'd gotten the poison from the pudgy little man. "It's written in the ancient script and looks much like the pages in your *Book of Stones*. I thought it might be of interest to you."

Feydir's dark sunken eyes scanned the letters swiftly. Excitement surged through him, and he slipped the Stone back into his robes lest it reveal the emotion. It pulsed warmly against his chest in time with his heart. Eyes hooded, he glanced at Lucien.

"Where did you find this?"

"In Gosney's rooms."

The ambassador didn't demand to know why his nephew had been there. Instead, he tossed the paper carelessly onto his desk.

"Is it of use to you, Uncle?"

"Perhaps." Feydir turned away. "Let's discuss *you* for the moment. How has your day treated you?"

"Well enough."

"Good. The council still meets, but it must reach a decision quickly or risk civil unrest. I'll be called for soon." Reaching down, Feydir unlocked a drawer in the desk with a small key tied to a thong at his waist. He lifted out several pages of paper covered with his own neat, tight handwriting. "I want you to go back to your room and study these statements. Know them well. By midnight you'll be named heir to the throne of Wynnamyr, and how you speak to your people after will set the tone of your reign.

"You've been a spoiled, unlikable brat for the past five years, but in these pages you'll find a list of promises to make to the people. If you present this speech with all the charm I know you possess, then you may yet win their approval. It's vital that you do so."

"Feeling is high against Southerners at the moment," Lucien pointed out.

"You're not a Southerner. By blood you're a descendant of the Red Kings. And soon you will *be* a king. Let me deal with those who would oppose you." The older man pushed the papers into Lucien's hands. "You must leave me now. I've much to do before the council calls for me, and so do you."

Feydir hustled his nephew out into the hall. "Put on your finest clothing, something befitting a monarch. I will come for you later." He closed the door without waiting for a response from the young lord.

Trembling now, the ambassador returned to the desk to reverently pick up the parchment, unrolling it. The words leaped out on the page. *The king's bane is the sorcerer's lot.* The riddle of Orym's Legacy! This was the key to Kingslayer—the key to a power beyond imagining. He racked his brain in an effort to dredge up the reference to the sword he'd read in the *Book of Stones*, but it eluded him. Quickly Feydir reached for the base of the statue where the book lay hidden, then stopped himself. No. A search of the tome's pages would take much time, and there were other things to be dealt with first. He locked the riddle away in the desk, still trembling in anticipation. Soon, he promised himself. Soon.

* * * * *

He was so close, so very close. Katy had her head down, tearing hurried mouthfuls of withered poverty grass. Her fine little ears flickered nervously. Then Gaylon misstepped and rocky soil dribbled away down the incline. Katy's head snapped up. Gaylon froze.

"Ho, Katy," he called softly. "Easy girl."

She came up on her hind feet, pivoting gracefully, and with a defiant flip of her tail, leaped away through the trees. The boy had just a glimpse of late day sun rippling over coppery fur and she was gone. A childish oath exploded from the prince's lips, and he lashed out at a downed branch with a foot.

All day he and Daryn had followed the horses. All day! And this was the closest Gaylon had come to either of them. Most of the time he hadn't even gotten within a stone's throw, which was likely for the best. More than once he'd felt like throwing one at the blasted animals. Little good that would have done.

Troubled, Gaylon looked skyward. Clouds were massing to the south, black and ominous, and the wind carried the scent of rain. At this rate the storm would be on them by dark and to be caught without shelter would be bad.

He also worried about Daryn. He'd left the man resting beneath a tall lightning-struck fir, one that was uniquely visible for some distance in any direction. Daryn was painfully slow on his bad ankle and little help for catching horses. But the ankle wasn't what worried Gaylon. They'd stopped to drink from creeks along the way, and each time Daryn was violently ill afterwards. Because the water would not stay down, the duke grew weaker. Gaylon feared that soon Daryn would be incapable of travel, but the boy knew he could never leave him behind.

The prince's stomach grumbled, cramping uncomfortably. He couldn't remember ever being so hungry. Abandoning his pursuit of the horses, he pinpointed Daryn's fir tree and followed a dry stream bed back up the mountain. As he climbed, he wondered briefly if it were possible to hunt rabbits with a sword.

Daryn hadn't moved. He was still lying huddled in the damp fir needles. His eyes were closed, his face pale and drawn with pain. Gently, Gaylon touched his shoulder.

"Daryn?"

Slowly the man's gray eyes opened, and even more slowly they focused. "Do you smell it?" he mumbled.

"What?"

"The smoke. It still burns. The lodge still burns."

"You're dreaming, Daryn," Gaylon told him, feeling sudden anxiety.

"No," Daryn insisted, lifting his head to look about, seemingly dazed.

Gaylon turned slowly, sniffing the air. No. Wait. There *was* the faintest hint of woodsmoke on the wind. And something else. Food!

"You're right," he said, excited now.

Daryn struggled to his feet, leaning heavily on his makeshift staff. "No luck with the horses?"

Gaylon shook his head ruefully.

"No matter," the duke said kindly. "I think our luck has changed for the better." He glanced around him. "Which way?"

"The wind's from the south."

"Then south it is." He shuffled forward.

"The storm's nearly here," Gaylon noted as they negotiated the mountainside. He pointed to the approaching cloud cover. The light was failing, and they quickened their pace from a snail's to a turtle's. The smoke scent grew stronger, and before long Gaylon's sharp eyes caught sight of a cottage roof far below in a tiny sheltered valley. Smoke spiraled up from its chimney before being swept away by the winds in the upper reaches of the forest.

"There!" he shouted.

Daryn nodded and seemed to gather strength. Where the going was roughest, he simply sat and slithered down the slope. Gaylon crashed headlong through the brush beside him. Daryn's staff was lost, unnoted, in the scramble, and as they reached the valley floor the first heavy drops of rain began to pelt them. But they'd arrived.

The cottage was small but beautiful, the walls freshly limed, the thatch of the roof thick and sturdy. Light winked merrily from two small windows. Behind the dwelling sat a low stone byre, and palings marked off a large garden still sporting straight rows of cabbages and carrots. The appearance of the place as a whole was tidy and even inviting.

Gaylon offered Daryn his shoulder for support, and together they followed the path to the stoop. The long overhang deflected most of the rain as Gaylon reached out to knock loudly on the door. A long moment passed, but there was no response from inside. The boy had reached out again when the door flew open. Gaylon froze, hand still in the air. A monster of a man filled the entire doorway. He was dressed in plain but spotless homespun clothing, and in one beefy fist he clutched a long-handled axe. His face was ruddy, well fleshed, and healthy looking. Everything about him suggested great strength.

"Sir," Gaylon began, but his voice broke. He swallowed hard, looking to Daryn for encouragement, but the duke stood dumb in wide-eyed wonder.

"Sir," the boy began again. "I am Gaylon Reysson and this is Daryn, duke of Gosney. We—We met with great misfortune last night. My father, the king, was murdered and our lodge was burned. None escaped alive save we two. Daryn is injured. We seek aid and shelter for the night."

Throughout Gaylon's speech the giant remained impassive. With sinking heart, the prince said falteringly, "Sir?"

"Harry, who is it?" called a high voice from inside the cottage.

"Beggars, Misk," Harry grunted.

At that, Gaylon bristled. Pulling himself to his full height, which barely reached the big man's navel, the prince snapped, "Sir! What I have just related to you is true, but if you'll show no common courtesy, we'll go elsewhere."

"Harry, you great oaf, move aside!" cried the voice from within, and Harry, a sudden good-natured grin on his face, stood away, revealing a diminutive peasant woman in long patchwork skirts. She was as tiny as Harry was huge, and she looked the beggars over critically, then her face softened.

"Come in, come in, you poor things! I'm Misk, and this is my husband, Harry." She elbowed past Harry to grab Gaylon's hands, effusing sympathy and caring. Misk stood no taller than the boy, though her hair was silvered. A bit nonplussed, Gaylon let her draw him into the cottage. Daryn came after, stumbling on the single step.

The cottage—one enormous room awash with warm golden firelight reflected from the walls and polished floor—was as neat inside as out. In the eves hung row upon row of bundled herbs, which made the air rich with their scents. The fireplace took in nearly the entire far wall, and from it wafted the maddening smells of cooking food.

Misk gazed out into the yard one last time. "Where is the other child?" she asked.

"Beg pardon?" Gaylon dragged his eyes with difficulty from the pot on the fire.

"The little girl. Where is she?"

"There's no one else," said the prince, confused.

"That's odd," said the woman, closing the door. "Well, come sit by the fire. The rain's cold tonight. I'll put more water on to heat for the two of you." Then she smiled and her eyes sparkled. "First something to eat."

Gaylon sat as he was directed, on a bench at the long table before the fire. He eagerly accepted a bowl of stew and thick slabs of brown bread with sweet white butter. The bread was used to scoop up the savory meat and vegetables. For a time, nothing existed in the world but the food before him, and the prince had never tasted anything so wonderful.

"Aren't you hungry?" the little woman asked.

Gaylon thought she must be jesting until he realized that she spoke to Daryn. For the first time since their arrival he looked at the duke. The man had not touched his food, but sat silently, his face flushed with misery. Gaylon was seized by guilt. He'd been thinking of his stomach while his friend suffered still.

"Daryn?"

Misk placed her hand on the man's forehead. "Fever," she announced, and even as she spoke Daryn began to slip bonelessly from the bench. Between them, Gaylon and Misk caught him.

"Jack! Don't stand stupid. Get him to the bed."

"I thought his name was Harry," Gaylon said as the husband lifted Daryn in his arms and carried him to the big bed under a window in the north wall of the cottage.

"It is," Misk answered, directing the operation, then cooing, "Poor laddie, poor sick thing," as if Daryn were a pet dog. She brushed the tangled hair back from his face, revealing the blood-engorged swelling about the right eye and finding the gash above the temple. "Nasty," she commented. Harry-Jack produced a bowl of warm water in which Misk soaked a clean cloth. Carefully she cleansed the wound. Daryn moaned.

"His left ankle's the worst," Gaylon pointed out, hovering near her shoulder. "I couldn't get the boot off, and I was afraid to cut it." And suddenly the husband was there again with a knife fully half as long as Gaylon's arm. He sliced the soft leather away with absurdly delicate turns of his huge wrist.

Misk observed the swollen ankle. "That's not it," she muttered, almost to herself. "No, no. There's something else." Gaylon watched her pull Daryn's eyelid back from his good eye, peering closely. "That's it!"

"*What's it?*" the boy demanded, but she whisked past him to the fireplace. He followed anxiously, then stood nearby as Misk crumbled dried flowers, leaves, and other oddments into a piece of cheesecloth. At last she poured boiling water over all into a wooden bowl.

"What's that?" Gaylon asked. He'd been treated all his life

by the keep physician, Girkin, and his foul tasting concoctions, but he'd never actually seen the medicines prepared. And while Girkin was a strange little man, portly and self-important, he was at least familiar and inspired some small amount of faith. Misk, with her muttering and quicksilver movements, inspired nothing in Gaylon but confusion and doubt.

Misk had heard the question, but she took her time in answering.

"Ah," she said finally, when the infusion was to her liking, and removed the cheesecloth. She looked up. "It's a simple tea with peppermint, comfrey, and willow bark. A bit of this, a bit of that. It'll ease the pain and fever, help the body to heal itself."

"It won't stay down," said Gaylon stubbornly. "He can't even keep water down."

"So? If it comes up, we'll put more down." She studied the boy with glittering, bird-bright eyes. "A dose would do *you* no harm, and you could use a good scrubbing. Here." She handed him a washcloth and turned back to the fire for another of the numerous kettles hanging on iron arms that swung over the coals. For an instant Gaylon thought that he saw right through her, saw the fire flickering where it shouldn't. He blinked, eyes tearing, and the illusion was gone.

"Madam?" He touched the woman's sleeve, as much to assure himself of her solidity as to get her attention.

"Misk will do, child." She pulled a basin from a nearby shelf and filled it as she spoke.

"Misk," he said obediently, "will Daryn be all right?"

"In time." She laid a thick bar of lye soap beside the basin. "I'll warrant he's lost his taste for curry though."

Gaylon's head snapped up. "What did you say?"

"Say?" Her brow furrowed. "I believe I said, I must hurry now. Yes, yes, that was it. The tea is cooling, and I certainly must hurry."

In a flurry of movement Misk swept up the bowl and a spoon and skated across the wide floor to the bed. Gaylon shook his head and rubbed soap onto the wet cloth. How could such a tiny woman whirl about a room so quickly? Even standing still she seemed to be in constant motion. It wasn't really annoying—just breathtaking and perhaps a little unnerving. He stripped away his tattered shirt and attacked the grime on his body, listening the while to Misk as she fed the tea to Daryn, cooing and coaxing.

Finished with the bath, Gaylon reached for his shirt and found a clean nightdress instead. He searched in vain under the bench and table for the other garment. It had vanished. Mystified, he donned the clean gown and wandered across the spotless floor to the bedstead. Misk completed the final wrap of a bandage around Daryn's ankle. He, too, had been bathed and clothed in a voluminous nightgown that could only be one of Harry-Jack's.

"There." Misk stood back, viewing the results with satisfaction. Her husband came to tower over her, and when he leaned down she took his immense head in both her tiny hands and kissed him on the brow. "You're a good man, Jimi," she said. "Go on now and bring the firewood. We'll be fine here. And look in on the animals, too. There's a dear."

He grinned adoringly at her before retrieving an axe, taking the lantern from the wall, and heading for the door. Outside, the rain slanted in a wind that had found its way finally into the valley. With an accepting shrug of his great shoulders, the man stepped out into the night.

"I thought his name was Harry," Gaylon said again, casually.

"It is."

"But you've called him Jack and Jimi, too."

"Ah," she laughed. "His name is Haryld Jackson Jimison. Mostly I call him Harry. He's Jack when he annoys me and Jimi when he's a dear."

"Oh," said Gaylon, immensely relieved. This at least made some sense.

Misk pulled the quilts over the sleeping Daryn. "He'll settle now, never you fear." She gestured toward the table. "Sit a moment."

Without hesitation, the young prince collapsed on a bench. At last fatigue took hold. Still, Gaylon felt secure somehow, in this warm place with its incongruous couple. He ground fists into tired, puffy eyes, then looked up. Misk sat across the table from him, watching with an odd intensity.

"I've waited a long time for you," she said suddenly.

"How could you have? And why?"

Her expression became vague. "Why what?"

"Why have you been waiting for me?" he asked in exasperation.

"But I haven't. What makes you think so?"

Mad! The woman was mad. Now she held out a hand, and in her palm sat a small ebony brooch. A closer look proved it otherwise; the thing had no clasp. He reached out a tentative finger, wondering what she might do if he touched it, but she encouraged him with her eyes.

The brooch was cool, smooth as glass, and liberally sprinkled with minuscule jewels set in a seemingly random pattern. Curious now, Gaylon took it up in his own hand. Misk made no move to stop him. He ran a fingertip over the surface, desiring the raised feel of the gems that blazed there, yellow, red, blue, and white, but they were somehow caught inside, suspended like stars in an eternal night. Turning the object over, Gaylon found the gems visible still, from a different perspective, changed but unchanged. It must be glass, he decided, but however he turned the brooch it remained black. How did the light pass through to set the tiny pinpoints of color ablaze?

"What manner of magic is this?" the prince demanded.

"It's not magic," she informed him. "But it has power."

"What is it, then?"

Her answer was cryptic. "A thing."

"What kind of a thing?" he asked slowly, making each word distinct.

"A chart, a map."

He sat silent, afraid to delve deeper.

"You may deliver it for me." She curled his fingers over the object.

After all her kindness, this was the least Gaylon could do. "Where do you wish it delivered?"

"To where you're going, of course."

"To Castlekeep?"

She drew back. "No! That's not where you're going."

Immediately Gaylon's palm began to tingle. When he opened his hand the object was gone.

"Where did it go?"

Misk's face was serene once more. "Where did what go?"

"The thing! The map! The chart!" he cried in frustration.

"Hush," she chided, glancing toward the bed. "Silly child. It's lost and must be found." Then her eyes unfocused and she murmured, "You must find the one thing first, before the other."

Gaylon was much too tired to follow this insanity any longer. He laid his head on his arms. Misk was saying something more, but this made less sense than the rest. An arm slipped around him, an arm as thick as an oak limb and damp with rain. The boy felt himself lifted and carried to the bed. After that he knew nothing.

* * * * *

For seven days it rained, sometimes a gentle drizzle, sometimes a thundering torrent, but never once did the sun show its face. In that time Daryn began to heal. Gaylon did not. His wounds were much deeper and carefully hidden, even from himself. The nights were the worst. He'd slept in an exhausted stupor the first night. The second night, he'd dreamed vividly that he was home in Castlekeep. Nothing seemed changed. Daryn was there and Jessmyn, Lucien and Telo. But in the dream he couldn't find his father. All night he wandered the mazelike halls of the keep, going from room to room, searching for the tall, red-haired king, only to awaken in the morning, empty and heartsick.

He'd spent the day after the dream sitting on the storage chest under a window at the front of the cottage. Through warped and rippled glass he saw the rain caught like teardrops in the naked branches of the fruit trees in the yard, watched without seeing as a tiny nuthatch moved agilely up and down the tree trunks to its little stashes of summer seeds. All the while Gaylon thought of vengeance, of childish and cruel retribution, until his jaw was tight and his teeth ached from clenching. What went on within the cottage he cared little for. He only roused himself to check on the duke, and once satisfied that the man rested peacefully, he returned to the window to brood.

On the third night the boy's dreams took a nasty turn—filled now with fire, blood, and death, so that he woke crying. Disturbed, Daryn turned restlessly in the covers, reaching out blindly to capture the child in one arm and draw him close.

"Gaylon?" he murmured, his voice thick with sleep.

"I've lost it," the boy sobbed. "I've lost the stone."

"Stone?"

"The fire opal. It's gone."

"You'll find another one," Daryn muttered, drifting away again. Barely conscious himself, Gaylon fell back into troubled sleep.

Morning found the prince once more at his window, keeping angry vigil, waiting impatiently for the weather to break, for Daryn to recover enough to brave the long journey back to Castlekeep. When Harry laid a gentle hand on the boy's shoulder, he looked up in irritation.

"Come," said the giant.

Had it been a command, Gaylon might have balked, but the word was kindly said, and he rose to follow the big man out the door. The boy wore his own clothing again. Breeches and shirt had been returned to him, newly mended and laundered, though now they looked ragged—more like a charboy's attire than a prince's.

Outside, the air was heavy with mist, and clouds lay dark and threatening, promising another downpour and soon. Harry led the child quickly behind the cottage to the byre and inside before they could get very damp. Gaylon had decided Harry must be simple. His round face was too placid, his brown eyes too calm, and if he spoke at all it was in single words or grunts. Now the big man destroyed the boy's theory completely.

"They're bedded down in the back here. I've made 'em

comfortable. They ain't so bad off, just lonesome I expect."

He led Gaylon past the tails of the half-dozen cows, ridge-backed and high-hipped, that stood with their heads in mangers along the left wall. Along the right wall were a number of covered vats and cheese presses. Several cartwheel-sized cheeses were compressing under huge stones, the whey dripping into pails set in the straw on the floor. The air was tangy with the smell of souring milk that overpowered even the odor of cow dung.

At the back of the long low building were two bay horses. Katy lifted her small head and nickered a greeting. Joyfully Gaylon went to her and let her snuffle and nuzzle him. She searched for the carrots he always brought, and finding none she snorted in disgust and buried her face again in the sweet timothy hay in her manger. Amber eyed the prince suspiciously before returning to her own meal.

Gaylon stroked the pony's silky neck with its thickening winter coat. He glanced up at Harry. "Where did you find them?"

"Didn't," the giant said in his deep basso voice. "They come in before you. *She* called 'em. Has a way with all the critters, she does. She tells 'em to bring you and the duke and . . . well, here you be."

"Misk called the horses? How?"

"Talks in their heads, like she does in mine. Don't know how, she just does. I know sometimes she don't seem to make much sense, but she's a good woman, boy. You mind what she says."

* * * * *

Within the cottage, Daryn woke clear-headed and reasonably free of pain for the first time since his arrival. Misk sat on a chair beside the bed, a steaming bowl of porridge in her hands. The air held the full sweet fragrance of apples cooked into the cereal. Without a word, the woman handed Daryn the bowl and reached behind him to plump up the pillows. She smiled, and he studied her with open curiosity.

Her face was angular, the cheeks high and prominent, the nose narrow and straight. Below her lips, which were thin over a wide mouth, was a chin that came to a dimpled point. Her eyes were dark and slanted, catlike. Her silver hair, caught back in a tight bun, was wispy where the shorter pieces had escaped around her forehead, much like sheep's wool. And despite the smooth youthful skin, there was a sense of great age about her.

"Eat," she admonished, "before it grows cold. It's nothing your poor, ill-treated stomach can't handle. Why do you stare at me so?"

Daryn lowered his eyes to the bowl in his hands. "I'm sorry. It's just that you remind me of someone."

"Yes?" she prompted.

"My teacher, a sorcerer I knew years ago. You could be his twin."

"I am," Misk said simply, then picked up the spoon and pushed a gobbet of porridge into Daryn's mouth. "We'll speak no more of that cantankerous old fool. You'll see him again soon enough."

"I was forbidden to ever return to Seward Castle," said Daryn around the food.

"Yes, well, things are changing, are they not? How does your ankle feel?"

He moved the foot experimentally. "Much better, thank you." Another spoonful found Daryn's mouth, and he took the utensil from the woman in self-defense. "Do you wear a Sorcerer's Stone like Sezran?"

"Of course not. Let the men play with their toys; I have more important things to tend to. Eat!"

Dutifully, the duke filled his mouth once more, chewing reflectively. "You have powers. I . . . feel them."

"My powers are my own," Misk replied and then refused to say more.

After a long silence, Daryn spoke again. "If my ankle will support me, Gaylon and I should begin our journey to the keep."

"It will not," she snapped. "And only death awaits you at Castlekeep."

"I hope you're wrong," Daryn returned quietly. "Even so, my duty is clear in this. Gaylon is rightful king, and I must defend him against those who would usurp his throne."

"And so you will, but have a care for your life, Daryn of Gosney. Other lives depend on it." Misk smiled again. "Another week and perhaps you'll be healed enough for travel. As for *where* you'll travel—that shall be decided when the time comes."

The front door burst open, and there was Gaylon, standing in the shadow of Haryld Jackson Jimison. The boy looked around the room and, seeing Daryn awake, ran to the bed. The prince's hair was wet, bound in a net of fine rain, his face animated.

"Katy and Amber are here!"

"Are they?" the duke asked.

"They came before us. Harry says that Misk—" Gaylon canted his head to look up into Harry's face. "Well, anyway, they're here and we can go, if your ankle's well enough."

"A week's time, no less," said Misk.

"Surely on horseback—" the boy began.

"No. Your duke risks the return of the fever, and he's weak, no matter what he says to the contrary." Misk gathered up the empty bowl and turned her back on them.

Disappointment filled Gaylon's face, and Daryn took the prince's thin arm in a firm grasp. "A week's not so very long," he said.

Seven

❖

Daryn and Gaylon didn't leave when that week was over, or even the next. First Amber went off her feed, and the duke feared her ill, and soon after, another storm struck, fiercer than the first. Gaylon was kept busy. Misk took him in charge and began to teach him the uses of her herbs, and though he attended her at first with only half a mind, he found her lessons challenging and soon became engrossed. With Misk, the mornings were best, for it was then that she made the most sense. In the evenings she changed, becoming mysterious and even frightening, speaking in riddles and muttering nonsense. And in the shadowed corners of the cottage, Gaylon often thought he saw two or three images of the tiny woman at once. At other times he heard her voice call him from across the room when he stood right beside her. Before long he began to doubt his own sanity.

None of this seemed to bother Daryn. He rested on the bed and, using materials provided by Misk, spent his time sewing. Sometimes Gaylon would watch in fascination as the duke worked, his needle producing the fine tight seams of a shirt or a cloak. Once, Daryn offered the prince the needle.

"A king doesn't need to know how to sew," the boy said haughtily, and at that the duke grinned.

"He might," said he, "should his royal arse begin to show." The statement caused Gaylon to reach for the seat of his breeches. The material *was* wearing dangerously thin. He accepted the needle, and though his patching was hardly pretty and he pricked his fingers constantly, the child was proud of his work.

On the morning of the twenty-seventh day after his father's death, Gaylon woke from yet another nightmare. He lay for a while in the cold light of the tiny window by the bed. It was not the dream that disturbed him now. Something was wrong, and he couldn't quite decide what. Finally he sat up. Outside the window the world had turned white, and snowflakes fell silently, drifting and swirling in the chill air. He realized that he missed the sound of the rain, the constant hiss as it struck the thatching and ran off the eaves.

"What is it?" Daryn asked, awake now.

"It's snowing," the boy answered. He felt the bed move as Daryn rose, and together on their knees on the straw mattress, they peered through the glass until it frosted over with their warm breath. Without a word, Daryn turned and slid off the bed, gasping as his bare feet touched the icy floor. Gaylon watched the duke begin to dress.

"Quickly," said Daryn. "Put on your clothes. Dress warmly."

The man stacked on the bed all the clothing he'd sewn for them both—two extra shirts, breeches, a spare leather jerkin each, and cowled cloaks of a coarse heavy sackcloth. The cloaks were set aside; the rest was pushed hastily into a leather bag. Gaylon pulled on his stockings, then fumbled at the ties of his shirt. His fingers were stiff with cold. Overhead he heard a soft rustling and tiny bits of straw showered down. A glance up revealed Misk leaning over the rafters from where Harry had made them a temporary bedroom with lumber laid down to form a simple loft.

"What are you doing?" she demanded.

"Packing, madam," said Daryn without pausing in his work or looking up.

"Why?" She hopped birdlike down the rungs of the ladder.

"It's time for us to leave," the duke told her evenly.

Misk eyes widened. "You mustn't!"

"But we must."

Gaylon felt a twinge of fear. Misk had stiffened with anger, and in a flicker of movement, she spun and pointed a finger at the hearth. A huge log smoldering there rolled over and burst into flame. When she turned back her expression was cold.

"Don't speak such foolishness," she said harshly.

Daryn reached out and took her hands in his.

"Dear woman, we're grateful for all you've done for us. But if our fate awaits us, you must let us go to meet it." The man's words were firm, but there was such pleading in the duke's gray eyes that Misk was forced to look away.

"Damn you," she murmured and pulled her hands free. The woman lifted her chin. "Surely you're not in so great a hurry that I can't pack you some provisions."

The duke smiled, and grumbling, Misk went about the task dressed in her nightgown. She motioned Gaylon to her and directed him in filling small bags with an assortment of herbs. These bundles were to be placed with the cheese and bread she herself packed. The ladder creaked as Harry descended to the cottage floor, and together, he and Daryn went to ready the horses.

"And not even a hot breakfast to start you warmly on your way," Misk growled as she bustled around Gaylon, the long hem of her gown swishing about her ankles.

When the men returned, she handed the bulging food sack to Daryn, catching his arm in a small hand. The duke looked down at her.

"If," she said, "I have helped you in any small way, and if you're truly grateful, then I ask only one thing of you in return. Will you grant it?"

"If possible," Daryn said gently.

"East of this valley runs the South Fork. If you follow the river toward Castlekeep as you're so determined, you'll come to a small town called Riverbend. Spend the night there, but tell no one who you are. There is a metalsmith who lives on the edge of town. His name is Sep. To him and him only may you speak freely. He's a good man and will have information concerning the kingdom. Will you do this?"

After a slight hesitation, Daryn nodded. "We will."

"Good." Misk released the duke's arm. "I'll do my best to obscure your movements from those who might search for you magically. Other than that, I can do nothing to protect you."

* * * * *

The great hall was alive with music, with people dancing, talking, eating. Men attired in garish frippery rivaled the women in their full-skirted dresses of silks and satins. In a short month's time the court of Wynnamyr had undergone a bewildering change. Jessmyn sat in a large velvet chair and watched the posturing of the adults about her. For all its richness, the chair was uncomfortable. It was so large she was forced to either sit forward, her legs dangling well above the floor, or sit back with them sticking straight out. However she sat, she felt foolish.

The clothing the princess wore was beautiful, but smothering—a shift of fine satin with a dozen petticoats and over them all, a soft green camlet gown meant to flatter her jade-green eyes. Or so the Lady Gerra had said while trying to entice Jessmyn into wearing it. Her hair was done up in high curls held in place by a circlet of pale yellow gold, a delicate crown befitting a young princess. Those were Lucien's words. It was his wish that she attend all the court functions now. And during the day there were endless lessons in dance and music and letters. She was being schooled in the Xenaran language again. It wasn't difficult for her. Lady Gerra hadn't been lax in teaching the princess her native tongue, and the two of them had always spoken it when alone, but now that language was heard often in the keep as more and more of the Southern gentry came to visit and live. Even in the rain and snow, the gaudy caravans from Katay found their way north. A hundred leagues and more was apparently not too great a distance to travel to the court of King Lucien.

Jessmyn tucked one leg under her, leaned an unprincesslike elbow on the arm of the chair, and proceeded to blow little puffs of air aimed imprecisely at a loose curl dripping over her right eye. She was absolutely and positively bored, and not a little tired. Interest in her little game was quickly lost, though, and she began a visual search of the hall for Lucien. She found him at last among the dancers. The new king led Lady Marcel about the floor in the intricate steps of a Southern promenade. He'd been especially attentive to the young lady in the last few weeks. He was handsome and regal now in royal blue. And charming. In fact, he'd charmed nearly everyone with his generous parties. Even the merchants of Keeptown were not unhappy with the small boon that new trade negotiations with the South were bringing about.

Like everyone else, Jessmyn had heard rumors that in late spring trade would begin in earnest. Everywhere there was talk: of cutting the giant evergreens along the Great River and floating them to the new lumber mill to be constructed at the river's mouth; of mighty rafts of logs lashed together and guided to the Inland Sea and then to the shipyards in Zankos and Katay; of aqueducts to capture the river's fresh water and take it over the Gray Mountains, pumped by great windmills through passes built by Xenaran slaves. These wondrous promises of the future would result in wealth and riches beyond comprehension for Wynnamyr. The people were rejoicing, King Reys and his son already forgotten.

There were several ominous changes, as well. Feydir had begun hiring mercenaries from the South, and they, too, were pouring daily into the realm. These men were a harsh, brutish lot, many of them ex-slaves with their previous owners' marks still tattooed on their cheeks. Others had thick scars where the brands had been crudely removed. Some were men who had always been soldiers, and these were garrisoned within the keep. They strolled the grounds and corridors as though they owned the castle. Jessmyn had been badly frightened by a tall man with only a hole where his nose ought to be. He'd surprised her in the hallway, and she fled crying into Lady Gerra's arms.

The princess shifted in the chair again, her eyes still on the dancing couple. Lady Marcel appeared flushed, and while she laughed and smiled often, there were lines about her eyes and mouth that didn't belong on one so young. Or so, Lady Gerra said. Marcel's father, the Baron Graystone, sat on one of the many chairs that lined the walls. He had grown pale and thin recently, and moved with difficulty now.

Jessmyn felt a twinge of sorrow for the man. There were dark stories best spoken in whispers in the keep. The baron had been one of Feydir's strongest detractors and had voiced loudly and bitterly his opposition to the new king's ascent to the throne. The baron and several others of his group had been arrested and held in the vaults below the castle. Of them all, he had been the only one to return to court, and then only after his daughter had become more receptive to Lucien's attentions.

High intrigue had found its way into a simple country court, and it was swiftly becoming a creature of dark habits. To Jessmyn, this was both confusing and frightening at once. Lucien was good to her, as he'd always been, even while insisting that she behave as royalty. He told her she must call Feydir "Uncle;" though the tall gaunt ambassador terrified her, he, too, was kind in a distracted manner.

The music began a deeper percussive beat, and the room seemed suddenly too bright, too crowded, the laughter too loud. Jessmyn's dress felt stifling. Across the wide hall, Lucien was caught up in conversation with two Southern lords, so the princess decided that this moment was as good as any to slip away unnoticed. She wriggled out of the chair and wended her way through the revelers to the door of the southeast wing, ducking between the guards there, ignoring their stark looks of disapproval.

In the passageway, she snatched the coronet from her head so that her hair tumbled to her shoulders and started off at a brisk walk. The princess was hungry and thought about going to the kitchens to beg a snack, but with Ketti gone, the kitchens were no longer the refuge they had once been. Poor Ketti. She'd hung herself in her little room soon after hearing of King Reys's death. Jessmyn shuddered. Best to go back to her own bedroom where Lady Gerra waited. She no longer slept in the nursery, but had a large double chamber near the king's apartments. Lucien's wishes again.

"Jessmyn?"

He had come upon her silently, and she froze there on the lowest step of the stone staircase leading to the second floor.

"Where are you going?" Lucien asked, voice soft and kind as always.

"To my rooms, Your Majesty." She turned and curtsied politely, though her heart wasn't in it. Lucien demanded much respect from everyone.

"Your presence is desired in the hall," said the young king.

"I'm tired," Jessmyn snapped, losing both patience and courtesy at once.

Lucien held out a graceful hand to her. "Come now, I am king and you must obey me."

His graciousness only served to irritate her further.

"I won't obey you!" the child answered angrily. "And you won't be king for long."

That gave him pause. "What's this?"

"Gaylon will come home soon. He'll be king, and you'll be nothing again." Jessmyn was instantly sorry she'd spoken her mind, but instead of growing angry, Lucien took a seat beside her on the stair.

"What makes you think so?"

"The horses. They found them all, but not Katy and not Amber. That means Gaylon and Daryn rode away, and they'll come back."

"If that were so, then why haven't they returned already? It's been nearly a month."

The princess had no immediate response to that.

"Gaylon is dead, Jessmyn." Again that awful condescending kindness.

"He's not!" the little girl flared. "I would know if he were. I'd feel it! Here!" She tapped her breast where she thought her heart to be.

Lucien only smiled sadly at her, and, infuriated, Jessmyn flung herself past him and up the stairs, sweeping her skirts and petticoats up in one arm to keep from tripping. The king said nothing as he watched her go.

* * * * *

The snow had been falling lightly all day, but the wind waited until dusk to hone the cold to a fine cutting edge. The winter light faded quickly. Daryn stood up in the iron stirrups once more, trying to force the blood to circulate in his toes. It'd been some time since he'd been able to feel them, and his fingers ached despite the fact that he warmed them constantly, first in one armpit, then the other.

"How goes it?" he called to Gaylon who rode a pace or two behind on Katy.

"J-Just fine," the boy answered through chattering teeth.

"Well, we must be nearly there. The last signpost said it was only five leagues to Riverbend."

They'd found the old coach road in poor repair, but the going was a good deal easier than it had been in the forest. Here, in the lowlands, the ground still showed in small dark patches through the snow. There were tracks of other horses that had passed this way before them, though they'd met no one. The river rolled turgidly on their right, its waters black and slushy.

Daryn pulled his cloak more tightly about him and began to wonder what exactly they would do in Riverbend. He'd heard of the town during his travels in the South. It was really no more than a way station with a very bad reputation. Built upon the flood plain, its inhabitants scratched most of their living from the rich soil the river deposited in flood years—after it had carried away their homes. Each time this happened they stubbornly returned to build again, to plant again.

Before the wars, the wealthy had stopped their coaches at the town's only inn, where they gladly paid exorbitant prices for tiny rooms and awful food.

Daryn's fingers found the pouch at his belt, and he felt for the four silver coins Misk had given him. They were all she had, and he only hoped they would be enough. In his boot, the one he'd carefully restitched, was a dirk that Harry had given him. Gaylon still had his sword, but Daryn felt uneasy about going so lightly armed into a town as ill-famed as Riverbend. Yet he'd promised Misk he would search out the smithy, Sep, before going on. It was just as well; tonight was not a night to be spent in the open.

The duke had spoken to Misk of fate, and he felt its inexorable pull now. It seemed that the plans he made for Gaylon and himself were of no account, that fate was narrowing his choice of paths until there would be only one direction in which to go. Misk had hinted of that direction, and the very thought made his hackles rise. Daryn shivered, and not from the cold.

He was haunted yet—by his mother's lonely death, his father's inexpressible love, the old sorcerer's rejection. He felt he'd failed them all and was terrified he would fail again. But the memory of the king's hand on his shoulder remained strong. Yes, he'd lead the prince as long as he was able and then, when the boy was ready, Daryn would follow him as was right and just.

"Lights!"

Daryn heard Gaylon's whoop as the boy pushed Katy into a canter past him, disappearing into the white on white of the wintery eve. The duke nudged Amber with his heels, and, shaking her ice-rimed mane, the mare set out in pursuit.

The only street of the town was lined on either side by small shops, shuttered now, perhaps a dozen in all. The inn was the largest structure, a two-story ramshackle affair, impossible to miss. Light from its many windows spilled into the yard and raucous laughter sounded within. "Fickle River Inn," the sign over the door announced.

They halted the horses in the yard. As Daryn dismounted, the door banged open, and a man stumbled out. The fellow's nose was bright red, his cheeks fat, and his belly protruded well over his belt. He grinned at them as he staggered past, then turning politely away, began to relieve himself into the snow.

"If yer lookin' fer a place to stay the night, yer outta luck," he said over his shoulder. "The inn's full up."

"Full?" asked Daryn.

"Yep. Full," the fellow confirmed. "Place's bin busy ever since the soldiers started comin' north. You a mercenary?"

"Well, I—"

"Look, I can't see ya out on a night like this. Come in and warm yerself, and I'll see what I kin do. Owner's a friend of mine." He winked and refastened his breeches.

Gaylon still sat on Katy, and the man turned on him. "Well, boy! Don't sit like a fool. Git down and tend yer master's horse. There's a shed in back. I suppose ya kin squeeze in another or two."

Gaylon didn't move, but his nostrils flared and his eyes glittered.

"Ya deaf, boy?" the man roared. "Git down or I'll yank ya off!"

Daryn caught the prince's wrist as he reached for the small sword hidden under his cloak.

"Easy," the duke whispered. "Best do as he says."

Angrily Gaylon kicked his boots free of the stirrups and dropped to the ground. Pain shot up both legs, numb as they were, and he accepted Amber's reins without a word. As he led the horses away, the drunken fellow clamped an arm around Daryn's shoulders, steering him toward the door.

He was saying, "Good help's hard to come by, but where'd ya find such a scrawny little thing? Don't look worth feedin'."

Gaylon stomped his way around the building and not just to stave off the cold. A lighted oil lamp hung near the back entrance. He took it from the hook and carried it with him to the shed. There were no stall dividers, the horses instead tied to iron rings along one wall. The place was definitely crowded, but Amber laid back her ears and nipped a big dun on the hip. Squealing, the creature swung aside to give them room.

"Good girl," Gaylon told her with a short laugh, for he felt like biting someone himself.

He stripped the saddles from the mares' backs and put the food and clothing bags aside. The harness racks were all in use so the saddles were set on their noses in a corner, the sheepskin pads thrown on top of them. They were old-fashioned saddles with high wooden pommels and cantles, their leather seats cracked and peeling. Harry had found them stored in the rafters of the byre, and Gaylon had helped him clean and oil them. They were serviceable and reasonably comfortable, but as the prince rubbed the horses down he checked them for saddle galls just in case. Next, he found the grain bin and some feed sacks that had been cut into crude nose bags. He poured a double measure of crushed corn into a pair and tied them in place over the mares' ears, then sat and watched the two until they were finished eating.

Finally Gaylon gathered up the packs and started for the back door of the inn, but as he passed out of the shed his sword clanked against the jam. He halted, debating a moment before reluctantly unhooking the scabbard from his belt. A ten-year-old sporting a fine sword would only bring questions he and Daryn were unprepared to answer. The blade was carefully hidden under the straw behind the saddles before the prince crossed the narrow bit of yard to the inn.

The common room was as crowded as the shed, perhaps more so, and smelled little better. The air lay oppressively hot, and smoke from the lamps hung in a thick blue cloud over the men who sat or stood, talking and drinking. Gaylon shed his cloak while searching the room for Daryn, and found the duke on a bench by the massive fireplace with a wine cup to his lips. The man's boots were off, drying before the fire, and a woman in long skirts and tightly laced bodice leaned over him to refill the cup.

Gaylon shoved his way roughly through the crowd, ignoring the resultant complaints.

"'Lo, m'boy." Daryn grinned at him. His words were gently slurred and his breath smelled of cinnamon and cloves. Gaylon felt a sudden irritation.

The woman was very pretty, with long dark hair caught up in a tortoiseshell clasp, and wide, green eyes. Then she smiled. Her front teeth were missing.

"A cup of mulled wine for you, lad?" she asked with only a hint of a lisp.

Gaylon nodded mutely, and the woman turned to fill a another cup, but not before she'd run a hand along Daryn's jaw. She handed the boy his wine and left to answer a call for service across the room.

"Who's she?" Gaylon demanded.

With difficulty, Daryn focused on him. He'd drained his cup again. "That's Haddi, the pro-proprietress. She's offered us a place to sleep at a price we can't afford to pass by."

"That so?" Gaylon snapped, but Daryn missed the sarcasm. The man's gray eyes followed Haddi's progress across the floor.

"What price?" Gaylon asked finally and sipped his hot wine.

"A song," Daryn replied.

"A song," echoed Haddi, returning. Her lips brushed Daryn's black hair. "You'll sing me sweet songs tonight in my room."

The duke held out his cup to her, smiling.

"No more," Gaylon said sharply, and the woman paused. "We haven't eaten. He needs food, not more wine."

She looked to Daryn, and he sighed. "He's right."

"Well, darlin'," said Haddi, her hand again on the man's jaw, "dinner's long over, but I'm sure I can find something in the kitchen." She nodded toward a table. "Sit yourselves over there."

Daryn gathered his boots from the hearth and pulled them on, surreptitiously slipping the dirk back into place. He found his cloak where it had fallen behind the bench and followed Gaylon to one of several trestle tables. The men already seated there moved down grudgingly.

The food came: cold mutton, a trifle greasy, and bread, more than a little stale. Somehow, though, Gaylon was certain Haddi had brought Daryn the best she could find. The duke sobered as he ate, but his attention remained on the woman, and Gaylon's irritation grew. He was depending on Daryn to get them safely home, and this was certainly no time to be side-tracked. The prince wanted this night over and done, so he could be back on the road to Castlekeep.

"Well, friend. Now that I see ya in the light, I know ya ain't a mercenary."

It was the man from the yard with his fat cheeks and red nose. He leaned across the table toward Daryn, and Gaylon could see the tiny broken veins in the pale skin on his fleshy face.

"I told ya Haddi'd do right by ya." He seemed to think that funny and laughed uproariously. Gaylon frowned as the man continued. "Name's Tobi. Who might ya be?"

Daryn said carefully, "I'm Davlin, and this is Gar." He indicated Gaylon.

"Yer charboy. Git the horses bedded down, did ya, boy?"

"Yes . . . sir," Gaylon answered, but the one word stuck in his throat.

"There's a good lad." Tobi grinned, turning back to the duke. "Well, ya ain't a soldier. Ya got no weapons, least ways none I kin see. Whattcha do and where ya headed?"

"I'm a minstrel, and I'm headed north."

"You and just 'bout everyone here. Headed for Castlekeep?"

"We're . . . looking for a man. His name is Sep. Do you know him?"

"Sep? Know him? He's my brother-in-law. And ya don't need to go looking for him. He comes in for a cup or two every night. You a friend of his?"

"Friend of a friend."

"Still makes ya a friend of mine," Tobi said grandly. "He's a bit late tonight." He squinted at the door on the far side of the room. "Ah, that's him."

Sep had arrived, but not alone. The smith was not a tall man, or big. He wore no cloak, and his shirt sleeves were rolled back. Thick ropes of muscle were woven through his forearms and down into hands that seemed almost too large for him. Though his head was nearly bald, a great black beard streaked with gray framed his face.

The man that passed through the door with him was unusual looking, dressed all in black with a scaled leather cuirass. Under one arm he carried a helm and, at his hip, a mighty sword. A uniform of some sort, Gaylon decided. But this soldier's most striking feature was his lack of a nose. The two men spoke in low tones in the doorway, then parted company.

"Over here, Sep!" Tobi called above the noise.

"Good brother, how goes it?" the smith asked as he straddled the bench. "Haddi! Ale, here! Do you need a drink,

Tobi?"

"I could use a drop," said Tobi agreeably. Then, "Look, ya gotta friend here."

"Oh?"

"This is Davlin. He rides the road north."

"Don't recall the name or the face, sir. Have we met?" Sep gave Daryn an appraising look.

"No," said Daryn, again choosing his words carefully, "but a friend asked me to call on you—a woman who lives in the woods some leagues south and west of here."

Sep's dark eyes narrowed. He turned to Tobi. "Haddi's busy. Be a good fellow and fetch us some ale."

"There's no hurry," said Tobi.

"I'm dry, man."

Tobi's lips pursed, but he climbed to his feet and headed for the kitchen.

"And bring a tankard for our friend, Davlin," Sep called after him. He looked again at Daryn. "So Misk has sent you. Is she in need of anything? I owe that dear woman much."

"No," Daryn assured him. "She said you might have some information for us."

"Information? To what concern? And who is 'us'?"

Daryn put a hand on Gaylon's arm. "Misk also said we may speak freely with you." He paused. "My name is not Davlin. It's Daryn Emilson. I'm the duke of Gosney. And this is my young ward, Gaylon, heir of the Red Kings, prince of the realm."

"My gods!" Sep drew a sharp breath, glancing quickly over his shoulder. He leaned forward. "Speak not so loud, milord," he said, though their words could hardly be heard over the rumble of conversation all about them. He shook his head. "This is strange indeed. This very night, a man named Nankus—the one who entered with me—came asking for information of your whereabouts. I could tell him nothing."

Tobi arrived, slopping ale from big mugs onto the tabletop as he set them down.

"I've changed my mind," Sep said hastily. "I want a bottle of Haddi's best wine. And not that watered down stuff she serves everyone else."

"But—"

"Go on, and don't complain. I'm buying, aren't I?"

With a shrug of his shoulders, Tobi left again.

"He's not a bad fellow, but his tongue grows loose when he drinks," Sep told them, "and he drinks all the time." The smith chuckled, then sobered abruptly, his eyes on Gaylon. "Your Highness, we all believed you dead. Your father, the king . . ."

"Is dead," the boy finished softly.

Sep looked at him pityingly. "And Lucien D'Sulang has stolen your crown."

"He'll not have it long, I promise you," said Gaylon through his teeth. "We're on our way to Castlekeep."

Shocked, Sep shook his head. "You'll never make it, not as free men."

Daryn and Gaylon exchanged a glance.

"What do you mean?" Daryn asked.

"The man, Nankus, is a captain in the king's guard—though it's come to my ears that the guard answers to Lucien's uncle, Ambassador Feydir D'Sulang. Feydir, it seems, searches for the duke eagerly under the pretext of capturing an assassin, but there are hints of a darker purpose. What that purpose might be, I don't know. I know only that there's nowhere safe for either of you."

"I'm rightful king," Gaylon said.

"Does it matter? If the people think you dead already, it'd be easy enough for Feydir to make it truth."

"No, we'll—"

"Young prince, listen. In the month since your father's death, the realm has undergone great changes. Look about you. These soldiers move north to the keep to join Feydir's army, but that's the least of it. Pacts have been made with the merchant rulers of the Xenara, and these foolish people, my countrymen, *your* countrymen, dream now of great wealth. I wonder if they would help you should you even have a chance to seek aid. Greed blinds so many of them. They don't see as I do, that the army is being built to prevent revolt when the people finally realize that the wealth they've been promised, have tasted already, will never really come to them. It'll all pass into the hands of Feydir and his puppet nephew. Wynnamyr will be bled dry and its people enslaved." The smith's eyes grew troubled. "Evil times are upon us, and I'm beginning to doubt there's anything any of us can do to change that."

"Change what?" Tobi demanded, setting the bottle and wine cups before them.

"Nothing," said Sep gruffly.

A call rose now above the voices of the room.

"Listen to me, good people of Riverbend and you soldiers who guest with them tonight!" Everyone turned toward the door to see who had spoken. It was Nankus, an imposing figure in his helm. "Listen to me!"

The crowded smoky room grew quiet under that command, and the captain began to speak. His words were oddly articulated because of the missing nose.

"I am Nankus, a captain in the royal guard, and I am about the king's business this night. We search for a man. You've heard of him, I know. He's the assassin, Daryn Emilson. The king bids me tell you that he now offers a reward for any information that will aid in his arrest. A hundred golden decos!"

The crowd rumbled its approval. The man spoke of Southern gold, and a small fortune.

"And five hundred to the man who can bring him to us alive!"

Their whispers held awe now, and one man called out, "What does this fellow look like?"

Nankus answered, "He's of medium build and height, and black-haired."

"Half the men here fit that description," the same man growled.

"He wears a ring on the forefinger of his left hand."

"And if he takes it off?" another called.

"Let me finish, please. The ring bears a Sorcerer's Stone. He'll never willingly remove it, though it is known that he has little power over it."

This brought mixed reactions. Many didn't like the thought

of dealing with a magician, even a minor one.

Daryn had pushed Gaylon down, forcing him beneath the table as Nankus spoke, and now he covered his left hand with his right slowly, for men were beginning to look over their neighbors. Tobi observed the duke's moves and saw a cold fear pass across Sep's bearded face. The fat man's fingers crept to the hilt of the dagger at his belt.

Under the table, Gaylon saw the thick fingers take the grip and begin to draw the blade. Without thinking, the boy plucked the dirk from Daryn's boot and plunged it with all his might into the muscle of Tobi's left thigh. The fellow screamed and leaped to his feet, overturning the table. The room was suddenly in chaos.

At the scream, every man in the inn found his weapon. At the resounding crash of the table every sword or dirk was drawn, and some of the more drunken soldiers found themselves engaged in clumsy combat.

"Stop!" cried Nankus over the clanging of swords. "Stop, you fools!" He strode across the room, batting away drawn weapons as he came. He halted before Tobi, who cried piteously now. "What's happened to you?"

"He was here," Tobi managed to sob. He had a hand clamped over the wound in his leg, and blood puddled on the bench, dripping onto the blade of his dagger where it had fallen. "Daryn Emilson. He was right here beside me. I coulda taken him, but the brat stabbed me."

Nankus looked at Sep, and the smithy said sourly. "He's drunk. This isn't the first time he's done this."

"What do you mean?"

"I mean, he got drunk and sat on his knife. He's done it before."

Someone guffawed.

"Lies!" Tobi screamed.

"I've told him to be careful," Sep continued scornfully. "I've warned him he'll geld himself one of these days." That brought a ripple of appreciative laughter in the room.

"There *was* another man sitting with you," Nankus said suspiciously.

"Aye . . . a minstrel from Zankos on his way to sing for the court at Castlekeep," Sep lied. "Haddi took him upstairs a while ago. She'll have him singing all right, and soon, I'll warrant." More laughter followed.

"Well?" Nankus demanded of the whimpering Tobi.

Tobi looked at Sep, and saw hatred in his brother-in-law's eyes.

"I lied," he said softly. "I thought perhaps—"

"That you could claim a hundred gold pieces. Consider yourself lucky. You might have collected a hundred lashes instead." Nankus turned on his heel and left the inn.

Sep stood staring down at Tobi, who still fought to staunch the flow of blood.

"If it weren't for my sister, I would kill you," the smith said in a low voice, calmly, coldly. Then he, too, turned and walked away.

* * * * *

Haddi's room was dark, and from the window Daryn and Gaylon watched Nankus in the yard below mount his horse stiffly and head it away from the inn. Where the man would go, Daryn could only guess, but he felt certain the captain had not come alone from Castlekeep. He turned his horse northward and didn't seem in a hurry. There was likely a small company of soldiers encamped nearby.

A soft knock came at the door, and Sep called quietly from without.

"Haddi?"

The woman had been standing silently behind them and now went to the door to let the smith in. She passed from the room as he came.

"You're safe for the time being," said Sep. "Tomorrow, early, you'd best leave. Where will you go?"

Daryn had no answer, but Gaylon said clearly, "To Castlekeep."

"The roads are patrolled, lad. It'd be wise for you to return to Misk."

"No—" Gaylon began, but the duke put a hand on his shoulder.

"We'll consider your suggestion," he said to Sep.

Haddi returned bearing a lighted lamp, her face awash with its soft yellow glow. Silence fell in the room. She looked at them questioningly as she placed the lamp on the trunk at the foot of her bed.

"I can't say that I understand all that's happened, but if I can be of any help . . ."

"You already have," Daryn told her gently.

She smiled, revealing the wide gap where her teeth should be. "It's late. I must go back downstairs and tell my guests that it's time for me to close the common room." She held out her hand to Gaylon. "If you'll come with me, child, I'll make you a nice bed before the fire."

Gaylon looked at Daryn.

"Have no fears for your master," the woman said. "I'll make sure he's comfortable, as well."

Gaylon lifted his chin. "I have no fears for that," he said archly and, refusing her hand, walked from the room.

Sep closed the door behind them, grinning.

"He's a cocky one, and damn quick with a knife," he said. "The boy saved both your lives tonight."

"I know," said Daryn. "What of Tobi?"

When the smith replied his voice had grown hard. "He'll cause you no more harm." Then he grinned again. "It seems the prince would protect you from Haddi, as well."

"Do I need protection?" the duke asked solemnly.

Sep's grin faded. "What can I say? She's a strong woman, more honest than most folk, but I would keep my thoughts to myself. These are times when trust is a luxury that few can afford, and a hundred gold decos is a goodly sum."

Daryn nodded. "I'm duly warned then. Thank you."

For a long moment they looked at one another in silence.

"By the gods!" said Sep suddenly. "It's been years since I hefted a sword, but I was a fair hand once. I've nothing here to hold me, really. If you could use—"

Daryn raised a hand. "You've risked enough already."

"But I could—"

"No, Sep. If we should pass this way again we'll likely need your counsel. Bide here and gather what information you can."

"You're right. I've always been one for picking up tidbits of news. I've friends from Land's End to Zankos. And Kelsyn! Kelsyn is an armorer in Keeptown. We fought together in the South." Sep scratched his bald pate reflectively. "I'll bet *he's* got a tale or two for me." He paused. "Forgive me, milord. You're tired, and I must go. I won't see you again before you leave. I've done little to encourage the favor of my gods, but for whatever they're worth, my prayers go with you and the prince."

The smith offered his right hand palm up, and Daryn clasped the man's wrist. The duke felt his own taken in a strong grip. As he left, Sep closed the door gently behind him.

Alone in Haddi's room now, Daryn glanced about, taking in the rough furniture, the few personal items on table and shelf. He was trying to gain a sense of the personality behind the objects, but it eluded him. On one wall hung a lute. He took it down, and sat with the instrument on a stool by the bed. This one was not as pretty as his own Candilass, but old, hard-traveled, and badly out of tune. The neck was warped slightly. He played with it for a time. The lute had been well used; the varnish had worn away from the dark wood on the front just below the strings. On the back, where the body of the instrument rested against him, was a deep gouge in the wood. He fingered the scratch thoughtfully, trying to imagine how such a cut might have been gotten. For all the sad appearance, the lute's voice was rich in a melancholy way. Someone at some time had cherished it. How he knew this he couldn't say; it was just a feeling he got with the instrument cradled in his arms.

The door opened quietly, and Haddi stepped into the room. She carried a bottle of wine in one hand, another tucked under her arm, and she smiled at him. This time he noticed only the dimples in her cheeks, the sparkle in her green eyes.

"The child doesn't like me," she said, placing the bottles on a tiny table near the one window. There were cups on the wash stand, and she blew dust from two before filling them with wine. "Perhaps he fears I'll steal you from him."

Daryn accepted the cup gratefully. "Things have been very difficult for him of late."

"Oh? How so?"

Daryn drained the cup before speaking, and then it was only to ask a question of his own. "Shall I sing for you now?"

"I'd like that." She refilled his cup, and he emptied it again, hoping the wine would soothe the odd nervousness that held him.

The song he chose was a simple one, a sweet ballad of another age, of another man and woman in another land. When he was done, Haddi set her cup upon the floor and sat at his feet, laying her head against his knee, her hand around the calf of his leg. She'd let her long dark hair down, and he stroked it a moment before beginning another song.

There was an unusual quality in the tone of the lute that lent to the next song a certain eldritch power. As Daryn plucked the final note from the strings, Haddi took the instrument gently from his arms and stood, drawing him up beside her. The lute was put aside. The woman was very nearly his height, and as he wrapped his arms around her, Haddi put her lips to his. Her kiss was soft, her lips cool and moist and tasting of wine. Daryn found himself returning the kiss eagerly, but she pushed him away and began to unlace her bodice.

She made love with him on her narrow little bed, and her gifts to him were many. But he had gifts for her as well, and slow and gentle was the giving of them. After, she lay close and whispered her life into his ear. He caressed her shoulder and listened.

Her husband had beaten her for the first time only days after they'd been wed, and she had lost her teeth then. He was an old man, she barely fourteen. Ten years later he had died, and she'd been left with the inn to run. There had been many suitors at first, all of them convinced she would need a man to keep her safe. She took great pleasure in proving them wrong. Later, there had been a lover, a young man whose lute Daryn had played. One night, as he sang in the common room below, a drunken patron took exception to the tune and stabbed him.

He had tried to fend off the blow with the lute, and the blade had scratched the wood. Haddi held him as he died. After that she'd loved no one, though the stories about her said differently. She let the men think what they pleased; she would be every man's conquest and no one's. She'd planned only to flirt with Daryn, as she did with all the customers—it encouraged their return—but somehow that intent was changed over the course of the evening.

He kissed her hair now as she spoke, running his fingers lightly over her breasts. Her supple skin felt exquisite to the touch. He desired her again and found her willing.

Daryn had no memory of falling asleep, but a dull thudding sound woke him. A bell-like jingling from outside forced him at last to open his eyes. It was dawn. Haddi lay warm beside him, and he was loath to leave her. There came another thud as snow struck the window. Carefully he slipped from beneath the quilts and went to stand naked before the thick glass.

In the yard below, the horses stood, saddled and waiting. Gaylon, muffled in his cloak, peered upward, his face barely visible under the brown cowl. The boy waved, and the horses stamped, blowing great gusts of vapor into the icy air. Daryn turned back from the window and found Haddi standing by the bed. Her dark hair spilled over her shoulders, making the white skin appear almost luminescent. He wanted to touch her, to hold her one last time, but instead, grabbed up his clothing and began to dress. His boots were stiff with cold, and he struggled with them, acutely aware that Haddi watched his every move. That made him clumsy. Her silence hurt him somehow, but he could think of nothing to say to her. When he'd finished she finally moved, taking up the lute and holding it out to him in both her hands.

"Do not forget me," she said softly, and as he accepted the gift, she turned away. He felt as if some vast distance had come between them already.

Daryn took the stairs quietly so as not to disturb the sleepers in other rooms, unbarred the front door, and stepped into the morning. Gaylon had already mounted and led Amber to the door. After pulling his cloak from the saddle and donning it,

Daryn drew the hood gratefully around his face. With mind still, emptied of thought, he tied the lute behind the cantle.

"Daryn?" Gaylon held out a long, cloth-covered object. "Sep came back to the inn last night. He said that if he couldn't go with us, then you were to have this to remember him by."

Another remembrance. The duke slid back the cloth and found a sword, old and heavy—so heavy a man of strength might cleave bone with it. The hilt was of silver and carven with sea dragons, long snaking creatures with tiny ruby eyes and inlaid scales of iridescent blue-green shell. The scabbard, of oiled leather, was unadorned, and Daryn hooked it to his belt. The strange weight of the sword tugged at his hip as he mounted.

"He said her name is Squall, and he prays that she'll serve you as well as she did him in the Southern Campaigns."

The prince had spoken in the same neutral tone throughout. Daryn looked at him curiously, but Gaylon's face was a dark shadow beneath his hood.

"Where do we go?" the boy asked now, again in a carefully emotionless voice.

Yes, where? thought Daryn, trying to divine the future and experiencing only a dark, hazy nothingness, formless and without comfort. He thought of Castle Gosney. There might be refuge so far from Lucien, and perhaps friends among those who were once loyal to his father and the Red King he served. It was also near Lasony. There was a chance they would find support across the northern border, though that snowy kingdom was poorer in resources even than Wynnamyr.

"We go north," he said finally. "We'll avoid the main road as far as is possible."

Gaylon only nodded—one curt dip of his cowled head—and set Katy at a brisk trot away from the inn. Daryn started after him, but not without first looking up at a certain window in the upper story. He had hoped . . . but, no. The empty window stared blindly back at him.

Eight

❖

The *Book of Stones*. Even the look of it was intimidating. It held countless pages of extremely thin paper, bound together in leather and wood. Each sorcerer's tome was hand-copied in tiny runic symbols. The ink was black, but legend had it that human blood was required in the mixing. The pages had no numbers, the chapters no headings. A reader would find no punctuation, indentations, or spaces between the words. To study the book took incredible concentration and determination and no small amount of foreknowledge. But the rewards were boundless for those who won their way through. It seemed to be textbook and fairy tale both, and the lessons varied. The volume offered the reader knowledge in metallurgy, chemistry, physics, and philosophy, and chronicled the ages, as well. The key to the book was the Sorcerer's Stone, and the book, in turn, was the key to the Stone.

The *Book of Stones* held another key, and it was this other that Feydir sought. Somewhere within the pages was a small reference to Kingslayer, and he was determined to find that passage. For weeks now he'd spent every spare moment of his days and most of his nights in a methodical search. Now his eyes felt as if sand had been poured into them, and the lines on the paper blurred continually before him.

The ambassador sat in the king's own library. There was no longer any need to hide his powers, and he wore his Stone openly around his neck, exposed upon the breast of his robes.

This brought fear to the ignorant and caution to the wisest of his enemies. Baron Graystone had felt his displeasure and others had learned from the man's misfortune. It pleased Feydir to strike terror in the hearts of those around him. Lucien, on the other hand, gained popularity by playing off his uncle's fearsomeness, by seeming to be the defender of the people. They'd fallen into this game quite unconsciously, but it served them well. The young king had proven to be quite canny, and this pleased Feydir, also—but he was still wary of his nephew. It would be most unwise to be too trusting.

Turning another page, the mage forced himself to focus on the words before him. There was another possible clue to Kingslayer: Daryn of Gosney. Lucien had found the riddle with its cryptic allusions to the fabled sword of power in the duke's apartments, and Feydir was bent on having what knowledge of the Legacy Daryn might possess. First, however, he must find the man. He refused to believe Gosney dead. While Lucien had never admitted to engineering the murders of Reys and Gaylon, Feydir knew his nephew too well to ever doubt he was responsible. And Daryn would surely have perished with the others.

Only, somehow, Feydir felt certain the man still lived, even though a careful scrying spell wrought with his Sorcerer's Stone had revealed nothing. There was always the chance that the duke might counter such magic with some of his own. When all else had failed, Feydir put his captain, Nankus, with a dozen of his best men on the search. Should Gosney be found and captured, well . . .

Feydir's Stone pulsed in anticipation, and he reached to cup it in his palm, enjoying the fire-and-ice sensation.

* * * * *

Yesterday's storm had passed during the night, and the day proved clear. The sun glaring off the snow caused eyes to smart, and the air warmed considerably so that Gaylon and Daryn soon shed their cloaks. They rode high on the wooded mountainside west of the road, but the melting snow had turned the run-off creeks that fed the South Fork into raging cataracts, and the two were forced continually back to the main road to use the small wooden bridges. So far luck had been with them, and they'd met no one at these crossings.

Gaylon hadn't spoken once since they'd left the inn, and now he rode ahead, setting an exhausting pace. Whenever Katy balked at a downed tree or deep puddle, the boy sawed at her mouth and put the spurs to her. At midday they were impelled once more to find the coach road. Daryn decided finally that he'd had enough of Gaylon's moody silence and pushed Amber into a long canter in order to catch up with the prince before he reached the bridge.

"Gaylon!"

The boy ignored him, and Daryn had to reach out and grab Katy's reins to force a halt.

"Let go," Gaylon said through clenched teeth, and the suppressed fury in his voice gave Daryn pause.

"I want to know what's bothering you," he said.

What happened then shocked them both. Sunlight sparked silver in a descending arc, and Daryn snatched his arm back only just in time to avoid injury. Gaylon had slashed out with the dirk that he'd kept in his own boot since the incident with Tobi. Now the blade was held frozen in midair, and the boy's anger had turned to horror.

"Why?" Daryn asked as calmly as he could. "Why are you so angry?"

Gaylon turned his face away, letting the hand with the knife fall back harmlessly to his leg.

In the silence Daryn searched his own heart for possible answers.

"Is it because of Haddi?"

"No!" Gaylon said too quickly. Then, "Yes."

Daryn stumbled over his next words. "I don't know what to say. Perhaps you're too young to understand what . . . a man and a woman—"

"I understand all that," the boy growled in exasperation. His head was still turned away, but his shoulders shook gently.

Stiffly Daryn dismounted, stepping down into the muddy

slush of the road. He caught the child around the waist, pulling him from his horse.

"What is it, then?" he asked, mystified.

Gaylon spoke so softly that Daryn nearly missed the words. "I'm afraid."

"Of what?"

"I'm afraid you'll leave me alone again." The boy began to sob openly now.

"I wouldn't. I wouldn't leave you for any reason, and certainly not because of Haddi."

Gaylon looked at him finally, his face streaked with tears. "You didn't even know her. It was . . . it was as if she'd cast some spell on you. All night I lay awake, thinking she might harm you or call the soldiers to take you so she could have the gold. And I wouldn't be there to protect you. I wouldn't be able to save you!"

In dismay, Daryn took him and hugged him close. How had this come about? Somehow their roles had been subtly reversed. He'd thought himself the defender and found himself defended.

And, yes, Haddi *had* cast a spell, though it was no more than the earthy magic that was every woman's birthright. Daryn felt a twinge of shame. He'd been so unthinking, so uncaring of Gaylon's feelings, his very natural fear of being deserted again.

The tears had stopped. The boy held out the dirk hilt first.

Daryn shook his head. "Put it back in your boot. You may need it again one day. I failed to thank you for what you did last night in the tavern. I do so now, with all my heart."

Gaylon wiped his nose on his sleeve, his lips turning up in an almost-smile. His hazel eyes glittered. "I would have killed him had I the chance."

There was a callousness in those words, and Daryn felt a pang at hearing them from so young a boy.

"I'm glad you didn't," he said quietly, taking up Amber's reins.

Over the thunder of the watercourse, the drum of hooves was heard. Too late they looked up and saw horses approaching from the north.

Daryn grabbed Gaylon, throwing him up onto Katy.

"Run!" he cried to the boy as he vaulted onto Amber.

The prince seemed frozen, his eyes on the small troop of soldiers coming toward the bridge. Nankus led them, and with a shout from him, the double column of horsemen broke into a gallop.

"Go!" Daryn snapped, his hand already on his sword hilt. "I'll hold them here as long as I can. Go back to Misk!"

"No," Gaylon said and reached for his own small sword. "Run or fight, I stay with you."

"Then we run!" Infuriated, Daryn spun Amber and sent her plunging through the snowdrifts, up the slope, and away from the river. Gaylon raced beside him. They entered the trees, Nankus and his men close behind. Too close. Daryn found himself fighting to hold Amber back so that Katy, with her shorter stride, could keep up.

The horses leaped a downed log and found a deep gully beyond it. Under Daryn, Amber's haunches bunched as she gathered herself, and the duke leaned forward, lifting the reins. The horse launched herself over the brink, clearing the gully handily. Gaylon had cued Katy too soon, however, and the little mare fell short. She foundered on the far bank, digging madly for a foothold. The wet earth gave, and she tumbled over backward, Gaylon under her.

Daryn pulled Amber up savagely, reining her around. The soldiers had broken formation once among the trees, and the boldest of the lot now cleared the ravine. The duke managed one swift glance below, saw Katy struggle to her feet, saw Gaylon standing beside her, blood running from his chin, then the enemy was upon him. He drew Squall and dispatched the first man with a heavy, two-handed stroke across an exposed shoulder, severing head from body. Amber danced under him, obeying the unconscious commands he gave her with the shifting of his weight.

Leaving Katy behind in the gully, Gaylon clambered up the steep incline. He fought the slipping soil with one hand, his sword bared in the other, and gained the top just as another soldier found his way around the ravine in an attempt to flank them. The fellow swung his blade high as he bore down on Gaylon, but the boy stood his ground. At the last possible moment, he dodged under the charging horse's neck, coming up on the soldier's left as he thundered by. The prince drove his sword into the small of the man's back, piercing a kidney. The soldier shrieked, pitching forward on the animal's neck. As he fell, the horse spun to avoid trampling him. Gaylon was swept off his feet by the sudden move, his weapon torn from his hand.

Daryn had accounted for another pair of soldiers, but immediately there were a half-dozen more to replace them. Over the cries of pain and the bellows of rage, over the clash of blades, the captain could be heard shouting orders.

"Don't harm the duke! By the Unholy One, I'll kill the man who puts a blade to him!"

It was true, the soldiers had been using their weapons only in defense so far, but Daryn continued to hack at them with deadly accuracy, unhindered by the command. Another man fell.

Nankus watched his men cut down and, in a red-faced rage, finally entered the fray himself. At the corner of his eye, he caught sight of the boy scrambling to recover his sword. He ran his horse at the youngster to head him off, and, grabbing him by the hair, dragged Gaylon up beside him on the saddle. He pressed his blade against the child's throat.

"Submit, Gosney!" he cried. "Or the boy dies!"

Daryn hesitated, drawing a ragged breath, then lowered his weapon. Five men lay dead or dying at his horse's feet. Rough hands jerked him from the saddle and wrested Squall from his fingers.

"Don't hurt the boy," he called as his arms were pulled behind him. Coarse ropes bit into his wrists.

Nankus dismounted, dragging Gaylon with him to the huddle of soldiers. Despite the grip on his hair, the prince clawed and kicked—until the captain clouted him with a mailed fist. The youngster fell face down in a heap on the muddy, trampled snow.

Nankus turned to Daryn. "The boy. Who is he?"

"A beggar, an orphan," the duke answered quickly. "You've no reason to keep him. Let him go."

"Fancy sword for an orphan boy," said one of the soldiers. He held up the little blade for the rest to see.

"He killed Nickson with it," another growled.

"I gave it to him," Daryn snapped.

This seemed to satisfy everyone but Nankus. He nudged the child with a toe, turning him over. Gaylon's eyes were open, glaring up at the captain.

"That right, boy? Are you just an orphan who can wield a sword well enough to kill a man the first time he tries?"

Gaylon sat up slowly. "I am Gaylon Reysson, and I'm king of this realm."

"No!" Daryn cried and was cuffed smartly by the man nearest him.

Nankus ignored the outburst. His interest was still held by the child in the mud. "Does Your Majesty often travel in rags?"

"If you want me to show mercy, you'd better keep a civil tongue," the boy answered, drawing himself into a crouch.

Nankus laughed good-naturedly, the sound booming hollowly from his noseless face. "Unfortunately for you, child, there's another king on the throne. My orders are to deliver Daryn Emilson unharmed to Castlekeep. Of you, there was no mention, but there's nothing so useless as an extra king. I think I know what my orders would be concerning you." He sheathed his sword and drew his dagger, caressing the razor edge.

Daryn began to struggle, but there was no fear in the prince's eyes as he stared up at Nankus. The captain reached down and grabbed another handful of hair, jerking the boy to his feet, pulling back his head to expose the throat.

Before the captain could strike, a sudden sharp pain stabbed through his side, and he reeled back under the devastating agony, releasing his hold. Gaylon slashed another man's arm with the dirk as he ran, and Daryn flung himself in front of two more, tripping them.

In the uproar, Gaylon leaped from the edge of the gully

onto Katy's back and sent her at a dead run along its narrow floor and out into the forest beyond.

"Don't let him escape," the captain screamed. "Find him! Kill him!"

Of the six soldiers left alive, four found their horses and jumped to obey. Romy, Nankus's lieutenant, appeared beside him, trying to pry the captain's fingers from his side and expose the knife wound the boy had inflicted.

"I'm all right," Nankus snarled and pushed him away. He crossed to Daryn. Stagger, an old mercenary with a bad leg, had the man in a firm grip.

"Where will he go?" the captain demanded.

"Where you'll never find him," Daryn answered coldly.

Nankus drew back a hand to strike the man and then thought better of it as the pain jolted through him. He fought the urge to double over. Blood was a spreading warmth across his stomach. Damn the boy! He'd only just missed piercing something vital with his dirk, having come in under the cuirass on the left side. With effort, the captain controlled the muscles of his face and found the strength to walk away. Romy followed closely.

When the lieutenant began unbuckling the chest plate, Nankus made no move to stop him, but sat quietly on a rock, thinking. The lieutenant dressed the wound and bound it with clean cloth.

At last Nankus had the duke of Gosney, but where was the joy of a task successfully completed? Six men dead in twelve! Feydir had said Gosney had no real magical powers, and that seemed true enough, but he'd failed to mention that the duke was formidable with a sword. And the boy—a prince of the realm. This was something Nankus felt would be a revelation to Feydir. Things were not so simple as they had at first seemed.

Romy's hands were thick-knuckled and ugly, but gentle as he laid a final wrap of the bandage. If Nankus called any man friend it would be Romy. Fourteen long years they'd worked and fought together.

"Perhaps we should make camp," the lieutenant suggested.

His voice was chronically raspy from an old throat wound.

"No," Nankus snapped. "We can cover five leagues by nightfall."

"Then I think I should rig a litter for you."

The captain cast him a dark look, and Romy smiled wryly.

"At least rest until the others return." He handed Nankus a blanket and a skin of wine. "They shouldn't be gone long. The child couldn't have gotten far. Whatever else he may be, he's still only a boy."

"Only a boy," Nankus grunted, feeling the sharp throb in his side. He took a long pull of the wine and, wrapping the blanket around him, settled as best he could on the ground against a cold, wet rock.

Stagger put Gosney back on his horse, tying the man's feet to the stirrups and lashing the animal up close to a handy tree. Then he and Romy began loading the bodies of their fallen comrades onto other mounts. Nankus watched for a time without interest. Finally he upended the wineskin a last time and lay back, pushing the pain from his mind. He must have dozed. He thought he heard Romy sigh heavily once, but that was all.

The captain woke at dusk feeling slightly drunk and still in pain. Coz, a young soldier from the Inland Isles, squatted beside him with a worried look.

"I feared you was dead, too," the fellow said, swallowing hard.

Nankus shoved him aside. The duke was gone. Romy and Stagger had each been stabbed once, neatly, in the back. They lay within a pace of where the captain had been sleeping.

"How?" he cried.

Coz shifted uneasily. "The boy musta circled back. We thought we found his trail leading south, and we gone a long way 'fore we realized it was the old marks him and the duke made in the first place. We come back as quick as we could."

Nankus leaned back, cursing silently. Was this Gosney's magic or the boy's foul work? What did it matter? They were gone, and Romy was dead. By the Unholy One, someone would pay dearly for this!

* * * * *

Gaylon and Daryn traveled west across the coastal range. The journey was nightmarish, a dream through which they moved in maddeningly slow motion. The higher elevations were still heavy with snow, and the time came quickly when the horses, already exhausted, could carry them no farther. They continued on, leading the animals, stumbling over snow-concealed obstacles and through waist-deep drifts, climbing, always climbing.

When the light was gone, Daryn called a halt, and man and boy huddled close in the lee of a burned-out cedar stump to await morning. Gaylon dozed, but Daryn didn't. A light wind stirred the night forest and each time an evergreen bough dropped its burden of snow, the duke jumped. It was foolishness; he knew that Nankus and his men could no more travel in the dark than they, but his nerves were raw and his senses acute.

If Daryn closed his eyes, vivid bursts of color would dance behind his eyelids, revealing over and over visions of the day. He saw himself a captive still and Gaylon stealing up behind the two guards as they played knuckle-bones on the ground near the sleeping captain. He heard again Romy's deep sigh when Gaylon's dirk found his heart. Stagger looked in wonder as his comrade dropped forward onto the oilcloth, and then died with that wonder frozen on his face. In less time than it took to draw a deep breath, the boy had killed twice.

Gaylon wiped the blood from his blade on Romy's sleeve, then went next to stand over Nankus, to gaze down at the wounded man still lost in wine-dulled sleep. Daryn could see the indecision in the prince's stance, but he didn't kill the captain and turned instead toward Daryn. Gaylon was flushed and his eyes almost fever-bright. He cut Amber free before slashing the ropes from Daryn's feet and hands.

Silently they recovered their swords, and as the prince led Daryn to where Katy was hidden, the duke untied two of the horses carrying bodies. The boy looked askance, and Daryn murmured, "We'll turn them loose later on to give the others an extra trail to follow." Gaylon nodded grimly as he mounted.

When they were well away, Daryn had looked once more at the ten-year-old prince and wondered if ever again he could think of him as a child. Later, as dusk fell and they fought their way on foot, Gaylon had dropped in exhaustion on the snow and Daryn, fighting the weariness in his own limbs, lifted the boy and carried him the final dozen paces. It was then, feeling the bones of Gaylon's arms through their thin covering of flesh that Daryn recognized the vulnerability of youth in him still. He'd fastened a blanket over the tree stump so that it covered them tent-fashion, trapping even the tiny warmth of their breath.

"Daryn?"

The bitter memories dispelled, the duke turned in the direction of that small voice, though he could see nothing in the utter night that surrounded them. He felt Gaylon draw close. The child was trembling.

"What is it?" Daryn asked.

"I fear I'll never see her again."

"Who?" But he knew the answer even as he spoke.

"Jessmyn. Is she safe? Is she well, do you think?"

"She's never been a threat to Lucien. He has no reason to wish her ill."

Gaylon's mind wandered. "He prepared me well. It was Lucien who taught me how to murder swiftly and silently—taught me the place where the knife can pass easily through the back and to the heart. He told me there's hardly any pain if the edge of the blade runs properly along the spine as it goes. That severs the nerves. You need to give the hilt a twist at the last, so a great hole is rent in the heart."

Daryn felt suddenly cold, a chill far deeper than the winter night. "Hush," he said quietly. "You're tired, you've got to sleep."

"No, if I sleep, I'll dream." The trembling grew worse.

"The nightmares trouble you still?"

"Not as they did at first—but tonight they're all fire and blood. I dreamed of Jessmyn too, and in it she cried as though her heart were broken, and that was somehow worse. . . ." Gaylon's voice trailed off, then he began again. "I thought today that I might die, and I wasn't sorry for it. I thought perhaps it would be good, that I'd join my father and be done with this, but there are things yet unfinished."

"Hush," said Daryn again. "You mustn't dwell on death."

"I must. I killed three men today and there was pleasure in it."

"Gaylon!" Daryn said sharply.

"Wait. Hear me out. It wasn't the actual killing that gave me pleasure. It was the knowledge after, that *I* was still alive. Does that make sense? Do you understand what I'm trying to say?"

"Yes," the duke muttered, disturbed.

"He won't follow us now," said the boy.

"Hmmm?"

"Nankus. He's wounded, and he has only four men left to him. He'll go back to the keep first to make his report."

"Most likely."

"That'll give us eight days—more, if his wound festers. He might even die."

"We can always hope."

"So long as he lives to tell Lucien that I'm alive."

"That's why you didn't kill him when you had the chance."

"I'll rest now," Gaylon stated, clearly ending the conversation.

Daryn listened in troubled silence as the boy's breathing finally settled into the evenness of deep slumber. By concentrating on the hypnotic regularity of the sound, he eventually fell into an uneasy sleep himself.

Nine

❖

Man and boy crested the mountains by midmorning the next day. The horses were gaunted, and Katy favored her right foreleg. The little mare's knee was swollen and hot to the touch. Daryn wrapped the swelling loosely with a wide strip torn from the hem of his cloak and packed snow in the folds of the bandage. They moved on slowly, riding double on Amber. Gaylon had not come away clean from the tumble into the gully either. His lower lip was split and double its normal size, and one cheek was bruised and scraped raw from Nankus's blow. Still, with the resiliency of youth, he soon regained his enthusiasm for the day.

They found a large meadow, sunny and warm, well down the western slopes with the snow mostly gone from it. There was graze for the horses—coarse brown poverty grass—plenty of wind-fall firewood, and a small, noisy creek close by. Under the naked limbs of a great oak tree the duke decided to make camp. Together, they carried stones from the meadow to line a shallow fire pit Daryn had dug with his hands and a fat stick. But the cold damp wood the duke had gathered refused to ignite, and soon he was cursing it.

Gaylon laid out the oilcloths and blankets that would serve as their beds, listening the while to Daryn's fuming. He busied himself with taking out the cheese and bread that Misk had packed, and a small blackened pot in which to boil water for tea should Daryn get the fire going. Finally he wandered over to the pit to watch. The duke crouched over the wood, staring into the Stone in his ring, the fingertips of his right hand pressed to his forehead. His Stone pulsed dully. The wood only smoldered, and he uttered black oaths under his breath.

"May I help?" Gaylon asked.

"How?" Daryn said shortly.

"I can find you better wood."

"I can manage with what I have. I just need to concentrate. Leave me be. Please!"

Unoffended, the boy left Daryn to his work, remembering a downed fir tree by the creek. There was a little trick Gaylon's father had taught him that might make things easier for Daryn. When he finally relocated the rotted log, the boy proceeded to kick it apart. Inside, he found what he desired: a wealth of dry, pitchy wood—and a termite colony. This proved irresistible, and he spent a while poking and digging through it, laying waste to the insects' warm winter home before remembering why he'd come. Feeling guilty at the delay, the prince gathered some of the wood, breaking free the stubs of the branches, as well. Knots were denser and would burn hotter and longer than the rest.

Gaylon glanced up through the trees. Overhead, the sky was a pale washed-out blue and quite cloudless. With the setting of the sun would come bitter, freezing cold. There was already a chill in the late afternoon air. He'd turned to go when something strange glimmered at the corner of his eye, a momentary flash of color and light somewhere in the rocks along the bank of the creek.

The boy took a step backward and moved his head. The light flared again, this time a brilliant, deep summer-sky blue. Instantly he dropped his armload of firewood and with boyish enthusiasm began exploring the rocks in the area from which he thought the flash had come. The search turned up only a finger-length chunk of pyrite. Disappointed, he pocketed the piece and started away. The blue light struck his eye again, enticingly. He hovered, uncertain.

Finally he squatted, keeping the glitter in the periphery of his vision. Beside him, the creek rumbled and rushed, its white water foaming. He began to sidle toward the sparkle, feeling foolish, as if he were sneaking up on the thing—whatever the thing might be. Carefully, he reached out to the side and felt among the stones . . . and grabbed it! His fingers clasped something small, rough-surfaced, vaguely round, and sun-warmed. The object continued to glitter blue in his palm until he looked directly at it. Then it resumed an ordinary form—a plain, rather homely, gray river pebble.

Gaylon considered the bit of rock for a long moment. A thought dawned on him, but he discounted it as being too far fetched . . . until he felt an odd inner stirring. In his hand the stone awoke, pulsing softly with a pale blue glow. He gasped as power ran tingling through his body. Around him the world became crystal clear, the colors of the landscape brightened, and the creek sang in his ear. The stone turned cold, so cold it burned his hand, and he clutched his fingers over it for fear the pebble would leap from his palm to disappear again among its lesser brothers lining the creek. A Sorcerer's Stone! And it was his!

The icy feel faded, and the prince's senses returned to near-normal. He had no idea how he had caused the Stone to wake, but Daryn could tell him, Daryn could teach him. He started at a run for the campsite, then thought better of it and returned to dutifully take up the firewood. With the rotted fir piled to his chin, he headed back at a slower pace, wondering. Daryn rarely used his Stone and never spoke of magic at all. Perhaps the man would not be so pleased with this discovery.

It was nearly dusk by the time Gaylon entered camp. The sun was sliding quickly into the distant shimmer of the Western Sea. Daryn hadn't stirred from his place, and still there was no fire. He glanced up at Gaylon once, his face beaded with perspiration, and the stark look in his gray eyes made the prince's exuberance fade even more. The boy dropped the wood into a pile. This no longer seemed the proper time to reveal what he'd found. Perhaps later, after they'd eaten. The Stone was slipped into his jerkin pocket.

Gaylon dropped to his knees beside the pit and removed the wet wood. Daryn said nothing, only watched as the boy made a neat cone of rotted fir, stacking the larger pieces over the smaller.

"Now try," Gaylon said, climbing to his feet and dusting off his hands.

Daryn took a deep breath and leaned his forehead onto his fingers once more, while Gaylon crossed the little clearing under the tree to the packs. A fluttering had started in the bottom of the boy's stomach. What he was considering was foolish, but the temptation proved too great. His fingers found the Stone and drew it forth. He searched for that inner stirring, and it came quickly, even stronger than before. The tingling sensation flowed up his arm and throughout his body. Gaylon stared into the Stone as he'd seen Daryn do, then envisioned the fire pit, envisioned the wood burning.

With a loud *thump* fire erupted in Daryn's face, and the duke flung himself back to land sprawled on the ground. High in the air, a great ball of flame boiled skyward. On the earth below, a little blaze burned cheerfully in the pit.

"By the black beard of the Dark King!" the duke cried. "What was that?"

Gaylon helped him up, wide-eyed with concern. "Are you all right?"

"Aside from singed eyebrows and a roasted nose, I think so. Did you see that?" The man didn't seem to notice that Gaylon's hands were shaking.

"It must have been the wood. I'm sorry, Daryn. I only meant to help."

The duke scratched his chin. "No harm done," he said absently.

Gaylon nodded, but his mind was elsewhere. An exhilarating rush followed his initial fear for Daryn's safety. He could do it, had actually done it! Of course, one could also say that he'd overdone it. Just a bit. Why was Daryn so loath to use his magic? To the prince the feeling was tremendous, like the flexing of muscles he had no idea existed.

The twilight grew deeper, and they donned their cloaks to huddle near the fire. Tea water bubbled in the sooty little pan nestled in the coals, and a meal was made of stale bread and cheese.

"If I'd gotten the fire started earlier, I might have set some snares," Daryn commented around a bite of bread. "There's a warren not ten paces from our camp. Over there." He pointed off into the night-shrouded trees. "We're lucky to have what we do, but I can't help wishing for a tender rabbit roasting over the flames."

He was also wishing for wine in his cup instead of raspberry leaf tea, but of this he made no mention. Instead he looked across the fire at Gaylon. The boy was oddly quiet this evening. His sandy hair tinted red by the fire's glow, he stared into some distant place. In Daryn's eyes, the prince had never resembled his father so much as he did in that moment, but there was a tension in those small shoulders, a current of energy that the duke couldn't decipher. Gaylon had glanced up briefly when Daryn mentioned the rabbit and smiled, just a little.

The duke sipped his cooling tea. Nearby the horses grazed, and an owl in a distant tree questioned the night mournfully. The embers of the fire spiraled upward in the smoke, winking out one by one in a star-filled sky. It was bitterly cold only steps away from the fire, but near it there was warmth and silent companionship and at least a promise of the future. An image of Haddi slipped unbidden into Daryn's thoughts, bringing with it a sad, sweet ache. He tried to force the memory away. Someday, perhaps, he might return to the inn by the river. Someday. He'd gone from contentment of a sort to melancholy in a swift moment's time, and now came a strong urge to take up the lute and release the feelings with song.

Daryn found the instrument near their packs, leaning against the oak bole, but as he bent to take it, there came a rustling in the grass just outside the circle of firelight. He straightened, listening. The sound came again, louder, from another area, and he reached for the hilt of his sword, which also lay with their gear. Before he could draw the blade from the scabbard, a rabbit, moving with great temerity, entered the campsite. Very near the duke the creature froze, hunched, its ears flat to its little body. By the fire, Gaylon started to his feet, but Daryn put a finger to his lips, motioning the boy back. The duke slipped his cloak from his shoulders and moved slowly into a position to drop it over the animal. As he lifted his hands, the coney took notice and dodged suddenly to the side. Daryn corrected his direction by spinning on one heel and dived after it. Startled again, the animal leaped into the air, turning back at the last moment, and too late, Daryn tried to check his forward lunge. He landed rolling in the damp grass, tangled in his own feet. And then it seemed that the creature jumped right into his hands.

He stood with the soft silvery-gray rabbit cowering in his arms. It made no move to escape, but lay quivering in fear. Still seated by the fire, Gaylon began to chuckle. Daryn felt a soft touch at his leg and looked down. Another rabbit, standing stretched up upon its hind paws, tapped his knee just above his boot. Then another scurried between his feet. And another. Suddenly there were hundreds of them everywhere.

It was too much for Daryn. With a wordless croak, he dropped the one he held and bolted for the fire, crying, "Shoo! Get away!" The coneys scattered in mad confusion before him. Gaylon doubled over with laughter and clutched his sides helplessly, tears leaking from the corners of his eyes.

Daryn arched one dark brow, scowling. "I seem to have missed the grand comedy in this."

"But, milord duke," Gaylon said with forced sobriety, "there's an excellent lesson to be learned here."

"And that is?"

"You must be very careful what you wish for."

It struck Daryn then, the utter ridiculousness of the whole affair. He coughed, trying to stifle his own amusement, but that set Gaylon off again. They laughed until it hurt. And there was rabbit to eat after all—but only because Daryn, in his mad dash to the fire, had trod on one hapless creature, killing it instantly.

* * * * *

Tired, Gaylon went finally to his bed. He rolled himself into his blankets fully clothed. Sleep didn't come easily, however.

The excitement of the last few days had yet to wear thin, and he lay on the bed listening to Daryn sing. How strange to hear such touching notes from the battered old lute. The hillsides echoed back Daryn's voice as it rose and fell with his song. He sang a ballad about the ghost of a beautiful girl who returned to haunt her lover, a man who'd proven false. The song told of his repentance and subsequent suicide, and of the happy ending, if it could be called such, in which the lovers were reunited forever in death.

With his Sorcerer's Stone snug in one hand, and Daryn's lilting voice in his ear, Gaylon slipped at last into sleep, to dream of coneys, maids, and magic. And then into another dreaming—

Here starlight shed a faint glow on a garden mantled in snow. Statues stood wraithlike nearby, and ice-covered fountains lay still. His perceptions were acute in this, and Gaylon felt the dreamlike quality of the scene fade. The snow had formed a crust and crunched beneath his boots. Icy air filled his lungs. He reached down and touched the snow with a tentative finger. Cold, yet not cold.

With a heart-pounding wrench, it occurred to him that this was somehow not a dream, that he was actually in this place, not asleep in the camp. The panic brought him awake with a jerk. He lay for a time, clinging to the reality of the earth beneath his blankets. Daryn still sang.

The prince clutched the Stone tightly and closed his eyes again, forcing himself to relax, to drift once more into sleep. The dream had changed subtly. He was no longer alone in the winter garden. A tiny figure, cloaked and hooded, stood among the statuary as motionless as the marble. He recognized his surroundings now. These were the gardens of Castlekeep. And he knew the child standing in the snow.

"Jessmyn," he called softly into the cold hush.

The princess turned toward him, searching, pulling back her hood. Starlight glittered on her cheeks. She was crying quietly. Distressed, Gaylon moved toward her, but as he came near she gasped. He was close enough now to see the sudden terror on her face, then she turned and fled away, back to the keep.

"Jessmyn," he cried, unwilling to chase her, to frighten her further. She was gone, and he felt lonely, lost. The prince closed his eyes, willing himself to wake. Dizziness came, then a whisper of sound—Daryn's voice in some distant place, singing:

"With fingers of moonlight she touched his cheek.
With lips of ice did she seek
To kiss him one last time,
To ki-iss him one-un last time."

The last note faded to silence, and then came a dry rustling like autumn leaves stirred by a wind. The prince opened his eyes. He was in his father's library. The room was fireless and dark except for one thick candle burning on the desk, creating a single pool of light. Someone sat hunched over a massive leatherbound volume, turning its brittle pages slowly, one by one. Gaylon stood motionless, watching. The man at the desk paused. Then, with a quick movement, he spun on his stool and peered into the recesses of the room. His eyes passed unseeing over Gaylon.

"Who goes there?" Feydir demanded.

Gaylon remained still, and the ambassador leaned across the desk to blow out the candle. The library was plunged into complete darkness. There came another sound of rustling, this time of cloth against leather. A faint pulse of blue light began at the center of the room, and an uneasiness gripped Gaylon, growing quickly into fear. Feydir wielded a Sorcerer's Stone. Even now the man began to mutter, and his fingers, stained blue by the light of the Stone, began to trace something in the dark air—a straight line, etched in glowing beryl. More muttering and another line met the first at a right angle.

Gaylon's fear heightened. Some deep instinct told him he must flee, that with the completion of Feydir's eerie design, he'd be hopelessly trapped. He closed his eyes once more, again willing himself away, but the old man's voice continued, deadly and sure. The boy reached out carefully to his right, felt the bookcase there and began to follow it along the wall toward a remembered doorway. There was a dragging at his limbs now. Every step taken required more effort than the last.

Bitterly the prince realized what a fool he'd been. He'd thought it so easy—the fire, the rabbits, both had obeyed him, but in this dream-that-was-not-a-dream, he had no control. His legs began to give out, and he felt himself falling.

In terror, Gaylon flung back his head, eyes closed, and screamed, "Help me!" There came a wrenching, a rending, and it felt as if he were being torn apart. Vaguely he wondered if Feydir had completed his spell, but no. The prince opened his eyes and found light. The library was gone. Now stone walls surrounded him, cold and barren. This room was lit with many candles, all fighting the gloom without much success. The dark walls, resenting illumination, seemed to absorb the light. Rough-hewn tables crowded the chamber, each table in turn crowded with jars and bowls, mortars and pestles, instruments and medicaments of all kinds. A wizened little man in deep blue robes stood at one of the tables, his back to Gaylon. His hands danced over the cluttered tabletop, grabbing handfuls of this, pinches of that, apparently throwing them haphazardly into the container in front of him. At last he took up a kettle that sat on a tripod over a candle and added its contents to the rest.

"There," he said with satisfaction. "Now it must steep a while before straining." His back still to Gaylon, he lifted his head. "What do you want?"

The boy remained silent.

"Come now," the fellow said with irritation, "have a civil answer. What do you want?" He turned to face the child, staring directly at him. A Stone hung from a gold chain around his neck.

"You knew I was here?" Gaylon asked, his eyes on the man's Stone.

"Of course," the little fellow snapped. "I can sense a Dreamer. Now, why are you here? Do you hope to steal my secrets? Who sent you?"

"No one," Gaylon stammered under the barrage of questions. "I'm lost."

"You're not lost! You're here."

"But I don't know where 'here' is."

"How unfortunate for you. Now get out."

"I don't—"

"Enough! Get you gone, I say—" the old man waved a bony finger threateningly "—before I send you somewhere you'll like far less!" For emphasis he grabbed up the Stone at his breast, and it began to pulse blue.

Gaylon turned tail and ran, heedless of direction. He found a doorway, a long twisting passage, then another, and didn't halt until he'd burst out into the open. It was still night. Here, the stars' frail light revealed an expanse of meadowland, rock-strewn and treeless. The air smelled of salt and moisture.

A wind howled out of nowhere to buffet the prince, to push him away from the high stone walls behind him. It seemed to drive him, herd him toward the far end of the sward. Was this the old man's doing? Gaylon had little time to contemplate. The meadow ended suddenly at the top of a cliff. Below, a storm-restless sea surged onto jagged rocks. Foam from the slamming waves flew skyward, whipped into salt spray by the wind.

On the very edge of that cliff, Gaylon teetered, mesmerized by the thundering surf below him. A great gust caught him from behind, lifting him up and over. Even as he began the plunge to the rocks, another gust tossed him upward, whirling like a leaf. Instinctively the boy threw out his arms and legs, stabilizing the spin, and found himself soaring out over the ocean. Terror turned quickly to elation, and Gaylon laughed and shouted his joy at being airborne, carried as thistledown before the wind. Higher! He must go higher! And the wind obeyed.

The earth fell away. All about the prince was black unending night, lightless and cold, but drunk with power and freedom, he no longer cared.

Then stars reappeared, far more and far brighter than any he'd ever known, shining with a brilliant, steady light. Thus distracted, he failed to notice the ground coming swiftly toward him. It was a soundless impact onto a springy, resilient surface that sent him rebounding outward again. Confused, the boy flung out his arms, grabbing at odd colors that flashed by. His fingers snagged a slender vertical something he mistook for a tree bole. It stretched with his momentum, his hands sinking into the pliant surface, then the something bent gracefully over to drop him upright on the ground.

The "ground" was a bright lemon yellow, and Gaylon's first annoyance was lost now in the wonder of his surroundings. Each dream the Stone had presented seemed more fantastic than the last. In this place, the landscape consisted mostly of a yellow plain that rolled away to a distant horizon—a gently curving line that divided the plain from the night sky. The "trees" were nothing more than rubbery blue-green spikes, set in clusters here and there. He studied the stand nearest him. The spikes varied in height and thickness; the smallest was perhaps waist high, the largest towering far above him. He could find no light source other than the stars, but the plain seemed to reflect the starlight, intensifying it. There was something profoundly soothing in the colors, the lines and angles of the land against that black velvet sky.

The prince began to walk, marveling at the indentations his feet left in the ground behind him. The prints filled in slowly as he moved away. Far off, near the horizon, there was movement. In moments the blur grew close enough to identify as separate moving objects or bodies, dozens of them. They rolled and bounced at a fantastic speed in his direction, tumbling and caroming off the "trees" and each other. Their shapes were indistinct. Sometimes they seemed round, other times barrellike, but the tumblers never stopped moving, closer and closer.

Gaylon became aware of music—nothing his ears could detect, but a vibration felt through the soles of his feet. Rhythmic, it possessed tones that were also felt, not heard. The beat was impelling, growing stronger as the tumblers grew nearer. Then, in a flicker, the creatures were bouncing around him, stretching and changing color and shape.

Enthralled, Gaylon watched as they encircled him, their movements slowing to a graceful swaying and finally to stillness. For several long moments the creatures remained motionless, then began to move again simultaneously in a wonderful, intricately choreographed dance. When they had gained momentum, one broke free to swing inside the circle; it slammed into Gaylon and threw him back. In that instant of contact came a sunburst of emotion, a feeling of intense joy, a fierce surge of happiness. The little creature elongated and flipped end-over-end, back to its place in the design of the dance.

For the first time, Gaylon noticed a hole in their pattern. The unheard music drew him into the circle to take his place. As he moved within the design, each step taken became a note, uniquely his, adding to their symphony of feeling and motion. The prince joined the dance, to careen and caper with the shifting tumblers across the yellow plain.

* * * * *

Somewhere far away an owl hooted, a warm sleepy night call. A cool breeze touched Gaylon's face. Close by came a whisper of movement in grass, a tearing, a chomping of horses at graze. He smelled woodsmoke, an acrid irritation in his nose and throat for an instant, and then it was gone. He opened bleary eyes.

Daryn paced the clearing by firelight, and his movements had a sense of nervous exhaustion about them. The man stopped long enough to bury his face in his hands, almost a gesture of despair. Gaylon wanted to ask him what was wrong, but couldn't seem to form the words. He tried to lift his arm and found it too heavy, the effort beyond him. Finally the boy opened his lips, summoning every bit of willpower left within him.

"Daryn." The word came out sounding all wrong, a mere croak, scratchy and barely audible.

But Daryn heard. He stopped dead in his tracks and swung around. His whole body seemed to slump, the tension slipping away. From beside the fire, the duke picked up a cup and crossed to where Gaylon lay.

"Have I been sick?" the prince whispered.

"No." Daryn's face remained expressionless. "No, you've

been . . . away. Here drink this. It's not too hot."

The cup came near Gaylon's lips, Daryn's arm supporting his head. However, his senses seemed heightened. The smell of meat broth was so intense it turned his stomach.

"I'm not hungry, please." He tried to turn his face away.

Daryn's angry reaction shocked him. "Drink it, you little fool!"

The boy choked the broth down obediently and, with its warmth, realized how very cold he felt, how very weak.

"How long?" he managed to ask.

"It's been six days, Gaylon. Six days!"

"I had a dream."

"I know," said Daryn, his voice dull with fatigue.

"You know?"

"Yes, I do. It's so beautiful there," the duke murmured, the words filled with an inexplicable sorrow. "The sky is always night. So many stars." He stared skyward now, his eyes dark sockets in a shadowy face. "And the dancers. You loved them, didn't you? And they loved you. I know you wanted to stay forever, to dance forever, because I did, too. Once." He smiled wistfully.

There was an edge of madness in the man's voice, and Gaylon began to fear for him. But Daryn was only tired, only remembering.

"You have a Stone, don't you, Gaylon?"

"Yes," the boy answered quietly.

"The fire. That was your doing. And the rabbits?"

Gaylon nodded, the barest movement of his head.

"By the gods! How did I miss it? How could I have been so stupid?"

"I wanted to tell you, but I was afraid."

Daryn's exasperation was plain. "You had every right to be afraid, but not of me. Now you must rest. We'll talk of this in the morning. Sleep."

"But—"

"Put the Stone in your pouch. Not in your pocket. It mustn't touch you."

Gaylon's hand had clutched the Stone for so long that the

fingers didn't want to open. With care, he slipped the Stone into the leather pouch. One part of him resisted, was loath to give it up. The prince knew, however, that he'd do as Daryn asked. And he did feel tired, so very tired. He closed his eyes.

Several times during the night, Daryn woke the boy and made him drink more broth. It tasted good now, even delicious. Those were his only lucid thoughts, then he would fall back into deep, dreamless sleep.

Warm sunlight on his cheek woke Gaylon sometime late in the morning. The fire had gone out, and Daryn had finally fallen asleep where he sat with his back against the oak, his cloak wrapped tightly around him. There were hollows in his cheeks, visible through a half-grown beard. He'd lost weight, weight he didn't have to spare. Gaylon studied the fine-boned face. Even in exhausted sleep there were trouble lines on the duke's forehead. The prince took one of Daryn's long-fingered hands in his.

"All is well, Daryn," he whispered. "I will guard your rest. Be at peace."

As the boy watched, the lines seemed to ease from Daryn's face, and his breathing grew more regular. Satisfied, Gaylon turned his mind to more pressing matters. He was hungry, thirsty. He threw back the blankets, struggling free of their considerable weight. Daryn had piled them all on him, horse pads included.

Without thought Gaylon stood and started toward the cold ashes of the fire pit. One step was as far as he got before his legs gave out, sending him down in a twisting, boneless fall. He waited for the world to stop spinning before he attempted to rise again. Daryn slept peacefully on.

His muscles remembered their functions at last, just as his stomach desired food. Gaylon found boiled rabbit and ate sparingly, but drank plenty of water. He wanted a fire and debated using his Stone, feeling for it in his pouch, then set about erecting a neat structure of wood in the pit. He had the Stone in his hand again when an eeriness seemed to invade the small clearing. Several times he was sure there'd been movement on the periphery of his vision. Each time he turned quickly and found nothing. With difficulty the prince forced his attention back to the task at hand.

Finally, a small fire burned in the pit, though directing the Stone's energy had been costly. Exhausted, the prince reached for the battered old tea pan and noticed a tall slender man leaning on a young tree at the edge of the camp. Pale sunlight through bare branches made the stranger's visage shadowed and indistinct, but he appeared fair of feature. He wore a russet leather jerkin and dark hose and carried no visible weapon.

"Greetings." His voice was melodic, friendly.

"Greetings," Gaylon responded, feeling only a touch of alarm. He glanced at the sleeping Daryn.

The stranger offered nothing further. The silence lengthened.

"Is there something you wish?" Gaylon asked finally. "I can offer you tea or some rabbit if you're hungry."

"You're gracious, but no," said the man. "There is something *you* wish. You have called, and I have come."

Confused, Gaylon shook his head. "I called no one."

"You called no one. You called me. You desire to know my secrets." The stranger stepped away from the tree, a supple, fluid motion. As his face cleared the shadows his gaze caught Gaylon's. His eyes were the brightest of blues, hauntingly beautiful, and something glimmered deep within them, something vaguely familiar. The longer Gaylon looked into them, the larger they became.

And then somewhere, everywhere around the prince the man's voice sang, "Will you walk with me? I will answer all your questions."

Mindlessly, Gaylon rose to follow.

In the distance someone began to shout. The sound irritated the prince, distracting him. Something moved into his way, blocking that incredible blue gaze. Gaylon tried to force his way past, angry now, so angry he began to shake. No, he was being shaken.

"Gaylon!" Daryn had him by the shoulders, shaking him violently. "Look at me! Damn you, look at me!"

Dazed, the boy tried to focus on the duke's face. By comparison, Daryn's slate-gray eyes were unremarkable, his features plain. How dare he get in the way? Gaylon peered over Daryn's shoulder. The blue-eyed stranger was gone.

"Where is he?" the boy demanded angrily.

"There was no one here," said Daryn.

"There was! A man. He stood right over there."

"That wasn't a man. It was a spirit."

"What?"

"A spirit, a teacher, a guide. That's as close as I can come to describing it." Then with urgency, Daryn cried, "Gaylon, promise me you won't use the Sorcerer's Stone again!"

"No!" It was a defiant word, spoken without thought.

"Sit and listen to me," the duke commanded.

Gaylon sat, and Daryn paced, agitated, his cloak billowing out behind him.

"At first your ignorance protected you. You were innocent, but you've used the Stone enough now that you're no longer safe. No, don't speak. I know how you feel. The power is there, but you have no training. If you'd followed that 'man' into the woods, you would have died."

"The spirit is evil?"

"No, no. Not evil, but not good. Just powerful, an elemental force that answers the call of a Stone bearer. It's like . . ." Daryn cast about him for an example. "Like fire. Neither good nor evil, it can help or harm. You must treat fire with respect. You must learn to control it. So the Sorcerer's Stone must be controlled."

"Then teach me! Teach me to use the Stone," Gaylon pleaded.

"I can't," Daryn said simply.

"Why not?"

Daryn looked away. "Because I'm afraid."

"No!" the boy cried. "You're not afraid of anything!"

The man shook his head. "Gaylon, only a fool fears nothing."

Gaylon refused to listen. He knew Daryn too well. The duke laid waste to his enemies with his sword, conquered people with only a lute.

Daryn anticipated his next words and said, "Why do you think I use my Stone so little and so poorly?"

"I don't know," the boy muttered sullenly.

"Because I'm afraid. I went to that dreaming place. The temptation to stay was, as with you, nearly my undoing. You can't know what it's like to stand helplessly by and watch someone you love waste away. All I could do was wait and worry. I was certain you had a Stone, but I couldn't get your hand open, and even if I had, I couldn't have taken it from you. If I had, you could never have returned."

In his mind, Gaylon saw the night-black sky against a yellow plain and remembered joy. "If I'd decided to stay in that place, what would you have done?"

"Bury you. In time the body dies. Many have been lost that way. It's a difficult and dangerous path you wish to travel, Gaylon Reysson. No king of this realm has had the courage to follow that path in a thousand years."

"I can do it, Daryn! I can! Let me try." Gaylon watched the dark-haired man turn his face away once more.

"I can't teach you, but I'll take you to someone who can." He refused to look at the boy. "Only if you give me your oath that you won't use the Stone for the time being."

"I do so," Gaylon said quickly, eagerly.

Daryn turned to him finally, his face gone hard. "If you fail to keep your word, then we're finished. I'll ride from you that moment, and I won't look back. That is *my* oath to you."

With satisfaction, Daryn saw fear touch the boy's eyes. Gaylon was strong-willed, proud, and brash, and the journey to Sezran's castle by the sea would take many days—a long time to keep a youngster's curiosity in check. But it had to be done.

And Sezran. What of him? Daryn felt a thread of fear wind around his heart, and it was some time before he could push that feeling of dread aside.

Ten

Nankus returned to the keep with his four remaining men and Romy's body. Ignoring the questioning looks on the faces of the soldiers in the barracks, he ordered a burial detail and went to his quarters to change. He dressed the wound again with a less-than-perfect bandage, refusing to let a young aide call the physician. It would be after-the-fact to call Girkin now.

The wound had festered badly, thanks to the boy's filthy blade, and without Romy's careful tending, Nankus had lain with fever for nine days in Riverbend. The men had wanted to bury all the dead there. Even in the height of delirium, Nankus refused to leave Romy in some unmarked soldier's grave along a road.

Now, his wound tended, the captain went directly from the barracks to Feydir's apartments. This was not a meeting he would relish. It was not in his nature to enjoy reporting defeat. One of the ambassador's servants met him in the hall. The guards at the door saluted smartly, a snap of the right forearm across the eyes, a ritual offering of blindness, vulnerability. Nankus didn't return the salute; he offered his life to no man. The young servant, bowing and scraping at his elbow, opened the door and ducked in. He heard the boy say:

"Ambassador D'Sulang, your captain of the guard, Nankus."

The word "your" rankled, but was no less than truth. The captain entered the chamber and glanced around once, noting the position of furniture, drapes, and windows, then stationed himself with his back to the one bare wall.

"Your lordship," Nankus said, giving the tall thin man standing by the desk a curt nod. By this he acknowledged Feydir his better, and there were few he considered as such. Feydir D'Sulang was not a military man, but Nankus recognized him as a man of vision, cold and calculating, deserving of respect. The captain had served the ambassador once, years before in Zankos, on some minor assassination work, and had found Feydir's network of spies equal, if not superior to, the Southern monarch, Roffo's. Yes, Feydir he would serve, but not that obsequious young pup of a nephew who called himself king.

The glance, the nod, the choice of position, none of this was lost on the ambassador. Nor the lack of fear. Nankus was not intimidated by Feydir's open display of his magical powers. The captain knew his own worth, and so did Feydir.

"Kyle, go now," the gaunt lord told the servant.

The boy bowed deeply, backing his way from the room, and the captain felt a touch of disgust for all such mincing, fawning creatures. Even a lowly servant should have some sense of self, some strength of character.

"Captain." Feydir poured two cups of wine and offered one to Nankus. "I am told you return empty-handed. Do you at least have news for me?"

Nankus took the cup, but didn't drink. "I have much news, none of it pleasant," he said with care.

Feydir eyed him thoughtfully. "Go on."

"We captured Daryn Emilson on the coach road, a day's ride north of Riverbend, but he later escaped. Of the twelve handpicked men who were with me, only four survived the encounter." He paused. "The duke was aided in his escape by a boy who rode with him."

"A boy?"

"Yes, milord. A boy who called himself Gaylon Reysson—who called himself king."

Feydir's face remained impassive, but his fingers tightened on the wine cup. "The men who came back with you, you cautioned them not to speak of this."

"Of course, milord, under threat of death."

"Then give me the details, Captain." Feydir looked away. He didn't enjoy staring into that ugly noseless face so like a skull.

Nankus related the story in full, from the odd happening that night at the inn and the disaster on the road the next day, to the questioning of a silversmith in the town later. He made no excuses and pointed no blame in any direction. Feydir listened with growing apprehension, with a seed of fury. Lucien! That bumbling fool was responsible for this—not even capable of murdering a mere child!

"The smith would say nothing before he died?"

"No, milord, and we were most persuasive. I believe he knew nothing of the duke's plans."

Feydir turned back. "Where will Gosney take the prince now?"

"I cannot say."

"You must have some notion." The ambassador's voice was tight. The Stone on his breast glimmered, betraying his irritation.

"My lord," said the captain, "your guess would be far better than mine, but I can tell you what *I* would do were I the duke."

"Yes?"

"I should take the boy north to Lasony and demand sanctuary, and from there begin to spread the word that the true prince lives . . . with hope of finding support in the nations south of Xenara. I might even attempt to embarrass Roffo into declaring war on the false king of Wynnamyr."

"The merchant families would never allow that," snapped Feydir. "They stand to gain much with Lucien on the throne."

Nankus smiled thinly. "But they might allow it if Gosney promises to honor whatever bargains you've struck with them."

Feydir's eyes were on his own untouched wine now, his jaw taut. "When did you see Gosney and the boy last?"

"Over a fortnight past, milord. Still, their travel—whatever direction they take—will be slow of necessity. They dare not use the roads. Word of the reward is in every town, every hamlet by now."

"And your wound, Captain?"

"Healed, your lordship," Nankus lied.

"Then you will leave the keep in the morning for the northern border. Go with all haste and take what men you feel necessary. You will carry a dispatch to the King of Lasony that I shall draft tonight. You'll deliver it to Sorek personally."

"Yes, milord. What are your orders concerning the prince when he's found?"

"Your first instincts were correct, Captain. Kill the boy. Bring Gosney to me."

Nankus nodded, and Feydir saw the brief satisfaction that flashed behind the man's cold, hard eyes.

"And, Captain."

"Yes, milord?"

"I want no word of this discovery to reach the king under any circumstance. The four men who returned with you are to be killed."

If there was any hesitation, Nankus hid it well. He nodded again. "As you wish, milord."

"Leave me now," Feydir said shortly. "I have much to consider."

With another curt nod, the captain let himself from the chamber.

Seething, Feydir paced for a time. Yet his fury at Lucien's ineptitude as an assassin was tempered by his relief at knowing Daryn of Gosney still lived. Finally, he took his seat at the desk, found paper and stylus, and set out the ink bottle and sand. He had more than one dispatch to draft this night. Nankus would carry one north, but Feydir would take no chances. His people in the South must be alerted, for while the harbor at Full Moon Bay near Castle Gosney was closed by winter weather, there was still a possibility that the duke would go with the boy to the Inland Sea and try to take ship for some sympathetic nation, where he might raise an army to dispute the crown.

No, the ambassador concluded, the prince must die and

Daryn must be captured at all cost. Only days before, Feydir had found at last the reference to Orym's Legacy in the *Book of Stones* and the translation was engraved in his mind:

In that century the Red Kings were given two terrible gifts. The first was the Sword with its riddle to keep secret, and the second was the Sight so that a Red King might recognize his own mortality and know the time for the passing of the weapon from the left hand to the right. And the good right hand must hold the Legacy in trust that it be given to the next Red King as he mounts the throne. So shall it be until Kingslayer be taken up once more, and then will the Sword know its master by the Stone he bears.

The Gosneys were the Red Kings' good right hand and Reys, feeling his death near, would have given Orym's Legacy to Daryn. The duke had hidden the sword cleverly, for Feydir had taken the man's rooms apart and found nothing. A similar, though furtive, search of the keep had been as futile. Easier by far to force Gosney to reveal his hiding place. The ambassador had no doubt of his ability to break Daryn utterly. And then Kingslayer would be his, along with all that its power could bring him!

The dispatches. He must concentrate on the present in order to win the future. But another stray thought came to nag at the ambassador. A thing had happened on the night he'd discovered the key passage in the book, a thing that haunted him yet. Sitting at the library's high desk Feydir had felt a presence. When he'd blown out the taper and taken up his Stone, a ghostly image had wavered into existence in a far corner. The blue nimbus that outlined the figure named it a Dreamer, a bearer of a Stone, but it was small, child-shaped. His attempt to trap it had failed, and he wondered yet at the significance of the event. Who would come to him in such a manner, and why?

Dispatches! He forced his attention to the paper on the desk before him, then took the stylus in hand and began filling the page with neat, terse phrases that would convince Sorek, King of Lasony, to cooperate with Nankus—to convince him also that to aid any fugitive from Lucien's justice would bring about immediate and dire consequences.

* * * * *

"The old wizard? Oh, aye, he's still there. Why do ye ask?" Roddi, an elderly fisherman, skillfully tied another intricate knot in the line he was using to repair his net, bit the line through with a sharp tooth—one of the few he had left—and peered up at the man and boy standing by their horses. His old eyes were squeezed into a permanent squint, partly from poor eyesight and partly from long days in bright sun over the ocean's reflective water.

"Is there someone in the village who'd care for our horses? We could pay a little. Not much, mind you, but some." Daryn ran a hand over Amber's velvet soft nose. Her lips twisted sideways to plop affectionately at him, her huge tongue scratching the back of his wrist seeking the salty taste on his skin.

"The Widder Matson's boy would probably love to look after 'em. He keeps watch on the village goats. Good wid animals, too. Why?"

Gaylon saw the curiosity written plainly in the fisherman's face and saw no harm in answering. "We're going up to stay at Seward Castle." Too late he caught Daryn's warning shake of the head.

Roddi looked them up and down again. Fine looking folk, he decided, but come to hard times by the look of their worn clothing and lean faces. Normally he had little truck with strangers, but the fisherman felt a warning would be a kindness here.

"Yer daft ta go enywheres near the place."

"Thank you," said Daryn quickly.

"Why?" asked Gaylon.

"He don't like mortal folks like you an' me, lad," Roddi said, warming to the subject. "Eats 'em. Kills 'em dead and eats 'em. Nothin' but bones bleachin' in the sun, that's the fate of 'em what goes to Seward Castle." He nodded with satisfaction as the boy's eyes grew wide with alarm.

"Where can we find the widow?" Daryn asked.

Roddi put the net aside. "Foller me. It's easier to take ye there. This way." He led them down the dirty main street and back though a row of shabby huts. "Ye ain't goin' up there enyway, are ye? I'm tellin' ye, he'll suck the marrow from yer bones."

Daryn gave the old man a hard look. "He doesn't eat flesh, neither animal nor human."

"An how would ye know, stranger? I've seen the bones, I have." Roddi halted, pointing out a mud and driftwood affair at the end of a well-worn path, then turned and ambled away, muttering and shaking his head.

Gaylon watched the fisherman move off, back down the street, agilely skirting the mud puddles. The gulls kited above the old man and sounded their odd mewling cries.

"Gaylon?" Daryn called from the door of the hut, and the boy turned to follow.

* * * * *

"This is Seward Castle?" the prince asked in awe.

Daryn, standing beside Gaylon on the broad grassy incline, was silent for a long moment. A late evening wind blew chill off the ocean, snapping the edges of his cloak. "He's been building onto it again." Apprehension edged his voice.

On the rolling sward the castle lay waiting, gray stone and mortar, alone on a knoll like some dark beast curled slumbering in the thin winter sunlight. Gaylon wasn't at all sure he wished to awaken that beast. It resembled no man-made structure known to him, and as the path had zigzagged up the low meadows, Seward seemed to change shape as readily as they changed direction.

Now they stood before the castle's western face. Here it might be a dragon with great rounded shoulders and long tail tucked close, while earlier, from farther back, the huge structure had appeared to be a giant mountain lion, gathered and ready to spring. Every step nearer had brought with it a growing uneasiness, an unsettling of the spirit.

Daryn had denied the fisherman's tales of horror, had insisted there was no danger, but his whole manner spoke the opposite. Standing next to the bundles they'd set down in the short grass, the duke seemed to be gathering strength around him like a mantle. He unpinned his cloak with careful deliberation and laid it neatly by his lute, then got down on one knee so that he was eye-level with the prince.

"Gaylon, you've got to wait out here."

Briefly the boy allowed himself a tiny shiver of relief. The very last thing he wanted was to walk into the gaping maw called Seward Castle. But he squared small shoulders and lifted his chin. "I'm coming with you."

Daryn grabbed him roughly by the arms. "I didn't give you a choice. And I need another promise from you."

"What?"

"That you'll remain out here for now, that whatever happens, you won't interfere. Promise me!"

Daryn's grip tightened, bringing pain, and Gaylon tried to back away, to break free. "Why? We've come here for help. If he was your master, why should we fear him?" And when Daryn gave no answer, "If there's danger we'll face it as we have all else, together. I'll defend your back."

"You'll do as I say," the duke snapped and put out his hand, palm out. "Give me your dirk and your sword."

Resentment welled in the prince, followed quickly by defiance. "No!"

Daryn slapped Gaylon abruptly with the proffered hand, jerking the knife from his boot with the other before he could step back. The sword was likewise taken. The prince stood rigid in outraged shock, a hand on his stinging cheek, his eyes sparking anger.

"Stay here," Daryn commanded gruffly. "Don't wander from this spot. Don't go near the Shadows of the castle for any reason, and above all else, remember your promise concerning the Stone."

He turned his back on the boy, hiding his regret, but the last thing needed at this point was Gaylon rushing to his duke's defense with a small and utterly useless sword. All the same, Daryn felt suddenly terribly alone. The monstrous castle doors lay only a half-dozen steps away. He crossed the bit of sward with determination, then put a hand on a rusted gargoyle knocker and boomed his presence to the inner court. Gaylon's dirk was slipped into his belt.

The doors remained closed. After a time, he gestured with his ring and they swung partially ajar, creaking complaint. By the sound, they hadn't been opened in a very long time. The duke paused in the red evening sunlight before passing into the dark. This was no longer his world, and he felt at a great disadvantage. Gaylon's little sword was placed against the wall just inside.

It took several long moments for the duke's eyes to adjust to the gloom. He peered about, trying to orient himself before moving away from the small comfort of the doorway and into the great hall. What little that could be seen was as he remembered—empty expanses of gray flagstones. The air, though, felt colder, smelled mustier. All around, the darkness throbbed, a trick of the eye, a trick of the mind. From the corners of his eyes Daryn saw the blackness scrabbling away, crawling back. It clamored for his attention, an attempt to confuse him. That much he remembered as well and was able to ignore the effects of the spell. The duke directed his attention to the bit of blackness that didn't move: a dim form in a high-backed chair near the far wall.

Still as death, Sezran sat, almost as intangible as his living night. Daryn would have thought him dead if not for the faint blue pulse from the Stone at his throat. There was an answering glimmer from the duke's left hand.

"Master," Daryn said softly, but the word seemed to thunder in the silence of the hall. The form in the chair never stirred. "Master," he said again, fighting to keep the quaver from his voice. He remembered this old man, this *ancient* man, with love. Only it was a love borne of respect and awe . . . and fear.

The sorcerer had never been one to waste emotions or words. And so it was now.

"Get out." The thin piping voice came to Daryn from the vicinity of the chair.

"Hear me first, master." The duke ventured closer.

"No." The word was final, irrefutable.

Daryn very nearly turned away then, but there was nowhere

to go. Gaylon had no one else to turn to. Whatever the cost, he must somehow make Sezran understand. He fought through a confusion of thoughts, trying to find the right words.

"You can't say no until you've heard what I have to say." His own pleading tone angered him.

"No."

"Listen to me!" Daryn shouted in frustration, and the castle walls reverberated. He braved several steps more toward the chair. A deadly glow began to emanate from the Stone on the wizard's breast, but what brought the duke up short was the flash of warning in Sezran's dusky eyes.

But there was no turning back now. Painful memories had been triggered, bringing with them a flash of insight.

"You've never forgiven me, have you—for failing, for not being strong enough?" Horrified, the duke found his eyes brimming, overflowing with unbidden tears as if he were a mere boy again. He choked in misery on the next few words. "I nearly died, and you've never forgiven me!" Daryn felt desolate, ashamed, then angry by turns. He was here on Gaylon's behalf, not to dredge up old hurts. "Well, I've brought you a child who promises to be all that I was not, a prince to be tutored from the *Book of Stones*."

"Get out!" Sezran snapped with such force that the command cracked on the air like a whip. Daryn flinched.

"Not until you've heard me out, damn you—" The duke was cut off by a rumbling that started deep within the foundations of the castle. The withered creature in the blue-black robes straightened in his seat.

"You overstep yourself, Daryn of Gosney." Sezran lifted a clawlike hand from the folds of his sleeve and touched his Stone. "You should never have come back."

This is going badly, Daryn told himself, feeling helpless in the undertow of emotions. He'd needed to choose his next words carefully, but found that he couldn't. Instead, he growled, "Yes! And what will you do, old man? Turn me into a toad? Kill me?"

The duke backed slowly into the center of the floor. Not a retreat—there was no retreat now. Every line of his body had tensed in a catlike readiness to fight. He didn't draw his sword. It was useless in this. Instead Daryn raised his ringed hand to eye-level and began to reach deeply for that inner power he'd denied for so long. The Stone on his finger began a steady intense glow.

In disbelief, Sezran leaned forward. "You challenge me with your infinitesimal powers? You *are* mad!"

"Will you hear me?"

"You're no match for me, you fool. I warn you one last time. Leave safely while you yet may."

"I'll go, but the child must stay."

"If you leave him, I'll destroy him. Get out!"

"No," Daryn replied.

Sezran stood and took up his Stone. Its color heightened. "Then die." He loosed a sudden bolt of blue fire.

Daryn flung himself aside, covering his eyes as the ground exploded where he had stood. His own response was immediate, though each moment seemed an eternity. The power had started somewhere inside him as a low vibration, then spiraled upward. The energy built on itself, fed by the tension, the fear, the frustration. When it snapped suddenly free of his Stone, Daryn was as much surprised by the intensity as Sezran. The power was far beyond the duke's own conception of himself.

Cobalt lightning lashed out, violent and terrible, but struck an empty chair. The wood burst into flame and threw the room into brilliant relief. A thick smoke filled the air. Just as quickly, Sezran retaliated from where he stood now, behind Daryn. Even as the young man spun about, flinging up his hand to parry the blow, a wave of cobalt fire swept over him, slamming him sideways and down.

Partially blinded by the glare, Sezran sensed more than saw movement from where Daryn lay. He lashed out a last time, a final, killing blow. Too late the wizard realized what he'd actually seen—a child crouched at Daryn's side—then the flame enveloped them both.

When Sezran's vision cleared once more, he found the boy, unharmed, still on his knees beside the fallen man. He held something cupped in his hands, and as he opened them the hall was bathed again with a blinding, icy light that faded slowly. A Sorcerer's Stone, unset, lay in the child's small palm. He'd diverted the blow with it.

In disbelief the old wizard crossed the floor to where the boy knelt sobbing. "Stand back, child," he said gruffly.

"No!" the boy cried. "I won't let you hurt him anymore!"

"I know." The touch of his hand on the child's shoulder was not unkind. "Move aside and let me see to him."

Reluctantly the youngster did as he was told, watching anxiously while Sezran unfolded the smoldering heap that was Daryn of Gosney, patting at the cloth where it still smoked. The duke was unconscious, but the damage seemed not so extensive as Sezran had first thought. The left hand was horribly burned, and over the left eye a thick lock of hair had gone white. Gently, almost tenderly, the master of Seward slid an arm under his former student's neck, the other under his knees, then with no seeming effort lifted the injured man.

"Here now!" he said sharply to the child. "Stop sniveling, boy, and get the door."

The old sorcerer carried Daryn across the great hall and along a cold passageway to his own crowded bedchamber, one of the few rooms in use these past years. The bed was narrow with a hard straw mattress and seldom occupied. At the barest glance, a fire burst into life on the hearth, and Sezran began his ministrations, using the medicaments on the many tables and shelves. The burned hand—what was left of it—was cleansed and covered with salve, then bandaged.

A small boy with an unset Stone had defended Daryn of Gosney. That completely amazed the wizard and gave him pause. While part of him still wanted nothing to do with the outside world, another part remembered Daryn as he once was, so young and eager and full of hope. Sezran frowned. He might come to regret this foolish act of charity.

When at last he'd done all he could for the injured man, the wizard sat back and contemplated the passive face of his patient. Daryn was dying, of that he had no doubt. There'd been a time when he might have felt sorrow, but no longer. Now he must decide how best to deal with the boy waiting outside the door. He clapped bony hands to bony knees before standing and shaking out his crumpled robes.

The boy sat on the cold stone floor with his back to the wall. As the door opened he looked up, eyes dry, but face streaked with dirt. He'd wielded a Stone with unbelievable power and yet he was nothing more than a filthy, scruffy child now—very much like Daryn had been when he'd first come to Seward. The boy still clutched the Stone in a grubby fist as he climbed wearily to his feet to face the sorcerer.

"I've got to speak with Daryn," he said quietly.

Sezran, with a bare shake of his head, said, "He can't hear you."

"You don't understand." The boy's voice began to rise. "I'm foresworn."

"How so?"

"I used the Stone. I swore not to. I gave him my oath."

"He'd forgive you."

"He said he'd leave me if I used it. . . ." Gaylon searched the sorcerer's passionless face. "Would the . . . could the Stone . . . ?"

"No," said Sezran simply. "In this the Stone has no power." He paused, seeing fear in the boy. "Do you love your master?"

"Yes!"

"Then you have within you the only power that can help Daryn. Go to him." Sezran drifted away down the passage without a backward glance.

Gaylon feared what he might find when he entered the room, and hovered a long time in the doorway before gaining the courage to cross the threshold. Within, the air was warm and close and filled with an admixture of curious smells. He passed shelves of old books, row upon row of them, and table-tops crowded with all manner of strange things. In the center of one sat the squat form of a massive stone mortar nearly lost in a forest of earthenware containers. The prince was touched by a vague sense of familiarity in wending his way to the hearth, but the feeling passed as he stoked the fire. Finally, because there was nothing else for him to do, no other way to avoid the inevitable, he moved listlessly to the bedside.

Daryn's face was ghastly pale against his dark hair, his features strangely slack, and for one awful moment, Gaylon thought him already dead. Dropping his head to the still man's chest, he caught the sound of a faint heartbeat. At first glance the injuries seemed minor, with only the left hand lost in thick bandages. But the animation was gone—all that was Daryn of Gosney, awake or asleep, was missing.

"Daryn?" the boy murmured, fighting a wave of panic, knowing himself helpless in this.

The prince began to talk, haltingly at first, a rambling narrative, a monologue of shared experiences as though, through memory, he might hold Daryn in this world. He sang the songs Daryn had taught him, wishing for the lute to accompany himself. His throat grew raw, swollen, and constricted with pent-up tears. Time ceased to exist, and he was unmindful of Sezran's periodic visits to change the bandages on Daryn's hand. The food and drink the sorcerer left for him was ignored. Gaylon slept fitfully only now and then, but from Daryn there was no response. The duke's heartbeat grew weaker.

Finally the prince had talked himself out. When his words had become tasteless, dried husks on a sluggish tongue, Gaylon broke down. Filled with bitter defeat, he sobbed his hopelessness and misery into the coarse woolen blankets that covered his friend.

Daryn heard. In some distant place the sobs had found him, but he refused to listen. When Sezran had struck him, his Stone had exploded, the force propelling him outward. The duke had found by chance that light, soft world where feeling is sound. He'd joined the dancers with a freedom he'd never known, and moved with them across their endless yellow plain under black starry skies. He had no desire to go back and face the pain and sorrow that awaited. Daryn danced with fierce joy because he knew the thin thread of energy that anchored him to life would soon snap. In that instant, he'd be gone.

Through it all, the man had heard a soft, insistent voice. The more he tried to ignore it, the more the sounds nagged at him. Then, somewhere, a child began to cry, endless sobs that brought Daryn pain. His dance slowed and finally stilled. Was there something he'd forgotten? Some important thing yet to be done? He'd done all he could; his work was finished. "No!" he shouted soundlessly, and the word rolled like thunder through the yellow plain. The dancers fled before that cacophonous beat, leaving him alone to listen to his own name being called over and over.

"Daryn, please don't leave me. Daryn. Don't die. I broke my oath, and I'm sorry. Please, Daryn, don't go." In Gaylon's fingers the Sorcerer's Stone began to glow, and he looked at it with loathing. "I'll never use the Stone again—ever! I'll throw it away."

"No." Though it caused him horrible pain, Daryn lifted the bandaged hand and touched the boy.

Gaylon felt the touch, heard the voice at first without comprehension. Then, in complete exhaustion, he closed swollen eyes and laid his head on Daryn's chest, instantly asleep.

Some time later Sezran entered the room. The boy slept deeply, his breathing ragged with spent sobs. Daryn of Gosney stared sightlessly at the ceiling above the bed, his ruined hand resting lightly on the boy's back. The mage watched the pain fall in crashing waves over the injured man, then went to the fire and poured a decoction into a cup. When he placed it to the injured man's lips, Daryn made to turn away.

"Drink!"

"What?" The effort of speech was awful, the word distorted, slurred.

"For the pain. Drink or the pain will surely kill you. Don't be a fool. Don't revel in your misfortune." With efficiency Sezran got the liquor into his helpless patient, then stood back.

Daryn's eyes followed the wizard. "My arm," the young man mumbled, his voice barely audible. "Leg . . . move . . ."

Sezran nodded grimly, noting the downward pull at the right corner of Daryn's mouth, the flaccid muscles of the cheek, the drooping eyelid.

"It is as I suspected," the sorcerer said, turning away. "You might as well have the worst of it now. I didn't expect you to survive, and you may yet regret the fact that you have. But, you *are* alive. Some think that that alone is enough. For you it may have to be."

Sezran made a nest of blankets in the leather armchair before the fireplace. As he lifted the sleeping boy and placed him there, he continued to speak.

"Your left hand is badly burned, but will heal—what's left of it." He returned to the bed. "The scarring will render it very nearly useless, though. Most of the damage was done here." He tapped Daryn's forehead gently just above his left eye. "This is the reason you can't move your right arm or leg. I don't profess to understand why, but your entire side is likely paralyzed. This could effect your vision, your speech, and perhaps even your thinking."

The drugs were taking effect. Daryn closed his eyes. The pain became a distant, curious phenomenon, drifting away. Drifting with it was any care for what Sezran said. Perhaps the old man had timed it that way.

"Daryn, you will not play the lute again. You will not use the sword. More than any of this, you have lost your Sorcerer's Stone, which was destroyed along with your magic. All of this you have given for one small child. I can only hope you find him worth the price."

* * * * *

Three days passed. Before dawn on the morning of the fourth, Sezran came into the bedchamber as he did several times each day. The fire had burned low, and he stopped to rebuild it. The child slept in the armchair, lying length-wise across the seat, his head lolled back, a book spread open in his lap. Sezran glanced at the page heading as he passed the chair. "Conjectures on Dementia and Other Brain Dysfunctions." The book was several hundred years old and as full of superstitious nonsense as any proper medical knowledge. With irritation he noticed that several of the tomes on his shelves had been disturbed.

He prepared another potion and swirled the dark liquid in the cup as he carried it to the bed. Daryn was nearly awake, his face contorting in half-grimaces, but he roused when the cup touched his lips and swallowed eagerly to the bitter dregs the contents. In moments he had slid back down into unconsciousness.

Sezran straightened and turned to find the prince watching him from the chair.

"Did I wake you, boy?"

"My name is Gaylon Reysson," the child said stiffly.

"Then, Gaylon Reysson, did I wake you?"

"No. I was only resting." Gaylon's eyes narrowed, and he looked hard at the old sorcerer. "I *know* you. You're the one who set the wind on me the first night I used my Stone."

"The wind obeys me, yes. You remember our first meeting. I wondered how long it would take you."

"You tried to kill me."

"No, but I could have. The Dreamer is vulnerable to many dangers. Dreaming is not a thing to be done lightly. It is a hazardous undertaking, even for those who've mastered their Stones. How long did you dream?"

"Daryn said I slept for six days."

"Only six? You are indeed strong. Daryn was gone over forty days. I nearly lost him. He was undisciplined and careless."

"The pupil is only a reflection of the teacher," Gaylon said coldly.

Sezran drew a sharp breath. "You've a sharp tongue, boy, but you know nothing of the risks inherent in the Sorcerer's Stone."

"I wanted Daryn to teach me, but he refused."

"Tis well he did."

Gaylon rolled the little Stone in his fingers now. "It doesn't matter. I'll teach myself."

"Do you think?" Sezran laughed shortly, without humor.

"Yes!"

"Then listen to me carefully. You're strong, of that I have no doubts, and one day your powers may even be great. If I were a mere man I would tremble in terror of you. It's only a matter of time—and not a long time—before the Stone destroys you. You must stay here, and I must instruct you. *I* will be your teacher."

"You can say that," Gaylon demanded hotly, "after nearly killing Daryn when he asked you for help? Why should you change your mind?"

"My reasons are my own and of no concern to you." Sezran watched the boy's Stone flare. "Shield your Stone or still it. The glow reveals more of your thoughts than should please you."

Gaylon made a fist over the pebble, and blue light streamed out between his fingers. He willed the Stone dark and slowly the glow faded.

"Very good." Sezran nodded. "Already there is control. Of a sort. You'll be an apt student . . . if you live long enough."

The book caught in his arms, Gaylon shifted in the chair and brought his feet to the floor.

"And another thing," continued Sezran. "I don't approve of you touching my books. Children have dirty hands and careless fingers."

The boy's face reddened. "I've done them no hurt!" His Stone flared brightly.

"The Stone, child! How quickly you lose what little control you have." The old man shook his head, then, in a more kindly voice, he asked, "Do you understand any of what you've read?"

"Some," Gaylon answered quietly. "It's hard to weed out all the foolishness from anything of value, however. See here?" He pointed to a paragraph on one of the pages. "It says paralysis can be cured by shaving the patient's head and spitting on his scalp three times a night during the second phase of the moon. But first you have to eat two handfuls of garlic."

"That, boy—"

"Gaylon."

"That, Gaylon Reysson, is one of the more scientific cures."

The prince closed the book, carried it to the shelf, and replaced the volume among the others.

"I want you to stop giving Daryn the poppy milk," he said

suddenly as he turned back.

Sezran studied him a moment. "You wish him to suffer?"

"No, but he can't live forever in a drugged stupor."

"Let him have his dreams, child. They're all he has now."

"One of the books says the limbs can learn to function again if they're exercised, made to work. If the muscles aren't used they de . . . degenerate. How can I help him if he's always asleep?"

Sezran saw the determination in the young face. "All right, but not just yet. Let the hand heal a while longer—a few more days. Then we'll begin to lessen the amount of the potion given him." He paused, his features softening. "You must understand, Gaylon Reysson, that Daryn is a cripple in other ways, as well. He may not thank you for your help. Now! Leave my books alone and touch nothing in this room without asking." The sharp angles of Sezran's thin face hardened, his countenance changing once more to that of a powerful and angry wizard.

Gaylon nodded slowly in obedience.

Eleven

The door slammed open, and Gaylon burst into the passageway. Sezran got one good look at his ashen face before the boy turned and fled away toward the great hall. The old sorcerer stepped into the bedchamber shaking his head. From the mattress, Daryn turned smoke-colored eyes on him. A bowl of soup lay upset on the floor beside him.

"What did you say to the child?" Sezran demanded.

Daryn's eyes shifted aside. "Nnnothing."

"And your soup?"

"I . . . am . . . nnnot . . . hhungry." Each word came painfully, articulated with care, heavy with sarcasm.

"Humph!"

Sezran took the chair Gaylon had abandoned, sitting sideways to avoid setting his buskins in the mess on the floor. He lifted the grotesque thing that had once been Daryn's left hand and drew it into his lap. It was healing well, the stumps of the fingers covering over with thick scar tissue. The wizard had brought a new salve he felt might ease the scarring.

"Your behavior of late has been unconscionable," he observed, rubbing the ointment into the skin. "Why do you treat the boy so cruelly when he only wishes to help?"

"Hhhhe . . . knows," Daryn growled, fighting his tongue, "what . . . hhhelp . . . I nnneed."

"And that is?"

The duke remained silent, his eyes drifting unfocused, his

face unreadable. Sezran replaced the hand on the blankets beside him. It was as lifeless as the paralyzed right one.

"Do you desire anything?"

Again there was no answer, and the old man stood. He stared for a time at Daryn, then took himself out into the passage and went in search of the child.

Gaylon had left the castle through the unshadowed west portal, taking the path across the meadow to the cliffs. There Sezran found him standing on the brink, gazing fixedly on the rocks below. At the sound of the sorcerer's steps the boy looked up. Against the color of the winter ocean his eyes were very nearly green, and a spattering of freckles stood out starkly on his pale cheeks. But the old man saw a subtle maturity in his stance. Gaylon's youth was already a fragile thing, slipping from him with every passing moment.

"Come away from the edge," Sezran said gently. Even as he spoke the ledge crumbled under Gaylon's right foot. The boy caught his balance quickly and stepped to safety, but his eyes traced the dirt's long fall to the gray-green water.

"I wouldn't have fallen," he muttered sullenly, then his teeth clenched. "Do you know what he said to me?"

"He wouldn't tell me."

"He asked me—no, he begged me—to set him free." The words were choking the boy, and tears spilled from the corners of his eyes. He held up his hand and shook it at Sezran, showing him a dirk. "He wanted me to use this! He said that if I truly loved him . . . I would do this one thing for him. He wants to die and can't do it for himself."

"He doesn't want to die."

"He does!"

"If he wanted to die he would have asked me. He knows well enough I'd perform the task without hesitation. He says these things to you because he suffers and wishes you to suffer, also."

"I was wrong, wasn't I, to have you awaken him?"

"There's no right or wrong in this."

"Would you . . . would you really take his life if he asked?"

"I would."

Gaylon drew a ragged breath. "You mustn't."

"He hasn't asked."

"And if he does?"

"Look, a storm on the horizon." Sezran's eyes had strayed into the distant west. He smiled faintly. "It comes. Soon there'll be a wind." The mage's hair, unkempt, lifted from his face and streamed back as if he stood already in a gale. The Stone on its golden chain around his neck took life and color, and his dark eyes sparked when he turned them again on the boy. "Do you feel it? The power comes!"

With the tangled sheep's wool hair gone from his face, Sezran was fully visible to Gaylon for the first time. The boy took note of the pointed chin, the narrow nose, and the gentle slant of the eyes.

"Misk!" he gasped, and Sezran's sharp features suddenly hardened.

"Misk," the sorcerer snarled. "What do you know of Misk?"

Now Gaylon trembled. It felt as though the storm had already arrived and stood before him, mercurial in wind-swept robes of midnight blue.

"Tell me!" Sezran cried.

The boy took a step back, nearer the cliff, the dirk poised ready in one hand, his Stone clutched in the palm of the other. Sezran recognized the danger in the situation and fought to calm his inner turmoil. His hair, his robes settled about him.

"Be at ease, Gaylon Reysson. I won't harm you. Only you *will* tell me what you know of Misk."

"She . . . she sheltered us after my father was slain. Daryn was sick, and she healed him." There was accusation in that, as if Sezran were failing where Misk had not.

Irritated, the wizard waved his hand. "Yes, yes. What else?"

"She's very strange."

That brought a small, tight smile to the old man's lips. "You are kind. Misk is a madwoman."

"She divines the future," Gaylon said defensively.

"That's too simple a term for it. But tell me, what does my sister say of the future?"

"She said I'll find a thing of power . . . a black stone with stars caught in it. She said, first I must find the one thing before the other. And I found this." The boy opened his fingers, and his Stone winked blue in the afternoon light.

Sezran's face had relaxed once more into inscrutability, but in his mind, thoughts raced. The storm grew nearer, dark clouds scudding eastward before a driving wind. The mage felt suffused with its raw power. He longed to lift his hands and direct the tempest's path of destruction, longed to wreck havoc on this world, to bring oblivion to every living creature within his reach. The thought brought a deep pleasure. It was enough to know that he could if he so chose.

He glanced back and saw Gaylon standing in his innocence, his eyes on the advancing weather. The old wizard reached out through his Stone and touched the power that seethed within the boy's small being—and recoiled instantly. At that nonphysical touch, Gaylon looked up.

To cover his disquietude, Sezran said gruffly, "Go, Gaylon Reysson. Return to Seward Castle. Leave me to my storm."

* * * * *

Misk didn't remember that he would come, riding the storm, his robes wind-whipped, his eyes flashing hatred. But it was late in the day and her control was thin, her future memories vague. The warm, cheery cottage filled with cold, moisture-laden air, and there he was, a dark form in the center of the floor.

She attempted a feeble smile, a frail shield against his anger.

"Misk!" Sezran thundered.

"Brother," she answered in a voice as mild as his was not.

She realized Jimi wasn't here and thought fleetingly that this was best. He'd gone to Riverbend with the cheese to sell. Her husband would get a good price—sixteen silver coins, eight coppers, and four black hens. One of them would never lay. The big man would buy their supplies and a bit of Zankos silk that caught his eye as a present for her. Gaudy red it would be with green—

"Misk!"

She blinked and remembered where she was and in whose presence.

"Welcome, Brother."

She could see Sezran's fury fading as it always did. Misk was the calm at the center of her brother's storm, but he clung to his anger as long as he could, rumbling and flickering.

"How dare you?" he demanded. "How dare you send them to me!"

"The boy must learn—"

"Learn! Do you think me such a fool? Shall I train him so that he may steal Kingslayer from me?"

"He cannot steal what is already his."

"It's not his!" Sezran raged hotly. "It's mine! Mine!"

"You traded the sword for that bauble on your chest, my brother. And you forget, the gem that powers Kingslayer was never yours in the first place." When he made to answer, she cut him off. "What of Daryn?"

Sezran's lips curled back over his teeth in a malicious grin. "You knew I would kill him. You knowingly sent him to his death."

Misk felt a curious ache in her chest. She'd carefully, magically, hidden Daryn and Gaylon to protect them from the Southern sorcerer, Feydir, then sent them into even worse danger at Seward.

"Then Daryn is dead," she whispered sorrowfully.

"No, but he wishes he were, and I may grant that wish."

"Brother, please. Don't kill him to punish *me*."

"Tell me where I may find my sword."

She lowered her eyes. "You know I can't."

"Damn you!" he flared. "Damn you, then! I'll destroy them both!"

Her mind wandered, traveling the tunnels of time, and she saw Daryn dead, and Gaylon, too. But that was another path, another future, one that led elsewhere.

"No," Misk said softly. "No, you'll only wait and watch."

"Is that what you see, sister dear?" he snarled. "Then you're blind!"

"I see . . ." she muttered. "I see . . . that you shall have what you desire. I see that Gaylon will place it in your hands, one day."

Sezran quieted, watching his sister closely, as if he might find some sign of deception in her face, but knew she was incapable of it.

Misk smiled suddenly. "I see another thing." She caught his eyes with her own. "I see a spark in that cold black heart of yours, my brother, a tiny ember of warmth, a thing I never thought possible." Her words had a curious effect. He drew back. "It's for Daryn. You *do* care for him."

She might have stabbed Sezran, his reaction was so violent.

"Foul creature!" he cried, his fury renewed. "Meddler! Look now ahead, woman. I will make the future mine, and nothing you may do will stop me!"

He was storm again, swirling clouds of blue-black. A gust of wind, a roll of thunder, then he was gone.

* * * * *

Gaylon failed to return to the bedchamber, and bitterly Daryn realized how very slowly time passed in this place. He studied the ceiling, though he knew every crack by now, every cobweb as once he had known the backs of his hands. Hand. He moved the left one and brought it jerking with palsy before his face. His right eye wandered in another direction so that for a moment his vision doubled. Impatiently, the duke waited for the blurring to end so he could see this monster's paw.

How much time had truly passed since he'd become a prisoner in his own body? Enough for the hand to nearly heal, for the scar tissue to web between the nubbins of fingers. The hand looked as though it now belonged to some amphibian creature rather than a man. The sight sickened him, and he let the grotesque thing drop to the bedcovers. The burns throbbed still so that he was ever aware of them, and even more aware of the fact that he felt nothing whatsoever on the right side of his body. Daryn closed his eyes and willed himself dead, though he knew this was foolish. His spirit clung stubbornly to life, even while his mind sought release.

Fury washed through him, a sudden wave of burning choler, followed quickly by anguish. He wanted to scream his outrage, but was afraid—afraid that once the screaming began he wouldn't be able to stop, afraid that his cries would bring Gaylon running, effusing love and understanding. The boy's pity was the hardest thing of all to bear.

A breath of cool air brushed his face, and the duke opened his eyes. The candle by the bed guttered briefly, and he turned his head toward the door. Sezran had come into the chamber. Alone. The wizard crouched at the hearth, feeding the fire.

"Gay . . . lon?" Daryn queried.

"He studies the *Book of Stones*." The sorcerer stood and crossed to the bed. He carried something in his hands and, as he neared, Daryn saw a chalice of gold, chased with blood rubies. The cup gleamed richly in the candlelight.

"Do you wonder what I have?" Sezran asked. He turned the chalice in his hands as if admiring it. "I bring you a gift, Daryn of Gosney. In this cup I bring you death. Does that please you?"

Daryn blinked twice, slowly, but could find no words.

"The boy told me of your wish, but a knife is so crude and painful, however quick or true the stroke." Sezran brought the chalice closer. "In this potion are dreams, gentle and sweet, and finally, a sleep without dreams—an endless sleep. Is this your desire?"

Daryn's lips parted slightly, and he ran his tongue over them. He stared at the cup, then lifted his eyes to Sezran's. They were wide pools of darkness, and Daryn could see his own reflection in them. Finally, the duke nodded.

Sezran smiled. "Then, it will be yours." He set the cup beside the candle. "First I must know of your plans for the boy. With your death, the responsibility falls to me. You called him a prince once. If this is true, then you must know a thing: I can train him in the ways of sorcery, but the ways of royalty are not mine to teach."

"Hhhe . . . will be . . . a king."

"Ahhh, I fear he'll not be suited to the task when I've finished with him."

"Hhhe . . . *mmmust* rule."

"No doubt he will. His strength, his power even now is beyond understanding. If he chooses to rule, there'll be none to stop him. But, mark my words, the kingdoms to which he turns his hand will rue the day. He'll make them forget the Dark King. Orym will be a sweet memory by comparison."

"Nnno!" Daryn cried softly.

"Yes. You've seen the hatred in him. It's his driving force. He barely holds the rage in check. His temper flares at the slightest provocation, and his fighting instincts are already fine-edged. He's a killer by nature, and his reign will be terrible and bloody."

Daryn's scarred hand jerked reflexively. His facial muscles twitched.

Sezran went on, watching the duke closely. "All that I have said will come to pass if Gaylon is given Kingslayer. With the sword he will be virtually omnipotent."

"Hhhiss . . . hhheritage . . ."

All along, the sorcerer had spoken calmly, reasonably. Now his voice rose.

"That is *not* his heritage. The sword is mine, Daryn. *I* am the one who forged the blade, and it's mine. Like a fool, I gave it into human hands, but Kingslayer must be given back to me." He lowered his voice, drew closer to the duke. "You know I'm right. If you have put your hand to Kingslayer, then you know what I say is true. It must *never* again be taken up by a human who wields a Stone."

Memory came in vivid flashes, and Daryn felt his heart pounding against his ribs. The taste of such power! He hungered for it even now, when it could never be his.

"Mmmy . . . ddduty."

"Your duty ends with death, and you've chosen to die." Sezran picked up the cup and brought it near Daryn's lips. "Tell me where Kingslayer is hidden, and the drink is yours." The wizard's eyes glittered slyly. "Does the boy know? Have you told him of the sword?"

Daryn, his gaze fixed on the chalice, shook his head.

"Good. Now tell me where it is and gain your freedom."

The cup tilted, and Daryn could see the dark liquid w golden light dancing on the oily surface. He longed fo e dreams the potion promised, for the oblivion. But what of Gaylon? It was true—the child was governed by hatred, and Sezran could never teach him compassion, could never temper the forces that drove the boy. How could a cripple succeed in those tasks? he wondered bitterly and railed mentally against his ruined body.

"Speak to me," Sezran demanded.

Daryn pursed his lips, turning his face to the wall. A long silence followed, then the chalice clanged against the stones of the fireplace and clattered to the floor. Daryn heard the echo of the sorcerer's footsteps moving away.

* * * * *

The young woman's beauty was breathtaking, her lips warm. She pressed close, enticingly close. So why did he feel only annoyance? Gently Lucien pulled back, disengaging Marcel's fingers from his neck, and stepped away to retrieve her red velvet cloak from the bed. He slipped the cloth over her shoulders, pinned it neatly in place, and pulled the hood up around her face. Her hair hung loose, and where it fell across her breast the firelight made the locks shimmer red and gold.

"Your Highness," she said softly, hurt in her voice.

"Hush," he murmured, and touched her lips with his fingertips. "You're as desirable as always, Marcel, but . . . there are things I must think on tonight. I need to be alone."

Lucien led her by the hand to the door behind the drapes—the bolt-hole—for the lady's midnight visits had to be discreet. He watched her pass silently down the steps, then closed and locked the door and moved back into the room.

For a time, the king paced before the fire, restless but unable to decide exactly why. The bedchamber lay in shadowed darkness, the lamps and candles unlit. He'd once desired Lady Marcel badly, and now that she was his, he no longer wanted her. The fact that she was to have been Daryn's had made her very attractive at first, but now she bored him. Everything bored him. Three months a king and already his tastes were jaded.

Lucien paused by the alcove window and looked down on the wintry gardens. A cloaked figure stood in the snow, in the starlight. For a moment he thought it Marcel, but the form was too small. It could only be Jessmyn. Anger came briefly. Why does she stand out in the cold so late at night? He thought about going down to the courtyard and scolding her severely, then decided against such action. The young king knew well enough why she walked the gardens alone.

Each day, Lucien had dresses of fine lace and silks sent to the little princess. He brought her delicacies and fed them to her with his own fingers and yet, each day, she grew paler, thinner. She mourns, he thought, and I can do nothing to ease her hurt. That brought a small ache deep within him, and he observed the pain with wonder. This was something new to him, this caring for another.

The king had brought his worries for Jessmyn to his uncle, a thing rarely done, and Feydir had told him to speak with Girkin. Girkin! That fat little idiot. He wouldn't trust the man with a favorite horse, let alone the princess.

Why should Jessmyn grieve, refusing to believe Gaylon gone? The king knew his uncle still searched for Daryn of Gosney, knew he offered huge rewards for any information concerning the duke. The old man seeks Gosney in desperation, hoping for information about Kingslayer, Lucien decided. But the weapon could never be his. Daryn, Gaylon, and Reys were long dead. Let the fool continue his hunt, though. That at least kept the sorcerer occupied and out of Lucien's way.

Finally Lucien pulled the curtains across the window, no longer able to watch Jessmyn alone in the garden with her sorrow. After lighting the lamps, he went to stand before the full-length mirror by the dressing table. The handsome youth that stared back at him had gained weight in the three short months he'd been king. There was a hint of jowl at the jawline, a small bulge at the waist. He held up his hands and looked at them critically. The nails were long, buffed until they shone, the fingers and palms soft. Gone were the thick calluses on the right hand, the hand that had once held a sword for long periods of time each day. He'd not taken up a sword since Daryn destroyed Galimar.

Irritated, Lucien pulled his dirk from its belt sheath and pared his nails back crudely, took a handkerchief from a lace cuff and rubbed the rouge from lips and cheeks, the kohl from his eyes. He'd played the fop long enough. For five long years he'd craved the delicate company of his Southern peers, but they were his peers no longer. A king should set trends rather than follow them.

His soft dance slippers were kicked off, and all the formal gold-embroidered finery was left in a heap on the floor. Dressed once more, he returned to the mirror to view his reflection; he now wore short riding breeches, high black boots, and a plain white linen shirt under a dark, short-sleeved leather jerkin. His pale hair had grown too long, the young king decided. It would be cut tomorrow. For now, he tied it back with a leather thong, then unracked the sword Roffo had sent him.

Dear cousin Roffo, a king in name only. The Xenaran merchant families held all the true power, the power that great wealth could buy. Lucien would not willingly follow that old man's lead. Roffo had sent the weapon along with his blessings. The old man was perfectly willing, perfectly happy to give his daughter, Jessmyn, to Lucien in marriage as Feydir wished. However the wind blows, eh, Roffo? Lucien's nostrils flared with disgust. Nearly ten years would pass before they would be wed. He couldn't imagine the marriage; Jessmyn was a tiny porcelain doll yet.

He hefted the beautiful blade with appreciation and dropped into an *en garde* before the mirror, admiring himself. Finally the scabbard was clipped to his belt, and the sword slid home. He went to the door that opened on the passageway. The two soldiers outside came to a clumsy attention, caught off guard. Their half-armor—cuirass and helm—clanked as they saluted. Lucien eyed the younger of the two, and the man smiled at him. His behavior was too familiar, lacking in respect.

"You!" Lucien snapped. "Come with me to the arms room. I wish to practice with swords for a while tonight."

The young man grinned, throwing a glance at his partner, and Lucien strode away down the passage. Let the fool grin, the young king thought, the fellow close on his heels. This night Lucien would sheath his new blade in the soldier's flesh, and by the man's blood the sword would be named.

* * * * *

Sezran disappeared completely for three days. He returned even more mysterious and reserved than usual, his wild hair singed, his nose soot-smeared, his mood foul. Gaylon tread lightly in his presence and reserved his questions concerning his lessons in the *Book of Stones* for another, more propitious time. Two more days passed with the sorcerer coming and going at odd moments. And at night, a roaring and clanging could be heard dimly from deep within the castle.

Gaylon had brought the *Book of Stones*, with Sezran's permission, to Daryn's bedchamber and studied now at a table in front of the fireplace. For the first time in a long while the boy felt something close to happiness. Daryn was no longer a plaintive querulous patient. He even allowed the boy to massage and work the paralyzed limbs, and his speech grew clearer with each passing day, though he would stumble over his words when tired or excited. The duke was still subject to spells of black depression, but Gaylon had learned to recognize the signs proceeding them and would take up the battered old lute and sing the bawdy tunes and shanties Daryn had taught him. This never failed to bring a cockeyed smile to the man's lips.

This day Gaylon sat at the table as he did every day, slaving over his pages, laboriously translating the tiny runes onto a clay tablet with a sharp stylus. Sezran allowed no copies made on paper and, once memorized, the clay was wetted and the translation destroyed. On the bed, Daryn had fallen into a fitful sleep.

The prince lifted his eyes from the page, tilted his head, listening. Faintly at first came a rumbling, as of distant thunder, which quickly grew louder. Daryn came awake with a start.

"What?" he asked.

Gaylon stood. The rumbling had taken on a clatter, seemed to be coming closer, and now, a squealing was added that set the boy's teeth on edge. The walls, the floor, the furnishings vibrated, and just when the prince decided he could endure no more, utter silence fell. He looked at Daryn, and together they looked to the door as it opened. Sezran entered pushing a wheeled chair before him. The metal-rimmed wheels howled piteously as they rolled.

"What is . . . ttthat?" the duke demanded when it was quiet once more.

"A conveyance for a cripple," the old man snapped. His eyes were bloodshot, and his hair stood up from his head in wild disarray.

"It's loud," said Gaylon, stating the obvious.

Sezran scowled at him. "The wheel rims will be wrapped with leather, and the hubs will be packed with lard. This will be your work. Come here, child!"

Gaylon stepped forward, and the sorcerer held out a square of silk, open on his hand.

"Give me your Stone," he commanded.

For a long moment the boy stared without comprehension, and Sezran waved the cloth under his nose impatiently. "Give me the Stone!"

Gaylon turned frightened eyes on Daryn, but the duke only watched silently, without expression.

"Why?" the boy asked faintly.

Sezran snorted in disgust. "Do you think I mean to steal your little pebble? It must be set, Gaylon Reysson, and the time is come. You can't carry the thing forever in your fist. Now, lay the Stone here in the silk."

Slowly Gaylon complied, saw his Stone wrapped carefully and placed in a pouch. Without another word the sorcerer left the room. The prince, standing motionless beside the table, looked long at the door.

"Gaylon?"

The boy turned, and Daryn saw tears rolling silently down his cheeks.

"Come to me," the duke said gently. As Gaylon came to the

bed, he added, "You mmmustn't . . . worry."

"I'm not worried," the boy whispered. "That's not it." And Daryn realized there was pity on his face, not concern. "Oh, Daryn! I feel as if my eyes have been taken from me, my sense of touch, my hearing. It's as if some vital part of me has been ripped away!" The tears continued to fall, and Gaylon took up Daryn's twisted hand. "This is what you suffer! I never thought, I never understood what it would be like to lose my Stone as you've lost yours."

The muscles of Daryn's stomach knotted, and he closed his eyes. Yes. That was how it felt. To be emptied, to be only half-alive, but the boy must never know that. The duke said thickly, "No, Gaylon. It isn't the same for me. I was . . . nnnever attuned to . . . mmy Stone as you are to yours. Do nnot . . . think I suffer." As much as he was able, the duke forced himself to believe that, as well.

* * * * *

In Seward's deepest chamber, Sezran waited impatiently for the forge to reach the necessary temperature. The coal found locally was soft and miserable to burn, sooty and foul, difficult to work with. When finally the heat was sufficient, the old sorcerer used tongs to pull the little crucible filled with molten gold from the fire. He tipped the trace elements into the bright liquid, then watched as the impurities sizzled and flashed. This was a primitive world, without the advanced technology of Sezran's home, but he'd learned to make do with the available materials.

While the metal cooled, Sezran took the Stone from his pouch and set it on the workbench. Sorcerer's Stones were a rare but natural phenomenon in this world: a crystalline essence with a dim self-awareness. Those humans capable of bonding with the Stones were also rare, but once a bond was established, the psychic energy generated between the two could be wondrous.

For all its plain appearance, Gaylon's Stone was a truly remarkable little pebble, the crystalline structure very nearly perfect. Sezran approached the unset gem through his own, reaching out mentally, and was rejected immediately. Already the restructuring had begun, the subtle imprint of each upon the other, boy and Stone. How unfortunate that this world's sentient species should be so short-lived. The degree to which empathy had been established would render this particular Stone useless with the demise of Gaylon Reysson. But how brightly the small gemstone would shine in its brief life.

Daryn's Stone had been very different. It had belonged to a distant Gosney ancestor and had been passed down for hundreds of years until the birth of a child capable of bonding with it again. While an uncontrolled Stone was highly dangerous, with careful handling it could be preserved. Sezran doubted this would be the case with Gaylon's. The boy's Stone seemed as powerful and erratic as its master.

He left the pebble wrapped still in the bit of silk and began to work the gold, tapping, drawing, bending. Gold was a joy for him to work with. His movements were slow and deliberate, exacting. The ring must be fitting for so fine a Stone. He knew the child fretted and suffered with this separation. If anything, that slowed him even more. Let the boy know what Daryn had lost.

"Hmmm . . . Very lovely," came a whisper from above.

Sezran glanced up. On a rocky ledge overhead, a small creature sat in shadow. Two ruddy pinpoints of light marked its eyes, and the shape in the dimness hinted at a pointy nose and bristling whiskers.

"Digger." The sorcerer acknowledged the rat and returned to his work.

The creature trundled across the ledge, leaped agilely to a lower overhang, then bounded to Sezran's shoulder. It balanced there precariously for several moments, its prehensile tail whipping back and forth. Finally Digger settled, tail curled tight around the old man's neck.

"There are humans in the castle," the rat observed. "I'm very hungry."

"So? You know your way to the pantry."

"Yesss—but the boy-child tried to skewer me with his knife.

He's very quick, very vicious. I do not like humans."

"And they care little for rats," Sezran returned.

"Hmmm. What are you making? It's very pretty, very shiny." Digger waddled down the sorcerer's arm to the workbench.

"Here! Watch your step, and don't touch anything. I'm setting a Sorcerer's Stone for the boy. You're fortunate he didn't have it when you met."

"Hmmm . . . The sick man, will he die?"

"No."

"Ahhhh," said Digger with just a trace of disappointment. "Well, I am just returned from a visit to relatives in the South. It was a very long, very dangerous journey." The rat tilted his head and peered up at the sorcerer with one bright beady eye. "But for me the journey was not difficult, for I am Digger the Bold, Digger the Brave!"

"You are Digger the Braggart," Sezran commented.

"Hmmm. Well, I am returned. A familiar must serve his master."

"You're not my familiar, you pest. You come and go as you please. You make your own choices always."

"If that is so, then I choose to be your familiar as my father did, and his father, and his. For your gift of speech, we serve you faithfully."

Sezran grunted irritably. "You serve faithfully only when it pleases you to do so, or when your belly is empty. I have, on more than one occasion, regretted gifting you and your forbearers with speech."

"Hmmm . . ." The rat had come upon the piece of silk. "Very soft, very smooth," he whispered, feeling the cloth with tiny handlike paws. He unwrapped the Stone.

Sezran paused in his work. "I told you to touch nothing! The Stone has strong defenses. If you touch it with bare flesh, you'll lose your life."

Digger hopped gracelessly backward, bumping into a hammer. "Hmmm!"

Sezran took up the Stone, still in the silk, and settled it in the clasps of the ring. Slipping the cloth out from under, he said, "Now, stand well back and cover your eyes."

Digger scurried to the far edge of the bench and placed his paws over his eyes. Sezran reached out and touched the pebble with the tip of a naked finger. The Stone flared brilliantly, and blue light rushed into every hidden corner of the chamber. When the glare had faded, the wizard picked up the ring. The Stone was fused for all time to the gold.

Digger trotted back to leap and cavort under the old man's hand, chanting, "Gold, gold, sorcerer's gold. Make it hot, then make it cold!"

"Get away, you little fool, before you're hurt."

"I am not afraid. I am Digger the—"

"Be quiet!"

"Hmmm . . ."

"If you wish to serve me, Digger, I'll give you a task."

"Yes, yes, very yes!"

"The sick man, whenever he talks alone with the boy, I want to know of what they speak—especially anything concerning a sword called Kingslayer. Will you do this?"

"Yes, yes, very—"

"Stop it!"

The rat sobered. "Of course. I'll do as you ask, but I'm very, very hungry."

Twelve

❖

Gaylon stalked the secrets of Seward Castle as a hunter might stalk lion and bear—with caution. The great stone structure was as eccentric as its creator and equally as dangerous. Sezran had laid the castle stone by stone through the centuries, and it sprawled with chaotic grandeur over the heath. The outer walls appeared solid and stable, but each blink of the eye proposed a drastic change of angles, and Seward's Shadows wavered continually like the shadows of trees in a strong wind. The high walls were gray expanses unrelieved by windows, and there were only two entrances—one in the east wall and one in the west, accessible morning and evening depending on the position of the sun. To venture into the castle's Shadows was to invite death, and not a pleasant one. This seemed confirmed by the white bones, both human and animal, scattered in the meadows that surrounded the castle.

To traverse Seward's inner passages took concentration and purpose. Gaylon learned this early—to lose track of where you were going was to end up back where you had begun, even if you walked a straight line. There were stairways that led nowhere, hallways that led to blank walls, and a myriad of rooms, some locked, some not, some empty, some not. There were chambers devoid of physical objects, yet full of disturbing sounds and smells. To some of these Gaylon would never return for fear of his life and sanity.

Two rooms in particular became the prince's favorites, and

he visited them again and again. One, deep within the ground below the castle proper, was filled with time-keeping machinery that never failed to awe and entertain.

Centermost in the chamber was a great water clock. This marked the time, drop by drop, the cogged wheels turning almost imperceptibly. The walls of this room were hung with innumerable time pieces of every shape and kind. Tocking, clacking, ticking, they observed moments with symbols that Gaylon could not decipher. Some had figurines, carved and painted, that danced to the music of gongs and bells. The chamber conveyed an overall feeling of momentum, a forward rush that gave way eventually to giddiness, and Gaylon found he always stayed there longer than he intended.

The other room the boy favored was on the ground floor at the very center of Seward. This chamber had eight walls of differing lengths that met in odd corners, and each wall contained a window, barred with heavy iron. These windows opened out on scenes of pastoral beauty. The landscapes were all very different from one another and displayed various seasons and times of days or nights. It was well the windows were barred, for Gaylon often leaned on the stone sills, face pressed to the iron, longing to climb through and follow this road or that path beyond the hill or mountain or forest. During the winter he stood for long periods before a casement that offered a world where the trees flowered and mockingbirds perched singing in the petalled branches. It filled him with a dichotomy of emotions—a strange peace and an even stranger discontent.

For Daryn, the time slipped by almost unnoticed; winter, spring, summer. It took over a year, but he eventually abandoned his bed and even the wheeled chair to shuffle along the passageways of Seward, slowly—step, thunk, slide—his right hand gripped weakly about a staff the prince had carved from a seasoned yew pole. In the beginning Daryn's grip failed him frequently, and he fell several times until Gaylon fastened a loop of leather to the staff in which he could secure his wrist. The duke wore dark robes now and had grown a full beard.

Daryn wasn't happy, and his emotions floated in a slender

space between depression and ill-humor, but he had found a purpose, and this—the formal education of the prince—he pursued with quiet fervor during the next several years. He was a much harder taskmaster than Sezran. Using books and scrolls from the wizard's collection, he put the boy through his paces in the more mundane studies of mathematics, letters, and history. And, from a chair, he continued the boy's training in weaponry, coaching and cajoling as Gaylon stabbed and slashed at a worn dummy.

Sezran went about his own mysterious business as always. He showed little interest in Gaylon and even less in Daryn now that the duke no longer required medical attention. What lessons the wizard offered the prince were mostly impromptu and enigmatic, and more often than not they left Gaylon disgruntled and frustrated, or outright angry. But sometimes, when the mood struck him, the old man could change radically, becoming ebullient, almost genial, and he would bring precious gifts of insight and knowledge to the prince. These lessons the sorcerer presented with an intensity that made them clear and comprehensible.

Late on a summer night in his second year at Seward, Gaylon came awake. His small room was dark, but charged suddenly with an energy that could only be Sezran's.

"Come!" the wizard said, and without a word Gaylon slipped on his breeches and sandals. He held up his hand, and the chamber filled with a soft blue light from his Stone, set now in a fine gold ring. From the doorway, Sezran growled impatiently, "Humans have useless eyes." He strode away.

The air outside the castle was warm and sweet with summer growth. In the east, a tiny sliver of moon rose, but the stars were numerous and bright enough to give definition to the hills and meadows. Gaylon followed the wizard up the path that led away from the castle, toward the brushy slopes near a large pond. At the water's edge they halted. The wizard put out a hand to motion Gaylon still, then cocked his head, staring into the darkness.

"Listen!" he said.

The hair prickled at the back of Gaylon's neck as he searched the night with both eyes and ears. "I hear nothing," he whispered huskily.

"Sit." Sezran followed his own direction, then leaned close to the boy's ear. "Be still. Use the Stone and listen."

A thousand questions chased one another through Gaylon's thoughts, and he fought to quiet them. The fighting only made things worse. With trouble he calmed himself, and his Stone began a gentle pulsing, nearly invisible. With head bowed, he emptied his mind and opened his ears.

The sounds of the night flowed into his consciousness, the rustle of the grass, the click of reed on reed, the chirrup of cricket, the croak and boom of frog and toad. At first the noises nagged at him, random and grating on the stillness of his being, then a change became apparent.

A pattern began to surface on that flood of sound. Pitch and rhythm separated, becoming purposeful, somehow orchestrated. Even the wind seemed to know its individual part in the whole. No creature or element spoke or moved or sang out of turn. Insect and reptile voices blended in *a cappella*, and the water gurgled at only the proper moment. Like a concerto, the sounds rose and fell with noticeable phrases, with beginnings and endings. Gaylon felt himself submerged in the music. It rippled around him like a warm current.

The music began to build in intensity, climbed to a throbbing crescendo, and ended abruptly. The absence of sound was complete, painfully so. Gaylon felt drained and empty, but peaceful. A great sigh escaped him, and he looked at Sezran.

"Did you hear it?" he asked the old wizard and was appalled by the harshness of his own voice against the silence. Sezran made no answer. Somewhere, timidly, a lone cricket sounded, an invitation to the rest to begin again. But the old man rose, his robes voluminous curtains in the night, before the song started anew. Reluctantly the boy followed.

* * * * *

On the morning of his thirteenth birthday, almost three years after his arrival at the castle, Gaylon stood in the western portal watching Seward's fell Shadows chase over the sward to the sea. The play of cool autumn sunlight on the green meadows tugged at bittersweet memories of Castlekeep far to the north. There, the grasses would be yellow now, long and heavy with ripening seed, and the air would be chill and dry without the heavy taste of sea salt. There, also, a certain young girl would be celebrating her ninth birthday. The prince leaned against the splintered wood of the door and tried to suppress the unhappiness, the longing. Does Jessmyn even remember me? he wondered.

A high, shrill squeal of pain dragged his attention back to the meadow nearest the portal. A hapless mouse had wandered into the castle's Shadows, and the tiny creature raced in circles now trying to escape some unseen foe. The boy watched in sick fascination as the animal leaped and twisted high in the air only a short distance from him. Come closer, he willed it, hoping for some chance to save the little rodent and, though his Stone glowed in response, the mouse's terror was too complete for it to feel Gaylon's call.

He had only to take a single step to save the creature, just one step into the castle's Shadows. With a last cry, the mouse dropped to the ground and lay still, bloody and broken. The meadows were quiet and serene again, a gentle breeze stirring the grasses and flowers. Gaylon closed his eyes, angry at his cowardice. A single step in the Shadows could have brought him no harm, no matter what Daryn and the old sorcerer said.

Finally the boy slammed the huge doors closed with a wave of his ring and went in search of Sezran down long, dark corridors of stone. Most recently, the old wizard was spending his time in the uppermost reaches of the castle, in a round lightless chamber that could rotate in a full circle on Sezran's command. There he taught Gaylon the names of the stars, which were visible through a hole in the roof—even in daylight. Sezran had devised a great metal cylinder with pieces of thick glass fixed to the ends. These had been ground into what he called convex and concave lenses, and made distant objects look very close.

Gaylon had seen a telescope before. The keep physician,

Girkin, had had a small one brought at great expense from one of the nations beyond the eastern desert. But Girkin's toy did little more than enlarge the pocked face of the moon; Sezran's telescope revealed entire worlds that shared orbits with their sun.

It was also in this stargazing chamber that Gaylon learned the art of Dreaming. Under Sezran's stern guidance, the boy had discovered the vastness of the universe around him. He had stood in the crumbling ruins of ancient alien civilizations and rode fire storms on the surfaces of stars—and once again visited the bizarre world of the dancers. In one hundred thousand lifetimes, the Dreamer could never hope to see everything. And with his inextricable ties to the fragile human body, a Dreamer's greatest danger was the loss of time sense that came with Dreaming. But Sezran taught the prince well with harsh and often painful lessons.

Now Gaylon arrived at the chamber and entered, his hand held out so the blue glow of the Stone in his ring sent light into the deepest corners.

"Get out!" Sezran snapped, standing beside the dark cylindrical shape of the telescope, near the center of the small room.

"I want to ask you a question."

"Later. I'll call you when it pleases me."

"No," the boy said, risking the old sorcerer's displeasure. "I want to learn more of Seward's Shadows."

"You know all you need to know of them."

"All I know is that I'm not permitted to walk in them."

"That's true. Now get out! You disturb my work." Sezran's Stone began to pulse gently.

"I'll discover the secret of your Shadows on my own."

Sezran struck a hand against the mechanism that turned his telescope. The sound boomed against the walls. "If you do, you'll likely die. And should you not perish, I'll make you wish you had! Perhaps punishment should be rendered first, meddlesome boy." The Stone at the wizard's throat flared a brilliant blue.

Gaylon took a quick step backward to the entrance, but the door slammed behind him, cutting off retreat. It wasn't wise to pressure the tiny sorcerer. Gaylon had learned that from experience, but time and again he'd tested the boundaries. And time and again he'd regretted it. There would be considerable pain of some sort meted out. Gaylon steeled himself.

Instead, he heard the door swing open once more. Yellow candlelight flooded into the chamber.

"Gaylon?"

Daryn's voice came from behind him. The boy looked back and found the duke with his staff in one hand and a candle in the other.

The man offered a rare smile through his thick beard and spoke. "There you are. I thought I'd never find you. This blasted castle seems to get larger by the day. Or am I only getting older?" Daryn nodded at Sezran across the room. "But you're at your lessons and I've interrupted. Forgive me. I only wanted to wish you a joyful birthday."

Gaylon forced a smile to his own lips. "Thank you."

"I haven't a present. I'm sorry."

"Your wishes are present enough," the boy murmured and glanced at the old wizard.

Sezran's Stone had lost its ominous glow. Daryn may have saved him from a thrashing, and that would make for a joyful birthday indeed.

"Well, I won't keep you from your studies . . ." The duke turned slowly, moving away. The door closed behind him.

"A birthday," Sezran echoed. "How old?"

His tone made Gaylon tense again. "Thirteen."

"Thirteen. Hardly time enough to learn to live, let alone to learn to be a sorcerer." The old man's voice gentled slightly. "If you wish to see another birthday, Gaylon Reysson, forget the Shadows of Seward. They're not nearly so important as your life." He motioned to the boy. "Come here! Let me show you a thing that can't be seen. Your Stone will serve you in this." Sezran gestured to the sky beyond the telescope. "Out there in your galaxy are dying stars collapsing in on themselves until they grow so dense that nothing escapes their pull. Not even light. We'll explore one."

The Shadows of Seward forgotten, at least for a while, Gaylon let the old sorcerer lead him once more into Dreaming.

* * * * *

"Recite the lineage of the Black Kings," Daryn said, and with the end of his staff rapped fifteen-year-old Gaylon gently on the shoulder from behind.

Startled, the boy jumped halfway out of his chair. All elbows and knees at this age, he thumped hard against the table, upsetting the candle. Hot wax ran across the wood as the prince scrambled to pull one of Sezran's precious books from the path of disaster. They were using the old sorcerer's cluttered bedchamber for Gaylon's studies this morning, and it would hardly do to damage the master's things.

"You're not paying attention," Daryn growled when the candle was righted.

"You're not saying anything of interest," Gaylon snapped.

The duke ignored the insolence, saying patiently and firmly, "These are things you must know. Now, recite the lineage of the Black Kings."

The boy groaned and rolled his eyes, but began. "In the year five eighty-three of the second age, Thesper . . . Thesper gathered under him the hill tribes of Wyndland, which we now call Wynnamyr. He then took . . . took . . ."

"Glyra."

"That's the one. Thesper took Glyra to wife and they begat Semel, the first of the sorcerer kings, in five eighty-seven. Semel married Glyra's niece, Velnar—"

"Lirra!" the duke interrupted. "Velnar wasn't born for another three hundred years. And he was a sorcerer king, not someone's wife."

"Lirra, Velnar! What can it possibly matter?" The young prince leaned his elbows on the table and put his chin in long thin hands. "They're only names, Daryn, an endless list of boring names."

"You're right. Their names hardly matter, but how they reigned does. How each king ruled is of extreme importance because you have to learn from their successes and failures. And as soon as you've memorized the deeds of the Black Kings and the Red, we'll start on the Lasony kings, then the Xenaran."

"Please, no," Gaylon pleaded.

"Yes. Now, begin again."

Muttering, the boy closed his eyes, and this time the names came more easily. The prince's Stone glowed faintly while he spoke, and Daryn smiled. While the Stone couldn't provide Gaylon with the information, it could enhance the memory, and that took considerable concentration. The duke settled finally on another chair, listening to the recitation, correcting the boy occasionally. There were eighty-seven successions to the Wyndland throne in just under one thousand years. Several kingships had lasted less than a fortnight.

"And Golir married his mother, Kisna, and in the year nine twenty-one of the second age they begat Orym, the last of the sorcerer kings," Gaylon said quietly. "Until now."

Daryn looked up, and the gleam in the prince's hazel eyes troubled him.

"I want to go home," the boy said, voice tight. "I want to go back to Castlekeep and kill Lucien and claim what is rightfully mine."

"No." The duke glanced away to hide his fear. "You're not ready yet. Open the text to page two hundred and twelve. We'll start on the next lesson."

"Daryn—"

"I said, no. When you've learned to put your kingdom and your people above all else, above your hatred and your need for revenge, then you'll be ready. But not now." The Stone in Gaylon's ring pulsed lightly, revealing some strong emotion, and Daryn tried to ignore it. "Open your book, and find the passages on Orym. His reign is probably the best example of how not to rule a kingdom, although, as the text points out, Orym was not a bad monarch in the beginning. Read aloud, please. From the bottom of the page."

* * * * *

"Dearie, drink your tea before it gets cold."

At Lady Gerra's gentle words, Jessmyn, a slender young woman now, stirred in her chair and took up the cup from the little marble table in her sitting room. Warm fall air drifted in through an open window, sweet with roses, and children laughed somewhere out on the lawns. But the smells and sounds were muted, lost behind a wall of sorrow. Today, the princess was fourteen, and Gaylon, had he lived, would have been eighteen, a young man now.

"Drink, sweetheart," Lady Gerra chided softly.

"I don't want it. I'm too tired."

"Girkin says this tea will stimulate you appetite. Please try."

The worry lines in the old woman's pudgy face were deep. The princess sipped the cooling tea dutifully. It tasted foul and smelled worse, and the effort of holding the cup only added to her fatigue.

Each morning, Jessmyn woke exhausted, and that weariness followed her all through the day. The waking world held little interest for her; every meal was tasteless, every court function dreary, and the company of others distressed her. She wanted only to be left alone with her unhappiness, left alone to wait for darkness.

Alone in the night, in dreams, the princess found solace. Then Gaylon would come to her, and sometimes Daryn, bringing with them the peace and joy of years long past—if only for a while.

"Jessmyn?"

The melancholy had deepened, and the princess blinked. Somehow she was in the window seat now, staring down into the gardens, the teacup forgotten on the arm of the chair. A tiny thread of anger touched her. Where was the little girl who had spied on the weapons yard in hopes of learning to use a sword, who could outride and outrun many of the boys her age? Where was she now? Lost.

* * * * *

Lucien tried to remember the exact moment he had first realized he loved Jessmyn, but couldn't. It was even more impossible to remember a time when he hadn't loved her. When the princess was eight, he gave her a pony, a roly-poly little dapple gray mare. But she named it Thistledown after Dayrn's song, heard so long ago, and that hurt the young king. There seemed to be nothing he could do to wrest her thoughts from Daryn and Gaylon. Soon after, the pony threw her, breaking her arm, and in a fit of temper Lucien ordered the animal destroyed. He regretted the action later for she would have nothing to do with subsequent ponies, saying she would never ride again. And for six long years now she'd been true to her word.

At eleven, she had still been a sickly child, pale and thin. He'd brought in physicians from Xenara, but they had agreed with Girkin's findings. There was nothing physically wrong with Jessmyn. Melancholia, they called it. A nervous disorder, a mental illness. With polite words and sympathetic cluckings, they dared to call the princess mad. Lucien had listened to their prattle with a tight jaw, his hand clutching his sword hilt. Only Feydir's presence during that final consultation had kept Lucien from killing them all.

A year ago, for Jessmyn's thirteenth birthday, he had planned a huge ball and sent her a bolt of scarlet velvet for a gown and skins of Lasonic ermine to trim it. He remembered now how quiet the great hall had fallen when she arrived. Every eye of that crowded room had followed her as she moved across the floor to curtsy before him, thanking him for his gifts. His mind had reeled when he bid her rise, for he'd noticed the long, slender slant of her neck and shoulder. The dress, though chastely cut, could not conceal the fact that the princess was no longer a child. She had smelled of warm summer nights, of jasmine and honeysuckle, and he'd held her hand far too long, the guests, the music all forgotten. Everything about Jessmyn had disturbed Lucien that night. He'd felt awkward and gangling as he danced with her, and the few times the steps brought them close enough to touch, he knew something akin to pain, something exquisite. But she only danced the once and picked at her food throughout the long dinner. After, when the revel began again, the young princess had begged the king's permission to retire, pleading illness, and she was, indeed, even more pale and drawn than usual. Unhappily, he'd let her go.

This afternoon Lucien came alone to the princess's chambers bearing another gift. There would be no grand celebration for her fourteenth birthday. Girkin had already informed Lucien that Jessmyn was too weak to suffer such excitement. The king heard stirrings behind her door, but waited long moments before his knock was finally answered. Eventually, Lady Gerra stepped into the passage, pulling the door closed behind her.

"I wish to see Jessmyn." Lucien's tone was not friendly.

"Your Majesty, milady is ill and wishes to see no one today."

Lucien refused to be put off. He looked the dowdy governess up and down, taking in her untidy dress, her careworn, pudgy face. His eyes narrowed, and she reddened under his gaze.

"Tell your mistress I am here. She will see me."

"Sire—"

"Now!" he snapped, and the woman dropped a quick curtsy, wheeled about, and fled into the inner room. A moment later the king was led through the antechamber to the sitting room proper.

Jessmyn sat in a window seat, gazing through the leaded windowpanes at the gardens below. The light haloed her hair, which shone like spun silk, honey and amber, but her face was colorless and wan. She was dressed in the palest of blues, a hue that only emphasized her pallor, and her hands lay thin and lifeless in her lap. All his tautness, all his anger slipped away, and Lucien was moved to drop to his knees on the rug beside her, lost in her beauty. He laid the small box that held his gift by her hands.

"Milady?"

She took notice of him and then the box, but seemed disinclined to touch it, so he removed the lid for her. Inside, laid in red satin, was a tiny carven rose of jade in perfect detail, sea-green like her eyes. The princess stared at the little flower dully before looking at Lucien again. He'd hoped for a smile, some small indication of her pleasure, but it was obvious she felt none. He sat back on his heels, the offering still held in his fingers. Bowing his head, he felt a sudden ache in his throat.

"How long?" he asked bitterly and looked up at the girl.

"How long will you mourn? Do you still refuse to believe Gaylon dead?"

The pain that crossed her face was a knife in his heart.

"No," Jessmyn said softly. "I can believe nothing else now. I'm no longer a child."

"Is there no place in your life for me, then?" he pleaded.

"I'm promised to you in marriage. What more can you ask?"

"Your love! I would ask for your love!"

She smiled sadly. "How can I give you what I don't have?" The princess reached out and touched his pale hair lightly, then the hand was set lifeless once more in her lap. Her eyes returned to the window, and she stared into some distant place.

Fingers trembling, Lucien set the jade blossom in the box and rose to leave. Tears burned in his eyes, and he hated himself for such a display of weakness, hated the ghosts of Gaylon and Daryn whom he'd killed so many years ago. Yet somehow they haunted the princess still. Lucien turned to glare at Lady Gerra, and, flustered, she scurried to let him from the chamber. He walked quickly to the throne room.

As the king parted the drapes that led out onto the dais a hundred faces turned toward him. Feydir appeared at his elbow, pressing a sheaf of papers into his hands, whispering, "You're late." Then the anger boiled up in Lucien, and in pique, he threw the papers into the sea of faces. Petitions and proclamations fluttered to the floor.

"Out!" he shrieked. "Out!"

The guards emptied the room quickly with only a scuffling of feet and murmured word of direction. Lucien settled on the throne and endured his uncle's speculative stare.

"Some of those men have waited months for this audience," Feydir remarked in a noncommittal tone.

The king regarded him coldly. "Then they won't object to waiting a short while longer. We shall talk first, you and I."

"All right. What shall we talk about?"

"I want you to prepare a love charm."

That seemed to catch Feydir completely off guard. "A love charm!" He very nearly laughed, but stopped when Lucien glared at him. The older man gave a little cough instead. "If that's what you wish, then go to the vendors in Keeptown on market day. Some old crone will gladly take your silver."

"No! I want a true charm, one you have wrought with the power of your Stone."

"For whom do you wish this charm?" Feydir asked suspiciously.

Lucien's fingers dug into the plush on the arm of his chair. "That is no concern to you."

"Then let me guess," the mage said. He leaned his sharp-featured face closer to his nephew's, dared to touch the blond head lightly—as lightly as Jessmyn's fingers had. "Who is so important to you that you are willing to snip a lock of your hair, to give a nail-paring and spill your life's blood?"

The young king kept his eyes forward, but his mouth contorted slightly. "You risk my anger, Uncle."

Feydir chuckled. "I risk nothing, but you . . . you risk much. Do you realize what a man of evil intent could do if you willingly put such items of your person into his hands? Of course, I, of all your subjects, am the one who holds the highest respect and affection for my king . . ." If there was sarcasm behind those words, he hid it well.

"No, such a move on your part would be madness, Nephew. And should a charm be made, what do you hope to accomplish? If you give it to a woman who already loves another—even the ghost of another—it could destroy you both. I'm not blind. I know the princess is the one you wish to charm. But in little more than a year, you and she will be wed. Then she can deny you nothing. You've waited this long, surely you can wait a bit longer. In the meantime, satisfy your hungers with the women who come willingly to your bed."

Lucien's lip curled. "You disgust me if you think my feelings for the lady are so base. I love Jessmyn and would have her return my love."

"Love!" Feydir growled. "What can you possibly know of love? Lucien, think! Why would you love her? Could it be only because she's something you can never completely possess?"

"No!"

"I've known you all your life. You're passionate in all things, Nephew, but love is beyond you. You're simply not capable of it."

Lucien came halfway up from his chair, his hand on the hilt of his dagger, but Feydir's Stone swung before him on its chain, glowing. The king slumped back in his seat. "All right," he said. "Believe what you will of me, but it's Jessmyn's life I fear for."

Feydir straightened. "Her life? How so?"

"You've seen her. You've heard the physicians. It's true, she loves a ghost and that love consumes her. Each day she seems to grow thinner, paler. I've done all I can to make her happy, but it can only be a matter of time before she takes a fatal illness. She has no strength with which to fight, nor the desire. There've been times I feared she would take her own life. How long can this go on?"

Feydir's hand stroked his chin, and his brow furrowed. "In this you have a point."

"I do! Our treaty with Roffo is built on the fact that I'll marry his daughter, that our firstborn son may have a claim on both crowns."

"Yes, yes, I know—"

"If she were to love *me*, I know she would regain her health. I'd see to it."

"A charm is not the answer."

"What then?" the king demanded.

Feydir caressed his Stone thoughtfully and said, "There may be no easy answer, but there is a thing that could be done."

"What?" Lucien asked, hardly daring to breath.

"A spell of forgetfulness. If she could be made to forget her love for Gaylon, then she would be free to love you. You'd have to earn that love, though."

"Only provide me the chance, Uncle," the young man said eagerly.

Feydir's dark eyes bore into Lucien's light ones. "If you think what we do will be easy, think again. Any spell that goes so against the grain of the subject is fraught with dangers—to her and to us." He took the stairs to the floor and began to gather up the scattered papers. "First you'll conduct the audiences. I will have Girkin prepare a sleeping draught for both the princess and her governess, something subtle but potent. I'll begin the spell tonight, but this will take several nights to complete. I shall require your attendance throughout. You'll assist me."

Lucien watched his uncle cross the room to the great doors, watched him open them. The petitioners began to flood back into the wide chamber, and the king forced a benign smile to his lips. His uncle refused to believe he loved Jessmyn, and Feydir was right in some things. Lucien had never truly cared for another person, but he had never felt before as he did now. What emotion, except love, could cause the hurt, the anguish he suffered both day and night?

* * * * *

Such a simple task to comb one's hair, but for Daryn of Gosney it meant total defeat. He fumbled with the comb. His right hand would not obey, and his left, with its stub fingers, could not. The room was chill, yet he sweated with effort. In a temper common to him these days, he dashed the wooden comb to the stone floor at the foot of the chair.

"Here, let me do that," said Gaylon gruffly, suddenly in the chamber. Just as suddenly the comb appeared in his fingers though he hadn't reached for it. The fire rekindled in the fireplace, flaring blue for an instant before dying back to a sedate yellow-orange. These actions weren't meant as a show of power, but were only an unconscious attendance to detail. They irritated Daryn nevertheless, and in a dark humor he submitted to the comb.

The boy had changed much in the eight years since their arrival at Seward. At eighteen now, he could hardly be called a boy, though it was difficult for Daryn to think of him as otherwise. Gaylon had his father's lean, angular build and fair complexion, with the rough-boned handsomeness of the herdsmen clans from which he was descended. He had failed to attain Reys's great height, but by very little. This made him a good deal taller than the duke—whose stature was considerably stooped now. And the prince towered over Sezran.

"We've let your hair grow too long." With deft, gentle fingers, Gaylon found the snarls and worked the teeth of the comb through them. "I'll cut it, if you like. I've not much skill with scissors, but I'm certainly capable of putting a bowl over your head." He gave a small forced laugh.

"Let me go, Gaylon," said Daryn softly.

The prince behaved as if he hadn't heard. "We'll wash your hair tonight and cut it tomorrow."

"You can carry on without me now. Sezran has much to teach you yet, but I've nothing more to offer. Let me go."

The comb paused. "What brought this on?" the youth demanded. "If you feel my education complete, then it's time we go north to claim my throne, to finally make Lucien pay in kind for the death of my father. I've mastered the Sorcerer's Stone well enough. I can do without Sezran's help, but you, you must be my sage council. A Red King is nothing without a Gosney by his side, Daryn. I'll have no talk of your leaving me. You're all I have."

"If I'm all you have, you're poverty stricken indeed," the duke said bitterly.

"Listen to me, Daryn!" Gaylon moved around to face him. "I've found a spell in the *Book of Stones*. There's something I could do for you." An odd eagerness had overtaken his words. "You can have another body. You needn't be captive in this one. I could do it. Easily. Do you understand what I'm saying? You can have any body, be anybody! You can be young and strong again! All we need do is find—"

"You're mad!" the duke cried and leaped to his feet, though he swayed slightly without his staff to steady him. "Do you hear yourself? Do you honestly think life so important to me that I would consider stealing another's form?"

"I only thought—"

"Thought! If you have any thought it's for power and revenge." Daryn's voice began to fail him, his words slurring with effort. Spittle flecked his lips.

The comb fell unnoticed from Gaylon's hand, and his face

flushed red. Daryn thought for a moment the boy would offer some angry retort, but the prince turned instead and left the room. Again in the chair, the duke bent to retrieve the comb and attacked the tangled ends of his hair with a fierce determination. His anger was self-directed now. First he had provoked the youth, then humiliated him. Gaylon was the one thing in this life he loved, and yet, he could never find a kind or approving word for him.

Through the years Gaylon had spoken often of returning to Castlekeep, and Daryn was running out of excuses to hold the prince at Seward. Yet he'd come to fear Gaylon as much as he loved him. It became more and more apparent that the young man was a force far better left within Seward's strong and magical walls.

Long ago, Daryn had tried to explain the unexplainable, tried to make clear to the boy the responsibility that must be shouldered by those who would claim sorcery as an avocation. He'd tried to tell Gaylon that one didn't flaunt his powers, that subtlety was all important; power—true power—was power over oneself, not the manipulation of others. But to tell the young prince that magic was not a form of theatrics was to tell a butterfly not to spread its beautiful wings and fly.

Gaylon had attempted to understand, but as the months passed and his power grew, it seemed almost hopeless. Every step he took, every word he spoke, every gesture he made then was charged with an unconscious energy so intense that, for a time, it was uncomfortable to occupy the same room with him. He'd been sixteen then, his voice deepening, his body changing so quickly that it made him joyful and strutting one moment, angry and hostile the next. Sezran had solved the problem in part.

Daryn had gone in search of the wizard and the youth that day, and found them in the meadow on the southern side of the castle. There the wizard kept a large vegetable garden. Gaylon often worked the ground with the old man, but that day there had been a one-sided shouting match in progress. Sezran was quiet-voiced and reasonable while Gaylon declaimed loudly. How the argument had started Daryn never knew, but that it was reaching a dangerous pitch appeared obvious from the prince's livid face and clenched fists. The youth shook the hand with the ring under Sezran's nose, and the boy's Stone had taken on a nasty glow.

A sudden fear gripped Daryn. It was as though he were watching a reenactment of his own bout with Sezran so many years before. But he was too far away and too crippled to move fast enough to separate the two. In helpless frustration the duke watched the scene unfold. Sezran backed away first, clutching the Stone at his breast, and all of Daryn's worst fears seemed about to be realized. Gaylon screamed some angry threat and gathered himself to strike, but Sezran was the quicker.

As the boy raised his ringed hand, the sky opened up over his head and a torrent of icy water poured down on him. In shock, he took several gasping breaths, his hair plastered to his skull, all thoughts of retaliation neatly washed away. Sezran lifted the hem of his robes and, with great dignity, sloshed away through the flooded garden, leaving the boy to stand alone, soused and shivering.

When the old man passed him, Daryn put a hand on his sleeve to halt him.

"Thank you."

"For what?" Sezran demanded testily.

"For not hurting him."

"The thought never occurred to me," snapped the wizard. "I was merely saving my own life." He frowned. "Look what I've done to my seedlings!" He chuckled as he moved on.

Daryn had never heard the old sorcerer laugh before. It was a truly frightening sound.

* * * * *

Jessmyn slept deeply now, so Feydir gathered his things from beside the bed and checked to make sure the princess's chamber looked in no way disturbed. Lady Gerra snored peacefully in the adjoining room. He nodded at Lucien and started for the door.

In the hallway the ambassador parted company with his co-conspirator. The king was pale, his eyes bleak. These past nights had been difficult for him, but Feydir had borne the brunt of the task. The casting of the spell was a long and tedious process. The memories could not be removed, only ferreted out and locked away in the subconscious—so deeply that the subject would unconsciously reject anything that might remind him or her of those forbidden remembrances.

The spell was complex, exhausting for the mage, who in turn had to draw energy from another source—in this case, Lucien. Feydir had performed a variation of the spell only once before and then with dubious success. He had his doubts about the success of this particular casting, too. In the few short years they'd been together, the princess had formed strong emotional ties to Gaylon Reysson. But there was something more involved, something that Feydir had never anticipated. Jessmyn had latent magical powers of her own, unfocused without a Stone, but present all the same. These, too, had been carefully locked away, for they might conceivably damage the spell of forgetfulness. Strong trauma of any sort might also damage it, but such problems could be hopefully avoided.

Now Feydir walked alone down the dimly lit corridors to the library to replace his papers. In the room he found only a single candle flickering on the desk, well burned down. The ambassador took a seat on the high stool and opened the *Book of Stones*. There was nothing in particular he sought, only the soul-soothing rhythm of its ageless sentences.

To the mind that seeks true power, let these words be well remembered. . . . He followed the solid line of runic letters, the Stone aiding him in the comprehension of what he read, but soon lost interest. His thoughts turned idly to the odd riddle of Orym's Legacy and his fading dream of gaining Kingslayer's power. In the past eight years not a word had come from any quarter concerning the Duke of Gosney and his young ward. It was as if the earth had swallowed them. By no means, magical or otherwise, had Feydir been able to track them. No one, of course, except Nankus and himself, knew that Gaylon still lived, and Feydir's people had known only that they searched for Daryn. If the man had so much as taken a dinghy anywhere along the shores of the Inland Sea, Feydir would have been informed, and Nankus had tirelessly pursued his own faint clues in Wynnamyr, all of which proved false. Now, with a trail that was eight years cold, the search had all but ended.

Lucien knew none of this, though more than once when the young king had mounted his high horse Feydir had thought of presenting him with the facts of his failed assassination attempt. Best that Lucien remain ignorant, the ambassador had long ago decided. His nephew was fanatical enough to cause all kinds of trouble should he think his rival for Jessmyn's love still lived, not to mention his rival for the throne.

Feydir rubbed his eyes and closed the book, staring at the thick leather binding. He hadn't given up hope of finding the Duke of Gosney, of finding Kingslayer, but that hope had been shelved for the time being. Meanwhile, his original plans moved forward slowly but inevitably. The face of Wynnamyr was changing daily. The coffers of the royal treasury continued to fill, and Feydir's political power grew, here and in the South.

The king, as always, seemed kindly and concerned about his people, offering largesse with one hand while emptying their pockets with the other. There was discontent among the merchants and the peasants, of course, but they were kept far too poor to do more than grumble. Any obvious dissension was severely dealt with by Feydir's army. Everything proceeded as the ambassador had planned, and with the marriage of Lucien to Jessmyn would come another fine thread of power woven into Feydir's tapestry. No, he was not displeased with what he'd accomplished in the last few years.

He ran a long yellow thumbnail across the closed pages of the tome until it caught between two. Opening the book carefully at that place, the ambassador read: "The Sending. A spell by which an enemy can be rendered helpless through his own dreams."

It was a spell that had always fascinated him, though he'd never had the occasion to use it. Feydir marked the spot with a bit of paper, something he rarely did with the *Book of Stones*, then took himself off to bed.

* * * * *

For eight long years Gaylon had stalked the large gray rat that haunted Seward's insane nooks and crannies. This might have been a game they played. He'd only seen the one, and for some unknown reason Sezran suffered the creature to live. Except for their first meeting, Gaylon had never gotten close to it, until now.

Today he'd finally managed to corner the thing in the pantry, but it was almost a shame to kill the rat. After some thought, the prince decided not to use his Stone. That seemed far more sporting, and he really had no desire to explain away some great smoking hole in one of Seward's walls. His control over the Stone had bettered with time and effort, but his magic could still get out of hand.

The youth pulled his dirk from his boot and put trust in his own quick reflexes. He closed on the rodent carefully, then crouched and feinted with his left hand. The rat dodged right, into the hand with the blade, and Gaylon struck. A narrow miss. The creature twisted in midair and fled back to the corner. There it stood panting, lips curled back over tiny, sharp teeth.

"Come, man-child," the little animal snarled, "kill me and feel Sezran's wrath!"

At first Gaylon's ears refused to register the meaning of those words or the small lisping voice that carried them.

"Well?" the creature demanded.

Gaylon found his own tongue. "You spoke!"

"Yes!" The rat pranced forward daringly. "I am Digger the Brave, Digger the Bold!"

"But you speak!"

"Hmmm. If you find fault in that, then it is Sezran's. I am his familiar."

"He's never mentioned a familiar to me," the youth said skeptically.

Little whiskers bristled now with indignation. "You gainsay me? Ask him! Yesşs, ask the sorcerer, man-child."

"All right." The prince replaced the dirk. "I'll ask. I can always kill you later."

Fear touched the beady red eyes briefly, then the rat chuckled. "You are welcome to try. You are quick, but I am quicker. *I* have passed safely through the Shadows."

"The Shadows of Seward?" Gaylon asked, his interest pricked.

"Hmmm."

"Tell me, what are they like?"

"Hmmm," said the rat again, glancing around him. "I am very hungry."

"I suppose you'd like something to eat?"

"Are there eggs? Eggs are very tasty." Digger scuttled between the youth's feet, headed for the table in the kitchen.

"We've a few," said Gaylon, following. "But I don't know if—"

"Two," Digger announced. "Two would be very nice." He leaped onto the coal scuttle by the cook stove and bounded to the tabletop.

Gaylon broke two eggs into a wooden bowl and set them before the rat. "Now, about the Shadows . . ."

"Hmmm," said Digger, attacking the yolks. "Yesss. The Shadows are not all that dangerous."

"There are some who would disagree—if they still lived."

"Hmmm. They did not fully understand what they faced. They were very ignorant. They were trespassers and fools. Now, me, I am Digger the Bra—"

"Just what are the Shadows?" Gaylon interrupted.

"Hmmm. For me, the Shadows come as huge cats or hunting dogs or birds of prey. For you . . . well, only you know what form your nightmares take." Gaylon was silent as the rat happily slurped the eggs. Digger looked up finally, wiping his whiskers meticulously with petite fingers. "*I* use the Shadows to test my skills. But they are not for the faint of heart. No, no. Not for you, surely."

"And why not?"

"Sezran forbids."

"I will try them nonetheless."

"Hmmm," said the rat, and his lips curled again, this time in what might have been a smile. "Your Stone has no power in the Shadows. Do you still wish to try them?"

With the barest hesitation the youth answered, "Yes."

"You will need a weapon."

"I'll get my sword. Wait here for me."

Gaylon fairly flew down the passages to his bedchamber. The sword was kept in a chest at the foot of his bed, and he flung back the lid. On his finger, the Stone pulsed to the beat of his heart. He fought to still the light for fear it would betray his intentions should Sezran or Daryn meet him in the halls.

The weighty scabbard was hooked to his belt. He'd long ago outgrown the small sword Lucien had given him. He practiced with Squall now, though he disliked the balance and heavy two-handed grip of Daryn's weapon. The blade slid with a hiss of steel into the scabbard. What form *did* his nightmares take? They'd changed over the years, but never diminished. He shivered slightly, then started back to the kitchen.

Digger was helping himself to a loaf of bread and looked up with a start when Gaylon returned. The youth grinned at the rat's stuffed cheeks, feeling more kindly disposed toward the little beast at the moment.

"Come," the prince said.

Digger pushed another bit of bread into his mouth, mumbling through it, "There is no hurry. The Shadows will always be there."

"Then I'll go alone." Gaylon started to walk away.

The rodent sprang to the floor. "Wait!"

They went to the eastern portal, and Gaylon pushed open the right half of the great wooden doors. It was early afternoon of a long summer's day. The sun shone hot and bright, the Shadows distinct despite their rippling movement. Gaylon drew his sword.

"How do I begin?"

"Go among them, of course," Digger answered.

"Are you coming?"

"Hmmm," said the rat. "I have nothing to prove. I will wait here for you." His tiny eyes glittered in the light. "You are very quick, very strong. But we shall see, shall we not?"

Gaylon didn't reply. He'd taken his first step into the Shadows. With the very next step, he was filled with a sudden foreboding. His Stone had gone dark, and the world had disappeared. Gone were the walls of Seward, gone the meadows and hills. The Shadows were no longer two-dimensional. They'd become a strange black fog that floated in thin wisps about him. The prince found he could no longer recall the direction from which he'd entered, and his steps slowed.

"What do you fear?" a voice whispered, and the youth spun around, his sword at the ready. There was only formless fog to face. The whisper came again behind him. "Do you fear death, Gaylon?"

"Who speaks?" he called and turned again, this time slowly.

A bit of fog detached itself from the rest, resolving into a slender shape as it came nearer. "It is I, Gaylon. I am your bravest hope—and your greatest fear."

The voice was familiar, as was the sweet smile, the pale hair. Only Gaylon's perspective had changed. Now the prince was taller than the man who faced him.

"Lucien?"

The blond man swung his sword through the black fog. Bits of dark vapor trailed after the blade.

"But Galimar was destroyed," Gaylon said, recognizing the weapon.

"A Shadow sword for a Shadow man," Lucien answered. "*En garde*, Gaylon." He struck the position, and the prince did the same, but with two hands before him on the hilt, his feet spread, knees and elbows flexed.

"We were friends once," said Gaylon, grief in his voice.

"There are only enemies in the Shadows, my Prince," Lucien replied tonelessly and drove suddenly forward.

Gaylon dodged to the left, beating the first thrust aside. It was a queer match—heavy Squall against the slender Galimar. And quickly the prince discovered his hours of drill on the manikin had little prepared him for this. He was being reminded of Lucien's flamboyant style all too well. It did no good to watch the man's eyes; those pale blue orbs might have been a corpse's for all they revealed.

The Shadow man gave Gaylon little chance to take the offensive. Each time the prince tried to push forward, using Squall's superior weight to forge an opening, Lucien danced out of reach only to come back all the harder. Gaylon felt himself tiring. There was no way of reckoning the time that had passed in that place, but it seemed that he'd been there forever, dodging Lucien's lightning strokes through smoke-colored fog. His chest ached with every breath drawn now, while his opponent never missed a beat, showed no sign of faltering.

The slender blade came in again, seeking Gaylon's flesh, and he pulled up, turning on the ball of one foot. As quickly as he could, the prince brought Squall across to strike Galimar down and away, but there was no resultant clash of metal. Lucien had rolled his wrist, and the blade rolled also, up and over his foe's defenses. Gaylon threw himself back, but not before the Shadow sword found his chest and very nearly his heart.

He landed on his back, gasping, arms outflung, and felt blood flowing hotly from the score on his breastbone. Beyond Lucien the fog thinned, and Gaylon saw snatches of sky, the outline of a hill. Slowly the Shadow man drew Galimar up for the final stroke, and Gaylon, exhausted, could only watch helplessly as the blade dropped in a seemingly endless arc. The Shadow man's form grew indistinct, and wisps of vapor seemed to hinder his weapon's descent.

The sword fell true. The prince felt steel bite into his neck and cried out. Over him, Lucien and his blade dissolved into nothingness, then Gaylon was left alone, a hand clasped to the shallow wound on his neck. The sun had set, the Shadows dispersed—until moonrise. He rolled over slowly, feeling an ache in every joint, and lay with his face pressed to the fragrant meadow grass.

A pair of buskins shrouded by the hem of a dark robe appeared in the grass very near his nose.

"Get up!" the wizard commanded.

Gaylon stood, jaw set belligerently.

Digger snickered from where he perched on the old man's shoulder. "I told him not to go. He knows it is forbidden. Punish him, Master. Punish him!"

"You little . . ." Gaylon growled, making a grab for the rat. Digger fastened his teeth in the boy's thumb.

"Stop!" the sorcerer bellowed.

"He's been in the Shadows himself," Gaylon accused, nursing his thumb, which burned like fire. "He told me as much!"

"You believed him? A rat? For that alone you deserve a beating. How could you be such a fool?"

"Fool, fool, the boy's a fool!" chanted Digger. The rat ducked close to Sezran's neck when Gaylon swiped at it again.

"Enough! Both of you!" The old man caught Gaylon's arm in an iron grip. "Perhaps it would have been best if you had died in the Shadows."

Gaylon jerked his arm away. "Is that what you feel?"

"Consider only this—you were lucky this time, but you will never enter the Shadows again."

"I will," Gaylon snapped.

"You defy me?"

"Yes. You would never speak to me of your Shadows. Could it be you fear them yourself? In what guise do *your* nightmares come, old man?"

Sezran's eyes darkened, and the Stone around his neck took fire. Digger gasped and cowered against the wizard. For once, Gaylon felt no fear. His Stone remained dark.

"I will go again into the Shadows," he said evenly. "And what's more, I want the use of your forge and your knowledge of metallurgy. I want another sword, one equal to the blade I faced this afternoon. I shall go again and again into your Shadows until I can beat them."

"Or until you are killed," Sezran said coldly. After a moment he nodded. "So be it."

Thirteen

Jessmyn's bell-like laughter floated over the voices of the company sitting at the dinner table, and, with something close to satisfaction, Feydir watched the young woman. She was no longer the frail sickly creature she'd once been. Her face had fleshed out, there was color in her cheeks, and even he, who had long ago vowed abstinence, had to admit that her beauty stirred his blood. The ambassador took a sip of wine from his earthenware cup.

Nearly a year ago, not long after casting the spell of forgetfulness, he'd still held doubts over its success. The memories of all that had gone before had been lost to the princess. She had begun to smile, at last, but it was a strange, vacuous little quirk of the lips. The effects of the magic had left her bemused. Her days at first were spent in absentminded wanderings, and she'd complained that her nights were filled with dreams she could not remember upon awakening. She hadn't seemed unhappy, but neither had she seemed happy—only distant and empty and lost.

But Lucien had been convinced of his ability to earn her love, and he'd showed a kindness, a tenderness that came as a revelation to Feydir. He'd never realized the depth of emotion to which his nephew had been made heir. This was the one thing, besides his sweet features, that his mother had given him, and it was so opposite to the young king's other traits that it gave Feydir pause. This strong a love also showed him a considerable weakness to exploit if the need arose.

Over the months, Jessmyn had responded to that tenderness. She had moved toward Lucien as an injured animal draws close to the hearth—in hope of healing, in hope of relief from suffering. Ever attentive and caring, the king had gradually drawn her back into court life until at last, in his unfailing love, she'd found a reality on which to build a life.

Her laughter rang again over some whispered jest from the young Southerner who was seated on her left. Feydir glanced at Lucien with an inner amusement of his own. From the head of the long table, the king frowned. Count Roric D'Loran was an outrageous flirt. He'd been at court less than a fortnight and already there'd been trouble over a merchant's daughter in Keeptown. He claimed Jessmyn as a distant cousin on King Roffo's side, and in his thinking, that kinship permitted him to behave in a more-than-friendly manner toward the princess.

Roric was a darkly handsome youth, full of himself and only newly come into his title. His father had died the year before of an unfortunate accident, but Feydir felt certain the son would be easier to deal with than the old count. The D'Lorans and D'Sulangs had been friendly enemies for more than a century. Young Roric was heir to a great fleet of merchant vessels that Feydir had been negotiating over for the past decade. Yes, the son would be far easier to seduce than the father.

Roric smiled across the table, and Feydir smiled back, lifting his wine cup. The count lifted his, then turned to Jessmyn to lean close and murmur in her ear. The princess's pale green eyes sparkled with mischief. On Feydir's right, Lucien dropped his wine cup to the floor. The sound of it shattering silenced the diners. Every head turned in the king's direction, and Lucien smiled sweetly about him, gesturing for his company to continue with their meal. Another cup was brought, one of gold, not so easily broken.

Feydir felt a surge of irritation at Lucien's petty show of power. Across the table, Roric pressed his shoulder to Jessmyn's. He chose a confection carefully from a platter and carried it to the princess's lips. But as she opened her mouth to receive the bit of candied fruit, Lucien rose suddenly, his knife clattering into his plate. He flung his napkin to the table, signaling to the servants, and the meal ended abruptly. In confusion, the courtiers dropped their utensils and stood while the food was hastily cleared away.

The king crossed to Jessmyn's chair and held out his hand to her. "Milady?" he said quietly.

Smiling, she placed her slender fingers in his, then stood and performed a deep curtsy. "My lord."

Their eyes met, and the current that passed between the king and the princess was not lost to the crowd or to Roric. The young count watched them sweep from the hall with just a touch of regret on his handsome face. Feydir caught his arm gently, and Roric looked up into the tall man's face.

"She is magnificent, is she not?" the count said in awe.

Feydir scowled faintly. "Count D'Loran, do you think it wise to alienate the king?"

Roric widened deep brown eyes hedged with long thick lashes in feigned innocence. "Certainly His Highness understands that I mean no—"

"It is best *you* understand quickly that this is not the Southern Court where the courtiers may, and do, take license with the king. Roffo plays the buffoon, and it's a role well suited to him." Here Roric's eyelids lowered to mask what Feydir believed to be anger. The ambassador continued, "Lucien is a young king and proud, and he'll brook no such behavior on your part." Feydir's voice softened. "We're not without our share of beautiful women, milord—as you well know."

The count's eyes widened again, and he grinned. "True!" he agreed with enthusiasm. "Though there can be none to compare with Princess Jessmyn, I am sure I can find one who will ease my broken heart."

The count executed a fluid, graceful bow, and Feydir returned the courtesy smiling. However foolhardy, Roric was a personable young man, and it was difficult to stay angry with him. The ambassador watched him make his way to the far end of the great hall, where, despite the king's unmannerly exit, a small group of Southerners still laughed and carried on. With a small shake of his head, Feydir left the hall to seek out the library and, eventually, his bed.

* * * * *

Someone ran shrieking through the passageways of the southwest wing of the keep. Feydir came bolt upright on the mattress and threw back the quilts. The ululating cry continued as the ambassador made his way through the darkened bedchamber to the door. The screams held a piercing, high-pitched hysteria that brought the guards racing from all directions, and Feydir's door was not the only one flung open.

It was just before dawn. Night candles had burned well down, and only one or two still flickered in the hallway where servants and soldiers milled in confusion. The screaming ended abruptly. Feydir saw Lucien's fair head among the rest. The king was dressed still in day clothing, and a small figure huddled sobbing at his feet: Roric's young man-servant, a slave boy of no more than fourteen. He began to wail again when a guard pulled him free of Lucien's ankles.

"Oh, please, sir! It's my master. He's sick, bad sick. You must help him!"

Feydir grabbed the shoulder of the guard that held the struggling youngster. "Get the physician!" he snapped, taking the child from him. "What's your name, boy?"

"B-Barri, sir. Oh, please, hurry!" He began to pull Feydir along the passage. Behind them the crowd followed.

In the well-lit guest chamber, the count lay naked on the bed, head thrown back in a terrifying convulsion. Foam speckled his lips, and his eyes rolled back in his head. The boy began to shriek again, and Feydir struck him.

"What has he eaten tonight since he came to his room?" he demanded. "Did he drink anything?"

"No food. Only the wine, sir," the child sobbed. "I tasted it first. I taste everything he takes alone, milord. I do it gladly! He's my master, and I love him more than myself."

"Here, move aside. Get back, all of you!" Girkin shoved his way roughly through the gawkers. The physician, dressed in a long robe that barely covered his generous bulk, turned to the soldier that had accompanied him. "Clear the chamber, man! Give me room!"

The soldier directed the gawkers into the corridor. Near the bed, Barri grabbed one of Roric's hands, trying to control his master's flailing. Feydir stood back and found Lucien beside him, stone-faced, impassive, watching the count die. Girkin would perform no miraculous cure this night. Coldly the ambassador watched while the sick man's agony heightened until his ravaged body could tolerate no more. At last he lay still, the horror frozen on his face. When he realized it was the end, Barri screamed and, tearing his hair, flung himself across the dead man.

Girkin took up a cup from the stand by the bed and swirled the contents, sniffing at the dregs. "Poison," he announced, throwing a quick glance at Lucien.

"No, sir! I tasted it," the boy cried, face haggard with grief. "Ask the lady." His swollen eyes searched the faces in the room. "Ask her. She must be here."

"There is no lady here," Girkin said.

"She must be. The lady that came to stay the night. She was beautiful, with long hair as pale as cornsilk. Her gown was blue like her eyes."

"What was her name?" Lucien asked quietly.

"She didn't say, milord."

"There was no woman," the king said tonelessly. "You poisoned your master."

"No! How can you say such a thing? No!"

Lucien snapped his fingers impatiently, and two guards dragged the boy from the bed and out of the room. His cries could be heard echoing hollowly down the passage. They were alone now, Girkin, Feydir, and Lucien.

The physician pulled a sheet up over the count's body. Scratching his balding pate, he said, "With your permission, milord, I'll send my assistants to prepare the body later."

"Yes, of course," Lucien waved him away, and when the man had gone, he glanced at his uncle. "Foul treachery. There will be a proper trial, then the boy will be executed. I promise you, his death will be no more pleasant than his master's."

"No," said Feydir sharply, and when Lucien blinked, he repeated himself. "No. You will have him garroted. It's enough that he must die for a thing he didn't do. He'll not be made to suffer any more than he already has."

Lucien's jaw tightened. "Just what do you infer, Uncle?"

"I infer nothing," Feydir snapped. "I only state the obvious."

"Be extremely careful how you speak," the king warned.

An unreasoning fury welled up in Feydir. On its chain, his Stone began to throb in sympathy, and he wrapped his fingers tightly about it.

In a deceptively mild voice the ambassador spoke. "You still have no conception of the power I wield. With a single thought I could turn you to ash."

"Then do it," said the king insolently. "But you dare not. You need me."

"Yes," Feydir murmured, "but there are things worse than death. I will yet take my due, Lucien. Believe it. It will be nothing so simple, so easy as death." He pointed a crooked finger at Roric's shrouded form. "Every man has his worth, every man, his use. You've been a wastrel, a fool. You take a life without a thought, without consideration."

"He looked at her!" Lucien flared. "He dared to touch her!"

"And you would give up a fleet of sailing ships for a look, a touch? You would risk our treaty with Roffo for a trifling?"

"You don't understand!" Lucien cried. "You can't know what I'm going through. Jessmyn loves me, yet she doesn't. She gives her love only out of gratitude. She feels obligated to me, feels it her duty to love me. It's somehow worse than before."

"What do you expect from me? Pity?" Feydir strode to the door. "Good night, Your Majesty. Sleep well."

"Wait!" Lucien called from behind him. The ambassador paused in the threshold, turning back. His nephew's face had changed, and some strange emotion played across his fine features. "Did you . . . Have you *ever* cared for me? Have you ever loved me?"

Feydir remained silent for a long while, then he smiled pleasantly. "Never. From the moment of your birth, I've loathed you. It was your mother I loved. Yet she cared only for you. For me there was nothing. You have never been anything to me other than a tool."

There was a pause, then the ambassador noted spitefully, "I sent your mother, Colena, to lie with your father. I made it possible for her to conceive. *I* created you. Your tutors, your swordmasters were all my minions. You have never drawn a breath, but that I suffered you to do so. Each move you make, I allow. You're a puppet. *My* puppet. The day comes when I will choose to pull the strings and then you'll dance, Nephew. How you will dance!"

Feydir watched Lucien's face throughout. The young man held his thoughts well. The muscles of his cheek and mouth were frozen, but his flesh paled and his eyes unfocused. The ambassador was moved to laughter, warm and full of derision, and at that Lucien lost control. He turned his face away to hide what might be revealed, and, laughing still, Feydir made his way down the corridor.

* * * * *

A fortnight after his first venture, Gaylon stepped once more into Seward's Shadows, this time just before dusk. The beautiful sword Sezran had forged was bared in one hand. The prince had thought long and hard on how to go about waging war in the Shadows. This time he would use wit and cunning to destroy his superior enemy. Daryn's careful lessons in fair play would not distract him. Fear and excitement nagged at the youth as the black fog billowed upward to obscure castle and meadow. All sound ceased, and his Stone went dark and powerless. The young man waited, watchful.

A whisper came at last behind him.

"Gaylon . . ."

"Show yourself," the prince commanded.

The fog shifted and Lucien stood at sword's length with Galimar in hand.

"You should not have come. This time you'll die, my prince." The empty blue eyes regarded him. "*En garde.*"

Gaylon flung himself forward, stabbing deep before the Shadow man could even raise his weapon. Lucien staggered back, and the blade pulled free dripping black gore. Another step back, and the man glanced down at the wound in the center of his chest, then the faint smile returned.

"You've no honor, my Prince. I've taught you well. But you see," the Shadow Lucien passed a hand over his chest, "you cannot kill me." The wound, even the cut in the material of his shirt, was gone.

The Shadow foe came at Gaylon suddenly and drove him into the fog. Their swords clashed and rang. The prince parried thrust after thrust, ducked and spun and danced away in order to avoid death. He fought for balance and a chance to force Lucien back. Finally the opening came, and Gaylon pressed forward hard. The Shadow man's blade slid shrieking along the new sword's razor edge. The prince trapped his foe's weapon on the guard and managed to hold firm. They were close, straining face to face.

"You can't be killed," Gaylon growled breathlessly. "Can you feel pain?" He slammed his left fist into the side of the man's head and caught him immediately in the right kneecap with a boot heel.

The leg gave way, and Lucien went down, the sword torn from his grip. Grinning, the prince tossed Galimar away.

"Did you feel the pain?" he demanded.

The Shadow man stared up at him and muttered tonelessly, "Yes."

"Good!" Gaylon brought his sword down in one quick heavy stroke, separating the creature's head from his body. The head, he kicked out into the fog. A thick black ichor oozed from the stump, but the chest continued to rise and fall, and air bubbled in the neck. The Shadow foe's hands felt blindly about it.

Disgusted, Gaylon walked away without the taste of triumph he'd hoped for. Sky appeared in snatches overhead, and a few moments later the wide meadows returned, bathed in fading daylight. The prince headed eastward away from Seward. There on a hillside he settled against a large rock and, frustrated, tossed the sword into the grass at his feet.

He'd beaten the Shadow Lucien, but it was a hollow victory over a bloodless nether-man. The real Lucien was the one he wanted to kill, and in order to do that he had to return to Castlekeep. But Daryn refused to leave Seward, still refused to believe Gaylon had mastered his Stone well enough to take back his crown. With clenched fists, the young man watched the sky to the west as the last fire of sunset slipped into the sea. He only knew that someday soon, with or without Daryn, he would have to depart Seward Castle.

* * * * *

In his small bedchamber that night, Gaylon worked the edge of the new sword by candlelight. It was still unblooded and unnamed. The Shadow Lucien's black bile was hardly suitable, and such a handsome sword deserved a handsome name.

He heard footsteps in the hall. Sezran's—they were too quick, too even to be Daryn's. Outside his door they paused.

"Come," the prince called, wondering at such a visit. Of late he and Sezran were not getting along at all well.

The door swung in of its own accord, and Gaylon looked up from his work. The wizard stood fast in the darkened passage for a moment. Something in his hand reflected back the light from the tapers. As the little man stepped into the room, the prince saw that he held a cup, a chalice of gold, chased in rubies the color of blood.

"What have you there?" Gaylon asked pleasantly enough. He'd seen the cup before, over the mantle in Sezran's bedchamber.

"I have made a mulled wine for Daryn to help him sleep," the old man said. "There is extra. Do you wish it?"

Gaylon nodded toward the chest at the foot of his cot. "Thank you. Just put it there."

Carefully Sezran placed the cup on the lid of the trunk. "You should drink it while it's still warm."

"I will." But when Gaylon looked up a second time, Sezran was gone. He laid the sword on the mattress before him and went to close the door. As it swung to, there came a sudden squeak of distress.

"You nearly had my tail," Digger cried indignantly. He pranced nimble-footed across the stones.

"Well, well. Tonight I have a wealth of visitors." Gaylon returned to his bed, taking up the blade again, pointedly ignoring the little beast. He could hear a stir and a rustle in the corners of the room as Digger explored.

"I thought perhaps your anger with me had dulled with time," the rat said, coming to the edge of the cot.

"Perhaps," said Gaylon noncommittally. He wet his sharpening stone from a bowl on the floor and drew it gently along the edge of the blade.

"Hmmm. Very nice. Very sharp. Is this the weapon with which you conquered my master's Shadows?"

"How do you know that?"

"I watched in the meadow. You didn't die. Is this the sword?"

"Yes, but alas, it remains unnamed. Of course, were it blooded on a rodent, I could always call it Ratslayer. What do you think?"

Digger's whiskers swept back in dismay. "You jest!"

"Perhaps," said the prince once more. "What is it you want, deceitful creature?"

"Nothing," said the rat in an injured tone. "And I am not deceitful."

"Oho? Digger the Brave, Digger the Bold? The rat who passes through the Shadows unharmed? Digger the False should be your name." Gaylon never once looked up from his task, but he could see the rat on the periphery of his vision, dancing in agitation. It was difficult not to smile.

"I did not lie! I didn't! I *have* been in the Shadows. But Sezran would skin me alive if he knew."

"Sezran would never believe you. Neither do I."

There came no immediate response, but the animal drew close to Gaylon's leg and stretched up tall to peer intently at the young man.

"It *is* truth. And here is another—I did not like you at first and I wished you ill, but I don't feel as I once did. You hunted me in the passages, but it became a game in time, hmmm? One we both enjoyed? Since you have come to Seward there are always very good things to eat in the pantry. You bake bread and bring meat. Meat is very tasty. Sezran will not eat it." He patted Gaylon's knee with a small paw. "Hmmm? I would be your friend . . . if that is possible."

The prince glanced down into a face that was trying hard for rodentlike sincerity. He choked back a laugh and said solemnly. "I've never had a rat for a friend."

"You do now! Oh, very, very, yes!" Digger performed a fanciful jig on his hindfeet. "Friends, friends, forever friends!" He paused. "Have you anything to eat?"

"No."

"Not even an apple core? A bit of melon rind?"

"Sorry."

"Hmmm," sighed the rat in disappointment. He scrambled to the top of the chest. "What's this?"

"Here! Don't knock that over."

"Hmmm." Digger circled the chalice. "It's very pretty, very shiny. Does it hold wine? I like wine."

"It's mulled wine, and I don't think you should have any."

"Just a little taste. Hmmm? A very little taste, friend?"

"A very little taste," Gaylon agreed. He began to wipe the sword with a soft dry cloth, admiring the blade. It was a marvelous piece of craftsmanship. He'd helped, to be sure, but it was actually Sezran's masterpiece. They hadn't slept for days and had hardly remembered to take meals. The memories were vivid yet: the constant thumping of the bellows as the prince worked them, the leaden ache in his arms, the metallic taste on his tongue. But there'd been no magic involved, no power beyond Sezran's keen eye and steady hand, his superior knowledge of his materials as he shaped the fiery metal. Gaylon turned the blade so it caught the light and scattered it over the bare stone walls.

"What do you think, Digger?" He struck the tempered

steel with a fingernail, and the sword sang in its own fine clear voice. "Isn't it beautiful?" There was no answer.

He glanced at the chest and saw nothing at first, only the chalice standing alone, then his eye found the small motionless form that lay beside it. "Digger?" The weapon was discarded on the blankets, and he slipped his hands under the rat's still-warm body, lifting it gently. The head dangled lifelessly; the little red eyes had lost their spark. "Oh, Digger," the prince murmured, feeling a strange grief.

Then came fear, sudden and icy, and he found himself in the passageway, racing madly through the murky castle. He tore a nail fighting the latch on the door to Daryn's chamber. It seemed forever before it opened. Within, a single candle guttered on the small table by the bed. An earthenware wine cup stood beside it. Daryn lay unmoving upon the mattress.

"Daryn!" Gaylon cried and grabbed the duke's shoulders, pulling him up from the pillows. The man's head lolled back. And then his eyes opened.

"What?" he mumbled.

Gaylon fell to his knees by the bed and buried his face in the coarse woolen blankets. His heart still hammered in his chest, and he couldn't seem to catch his breath.

"Gaylon?"

"I—I thought he'd killed you."

"Who?"

"Sezran! He brought me mulled wine tonight. It was poisoned!" Though his knees still shook, Gaylon straightened so that he could see Daryn's face, lost as it was in its graying beard. There was no surprise in those smoke-colored eyes.

"So?" the duke murmured, looking away.

"So? Is that all you can say?"

"Be calm. The wine was brought to me first, offered to me."

"You knew it was poisoned?"

"Yes, but I failed to realize what he'd do when I refused his gift again."

"His gift? Again? Daryn, I don't understand."

"It wasn't truly a gift. It was to be a trade."

"For what, and why?"

Daryn seemed to ponder for a moment. "If you didn't drink the wine, how did you know what it held?"

"Digger begged for some. I was sharpening my sword."

"The rat?"

"He was always hungry, always getting into things. And now he's dead. But you haven't answered me. What trade would Sezran make with you?"

"You mustn't think ill of him, Gaylon. He attempted this because he fears you."

"Why? And why won't you answer me?"

Daryn's ruined hand found Gaylon's arm. "All right. You deserve an answer, and it's time you knew. Before his death, your father entrusted me with a certain sword to be given to you when you ascended to the throne."

"Kingslayer," said Gaylon.

"You know of it?"

"Only a little. The *Book of Stones* has a passage concerning Orym's Legacy. It says Kingslayer was given into the hands of the Red Kings and passed down, father to son, over the centuries. But my father never mentioned it, so I assumed it was only legend."

"No. I've held it, felt its power."

"What has this to do with Sezran?"

"He fears you'll take up the weapon. He forged it and feels it's rightfully his."

Gaylon nodded. "Then he may have it. I want no part of its power."

"You don't know what you're saying—"

"Daryn, the sword turned on its master and killed him. It's Kingslayer."

"Orym was evil—"

"No. Remember your own lessons, teacher? History says Orym was a decent enough king, if somewhat self-centered . . . until he took up the sword. Under its influence he became a murderous tyrant."

"All right, but you needn't follow his path. I'll admit that at first I thought it best never to even tell you of the sword, but against Feydir, it may be your only chance to take your throne."

When the boy shook his head, Daryn snapped, "Gaylon, your father wanted you to have it."

"My father didn't possess a Sorcerer's Stone. He couldn't know . . ." Gaylon smiled suddenly. "The sword is Sezran's. I've watched him work, Daryn. If the sour old creature has any joy of this world, it's when he fires his forge and takes up his hammer. He's already given me a sword. Let him have Kingslayer. I think I've gotten the better of the deal."

"For your father's sake, at least lift the weapon . . . if only once."

"No! Sometimes it's more than I can do to control what power I have. Don't burden me with more."

"Gaylon, I hid it before we left Castlekeep. Let me at least tell you where to find it."

"I don't want to know where it is. I'll not be told. Tell Sezran, so he can recover it." After a pause, the prince noted, "You're right in one thing, though. It *is* time for me to return to the keep. If I don't have the power now to take back my crown, I never shall. Will you come with me?"

The duke settled back on his pillows and closed his eyes. "No," he said heavily.

"I thought not." Gaylon drew a deep breath. "It was wrong of me to hold you, Daryn. I see that now. It's your life. Any claim I may have had on you through my father, I relinquish. You're no longer duty-bound to me." Here his voice roughened, caught. "I shall miss you, my friend." He pressed his lips to the scarred hand and rose to leave.

Daryn said nothing, and his eyes remained closed, but a tear slid from the corner of one eye and disappeared into the tangled hair over his ear.

Gaylon returned to his own bedchamber. It seemed a bleak and barren place now. The fire was dying on the hearth. He carried the chalice to it and quenched the coals with the wine, then built a small bier of wood over the ashes. There he nestled Digger as if he slept, and with his Stone, set the structure ablaze. He watched the fire for a time, his mind emptied of thought. Finally he placed a larger billet over the collapsing pyre and began to pack.

His possessions were few, and in a short while he was finished. Daryn's lute he placed on the lid of the chest. He wouldn't take it with him. Empty of thought, he sat down on the bed to watch the flames crackle and consume the pyre.

* * * * *

"All right," said Lucien waspishly to his uncle. "I'm here. What matter is of such importance that you call me so late?"

It was well past midnight, and the king was tired. Feydir had left him to deal with the council alone, and the meeting had gone on forever. The bickering and petty squabbles of the members had left the king exhausted, but too edgy for sleep. Now he stood on the thick carpeting in his uncle's somber chambers, still dressed in the formal robes he'd worn at council. The thin gold coronet still rested on his brow, nearly lost in his flaxen hair.

Feydir sat at his desk and turned at his nephew's voice. The ambassador let his eyelids droop almost imperceptibly over dark, glittering eyes. "Relax, Nephew," he said, not quite a command, but his voice was rich and resonant, sweetly persuasive. He began pouring wine into a silver cup.

Lucien almost smiled, almost sneered. "I've known you all too long to fall for that."

Feydir laughed pleasantly and set the flask down. "I only think of your welfare. You've worked too hard today. You're tired . . . so tired . . ."

"Stop it!" Lucien snapped. "Try that once more and I'll leave."

"By the gods, you're a difficult creature."

"I was well taught." And when Feydir laughed again, the king asked, "What is it you wish, Uncle? I've a bed to get to."

"An empty, cold one."

Lucien turned on one heel and strode for the door.

"Gaylon Reysson is alive, and Daryn of Gosney as well." That brought the king to a halt, midstride, and Feydir leaned back in his chair. "It seems you failed to kill them." Lucien had spun about to face him.

"That's impossible."

"But true, nonetheless."

"How? Where have they been all these years?"

"Hidden from us. Apparently they found refuge with a hermit wizard along the coast—not a month's ride from the keep. One of our soldiers chanced on a fishing village there and learned the truth."

"So close! All this time! Call your man, Nankus. I'll take an armed force and finish what I started."

Feydir held up a hand. "Not so quickly, Nephew. I know of this wizard. He's extremely powerful. You can't touch them while they're under the man's protection."

For a moment it seemed that Lucien would lose his temper, but the years had matured him. Feydir watched with approval as the king pulled that once frenetic energy into a clear and calculating power.

"Then what do you propose, Uncle? Will your sorcery serve us in this?"

"After a manner." Feydir held up the cup, offering it to Lucien. "Yes, after a manner, it may serve us very well. Drink."

Lucien stood motionless, looking not at the cup, but at Feydir.

This time it was the older man who sneered. "What do you fear? Poison? That's no tool of mine. There's no death in this."

"There are worse things to contemplate than death—so you have told me."

"Well, choose, King Lucien. How little is your love of Gaylon or Daryn? How great is your love for Jessmyn?"

Lucien snatched the cup from his hand, slopping the doctored wine onto a lace cuff. "What is this and what must I do?"

"It's a sleeping draught, and you must dream a dream."

With a nasty grin, Lucien held the cup in a mock salute. "To whatever serves you best, Uncle, my death or theirs." It wasn't a question, but an odd toast, and he drank the contents noisily, then slammed the cup empty to the desktop. "What now?"

"Lie down and relax. Nothing more." But Feydir could no longer hide his eagerness.

Lucien sat on the bed, feeling an immediate light-headedness, and fought a growing fear. The room seemed to darken. His uncle took him by the shoulders, twisting him, pressing him back into the pillows, down, down, down . . .

"Let go of your fear, Lucien. Open yourself to wonder, for I shall weave you a dream such as you've never dared to dream." The gentle voice coaxed, the words echoing over and over. With difficulty the king followed their meaning until they faded away altogether.

The darkness was gone, the room suffused now with a soft, golden glow. Lucien sat up and swung his feet to the floor. He was alone in the chamber. The air seemed to sparkle, and motes of light swirled above the many candles.

"My lord?"

The sweet feminine voice drew the king's attention. Jessmyn closed the door behind her, smiling, and came to him from across the chamber. She seemed to drift, her gown of pale green sweeping over the rug as she approached. He held out his hand to her, and as she took it, the king drew her close, putting an arm around her waist, pulling her down on the bed beside him. She did not resist, but tilted her chin to receive his kiss, returning it with passion. He found the hooks that held her gown and began to loosen them, and she sat passively, watching him with wide green eyes. He undressed her slowly, taking each article of clothing and setting it neatly aside. When he was done, she took his hands and placed them on her breasts. He couldn't wait any longer and grabbed her roughly by the arms. The princess flung back her head, gasping when he bit her shoulder, then kissed the marks. All he had ever desired of her and more, she gave him willingly now.

Somehow the darkness had found Lucien again, wide and remote and very, very cold. He woke, teeth chattering, and opened his eyes on the gray light of dawn. Feydir stood over him, watching with catlike intensity. An awful feeling of theft possessed the king, and he roared in fury. The ambassador leaped away, but Lucien was on his uncle in an instant.

"You monster!" the king screamed, slamming the old man against the wall. A forearm across his throat, Feydir was pinned so that his hands could not reach his brightly glowing Stone.

"Gaylon will come!" the mage cried, his terror real as the king sought to crush his windpipe. "What you dreamed, he dreamed!" The words were being squeezed off. "Lucien! I meant no cruelty. It had to be done." The arm pressed harder. "It had . . . to be done!" He clawed at Lucien's arm, fighting for breath.

The king dropped his hold and stepped back, his eyes streaming rare tears. "Old man, if this fails, if she is never to be truly mine, I will kill you. Somehow, I will kill you!"

"He'll come, I swear it. What was joy to you this night was nightmare for Gaylon. Believe it, Nephew. He *will* come and bring Gosney with him, right here to Castlekeep where my powers are strongest. We'll have them both!"

Fourteen

❖

For most of the night, Daryn lay awake. Finally, mind still churning, he left the bed and made his slow way to Gaylon's chamber. What he would do there he had no idea, but if he hoped to ever gain peace, then a way had to be found to say good-bye. And he couldn't bury his hope of keeping the boy here. There had to be something he could say, do, promise, than would bind Gaylon to Seward yet a while longer.

The bedchamber was empty. The duke swept the candle before him, left to right, throwing its fluttering luminescence into the corners. His stub fingers clutched the taper's stem convulsively. The ashes were cold on the hearth, the trophies of childhood still neatly arranged on the stone walls. The battered lute lay on the lid of the trunk. Abandoned. The sense of it was overwhelming. Daryn set his foot on the threshold and slid the staff forward. The wood connected with some unseen object on the floor and sent it clattering across the stones. The candlelight revealed the glittering hilt of a sword, the broken blade lay at the toe of his right foot. He recognized it as the small weapon Lucien had give Gaylon so many years before.

Cursing his lame leg, Daryn headed for the great hall. It, too, was empty, but he no longer sought the prince. Even without his powers, it was obvious the youth had left Seward. No, only Sezran might help him now. The duke found him finally in one of his many workrooms. The old wizard peered intently into a huge, three-legged lead vessel on the floor, his sharp features lit from beneath by the blue glow of his pendant, which hung betwixt him and oily fluid in the great bowl.

"He's gone, damn you!" Daryn cried and thumped his staff in high temper.

Sezran looked up. "Damn me, is it? Damn me!"

"You tried to kill him!"

The wizard's eyes returned to the cauldron. "Don't tell me the thought never occurred to *you*," he said coldly.

The words came almost as a physical blow, and Daryn sagged against his staff. There *had* been a time, once, when he'd thought Gaylon better dead than a force loosed on an unsuspecting world. But to act upon the thought was inconceivable.

"So, he returns to Castlekeep," Sezran growled. "Did you tell him how to recover Kingslayer?"

"No," Daryn said quietly. "I tried, but he refused to hear me out."

The sorcerer's head snapped up. "He refused?"

"Yes. He said the sword is yours."

"Ah! The folly of youth, so good and so kind," the old man cackled derisively. "Tell me, then. Where may I find *my* weapon?"

"No. If Gaylon will not have it, no one shall. Least of all you."

"You try me, Daryn! I have been more than patient with you. I'm the least of Gaylon's dangers now." Sezran's lids lowered over his dark eyes, and his thin lips smiled faintly. "That Southern sorcerer, Feydir, is clever and ruthless. Last night he sent the boy a dream—a thing so intense that even I sensed the spell."

"A dream?"

"It's an ancient art called the Sending, in which one may unbalance his enemy by sending him nightmares so substantial, so true-seeming that they're nearly impossible to discern from reality. Such a thing was done to Gaylon. Without the peace of sleep in which to retreat, a man is soon undone."

"Is there no protection from the dreams?"

"Other than wakefulness or the death of the perpetrator, I know of none."

Daryn's hand tightened on the staff. "Then I must follow the prince, somehow catch up with him. He'll need me more than ever."

"Need *you?*" Impatiently Sezran snapped his fingers. "Look!" He pointed to the roiling liquid in the cauldron, holding his Stone at the end of its chain to light it. Daryn shuffled close and leaned over, watching the surface grow still. He expected a vision, some portent, but all that was revealed to him was the deeply lined, careworn face of a bitter, old man whose hair was far more gray than black. The streak of white over the left eye, his own left eye, no longer stood out. His injuries and the loss of his Stone had aged him far more quickly than a normal man.

"Of what use will Gaylon find a withered, crippled old man?" Sezran asked cruelly. He straightened, and his Stone fell back to his chest, mercifully throwing the water back into darkness. "Tell me where Kingslayer is, and *I* will help the boy take back his throne."

Daryn heard the lie in those subtly persuasive words. He looked up and saw the cold truth glittering behind the wizard's eyes. "No," he said carefully. "You mean to kill him."

Sezran reared back, his face gone to fury, and he struck the cauldron, knocking it over. The black water ran gushing and streaming across the floor, and the metal clanged hollowly.

"Begone then! Follow the boy, and you'll die together!" The wizard shook a finger at the duke. "But not before you've given the sword to Feydir. Let him take up Kingslayer and mold his empire with fire and blood. I've waited a thousand years. I'll wait another thousand. Time is not *my* master!"

Daryn gripped the yew pole, seeking its support. "It comes to me suddenly," he said, "that you cannot be as immortal as you would lead others to believe, or you would not have built this fortress and loosed your Shadows to guard it. If Feydir gains Orym's Legacy, he may well come for *you*."

Sezran paled, and he clutched his Stone. The brilliance of it caused the flesh of his hand to glow translucently. The air crackled, raising the tiny hairs of Daryn's face and arms. The wizard's iron gray mane lifted from his shoulders and miniature lightning ran dazzling through it. But Daryn turned his back, and stumped away toward the door.

"Stop!" Sezran raged.

Daryn kept on. Oddly enough, he felt no fear, and the sorcerer made no move to prevent his going.

In his bedchamber, the duke gathered some clothing that fit easily into one small bag. A peace had descended on him with the making of this decision. He took his boots from a corner, wiping the dust from them, and struggled into the stiffened leather, then ran his fingers over the seam he'd restitched. The thong had darkened with age until it matched the rest of the leather. The boots were heavy on his feet, uncomfortable, but they were far better suited to travel than his sandals. He stopped one last time at Gaylon's room and used a strap to tie the lute across his back. He chided himself for foolish sentimentality, but a deeper instinct told him the instrument had yet another role to play.

After so long within Seward's gray walls, Daryn was unprepared for the morning light that greeted him beyond the eastern portal. Slowly his eyes adjusted to the sun's brightness, and the duke looked about him for what seemed the first time. In all the years gone by, he'd left the castle twice and then only briefly. Now he was acutely aware of his surroundings as he found and took a deer path northward over the sward.

The grass was ankle deep and thick with dew that quickly soaked the hem of his robes. Small animals burrowed away through the sedge as he passed, and the scent of the disturbed blades came to him even on the cold, moist ocean air. Late blooming wildflowers dotted the meadows with color: yellow buttercups and dandelions, opening to the sun; pale red columbine and deep purple-blue royal trumpets. He came within ten paces of a small band of grazing mule deer. None looked up, save one—a young buck sporting a proud rack with three points over ears that twitched curiously in Daryn's direction. A thrush warbled, a meadowlark answered in high, sweet liquid tones.

After wishing for death for so long, Daryn was surprised to find himself glad to be alive. The fact that his pace was slow and jerking failed to bother him. Only once did he look back to see Seward against the pale, morning-blue sky. It was a single swift glance that allowed the castle no chance to begin its hypnotic wavering. He would never return to Seward. Daryn Emilson was a free man—crippled, but free. He had led Gaylon to Seward and now would follow the prince back to Castlekeep. Together they would win or lose a kingdom.

The duke came to the first of the many creeks that cut through the meadows on their way to the ocean. The way grew dangerously steep for a lame man. He crossed two streams, his boots filling with icy water, and decided to follow the next one through its small gorge and out onto the black sand beaches. The tide was at low ebb, and here on the sand the creeks fanned out over the shingle, making the crossings easier. Great boulders marched endlessly into a tourmaline sea, and Daryn wove his way through them to the water's edge, then turned northward once more, keeping to the firmer wet sand where tiny combers slid bubbling underfoot. He was tiring, but trudged on, relying heavily on the staff. Somewhere along this beach, he should eventually find the fishing village where he and Gaylon had left the horses nearly nine years ago.

By midday the duke was forced to rest often. His first doubts were surfacing. He'd brought no food, no cloak, and the wind blew chill out of the north. Worse yet, he followed a young man with two good legs—if indeed, Gaylon had even gone to the village. Daryn pushed on. The tide was rising, and soon he'd be forced inland again. But at last, rounding a final rocky promontory, he found the village, just as the stench of it found him; a mixture of woodsmoke and rotting fish brought on a wind that also carried the shouts of children and cries of gulls.

The hamlet was bustling. Tiny sailcraft were putting out across the small, sheltered cove. Others were landing. Barechested men dragged nets full of fish onto the verge of the town to a freshwater creek where women with knives cleaned and fileted them. Other women with scarves wrapped over nose and mouth carried panniers of the prepared fish into huts to be smoked.

Daryn was nearly among the villagers before the first child

noticed him and ran calling to his elders. Eyes turned, wide and staring, and all movement ceased. In the silence the sea gulls could be heard, squabbling and wrangling over fish heads and entrails. Self-consciously Daryn stopped beside a young woman who sat over a huge pile of salmon, her arms bare and bloodied to the elbows.

"Please," he said to her. "Where may I find the man called Roddi?"

Her eyes were dark and touched with fear. She said nothing, but glanced away toward a group of men also standing dumb. Their fingers were still snagged in a net they'd been dragging through the black sand.

"I be Roddi," said a wrinkled little gnome of a man, loosing his grip and coming forward bravely. He performed an awkward obeisance. "How can I help ye, Master?"

Daryn felt numerous eyes on him and wondered at the awe in the villagers' faces. He could not be so unusual a sight—an aging man in dark robes, stooped and crippled. Perhaps any stranger was good cause for awe. He looked at Roddi, a white-haired old fisherman with a toothless grin, his skin tanned to leather by the sun, and he remembered the fellow only vaguely.

"I seek a young man who may have passed this way today."

At that, Roddi broke in eagerly. "Oh, aye!" He bobbed in avid agreement. "It's Liam ye'll be awantin', sir. It were him that tooken care of the young master. Kessi! Get yer da!"

A boy broke from a band of youngsters, and sand showered from under his churning feet as he took the incline from the beach at a run. He disappeared among the shabby stick-and-mud dwellings. Around Daryn, the fisherfolk slowly returned to their work.

The duke leaned heavily on his staff, and Roddi said quickly, "Come, Master. Set yerself here."

A little stool was settled in the sand beside him, and, grateful, Daryn sat. He tried to thank the child who had brought it, but the boy backed away fearfully. All the villagers gave the duke a wide birth, so he waited patiently, content to watch the frenzied activity around him. Roddi had returned to help with the net. More of the boats landed, and as quickly as they were emptied of their cargo of fish, they set out again. Daryn suppressed a cough when harsh smoke drifted across the sand from a nearby hut.

The boy, Kessi, came soon enough with a thin young man in tow. Behind them trailed two toddlers, naked and pot-bellied, one with a thumb plugged firmly in her mouth. The man came to a halt before Daryn, and the little ones found a long leg each to cling to and peered shyly at the stranger.

"I am Liam, sir." The fellow smiled and bowed as Daryn rose from his stool. He was fair-haired with a long, narrow face, handsome in a disheveled fashion. Like the older boy, he wore only greasy leather breeches that ended above the knee.

The duke nodded to him. "My name is—"

"Daryn," said Liam, and his smile broadened. "The young master said we should make ye welcome."

"He's here, then?"

"Alas, no, sir. He came only to speak of the horses."

Daryn's hand tightened on the staff. "Did he . . . take them?"

"No. He wished to make sure they'd been well cared for and to pay us for their keep."

"But how? He has no money."

"Not in coin, sir. His was a far greater gift." The fisherman gestured out toward the cove. "He called the salmon to our nets."

"I know you," Daryn said slowly, staring at the young man's face. "You're the widow's son, the one we left the horses with."

"Aye!" Then Liam's smile paled. "My ma passed on two winters back. We lost many that year from hunger, and last winter, too. The salmon ain't returned to these waters in three long years. The Little River flows with mud in the rainy season now, and the salmon can't spawn. But this winter none shall starve!" His eyes met Daryn's. "I would be honored if ye would come to my hut."

"Thank you for your kindness," said the duke, "but I'd like your help in readying one of the horses."

Liam shook his head. "Come, rest first and eat. Kessi, run

tell yer ma we have a guest."

"Aye, Da," the boy answered and started away, the toddlers following.

"Can I help ye?" Liam asked timidly, taking Daryn's elbow to assist him up the slope.

Graciously Daryn accepted the hand on his arm, let himself be led down the wide goat path that passed for a main street. The squalor was appalling, and the flies and foul odors were so thick that even the wind failed to eliminate them. But the duke heard laughter, saw hope in thin faces, and knew Gaylon had put it there.

"You were but a boy when last I saw you," the duke said. "Now you have children of your own."

"Two fine sons and a sweet daughter," said Liam with a hint of pride.

"The people of the village, they seem almost fearful of me."

Liam hesitated before answering. "Sir, they have lived in terror of Seward and its black sorcery for as long as any remember. The young master has shown them that such power can be used for good as well as ill, but even now they find it hard to believe their good fortune. They fear yer wizardry."

"I'm no wizard," Daryn told the young fisherman. "I have no powers."

Liam gave him a curious glance, but they had arrived at his hut and the young fisherman hurried to pull open the rickety door. It was a small single-room dwelling with a dirt floor and a cook fire at its center. Afternoon light streamed in through the smokehole. Liam's wife was small-boned and thin and very pregnant. Her clothing was the same as every woman in the village that Daryn had seen—a sleeveless, sacklike dress that fell shapelessly to the ankles—but her ears were pierced and strung with tiny seashells and her wrists carried bracelets of larger ones. Though she lived in a state of poverty, her spirit was not impoverished. She was quick to smile, quick to laugh.

Almost immediately she handed Daryn a thick wedge of flat pan bread, heaped with golden salmon roe. He bit into it, the little eggs bursting with a snap between his teeth. The fisherfolk's world seemed permeated with a pungent, fishy odor; the air, the smoke, their clothing. One must eventually grow inured to it, Daryn decided. But salmon was a food he would never tire of, and he devoured the bread and another slice when it was offered.

They had bid him sit on a crude chair—the only bit of furniture of which the hut boasted. The lute and his bag had been taken from him and leaned against a wall, along with his staff. Liam did all the talking. From Mysha, his wife, there was only an occasional nod of affirmation or an eye of gentle disapproval and always, soft, affectionate laughter. The younger children sat at Daryn's feet and watched him eat with an air of wonder. Kessi had disappeared soon after their arrival.

"The young master said ye would come," Liam stated as he passed Daryn a wooden cup filled with weak tea.

"He was that certain?" Daryn muttered and sipped the hot beverage. It tasted of lemon grass and blackberry leaf, as well as the omnipresent fish.

"Aye, he was certain. He also said ye were not to follow him. He said that when he has settled his affairs, he'll come for ye at Seward and return all that was taken from ye."

"Not all," said Daryn softly and rubbed the scars of his left hand against his robe-covered knee.

"Yer hand's all gone," noted the tiny daughter solemnly. Her mother hushed her, but Daryn gave the child a small lopsided smile and, encouraged, she crawled into his lap. He looked down on her pale downy hair and watched a louse scuttle for cover behind an ear. Gently, carefully, he lifted her from his legs and set her back on the floor.

"Myrtle leaves and rattlesnake grass . . ." he said, half to himself.

"Eh?" asked Liam.

"For the lice."

The young fisherman seemed not to take offense. "That's what the young master told us. Only we call them pepperwood and horsetail. He said a wash of tea would kill the lice, and if we crush the leaves and put them in our beds, it'll kill the sand fleas and ticks, as well. We had hoped he would stay with us and teach us his herbal medicines, but so great a sorcerer would find little to please him here. Perhaps," he said hopefully, "ye would consider—"

Daryn shook his head. "My knowledge of herbs is limited, and my place is with Gaylon . . . the young master. I mustn't tarry any longer. If you would help me ready the mare?"

For the first time, Liam frowned. "He was very clear—"

"Then I'll continue on foot," Daryn said firmly and reached for his staff, using it to pull himself up. "At least tell me the way he's gone."

"He follows the Little River east, but it's late. Stay with us the night."

"No."

Liam drew a deep breath. "Sir, please. What ye do is unwise. The cold comes early this year. Already the animals have grown heavy winter coats. The birds and insects make ready. In our Sacred Cycle of Nine, this year precedes the one of renewal. It means a winter, bleak and long. Ye are not prepared for a journey in such weather. After all, ye are . . ." His voice trailed off.

"Crippled," Daryn finished for him, unable to conceal his bitterness.

Mysha put a thin brown hand on Liam's arm and leaned close to whisper in his ear, her long straight hair falling forward to conceal her profile. Liam studied the dirt beneath his feet and nodded slowly.

"I will bring the horse and saddle her," he muttered with resignation.

"I'll come with you," said Daryn.

"The way is steep."

"Nevertheless, I'll come."

With a bare nod of his head, Liam deferred. They met Kessi in the street, and the boy led them up the hillside away from the village, running ahead, circling back, impatient with Daryn's slow pace. The duke listened inattentively to Liam as he described the condition of the horses, his thoughts already on the journey ahead. Before long they heard the tinkling of the goats' bells. The meadows here were well grazed, the grass shorn close, the small stands of whitethorn and blackberry all but denuded by the foraging herd. Another small boy lounged against a stump, a pile of stones beside him to throw should the animals stray. He waved to Kessi. Nearby the goats clustered, watching suspiciously as the men approached. The horses cropped grass farther on, disdainful of the company of milk animals.

She will not know me, Daryn told himself. What dim and distant memory Amber might have would be of another man, the man he'd once been. He dragged his right leg forward, reaching out with his staff for the next step. They were upwind of the animals, and Amber's head came up, swinging to gaze in their direction. Her nostrils fluttered, tasting the wind, then she called out, a high pitched, ear-shattering neigh.

"Well," murmured Liam, beside the duke. The mare trotted toward them, but Katy circled away, agitated, distrustful of the men. Amber bypassed Liam and Kessi to stop before Daryn, lifting her nose and blowing great gusts of sweet, grassy breath into his shaggy hair. He cradled the staff in his elbow and reached out to stroke her cheek, brush the forelock from her eyes. She would be nearly twenty now, and showed her age. White hair flecked her blood bay coat, especially around the muzzle, and the flesh over her eyes was sunken. But she was sound, rounded with summer-fat, her fur long and thick in anticipation of winter.

He ran his hand along her neck, over the slope of her shoulder to pat her chest, then laid his forehead on her withers, remembering the feel of her beneath him, the strength, the willingness and desire to please. He spoke to her in low warm tones, promising her again that unique kinship they'd once known. "You must be my legs now," he told her.

They started back. Liam had brought a rope, but it was unnecessary. Amber walked close behind Daryn, and Katy followed at a safe distance. Liam talked as before, explaining that he'd kept their hooves trimmed as best he could with a fish knife, but that neither horse had been ridden in a long while.

"She'll be half-wild now, so ye must take care," the fisherman said as he saddled Amber in front of the hut. The saddle had been a sad affair at best, but now its leather was rat-chewed and dry.

Daryn refused the fisherman's help in mounting. He was determined to prove to Liam and himself that he was capable of some small effort. Amber craned her neck to look back at him as he settled in the saddle, but never moved a muscle. Mysha emerged from the hut, the lute in one hand, an oilcloth package in the other. Over her arm was a long full cloak of embroidered cloth, fancifully sewn with sea dragons—a finer garment than any the duke had seen in the village.

She stood silently as Daryn tied the lute behind him on the saddle. Liam helped him run the staff under his right leg and bind it in a way so as not to hinder Amber's movements. When they had done, Mysha handed the package to her husband to fasten near the lute.

"Smoked salmon," Liam informed him, "and pan bread."

The woman came close, holding the cloak up to Daryn.

"It was her da's," said the fisherman quietly. "The young master would take nothing for his kindness. Mysha hopes you'll accept this gift in his stead."

Unwillingly Daryn put out his hand. It was too fine a thing to give to a stranger, but Mysha laid it across his lap and took his fingers, pressing them to her lips.

"Safe journey, Master," she said in a strong clear voice, then the color rushed to her face and she backed away, head down.

Daryn understood now why she was so quiet: she was shy, painfully so. "Thank you," he murmured.

The mouth of the Little River bordered the northern edge of the village. The water was low, sluggish, and foul with algae. A small crowd followed the man and horse a short way along the bank. Kessi walked at Daryn's stirrup while his more timid peers watched in admiration. Finally the villagers left the duke to continue on alone with only Katy as a shadow, keeping well away, but always in sight. The sun westered, and Daryn donned the cloak against the chill, smiling to himself; he certainly looked the part of a wizard now, enfolded in the heavy dark cloth with its prancing red and green dragons.

A half-moon already hung in the heavens. It had risen early, would set early, but he had several hours of travel ahead before the light was completely lost, and here the way was easy, the river providing a fairly wide flood plain to follow.

He didn't push Amber, though he felt a strong urge. On the ground Daryn was clumsy and awkward, but on the mare his balance returned, and with it, his confidence. It was as if he'd never left the mare, never suffered Sezran's wrath. His ruined hand was sufficient to grip the reins, if nothing else. With Amber it mattered not that his speech was slurred, that his eyelid drooped or his mouth turned down on the one side. Theirs was a communication of body and mind, a thing no more easily forgotten than breathing.

The elation he'd felt that morning on the meadows near Seward returned tenfold, his spirits climbing with the river as it snaked its way into the coastal range. The twilight and the cold deepened as he drew farther and farther from the temperate ocean. Katy no longer trailed so far behind. She walked at Amber's heels now, even growing so bold as to come alongside and nip jealously at Daryn's leg until he caught her once across the nose with the end of the reins. He would have preferred to leave the little mare behind, but both animals would have suffered at the separation.

Gaylon had nearly a day's head start, but Daryn was no longer afoot. It could be only a day or two before he found the prince. He felt a twinge of worry. The Sending, Sezran had called it—nightmares to plague and beleaguer the lad, as if nightmares hadn't already been a bane to him since the death of his father. Daryn set the worry aside as useless and self-defeating. He would find the boy soon enough and help him deal with Feydir's spell however best they might.

* * * * *

The duke had thought to overtake Gaylon in no more than two days. He was mistaken. Four days passed, and a fifth. The way grew rugged, and the river branched as he neared its source. He took the northern tributary, for it would bring him soonest to the coach road, and he assumed Gaylon had done the same. Here the landscape was bleak. Some years past there had been a forest fire, a big one. It had destroyed the vegetation on both sides of the river up to the ridgetops and beyond. The scorched and dead trees left standing after the fire had been cut down and carried away. The river was clotted with debris, and erosion was rampant through the area. In every direction, Daryn could see an endless swath of destruction, devoid of wildlife, blackened and barren. This also accounted for the flow of muddy water in the winter and the loss of the salmon. Small plants were just now taking hold. On the north-facing slopes, the tiny redwood and fir seedlings might stand a chance, but on the south slopes, where the sunlight was strongest, the underbrush would thrive and choke out the young trees. A hundred years, even two or three hundred, would pass before the forest could renew itself.

Daryn used the man-made roads where he could, but they were washed out in many places. Even in this desolate countryside, the duke found little sign of Gaylon's passing. The prince seemed to be keeping to the river, and it seemed he never rested. On the evening of the sixth day, when Daryn was beginning finally to despair, he smelled the smoke of a campfire. The weather had been clear all along, but there was a biting chill in the air now, a moisture that heralded change. He turned Amber's head, urging her down the steep bank to the riverbed. He'd seen a dark plume of smoke drifting from a shelter of large rocks near the water's edge. The mare's unshod hooves clattered on the stones, and above the bank, Katy minced along the ledge, looking for another, easier way down.

A figure hunched over the small fire, mostly hidden in a brown cloak. Daryn dismounted stiffly. "Gaylon," he called softly. The figure looked up, and as the firelight struck the face, Daryn felt a deep jolt. The young man's eyes were dark pits, sunken in his head, his cheeks stubbled with the beginnings of a beard.

"Are you dream image or truth?" the boy asked hoarsely. Before Daryn could answer, he continued. "I will not fight you." His hand waved drunkenly in front of him. "No more. My friends are my enemies, my enemies mock me. I've died too many times. Where's your knife?"

Daryn moved toward him, but the boy cried, "Stand back!" The duke took another hesitant step, and Gaylon threw back the cowl of his cloak. "I'll trade dreaming pain for waking pain," he snarled between clenching teeth and plunged his left hand into the flames of the campfire.

Daryn stood frozen for an instant, horrified, then flung himself at the boy and tried to drag him back from the fire. The weak leg crumpled under the duke, and he fell, rolling, pulling Gaylon with him. They struggled a moment on the edge of the river, then the prince lay suddenly still. Daryn searched feverishly through the tangled cloak to find the burned hand and submerge it in the water. The skin was terribly blistered. This was obviously not the first time Gaylon had put it in the flames.

"Daryn?"

The man turned his head at the voice. The prince's tone seemed lucid now.

Gaylon licked his lips. "Is it truly you?"

"Foolish child," Daryn said gruffly. "If I had my staff I'd thump you."

The prince's dry chuckle became a groan. "There's a rock in my back. May I move?"

Daryn realized he had his knee on the boy's arm and was gripping the wrist with a force he'd not thought possible for his right hand. He loosened his fingers. "Let me soak the hem of your cloak. We'll wrap the hand in it."

"No," said Gaylon. "I need the pain." He rolled onto his side and, careful not to use the injured hand, got himself to his feet. He reached down to help Daryn rise. In the fading light the boy surveyed the duke, then eyed Amber standing several paces from the fire, Katy beside her. "You followed me despite my orders. I should be angry."

"Your *orders* is it?" Daryn snorted, limping to the fire.

"Yes. And what's this you wear? I've never seen the like."

"It was a gift from Mysha."

Gaylon grew quiet, staring, his eyes seeing things beyond gaudy dragons.

"Sit," Daryn ordered him.

The youth's gaze began to wander restlessly, but he sat. "Talk with me," he said urgently. "How was the village when you found it?"

"Busy."

"Ah," said the boy with satisfaction.

Daryn settled beside him. "They say you called the salmon to their nets."

"I think I may have." Gaylon smiled faintly. "The children were so thin. I remember thinking, 'These are my people and they're dying.' It seemed so unjust. I thought of the salmon coming to the cove. Perhaps my Stone answered, I can't be sure. If it was indeed magic, it was a most subtle kind."

"Subtle magic is the most powerful of all," Daryn said approvingly.

"Liam and Mysha are good folk. They may live in ignorance and poverty, but they have a strength, a peace that I envy. We gave Liam two small pieces of silver with a promise to return, and years later, even while they starved, they never once considered slaughtering our horses."

"And you've done them well." The duke fed sticks from a small pile into the fire. "What's this?" he asked, taking the prince's chin and turning it in the firelight.

Gaylon pulled away. "I've had no time to shave it off."

"I had no idea you needed to. Your beard will be red like your father's."

The young man shuddered slightly, gaze shifting away. He moved the left hand toward the flames, and Daryn grabbed the wrist.

"No!"

"You don't understand! I can't fall asleep!"

"Listen to me. Sezran told me of the thrall you're under. But you must rest. I'm here now to watch your sleep. I'll wake you if need be, but you've got to remember they're only dreams."

Gaylon's laughter had an hysterical edge to it. "Oh, they are *not* only dreams."

"Explain them to me."

"How can I?" The youth shuddered again. The pain on his

face was from more than the burns on his hand. "When I fought Lucien in the Shadows, I thought I had conquered my nightmares finally, but I know now that I had no conception of true nightmare." He hugged his knees. "Oh, gods! I thought I knew evil. I had no idea." After a moment, Gaylon stared at Daryn, a hard searching look.

"I'll tell you a gentle dream, a kind one in comparison with the rest. . . ." His eyes lowered. "In it, I walk with my father in the gardens of the keep. I'm as you see me now, grown. We're talking. I see the sky. I smell the flowers. I hear his voice, and I'm happy. By the fountain he embraces me, then stands back. Too late I see the knife in his hand. With a single stroke he opens my throat." Gaylon reached reflexively to his neck, but continued tonelessly, "The pain is quick, the blood hot, and I fall. He stands over me, cursing. And he curses my mother for giving birth to me."

"And then?"

"I die, and another dream begins." Even in so flat a voice the youth's horror was evident.

Daryn asked softly, "Do I also come to you in these dreams?"

"Yes." The boy offered nothing further.

"Do I . . . kill you?"

"No." The word was desolate. "But I beg you to."

Daryn put a hand on the prince's shoulder in hopes of bringing comfort, but Gaylon stiffened.

"Don't touch me," he said in misery. "I can't bear it."

"You must somehow gain control of the dreams."

"It's impossible. I've tried, but I'm helpless in them."

"No," Daryn said firmly. "You're only helpless because you believe you are. You must fight back. You've got to attack!"

"I've tried! Don't you think I've tried? I've been forced to fight against those I love as well as those I hate. Nothing I do makes any difference."

"What of your Stone?"

"It won't answer me in the dreams."

The duke searched Gaylon's gaunt face. "Does Feydir come to you in them? Lucien?"

"Feydir, never, but Lucien often." Here the youth began to shiver. "And Jessmyn."

"Jessmyn! How so?"

Gaylon's jaw set. "Don't ask. They're the foulest dreams of all."

Daryn slipped his cloak from his shoulders, and the cold air struck him, finding its way through his robes. He folded the embroidery to the inside, then rolled the cloth into a pillow. "Lie back. Close your eyes," he commanded.

"Please, no," Gaylon begged through clenched teeth.

"I'll help you," the duke promised, "but you've got to let me. Do as I say!"

The prince lay back slowly, and settled the cloak under his neck. The burned hand was cradled across his stomach. Daryn crouched beside him, brushing the hair from the youth's eyes.

"Relax."

Gaylon's eyelids fluttered, then opened. He'd fought sleep too long to let it come easily, but against his will exhaustion took hold. Momentarily Daryn's face floated before him, and the prince took comfort in the familiar heavy, gray-streaked beard, the gray eyes that glittered with firelight. A numbness began to spread through the youth's body as his hand ceased throbbing. Fog, thick and dark, slipped over his vision, and the duke was gone.

Panic gripped Gaylon, and his heart began to pound. Wake! he cried to himself. Wake! The fog melted away, but it had left him in dream.

He was in a chamber below the keep. There were wide cuffs of iron on his wrists, heavy chains secured him to a stone slab. Terror consumed him, and he began to struggle. He knew this dream. He'd been here before.

I am with you, came a whisper in his mind. *Call Lucien to the dream.*

"He's already here," Gaylon gasped.

Lucien stood before an open forge, working a small bellows, turning a metal rod in the coals. He pulled it free. The tip glowed orange, and the fair-haired man smiled as he crossed the room.

"No!" Gaylon twisted his wrists in desperation. The chains rattled.

"But, yes," Lucien said sweetly. "Shall we begin with the eyes this time?"

Fight him, Daryn whispered.

"I can't!" the boy cried. "My hands are bound. I have no weapon!"

You do, Daryn said. *You have your ring.*

Gaylon craned his neck to look at his right hand. The Stone was on his finger, but dark and lifeless as it had been in Seward's Shadows, as it had been in every dream.

"The Stone has no power here," the prince murmured hopelessly.

It does! It must! Try, Gaylon. Try!

Lucien's fingers twisted in the young prince's hair, holding his head still. "Pain is pleasure, Gaylon. Let me pleasure you." There was joy on his face as he pressed the rod into the boy's right eye. Gaylon screamed.

It glows, Daryn said urgently. *The Stone awakes. Use it!*

Excruciating pain swept through the prince, but with it came fury and power. Lucien's hand flew back of its own accord, the rod torn free, sailing end-over-end across the chamber. In shock, the man stepped back from the slab.

Take control now, Daryn commanded. *The dream is yours.*

Gaylon felt the Stone's power surging through him. He pulled at his wrists, and the chains snapped, falling away.

In Feydir's bedchamber at Castlekeep Lucien cried out, but did not awaken. The ambassador leaned over the king. Something had gone wrong, terribly wrong. He began to pace the carpet by the bed, slapping his palm with Gaylon's small glove, the one used to direct the spell. Lucien moaned, and Feydir halted beside him once more. His nephew's forehead was wet with perspiration, his hair soaked with it. But he had drunk the potion and couldn't be roused. Whatever was happening, Lucien would have to face it alone.

Gaylon was fighting back. But how? Feydir wondered. That really no longer mattered; the dream spell had been rendered useless. This was obvious. Throwing down the glove, the ambassador paced some more. He'd hoped to unbalance the boy completely before he reached Castlekeep, but he'd have to change his tactics. He would have to rely more on outside help—a thing that did not please him.

He went to the door, opening it a crack. One of the guards turned his head.

"Call Nankus to me," Feydir told him. "Immediately!"

Fifteen

The cottage was lit by firelight only. Misk brought the teacup to her lips. Her hand trembled slightly, and she fought to still it, to center herself. Nights were worst, when Jimi slept, when all the creatures of the surrounding forests rested and there was no gentle energy to tap, to help her draw the tenuous lines of her being more tightly together. Tonight as always her otherselves haunted the shadows of the room, distorted images of her many pasts and possible futures.

An emanation began in the center of the highly polished floor. Misk didn't move from her seat at the table. She knew who was coming to disturb her, but couldn't remember which meeting this was or how it would end. A curtain of blue gauze rippled before her eyes, and an outline formed, clarified until it was not quite substantial.

"Brother dear," she said calmly. "Welcome."

"Greetings," Sezran replied with a hint of echo.

"How long has it been since last you came to me without the aid of your Stone?"

"By this world's reckoning of time, seventy-two years, two hundred and fifty-one days."

"How clever my brother is," she said dryly.

"Do not begin this meeting on a sour note, Misk."

"Forgive me. I only hoped to see you in your corporeal body this once so I might offer you some tea." She took another sip of the scalding liquid in her cup. Her hand had steadied now.

The burning sensation on her tongue helped to focus her.

Sezran frowned, glancing about the room. His eyes settled on the sleeping Jimi. "How can you take them to your bed? The thought is disgusting. It smacks of bestiality, Sister." He saw he had hurt her and felt joy and regret both at once.

"You're a snob, Sezran," she dared to answer. "Physiologically the differences between our species are few. Perhaps it's your failing—to think of them as animals."

"You're a hypocrite," he snapped. "You've bred them like livestock."

"Only because their finest bloodlines were nearly exterminated. And whose fault is that, but yours? Their world has been too long in the dark ages."

"I want the sword," Sezran demanded without further preamble.

Misk laughed gently. "You shall have it, Brother. All in good time."

"The time is now! Where has Daryn hidden it? He's your creation."

"Poor Daryn is my failure, and you know it."

"Yes," the wizard said with obvious pleasure. "Daryn, who was to have been a prince—until Feydir saw an opportunity and seized it, creating Lucien—your careful scheme gone awry. How then was Gaylon chosen?"

"I make do with the available materials, as you have so often done."

"He's too powerful, too unstable."

"He's all I have!"

Impassioned, Sezran moved toward her. "Let me have the sword, Misk. It's not too late! With the star gem that powers Kingslayer, I can take us home. You needn't die here."

"Unlike you, I'm reconciled to my death."

"But not here! Not alone! Where is Kingslayer?"

She smiled sadly. "I don't know."

Her brother's rage was magnificent, but impotent. "You have traveled the lines of time. You must have seen something. What does the future hold?"

"Which future, my brother? Which would you have me

relate? I've seen your end. Shall I speak of it?"

Sezran averted his eyes.

"I thought not. I'll tell you this: A great change comes in which this world will finally embrace its future, a great acceleration of human potentialities. The cost will be high, as all such growth dictates, and the sword will be the catalyst. Sezran, *you* began the game. On your shoulders rests the blame of the last thousand years, but in the end, you will undo the wrong with the very tool of your ambition."

"Be warned, Misk! I'll fight this!"

"It's fate."

"I'm above the fate of this miserable little world." But Misk only smiled at her brother knowingly, and infuriated, he cried, "You're a madwoman!"

Yes, mad, Misk thought. She was tired, the effort of remaining clear had drained her. Her fragile hold on the present slipped, but she fought to keep it for a small while yet. There was one last thing to be said.

"We will be there, you and I, at the end, at the beginning. We'll be together."

He was still angry. "Stay well clear of me, Sister!"

Misk raised her cup again to her lips, but her hand trembled uncontrollably now, and the firelight trapped on the surface fragmented. Her thoughts scattered with it. "Too late. Too soon," she mused, and felt the backward rush of time—

"Are you a witch?"

She turned her head and found ten-year-old Gaylon standing beside her, young eyes questioning.

"Goodness, no, child! Witchcraft is far too inexact a science."

"Then what are you?" the little boy asked.

"I am Misk."

The answer didn't satisfy him. She could see that. "Witches work with pinches and dashes of herbs, a bit of cobweb, fungi gathered under a full moon. How can they ever find the same potency twice in their concoctions? Here, put out your fingers, like this." She turned his hands, palms up, straightening the forefingers, then took a tiny bit of salt and placed a single grain on the tip of each finger. "Now. Tell me which is the larger?"

Gaylon looked confused. "I can't. They're the same."

"They're not! Which is the heaviest? Feel the weight."

The young prince lifted one and then the other finger, carefully so as not to dislodge the salt. Finally he shook his head in frustration. "What you ask is impossible."

"Difficult, but not impossible. In time you'll understand. In time you'll gain the sensitivity required for the task, and then, perhaps, you'll know what I am."

Sezran watched and listened as Misk spoke to the empty air, as she pantomimed with a hand that was but a bare outline against the fire. However much he despised her meddling, he loved his sister, and it hurt him to see the madness upon her. How close they'd once been, but now a great rift separated them. The wizard closed eyes that were mirror images of Misk's and willed himself away.

* * * * *

"Your Majesty." There was a note of surprise in Girkin's voice, but he opened the door wide to admit Lucien. He looked once, quickly, into the passageway.

"I am alone," the king said quietly. He held out a tall green bottle to the physician and watched his eyes light.

"Milord, you're most generous, most kind," the fat man effused, peering closely at the label. "A wonderful vintage, a fine year. Please, please be seated. I'll open it immediately."

While Girkin rummaged for a cork puller, Lucien took a seat before the fire. The physician's rooms were beneath the keep and chill, even in the unseasonably warm weather they were experiencing this fall. He glanced around at the disarray, the curios that lined the mantle, that covered every available surface. It was a comfortable clutter somehow, even with the wide-eyed skulls staring sightlessly from dark corners.

Girkin brought a cup and poured the wine. He stood back respectfully, waiting for the king to taste it. Lucien smiled inwardly. Crafty old man, he thought as the full, fruity aroma of the grapes filled his nostrils. He sipped the wine feeling

Girkin's eyes hard on him. He thinks there might be something extra in the drink, Lucien mused.

"Sit, Girkin," he said gently. "I've come for companionship this night . . . and a little information."

Happily the physician settled his pudgy form in the chair beside the king, then sipped the wine and rolled his eyes appreciatively. "Milord has exquisite taste. This is fabulous. And how good of you to visit a lonely old man, but isn't it rather late?"

"I couldn't sleep," Lucien muttered.

"Ah," said Girkin. "Would His Highness like me to prepare a draught?"

"No," the king said, perhaps too quickly. Sleep was a thing he had dreaded since his last experience with Feydir's dream spell. "No, I want to know what more you've learned concerning Orym's Legacy, concerning the riddle." The bit of parchment had been written in the ancient script of Wyndland and was well known to Girkin; physicians, like sorcerers, did much of their studies in that dead language.

"I thought perhaps you'd forgotten about Kingslayer after all these years," Girkin commented pleasantly.

"Anything that interests my uncle, interests me."

"Yes, but if indeed the sword exists and is found, its power could never be yours, milord."

Lucien looked at him sharply. "Why is that?"

"Forgive me, Sire, but you're not a sorcerer. It's said the weapon answers only to one who bears a Stone." Girkin paused to drink deeply from his cup. "But all this is academic. Your uncle has searched the keep thoroughly, so you have told me, and it seems to me that the only clue to the weapon would be Daryn of Gosney. That's where the riddle was found, was it not? In Gosney's apartments?"

Lucien didn't answer. Instead he took up the bottle from the hearth where Girkin had placed it and leaned forward to refill the little man's wine cup. He smiled thinly.

Girkin prattled on. "Of course, Gosney's long gone. If he isn't dead, he's a thousand leagues from here. If Lord Feydir ever got his hands on the man, he'd talk soon enough—

especially with a little urging from that filthy creature your uncle made master of the dungeons."

"Rum is a good man in his way," Lucien said.

The physician wiped his mouth with a fat-fingered hand. "He gives me the shudders. Reminds me of a pale-skinned salamander. Belongs under a rock, that one." He gave Lucien an apologetic smile. "I'm a healer, milord, and I just can't abide what Rum does with those gods-cursed instruments of torture he uses. Seems I'm forever being called on to keep some poor devil alive a bit longer so Rum can do his dirty work.

"Now Gosney—there's a man I wouldn't care to see under Rum's knife. I was there at Daryn's birthing. And his mother, Edonna, what a beauty she was, a frail, sweet thing with black hair so long she could sit on it. Sad that she should die so young. A wasting disease. Nothing I could do for the poor woman. It was strange that she should ask for her body to be laid in the cairns of the Dark Kings."

Lucien took a sip of wine, hardly tasting it. The cairns. That thought nudged a distant memory of Daryn: the duke was caught in the light of a window one night long ago, ashes—mourning ashes—smeared across his brow. But the last thing the king wanted to hear tonight was the family history of the Gosneys. He turned a deaf ear to Girkin's discourse.

So, Kingslayer could be of no use to him. Then he would make certain Feydir never had any use of it, either. His uncle eagerly awaited the arrival of Gosney and the prince, but Lucien would somehow find a way to destroy them first. That thought brought a tingle of pleasure. Even deep in his own thoughts, he heard Jessmyn's name spoken and looked up. "What was that?"

Caught in mid-breath, Girkin went blank-faced. "Sire?"

"What were you saying about Jessmyn?"

"Oh. Oh, yes. I was merely commenting that I understood your sleeplessness. Were I awaiting my wedding day to such a lovely lass as the princess, I doubt that I should sleep much, myself. Difficult to believe she'll have her fifteenth birthday in two weeks. Why it only seems yesterday she was . . ."

Oh, gods! The man was an insufferable old bore. Lucien

leaned back in his chair, smothering a yawn, and resigned himself to listen a while yet. As Feydir was so fond of noting, every man had his use. Even Girkin.

* * * * *

The wagon thundered past Gaylon and Daryn on the main street of the town. It was drawn by a team of eight heavy draft horses with hooves fully as wide as dinner platters, flinging mud as they went. Daryn directed Amber well to the side. Katy was slower to respond, and the curtain of slush that spewed from under the wagon's huge wheels caught Gaylon full on. His curses were loud and colorful. Daryn pulled his cowl around his face to hide his amusement. The lad rode like a true aristocrat, straight-shouldered and proud, but on the mare, his feet dangled nearly to the ground. Now covered in mud, Gaylon looked anything but royal.

They'd argued bitterly over who would ride Amber. Daryn insisted that Gaylon should—with his bandaged hand and exhaustion from Feydir's dream spell. And he was, after all, a prince. But Gaylon would have none of it and finally silenced the duke by fashioning a makeshift bridle for Katy and climbing onto her bareback. She was a small mare, but larger than a pony, and the prince, though tall, had the thin frame of youth still. Katy endured him until he was almost settled, then she promptly threw him. Luckily he hadn't far to fall. The next time, he was ready for her and managed to stay put while she plunged angrily along the trail. In the end she acquiesced, but Daryn saw the impish gleam in her eye, and every so often disaster would strike and Gaylon would find himself straddling the little mare's neck or sitting on the ground. In this manner they came finally to Riverbend.

The town had changed dramatically in the last nine years. It sprawled over the flood plain of the South Fork, across the coach road and onto the hillsides. It boasted a marketplace now and several inns, the least of which was the Fickle River. That old establishment had been enlarged and smeared with a fresh coat of whitewash, neither of which did much to hide its age or shabbiness. The place was still the favorite among the townsfolk, judging by the size of the midday crowd Gaylon and Daryn found there. The inn was packed, not with soldiers now, but with a larger, burlier breed of men who came to pull the giant trees down off the mountains and send them on massive wagons by the inland route to Zankos and Katay.

Gaylon had been outraged and sickened by the camps they'd passed on their way downriver. Slave labor was employed in these temporary villages, and death was common among the men who worked with rope and chain on the steep mountainsides. It was a dangerous undertaking to bring the logs to the road where they could be loaded. But what hurt Gaylon most were the great scars upon the land. It had rained lightly several times during their journey to Riverbend, and after each rain, the night sky glowed with the eerie, ruddy light of forest fires, purposefully set to clear the lesser growth from the areas to be cut for timber. Daryn rode with a blind eye to the destruction and human misery around him, unwilling to accept the heartache Gaylon embraced. Still the duke remembered a night long ago in the king's bedchamber when Reys had warned him of just such a future.

There was a fence now around the front yard of the Fickle River Inn, but it was falling to ruin, sagging in many places. Gaylon, on Katy, led the way through the gate that hung aslant on rusty hinges. At the squawk of those hinges, the door of the inn opened and a barefoot youngster dashed out, leaping over the puddles and coming to stand in the mud before the two men on horseback. A small, dark-haired child, he looked up as he took Katy's reins. Gaylon performed a fairly dignified dismount, ignoring the boy's curious smile.

"You got mud on your face and all in your hair," the youngster pointed out helpfully.

Gaylon scowled, but rubbed at his bearded cheek with a ragged sleeve. The boy tugged Katy after him and went to take up Amber's reins. Daryn sat motionless, staring down at the youngster with an odd intensity. The child's hair was thick and curled at the neck, his features delicate. He turned cat-green eyes on Daryn.

"Sir?" he said as if the duke were perhaps some poor half-wit. "If you'll get down, I'll take care of your animal."

Daryn still didn't rouse. His gaze remained fixed, and the boy looked to Gaylon for assistance.

"Do you want help?" the prince asked, putting out a hand. Wordlessly Daryn shook his head and lowered himself to the ground. The boy started away.

"Here, wait!" Gaylon called after him. "Does Haddi still own the inn?"

"Aye," the child answered over his shoulder. "Haddi's my mum."

Inside, the tavern was noisy and packed with a dinner crowd, the air thick with the smells of roasting meat and baking bread. A young serving woman glanced at Gaylon and Daryn briefly as they entered, but their clothing was poor enough to cause her little interest. The prince found them a seat by the fire and guided his companion to it.

As the two men sat, the kitchen door snapped open and Haddi swung into the dining area with a great platter in her arms. The mutton roast she carried was blackened and shriveled, and Gaylon smiled. Whatever brought the patrons to the Fickle River, it was certainly not Haddi's cooking. She dropped the plate with a thump in the center of one of the long tables.

"Haddi, me darlin'! Come here," cried a man at the end of the table. "I wanna talk to ya."

She went to him smiling and leaned close to listen to his murmured words. If the town had changed, Haddi had not. Perhaps her waist had thickened a little, but her hair was still the glossy black of a raven's wing, caught up in fat braids that hung in loops over her ears. She was a beautiful woman, Gaylon decided, looking at her through the eyes of the man he fancied himself to now be. He glanced at Daryn. The man's expression was unreadable, but his eyes followed Haddi's every move as she left the patron and returned to the kitchen. Gaylon stood up.

"What are you doing?" the duke demanded, catching the youth's arm.

"I'm going to ask some questions." He paused. "And

maybe find us some dinner—such as it is."

Unhappily Daryn let him go. The prince skirted the crowd, making for the kitchen. Within, Haddi poured great dollops of soup from a ladle into bowls. She didn't look up as the door closed behind him.

"There's no room in here," she said brusquely. "Go back out front."

"I want to ask you a question," Gaylon said and popped a scrap of meat he found on a counter into his mouth.

"Later," she snapped and slapped his hand when he reached for another. The woman swept past the youth to a cupboard and began piling loaves of bread on the tray with the soup.

"It'll only take a moment."

She gave him a look of mild irritation. "What did you do, roll in the mud before coming in? You woodsmen are all alike. Lift your boot!"

"Beg pardon?"

"Lift your boot, I say! I don't allow hobnails on my floors." She glanced down as he turned an ankle to present the sole of one mud-encrusted boot. "Filthy," she said with disgust.

"Please, all I want to know is where I can find the smithy, Sep. His shop's been torn down and no one seems to know him."

That brought Haddi to a halt. "He's gone."

"Where?"

"Dead," she snapped. "He was murdered long ago by a captain in the good king's guard—a noseless bastard named Nankus."

Gaylon's stomach twisted.

"Now, go out, and I'll get your dinner to you all the sooner."

"I'm afraid I haven't any money."

Her lips drew up in a wry smile. "I can't afford to feed every raggedy scamp that passes through town—"

"Mum!"

Haddi turned at the call. "Davi, I've no time for you now."

The boy had come in through the back door, carrying the lute and Daryn's small bag. He smiled up at Gaylon. "I couldn't leave them outside in the shed, they might get thieved."

Haddi looked at the lute, then gave Gaylon a sharp glance. "Go out, and I'll feed you this once," she muttered, turning back to her tray. "Davi, put his things in the little room under the stairs. He can sleep there tonight."

"There's two of us, madam," said Gaylon quickly.

Haddi's hands froze on the edge of the tray, then she jerked it up and dodged from the room.

"That's all right," said Davi happily. "One of you can sleep on the floor." He led Gaylon from the kitchen, and they wended their way through the tables to the staircase. The room was indeed small. Its single cot was narrow and extremely short. There'd be no question of who slept on the floor.

"Can you play it?" the child asked as he placed the lute on the bed.

"Yes."

"I hope you won't be angry, but I strummed it a little. It's got a nice sound, even if it is sort of sorry-looking."

"That lute's an impervious old thing," Gaylon told him kindly. "Nothing seems to harm it anymore. Do you play?"

"Naw. I'm going to work in the woods when I'm big, though Mum won't like it. A woodsman's got no time for foolish things like music."

"Is your father a woodsman?"

Davi shook his dark head. "My pa's dead."

"I'm sorry."

"I never knew him," said the boy, shrugging small shoulders. "You best get to the table before the food's all gone. Where's the old man with the funny cloak?"

Gaylon smiled. "I left him on a bench near the hearth. Have you eaten? Would your mother let you sit with us?"

"I got chores yet, but I'll come see you later."

The prince returned to the common room. Daryn hadn't moved from his seat, though it was uncomfortably warm so close to the fire. He looked up as Gaylon sat beside him.

"Sep's dead."

"I feared as much," the duke said sadly.

"Nankus killed him—not long after we last saw him, I think. I'm to blame."

"No. If there's fault, it belongs to us both."

Gaylon drew a deep breath. "Well, let's find a space at a table. Haddi will feed us. She's even given us a room for the night."

Daryn remained seated. "What did you tell her of me?"

"Nothing. There wasn't any time. But I'm certain she recognized the lute."

"I'm not hungry," Daryn said suddenly. "I'm too tired to eat."

"Are you all right?"

The duke ignored the question. "Where's the room?"

"Beneath the staircase. It's more of a storage area, but there's a cot. Shall I bring you dinner?"

"When you've finished your meal, I want you to find me some writing paper." Daryn pressed a tarnished coin in Gaylon's hand. "Don't buy it from Haddi—find it elsewhere in town. Buy ink and a stylus, also."

Gaylon looked at the small piece of silver. It was one of the four coins Misk had given them. "You wish to write a letter?"

"Just do as I ask." Daryn pulled himself to his feet with his staff. "Say nothing of me to Haddi." He took up his cloak from the bench and made his way toward the stairs, his movements clumsy and slow.

Gaylon watched him go, feeling concern. Since leaving Seward, Daryn had changed. He'd grown stronger, more sure of himself, but now it seemed as if the black depressions were returning. Perhaps it had been wrong to insist they stop at the inn, but Gaylon wanted news of the realm and the Fickle River had seemed the likeliest place for gossip.

The prince stood finally and squeezed himself onto the end of a bench at the nearest table. The big man next to him was friendly enough, but smelled of old sweat, sour and strong, and Gaylon found himself fast losing his appetite. He washed down what he could of the dinner with ale, making certain to show interest in his neighbor's discourse. These woodsmen didn't seem a quarrelsome lot. To Gaylon's mind they brought an image of the great brown bear—a gentle creature, but powerful and unpredictable. So the prince nodded and laughed at the proper moments, skillfully avoiding any questions about himself. When finished with the meal, he thanked Haddi and received a curt nod for his effort. Donning his cloak, Gaylon went in search of Daryn's paper.

The afternoon was nearly spent when he returned to the tavern. Dinner had been cleared away, and those who had not gone back to work had sat down to drink and visit. The prince was hailed immediately by the fellow he'd shared the meal with and given a full tankard. He finished the one and was treated to another. The ale was good—thick and creamy and warm. He listened to the conversations around him, though some of the voices were thickly accented and difficult to understand. The men discussed wages, here and in the South, and the poor quality of slave labor. They also argued pleasantly over the demise of a friend who'd been crushed by something called, "a widow-maker." Gaylon was offered the dead man's job, which he carefully declined amidst good-natured jibes.

He'd left the small parcel containing Daryn's supplies under the folded cloak, and the papers were badly crumpled by the time he found his way to the room beneath the stair.

"What have you been doing?" the duke demanded as Gaylon entered. He sat on the bed, waiting, his back to the wall.

"I—"

"Never mind," Daryn said shortly. "I can see what you've been doing—and smell it on your breath. Where are my things?"

Gaylon dropped the package onto the blankets beside the man. The ale had served to make the youth somewhat morose. "Am I reduced to an errand boy? You mustn't speak to me in such a tone, Daryn. I may not look a prince, but I am."

Daryn's lips pursed. "Forgive me, milord," he offered, then removed the bit of string from the parcel. "I won't rest easy until this is done. I need your hand steady."

Gaylon took a sheet of the paper and straightened it, looking for a surface to use as a desk. There was only the floor. "What shall I write?" Taking the candle from the bracket on the wall, he set it on the floor, then sat down before it. The light was poor.

"Do you know the boy's name?"

"Haddi's son? It's Davi."

"Davi . . ." Daryn said gently. "He's my son, also."

Gaylon looked up, brows furrowed. "How can you know that?"

"I know." The duke's face was shadow and light, bearded and gray.

"He thinks his father's dead."

"Good. That's true enough." Daryn raised a hand to keep Gaylon quiet. "As I am, I've nothing to offer the child, but I can at least claim him as my son. Should we succeed in our venture, he'll be a duke one day and heir to my lands."

"Haddi has a right to know who you are, Daryn."

"No." The duke stared at his ruined hand. "The man Haddi knew is gone. Now, write . . . please."

Gaylon took the pen in hand. In his small neat script, he transcribed the softly spoken words, holding the paper up at last for Daryn's approval. The duke took the page and laid it across his knee and, accepting the stylus, scrawled his name painfully beneath Gaylon's characters. When the ink had dried, the duke rolled the paper tightly and handed it back to the youth.

"Will you take it to her now? I want to leave at first light tomorrow."

There came a small knock at their door. Gaylon slipped the document under his cloak on the mattress, shoved ink bottle and stylus under the bed.

"Come," the prince said after another knock.

Davi entered bearing a small tray with a bowl of soup.

"Mum says this is for your friend." He brought the food to Daryn, and they were, for a moment, face to face, man and boy.

Gaylon saw the similarity in the bone structure, the cheek and nose, and wondered how he'd missed it before. The child turned his green eyes, bright and searching, on the prince. Then Davi was his mother's son again, completely.

"I can visit for a little, until the soup's all gone."

Gaylon smiled at him. "Will you keep . . . my uncle company, then? I've got to go on a small errand, but I'll return as soon as I can."

Davi hid his disappointment well. "Would you play me a tune on your lute when you come back?"

"If you'd like," offered Daryn, his eyes downcast, looking at but not seeing the bowl of soup in his hands, "you might play a tune yourself."

"I don't know how."

"I could show you."

Gaylon took the cloak with the paper hidden in it and left Daryn and the boy talking. The inn was near empty. A young serving wench was mopping the floors and gave Gaylon a look of disgust when he crossed the area she'd already cleaned. He grinned placatingly, and her expression softened.

"Is Haddi in the kitchen?" he asked her.

"No, upstairs," she answered. "But she don't like none to bother her this late."

"I won't bother her," he promised and took the stairs two at time. First door on the left, he remembered. He knocked on it gently.

She was a long time in answering and then only opened the door a crack.

"What is it now?" the woman demanded.

"I was charged with a letter for you."

"A letter?" The door opened a little wider.

"Please, I need to speak with you."

Reluctantly she stood away to let Gaylon by. The room was not much larger than the one under the stair. It had changed no more than Haddi—still furnished simply and very private. She showed him to a stool and went back to her narrow bed to take up the sewing she'd put aside.

"Did Davi bring the soup?" she asked.

"Yes, thank you."

"The letter?"

He fumbled for it in the folds of the cloak, then leaned to place the paper beside her. She glanced at it, but continued with her sewing.

"It's from the boy's father," he said.

Now she looked at him, green eyes narrowed. "And where is his father that he sends me a letter?"

"He's dead," said Gaylon, the lie coming too easily to his lips. Her only reaction to the words was to take up the sewing again, aligning the seams and beginning the stitches with quick, sure fingers. He watched the lamplight flash from her tiny thimble, grateful that she didn't ask him to elaborate on the lie. "The letter holds the boy's heritage."

"The inn is his heritage," Haddi said tonelessly.

"Davi is a duke's son."

Her fingers stitched on, and she remained silent.

"Won't you read the letter?" he asked finally.

"No," she said, and hostility crept into her voice. "I know already what it says—that Davi is the son of Daryn of Gosney. It was knowledge of Daryn that bought Sep's death. It would buy my son's if any knew his bloodlines."

"But a change comes," Gaylon offered fecklessly. "The prince rides even now to take his throne from the usurper, Lucien."

"Where are your armies, Your Majesty?" she asked sourly. "Forgive me, I see them, there, on your finger, caught up in your little Stone."

She'd struck him twice without raising a hand. "You know me," he muttered.

"I know you. Nankus returned to Riverbend only a day after you left. He was sick, burning with fever from a wound, but he didn't rest. He sought out Tobi first, that fat slug, then went to Sep." Haddi paused in her work, trapping Gaylon's gaze with her own. "The smithy died hard. They burned out his eyes—"

"Don't," Gaylon pleaded, feeling nausea well up. His memory of the dreams and Lucien's torture was still strong.

But Haddi went on. "He came to me next. Unlike Sep, I told them all I knew. I was fortunate. Nankus's desire for revenge had been sated for the time with Sep. I received only a broken arm and the doubling of my taxes—and a promise of death if I failed to send word immediately should you come again to my inn."

"Then you've sent word?"

"No. My hatred of Nankus outweighs what I feel for you. But if you wish to go to Castlekeep in secret, you had best turn your ring so the Stone is hidden in your hand. Ambassador D'Sulang tolerates no other magicians in the land, and he pays his informants well."

Gaylon touched his Stone, and a ghost light flickered within it. He'd been so careful in the past weeks, making certain not to use his power, consciously or unconsciously. That hadn't been an easy thing.

"I'm grateful," he said, "for your warning and your silence. Should I win my crown, you'll bring Davi to the keep. A ducal heir needs training, a formal education. He's a fine boy, and I'll be proud to have him stand beside me one day."

"My son will never serve you," Haddi said coldly.

"But it was his father's wish. It was Daryn's hope . . ." The prince paused. He'd spoken of Daryn twice in the past tense, and it brought him a sense of foreboding. "The Gosney holdings are considerable—"

"No. I will never let Davi follow you, Gaylon Reysson. You're a harbinger of ill luck. Death heels to you like some great hunting dog, and where you go, so goes misery." She spoke with quiet ferocity.

"Those who love you most will suffer most. Already the boy is drawn to you. His Gosney blood recognizes its king." The woman shook her head. "Be satisfied with the lives you've already destroyed, but leave Davi be. He's all I have."

Gaylon listened to the gentle tirade, and the words made an awful sense. He rose from the stool, feeling the weight of her accusations.

"I'm sorry," the prince said softly as he crossed to the door. "Everything you've said is true. But when the kingdom is finally mine, you *will* send the boy to me." With that, Gaylon left the woman to her sewing.

At the foot of the stairs, he heard the muffled plinking of lute strings. He stood listening by the door to the tentative melody. Some notes were clear and sweet, some misfingered and flat. Davi glanced up when Gaylon entered. The boy was seated next to Daryn, and he concentrated on the placement of his fingertips on the strings with his lower lip caught between his teeth. The lute was an armful for one so small, so young. Davi grinned at the prince happily.

"Listen! I can play something!"

"Davi," Gaylon said carefully, "you have to go now."

Confused, the child looked from Gaylon to Daryn and back again. "Why?"

"It's your mother's wish."

The boy accepted this and laid the lute down. "I'll see you in the morning, then."

"No, we must leave very early," the prince said.

This visibly upset the lad, and Gaylon went to one knee beside him. "Before you go upstairs, I want to give you something. I want you to have Katy, the little mare I rode in on. She's much too small for me." Davi's green eyes widened as Gaylon spoke. "She's not well trained, I'm afraid. She belonged to another little boy once who couldn't ride her as much as he might have wished. She'll need a firm hand, and you've got to be careful when you ride her. Your mother would never forgive me if you were hurt."

"I will! I'll be so very careful," Davi promised. He was halfway out the door before he remembered his manners. He looked back. "Is she truly mine?"

"Truly."

"Thank you!"

The tiny room boomed with the thump of his feet on the stairway. Gaylon took the lute from the blankets beside Daryn and settled on the floor before him. Unseeing, the duke stared at the door. Daryn had sacrificed much for his prince—his hand, even his magic. Sep, his father, and Telo were all dead.

For an instant Haddi's accusations overwhelmed the prince, but the feeling was quickly replaced by a numbness. Gaylon looked down at the lute and began to play, unable to do anything else.

Sixteen

Nankus shoved his way to the fore of the crowd. He stood watching a group of acrobats performing on the cobbled streets of Keeptown. Under the hot autumn sun, three young men and a young woman tumbled along the narrow stretch of roadway cleared for them. They were small lissome creatures, dressed as clowns, and the crowd roared with pleasure as the men pretended to vie for the young woman's attention, tossing her between them. Nankus scowled, unamused, and gazed into the throng.

There were none here who fit the description of the men he sought. He hated the horde of strangers that clogged his town and made his work nearly impossible. Even Zankos, a wide-open port, was easier to deal with than Keeptown as it prepared for the coming royal wedding. And to make his work harder, he was too well known in Keeptown, too well hated to gain the unreserved cooperation of the locals in his search.

Coins began to flash in the sunlight, clinking across the stones as the show ended. Nankus turned away, giving the crowd a last searching look. There was a sudden movement at the very back; a cloaked figure, cowled even in this heat, jostled the man next to him, then moved away swiftly. Nankus raised a mailed fist high in the air to catch the attention of two of his soldiers on the fringes of the throng. He pointed at the retreating figure, and with them, began to converge on the fellow from three separate directions.

The man saw them coming and took to his heels, weaving and dodging through the gawkers to make his way across the road and into an alley. The soldiers were not so gentle with those who got in their way, but by the time they gained the tiny side street, the man they chased was gone. For a moment the men stood in the filthy clutter of refuse and empty crates. Disgusted, Nankus sheathed his sword, growling a reprimand to his men, then his keen ears caught a sound—the careless shifting of a foot. In the silence that followed, their quarry bolted from behind a crate and fled back the way he'd come.

Nankus raced after the man and managed to snag a handful of his tattered cloak. The material gave way, and the sound of it rending was overloud in the narrow space between the two tall buildings. Still, the cloak held at the throat well enough to wrench the fellow backward and off his feet. Nankus grabbed the hand that came up wielding a dagger and slammed the knuckles hard against the ground until the blade was loosed. By then his soldiers had sword points pressed to the man's breast. Their quarry ceased to struggle.

The captain tore the hood away. The face revealed was young, contorted with anger and fear, but the eyes were dark brown, the hair color wrong. This was not Gaylon Reysson. Nankus felt through the cloak and found a pocket sewn within. In the pocket was a small pouch of coins with its strings neatly severed.

"By the Unholy One!" the captain snarled under his breath. "I seek a prince and find a cutpurse."

He stood away and let his men drag the captive to his feet, then poured the contents of the pouch into one hand. There were eight coins, only one of them gold, the rest, silver—poor pickings indeed. Nankus tossed each soldier a silver piece, which they plucked neatly from the air, grinning. The rest of the money the captain pocketed before he sent his men, the hapless youth between them, back to the keep, to the already overcrowded dungeons.

Once more on the teeming streets, Nankus paused on a corner to glance down the line of shops. In a doorway, under a garishly painted sign advertising fortunetelling, stood a tiny woman in long patchwork skirts. She watched the captain boldly, and he considered questioning her. But there was something strange about her eyes, dark and glistening, and never truly understanding why, Nankus turned and started away in the opposite direction.

* * * * *

Jessmyn unhooked the window latch and pushed the heavy wooden frame outward, then leaned precariously over the sill and listened for the faint music that had drawn her from her needlework. She heard nothing now but the murmur of the many voices of the keep: servants at their chores, the clanging of the armory, the cry of the drillmaster from the weapons yard. She leaned a little farther so she could see the edge of the gardens. The roses were in their last riotous bloom of the year, and she felt certain she'd never seen anything so glorious or smelled anything so wonderful.

Surely Nanny Arcana was mistaken in her prediction about the weather. More likely, Lady Gerra had misunderstood the old woman's words, since Nanny tended to speak in riddles. That was part of her mystique. Not that Jessmyn approved of her governess going so often into town to visit the fortuneteller. The princess had gone along once to see the strange little woman, but what Lady Gerra took for prophecy seemed only mindless wandering to Jessmyn. Still, Nanny's warmth and kindness made the princess look forward to visiting her again.

Winter of the Lost, Nanny had foretold. This was the ninth year of the ninth cycle and would bring the worst winter in eighty-one years. If this were true, why then did the sun shine so late into autumn? Why was the sky so clear and blue? Jessmyn drew a deep breath of rose-sweet air, the music forgotten. Nothing really mattered so long as the weather held for a short while longer. Tomorrow she would be fifteen and marry Lucien. Then she would be a queen. The thought filled her with anticipation and dread. She loved Lucien for his kindness, his tenderness, and wanted so badly to please him, but she also feared him somehow.

The music came again, maddeningly distant, maddeningly familiar, a thread of sound that tugged at her. She stepped back from the window, glancing across the room at Lady Gerra. The woman had fallen asleep in her chair, her needlework held loosely in her fingers. Without another thought, Jessmyn went quietly to the door and opened it a crack to look out into the passage. The way was clear, and closing the door gently behind her, she moved to the stairwell. Her slippers made only the lightest pattering on the steps as she descended to the ground level of the keep. The princess felt a delicious wickedness; she was never allowed from her rooms without an entourage.

The tramp of boots sent the young woman, heart pounding, into a recessed doorway to stand pressed into the shadows. Four guards marched past. When their footsteps had receded finally into nothingness, she stepped out, only to collide with a servant girl hurrying along the hall. For a brief moment they stared in shock at one another, then the girl, her arms full of linen, fell to her knees, head bowed.

"Milady!" she gasped.

She was hardly more than a child, no older than Jessmyn. The princess pulled her to her feet and placed a cautioning finger to her lips.

"Please!" Jessmyn said in a low voice, smiling. "You haven't seen me."

The girl smiled back hesitantly. "Oh, Your Highness, I have seen no one."

"Go, then."

Jessmyn watched until the servant rounded a corner, then set out again in the opposite direction, gaining the inner courtyard without further incident. Here there was far greater servant activity, though the noble lords and ladies were not about. The nobility spent their afternoons in rest and in the tedious, long preparations for the coming evening's celebrations.

In an open archway the princess waited, undecided, until the music came again to pull at her. She found the courage then to walk across the stone flagging of the yard, following the faint, melodious sound. Looking neither left nor right, the young woman moved purposefully but without haste, down the short span of stairs into the gardens, then across the lawns with their statues and fountains. The head gardener's small flock of sheep nibbled at the short grass and paid her no mind. No one called her name or even looked her way, and she felt giddy with this unexpected freedom.

Following the whitethorn hedge along the perimeter of the grounds, Jessmyn found the secret break that cut at an angle through the foliage. The way was narrow and the branches plucked at her skirts and hair. The music grew louder now, drifting up from the river far below, and she could identify the instrument finally—a lute. The path led in wide loops down the face of the hillside, through live oak and fir, myrtle and yew, through shadow and light. The sweet music continued, insinuating a subtle joy in her heart. As she started down the path, the princess held her skirts bunched before her, high off the leaf-and needle-strewn earth.

There were two men and a horse on the stony bank above the river. One sat with his back to the hillside, the other on a large rock, watching as she descended through the woods. His face was lost in long gray-black hair that met a beard so full, she couldn't tell where the one ended and the other began. He wore black robes with a long flowing cloak of the same dark hue over them. The outer garment's somber material was relieved by embroidered green and red dragons, their wings outstretched and claws extended.

It was the other, younger man who played the lute, and as Jessmyn reached the bank, he turned at last to face her. He was bearded also, but the beard was well trimmed and a deep red-gold in contrast to the short sandy-blond hair of his head. His clothing was of undyed chamois, a jerkin with short, flared sleeves over a white linen shirt. His breeches were of the same soft leather, tucked into high boots. He stared at her with solemn brown eyes shot through with green, but his fingers never ceased their playing. Fascinated, the princess watched the fingers as they danced on the strings. The melody was haunting as it wove its way through her thoughts until, from somewhere unknown, the words came to her. She joined her voice to that of the lute's:

Thistledown, Thistledown,
Where're ye goin'?
Ah, where the wind takes me,
Where 'er it's blowin'.

Thistledown, Thistledown,
And what will ye there?
Ah, how should I know then?
And why should I care?

Thistledown, Thistledown,
Please may I come, too?
Aye, if ye hold tightly,
Now see that ye do!

The sound of her own voice surprised the young woman. She couldn't remember when last she'd sung. Jessmyn stood mesmerized as the song died away, lost to the burbling of the shallow river over its rocky bed. She found both men's eyes were still on her and felt a rush of heat to her cheeks.

"You . . . you play beautifully," she murmured through her embarrassment.

"Thank you, milady," said the youth, humbly nodding. His eyes wandered to the old man's, and now they seemed to speak wordlessly to one another. The fellow in the cloak pulled himself upright with the help of a long staff and with careful steps came to stand beside the minstrel. He appeared to be badly crippled. The bay horse followed at his heels like a big dog.

The youth spoke again. "If it please milady, I would play another song."

The black-robed man shook his head slightly, almost a warning. "We mustn't keep milady overlong. We wouldn't wish to alarm the keep." He took the lute from the young man's hands. "If you will escort milady back—"

Was it apprehension that flashed so quickly across the youth's face? Jessmyn couldn't be certain, because he smiled as he took her hand and led her back up the path. The touch of his fingers was disconcerting. A twinge of guilt tugged at her. Lucien's touch didn't make her feel so strangely, or fill her with such odd excitement. Ashamed, Jessmyn pulled her hand away and saw clearly the hurt in the young man's eyes. She tried to think of something witty, something kind to say, but her thoughts refused to settle. All the long way up the hillside they were silent. At the hedge, he turned to go.

"Please," the young woman said, suddenly afraid of never seeing him again. "I would like to hear you play once more." He hesitated, and she rushed on. "Tonight! You'll play tonight at dinner."

"Milady, I don't think—"

"You must do as I ask," she said lightly. "I am a princess and soon a queen. I'll leave word with the guards to admit you, and you'll bring your master, also. I promise you'll both be fed and paid."

The minstrel hesitated again, a worried frown on his face, but there was a certain longing there as well. He bowed gracefully. "If Her Highness commands, I must obey."

She smiled and started into the break in the hedge, then halted. "Your name. You must give me your name."

Again the hesitation. "It's Thayne, milady."

She heard the falseness in the words, but chose to ignore it. "Good-bye . . . Thayne."

* * * * *

"This is madness!" Misk cried in a low voice, throwing her hands up in despair. The bell jingled in the front of the fortuneteller's shop, announcing a customer. She turned to Daryn. "You must talk him out of this." In a flurry of skirts, she swept from the room. The heavy curtains in the doorway fell closed behind her, but not before a breath of thick incense found its way through. They could hear her murmured greeting.

"She's right," Daryn said, his voice low for fear their conversation would be overheard. "I forbid you to go."

"Do you?" Gaylon laughed gently. He was applying wax to the lute in a useless attempt at making its appearance presentable.

"By the gods, Gaylon! Do you think I jest?"

The prince smiled. It was a pleasant turn of the lips, but his eyes were hard. "How will you stop me?"

"Think, lad. In a week's time Lady Gerra will bring Jessmyn here. Misk's arranged it. We can send the girl to safety with Jimi."

"A week! Tomorrow she'll be wed to Lucien."

"Keep your voice down," Daryn snapped. "We're not prepared to take action yet. If you confront them now, she could be hurt. We've got to get her well clear first. Misk's spent months working with the rebel faction here in Keeptown. With their help, we've got a real chance of succeeding. You've got to wait."

"No, tonight I'll end it. I won't have him touch her, take her to his bed. She's to be *my* queen, not his. There'll be no marriage."

"How can you stop it?" Daryn demanded. "Feydir knew we would come. I'm certain that is what he planned all along. Misk has seen the soldiers searching the town. They'll be waiting for us, Gaylon. The entire keep is a trap. Nankus will have you before you pass the first gate."

"You forget. I've got this," Gaylon growled, making a fist of the hand that carried his ring. The Stone in it flared with emotion.

"Fool! You've got power, yes, but no experience."

"Daryn, they'll never expect me to walk boldly into the keep. I have an invitation. *We* have an invitation. I'm Thayne, a simple minstrel, and you're my master. The entire castle is packed with lords and ladies come for the wedding, packed with entertainers of every sort. With any luck, I can weave a spell over the entire company with my music, then take my crown without a drop of blood spilled."

"Simpleton! I've raised a simpleton!" Daryn cried in anguish. "There'll be blood spilled, mark my words, and it'll be yours!"

Gaylon's face set with anger. "Stay behind, if you're so afraid."

The curtains parted, and the two men fell silent as Misk

came through.

"A customer?" Daryn asked her.

"A child with a bellyache. The mother came for an herbal remedy." She shot a glance at Gaylon, who applied wax sullenly to the lute, then looked at Daryn.

"He won't listen to me," the duke said.

"Gaylon," Misk said quietly. "Will nothing turn you from this course?"

"No," he growled.

"Then allow Daryn to bring you the sword."

"We discussed that earlier," the boy said harshly. "I won't take up Kingslayer. I don't need it." Then his tone softened, and he put a hand on Misk's arm. "I know you see the future. That's how you came to be here when we needed you, and once again we're in your debt."

"Gaylon, child," the tiny woman began. "Let me tell you what little I can see of the future."

"No. I want that no more than Kingslayer. You've got to have some faith in me. I'm no longer a little boy. I'm a sorcerer, Misk, and my powers are considerable. I'll have my kingdom back this night, or never."

"What of Feydir?" Misk asked. "I've kept the both of you hidden from him this past fortnight, but once in the keep, I cannot help you. The ambassador's powers must be reckoned with."

"He doesn't know I wear a Stone. See?" Gaylon turned the ring so the Stone lay hidden in his palm again. "By the time he realizes that I do, it'll be too late." He stood, taking up the lute. "Misk, I truly believe my life is somehow charmed. Nothing can harm me. I can't fail. Don't fear for me, either of you." He opened the back door of the shop and passed out into the alley.

Misk watched him until he turned a corner. Daryn came to stand beside her in the doorway, his cloak over his arm.

"He's a hotheaded young fool," he muttered. "I can't leave him to face this alone."

"Yes," she answered looking up at the duke, her face reflecting some deep sorrow. "You know what is to come, what awaits you at Castlekeep?"

"You told me that long ago." Daryn raised a shaggy brow.

"Feydir must not have the weapon."

"He won't have it."

Misk turned her eyes skyward. High in the narrow strip of cobalt blue seen between the rooftops small clouds were forming. Dusk approached swiftly.

"Do you smell it?" she asked. "Do you feel it?"

"What?"

"The storm. I've held the weather back as long as I can, but now Sezran comes." The tiny woman shifted uneasily. "Gaylon is right in one thing. Tonight it ends."

"Do you see that end?"

"Only in part. We've come to a millennial juncture, a vortex of possibilities, and I can only hope that what I set in motion will have the momentum to carry us through."

"Misk . . . I must go."

She reached out to pull Daryn's face down to her, meaning to kiss his forehead, but he brushed his lips to hers instead.

"Farewell," he said.

"Farewell, Daryn of Gosney."

The duke moved away from her, his staff tapping across the stones of the alley. For an instant her vision shifted, and Misk saw the young man he had once been. The image only brought her sorrow.

* * * * *

Jessmyn was vibrant, absolutely radiant. Could the thought of their impending marriage have brought about such a noticeable change? Lucien dared to hope as much as he led the princess to her seat at the table. The diners already stood beside their chairs. When the king took his seat, the others found theirs. There were only twenty at table tonight, taking their meal in a small private dining chamber. Lucien had had enough of his stately Southern cousins who had come for the wedding. The keep overflowed with distant relatives, merchants and nobility, known and unknown, friends and enemies. The passages were teeming thoroughfares, and the great hall a madhouse at dinner time.

Here it was relatively quiet, and Lucien could appreciate the food and wine, the few friends seated with him. He eyed Lady Marcel at the opposite end of the table, petulantly beautiful in her ice-blue satin gown. The woman was most unhappy about the wedding, but then, Lucien had never promised her anything. In any case, nothing need change between them. Seated on the king's right, Feydir had his mind elsewhere. He was much too absorbed in his search for Gaylon and Daryn. His uncle might think to use them to gain Kingslayer, but Lucien had other plans. The king's foes would die the moment they were found.

Lucien reached for his wine and took a long swallow. It troubled him that the two were still alive, but more recent memories were far worse. His throat grew dry whenever he thought of Feydir's dream spell and his own part in them. He'd taken great pleasure in torturing Gaylon, even though the prince had appeared in the dreams as the child Lucien had known nine years before. But when the dream had turned . . .

His stomach heaved at the memory. It could only have been Daryn's foul hand helping the boy, using his gods-cursed Stone to set the prince on him. Lucien had been paid in kind, then. He drained his cup and called for more wine. In wine there was comfort. Jessmyn, too, brought comfort. He found himself staring at her, adoring her, desiring her.

The last meat dish was served and cleared away, and the cakes and puddings brought to the table. The steward entered through the open doorway and tapped his staff lightly on the floor.

"Your Highnesses, milords and ladies, I present the minstrel, Thayne, for your entertainment, and his master, Meryl."

Beside the king, Jessmyn came to life, her smile suddenly dazzling. Confused, Lucien watched the minstrel enter. He was a tall young man, bearded, slender and graceful, well dressed in pale leather garb and carrying a lute that had seen far better days. Close behind him came an old man, much more heavily bearded, dressed in a gaudy cloak. This fellow took a stool in a far corner near the fire and leaned his staff across his knee. Lucien turned his attention back on the musician who'd already begun to play a quiet ballad.

Jessmyn laid a small hand on Lucien's arm. "I heard him earlier today. He was so wonderful, I had to invite him. I hope you're not displeased, my darling."

"Of course not," the king answered, but his thoughts were sails running before a high wind, and he looked to his uncle. The man's eyes were narrowed and his features frozen like a cat's when it first sights its prey.

Nankus appeared silently at Feydir's side, and they conferred in whispers. Across the chamber, the boy with the lute watched them thoughtfully as he played. Lucien dragged his gaze from the minstrel to look once more at his uncle. The captain was gone from the chamber as quickly, as quietly as he'd come. Feydir smiled pleasantly at his nephew and reached for his wine cup. The servants continued to move about the room attending to the needs of the diners.

What goes, what goes? Lucien asked himself, feeling a surge of excitement. He studied the minstrel more closely, the hair, the eyes. And the old man—could Daryn have aged so much? A disguise, perhaps? Surely, they'd never be so foolish as to come to the king's own dining chamber. Lucien smiled down the table at Marcel, beckoning her with a look, and she came to him happily, bending close to listen to his whispered instructions, then left the room immediately to do his bidding. Jessmyn, so enthralled with the music and the minstrel, noticed nothing.

Two guards with halberds positioned themselves by the door now, to stand motionless, behaving as furniture. There was an instant's uneasiness on the minstrel's face, Lucien was certain of it. But the old man sat in his corner without expression, listening, watching. By the gods, the king noted, the lad could play, coaxing tones from the old lute, creating echoes as if he were in some deep canyon. His voice matched the instrument's, both nearly magical. Magical . . . Lucien set his cup back on the table, determined to keep his wits, determined to miss nothing.

Feydir sat toying with some secret pleasure, his craggy winter-oak face almost benign. With a finger, he absentmindedly stroked his Stone. To Lucien's relief, his uncle was unmindful of Lady Marcel's return and of the tiny envelope she slipped into the king's hand as she curtsied before him. Someone called for a bawdy tune, and the minstrel obliged by beginning a song with lyrics so outrageous, so obscene that the ladies were soon shrieking laughter and the men dabbing at tears of mirth with fine lace handkerchiefs. Even the two guards had smirks on their coarse faces. Only Jessmyn didn't laugh. Her eyes were fixed on the musician, and it seemed as if she found no sense in the words he sang. She watched his fingers with such intensity that Lucien felt a sudden penetrating cold. She was so alive and happy this night, and now he understood why.

The diners joined in the chorus, their voices drowning out the minstrel. Lucien signaled his personal servant and had him bring a small tray with two filled wine cups. Under the distraction of the noise and merriment he spilled a minute amount of the fine powder Marcel had brought him into each cup. The song came to an uproarious end, and Lucien nodded to the servant. The tray was lifted from the table, on its way to the minstrel and the old man in the corner.

Then Jessmyn did an unreasonable thing. She turned, grabbing up one the cups from the tray as the servant swung past her, and put it to her lips. For Lucien the moment remained frozen, the cup, suspended, everything cast with the crystal clear light of horror. He slammed his fists to the tabletop and came halfway to his feet.

As Jessmyn tipped the cup it exploded in her hand. She screamed, the pottery shards and wine showering the front of her gown.

Havoc broke out. The minstrel flung down the lute and leaped for Jessmyn, but the guard nearest him was quicker. The soldier snapped the butt of his halberd in an upward arc that caught the young man hard below the left ear. The blow propelled him forward into a section of the trestle table, and man and table collapsed together in a rain of plates and cups.

Lucien grabbed Jessmyn by the shoulders, and dragged her to her feet.

"How much did you drink?" he cried.

Confused and terrified, she looked down at her gown, then at the minstrel sprawled at her feet. Lucien shook her roughly.

"How much did you drink?" he demanded again.

"I—I—" she stammered, then her eyes locked with his. "Only a swallow! Why?"

The king saw realization dawning, and she paled, her knees buckling. He swept the princess up into his arms.

"Get the physician!" he shouted over the uproar. "For all the gods' sakes find Girkin!"

Lying in his arms, Jessmyn convulsed suddenly. The poison was swift and cruel—the king had chosen it for those very reasons. He clutched her tightly to his chest and rushed from the chamber.

"Get out! All of you!" Feydir roared at the milling nobles and servants. "All but the guard!"

The lords and ladies made for the door, eyes wide with fright. They called to one another, couples seeking each other in the turmoil. Daryn had come to his feet, and Feydir pointed a finger at him.

"Take that man!"

The nearest guard moved to obey. Even as the man's hands gripped him, Daryn saw Gaylon stir. The youth turned his head, his eyes opened, and he witnessed the soldier jerk Daryn's staff from him.

"No! Don't!" the duke cried, too late.

A wind had been loosed in the chamber. In a whir of invisible motion it swept debris from the tabletops, extinguished candles, tore the tapestries from stone walls. The last of the servants ran screaming from the room.

His Stone bright upon his chest, Feydir shouted something against the rush of icy air, but the words were torn from his lips. The guard that held Daryn looked with amazement as the wind found him, tugging at his hair, his clothing. Beside him, the fireplace rumbled, a guttural noise deep in the throat of the chimney. The man wheeled, startled, and a wave of blue fire billowed out from the hearth to envelope him. He opened his mouth to scream and died then, his lungs filled with flame. Daryn stood alone now, untouched. The wind vanished as suddenly as it had appeared.

A foul greasy smoke filled the chamber and through it, the duke could see the throbbing light of two Sorcerer's Stones—Feydir's and Gaylon's. The two men faced each other across the room while the remaining guard stood cowed against a wall.

"Daryn!" the prince called, his eyes never leaving Feydir. "Stand clear!"

Cold foreboding filled the duke. He began to move slowly toward the door, but another figure darted in from the shadowed passageway. An arm caught the duke across the chin. Something cold was pressed to his throat.

"Be still!" Nankus hissed in Daryn's ear, dragging him to where Gaylon could better see them. Several more guards crept into the chamber.

There was triumph on Feydir's face. "Young sorcerer! Remove your ring or Gosney dies."

"No!" Daryn snapped. "I won't be your weakness!"

Nankus muzzled him with an arm, jerking his head back.

Out on the floor, Gaylon wavered. He needed time to think, but his head still pounded from the blow he'd taken. Nankus's knife pressed harder into Daryn's throat. A thin trickle of blood slid away from the blade.

Slowly the prince worked the ring from his finger. As it came free, the brilliant blue light in the Stone dimmed and failed.

"No," Daryn moaned.

Feydir crossed the chamber to Gaylon, hand out, a silk handkerchief laid across his palm. Numb, the prince set the ring in the cloth.

"A fine Stone," Feydir murmured, peering at it closely, then folded the cloth carefully over the ring. "How unfortunate it must be destroyed." He turned away. "Bind the boy."

"And this one?" Nankus asked, loosening his hold on Daryn.

"Bring him to the library. I must go to my rooms first, but I'll meet you there. The boy will be brought to me later."

Dazed, Gaylon watched Feydir leave the room, bearing the Stone away. Its loss left him empty and sick. He was only vaguely aware of Nankus's approach, of the nod the captain gave the guard that stood beside him. Something swung near the prince's head, a blur of movement on the periphery of his vision, and the butt of the halberd struck him again. White light exploded behind his eyes, and the ground dropped out from under him.

Awareness returned slowly, and when it did Gaylon found himself on the floor. Something heavy pressed into his back, a knee grinding against his spine. His arms were twisted cruelly behind him. It hardly mattered. He lay quietly while they bound him, his face pressed to the stone floor, the salty taste of blood in his mouth mixed with a sour defeat. Disaster and death. His thoughts whirled through a red haze of pain. Haddi was right, everything he touched withered and died. Even Jessmyn! Gaylon had seen the look of horror on Lucien's face when she'd taken up the wine. Without thought, he'd used his Stone to shatter the cup, but too late.

A boot caught Gaylon hard in the side, rolling him onto his back. The sharp agony filled him with helpless fury. Nankus stood over him, a death's head grin on his ugly noseless face.

"You know I'm the rightful heir to Wynnamyr," Gaylon said as calmly as possible. "Loose me, and I'll reward you."

Nankus laughed. "I can imagine how. No, I learned my lesson with you long ago, boy." The captain grabbed the front of the youth's jerkin, dragging his shoulders up from the floor. "You knifed Romy in the back, but you should never have left *me* alive. Now, I'll reward you for that murder." He drove his mailed fist against the side of Gaylon's face.

"Stop it!" Gaylon heard Daryn cry in some distant place. "He was only a child then! He was only protecting me!" But another blow fell and another.

* * * * *

"You know damn well what she took!" Lucien snarled in a hard, low voice. "You gave me the poison!" At the physician's look of dismay, he added, "If she dies, so will you—in a most unpleasant manner."

That promise was sufficient to send Girkin fleeing back down the passages to his apothecary. Lucien returned to stand by the bed. How pale Jessmyn was, her eyelids and lips a florid purple by contrast. He took up her hand. It was as cold as ice. Her fingers tightened over his until they threatened to crush bone. Another convulsion began. Her face contorted with pain, and he wept for her, bright tears welling from his pale blue eyes. Lucien felt no self-recrimination—this was Gaylon's fault, Feydir's, Girkin's, but certainly not his own. When the seizure ended he laid her hand down and raged through the chamber, vowing death and destruction to all those responsible should he lose her. The thought was untenable. Jessmyn moaned, and Lucien came to hold her hand again.

"My darling, my darling," he whispered anxiously.

Her eyelids fluttered open, and with difficulty she focused on him.

"How I love thee," she murmured, and he leaned close to better hear her words. Her fingers were tightening again even as she spoke. Her teeth clenched, the agony taking her once more, and she cried out. "Gaylon!"

Carefully Lucien pried her fingers loose from his own, straightening and turning away, his face gone hard. Girkin arrived finally, panting in his haste, a cup in his fat fingers.

"The antidote, Sire!"

The king eyed him coldly. "Give it to me."

"She must take the drink immediately!" the physician cried, but Lucien snatched the cup from his hands. Some of the precious liquid spilled to the floor. "Milord!"

"Leave," Lucien commanded. "Now!"

Swallowing words of protest, Girkin hurried fearfully from the chamber. Gently, the king placed the cup on a small table by the window. Without a backward glance, he went into the passageway, closing and locking the door behind him. The guards saluted, but he ignored them. As he started away, Lady Gerra rushed to him, going down to her knees on the cold stones.

"Sire!"

"The princess is dead," Lucien said calmly.

The woman began a high-pitched keening, and the king walked away, leaving her huddled on the floor.

* * * * *

The bit of parchment clutched in his fingers, Feydir waited impatiently in the library. He sat in an armchair, his back to the fireplace. At last! The mage touched the Stone at his breast, calming it, calming himself. Blast Nankus! What was taking him so long?

Finally the ambassador heard footsteps in the passage. From the doorway, Nankus inclined his head at Feydir, then stepped aside to let the duke enter. Daryn walked unaided. He'd not been restrained, but without his staff, his limp was pronounced. Even so, there was a strange dignity about him; his smoke-gray eyes met Feydir's without wavering. The ambassador resolved to use a gentle hand in this, at least in the beginning. Daryn the cripple, the sorcerer undone, would not be so easily broken.

"I don't know the circumstances concerning the loss of your Stone," Feydir said mildly, "but it would appear you fought a braver battle than young Gaylon. No doubt your suffering has been great. I promise you, it will soon be ended."

Daryn's face remained impassive, and Feydir went on. "You know, of course, why you are here." He held out the parchment with its riddle for the duke to see. "I'll have Orym's Legacy before this night is done, whatever else may happen."

The ambassador unrolled the paper and read:

"When royal blood has turned to rust,
So then does gold become as dust.
The king's bane is the sorcerer's lot.
What is not, is—what is, is not."

Feydir looked up. "Can you tell me what it means?"

"It means only that the sword is ensorcelled," Daryn answered readily, "that it does not appear as anything but an ancient, decrepit weapon."

"So, it is as I thought, " murmured Feydir, nodding. This was all too easy. "You hid it well, Daryn of Gosney. Will you tell me now where I may find Kingslayer?"

Daryn's eyes flickered in Nankus's direction, then back to Feydir. "I'll give you what you want, if you'll grant me one boon."

Feydir leaned forward in the chair, resting an elbow on one knee. "And that is?"

"Do what you please with me, but let the boy go. He has no knowledge of the sword."

"That I do not believe."

"It's truth, and without his Stone, he can't harm you. Exile him—only let him live."

There was a quiet passion in that soft-spoken voice, Feydir thought. He shook his head. "You would condemn him to suffer as you have? His powers are much greater than yours, and so his grief will be greater with the loss of his Stone. Better a kind death."

"He's young, he'll forget—"

"Do you truly believe that?" Feydir asked, lifting a thin dark brow. Daryn's silence was answer enough. "No. Gaylon Reysson came here tonight for only one reason—to take up Kingslayer against me. The only boon I'll grant you is a painless death for the prince and yourself. Now, tell me where the sword is."

Daryn's gaze drifted to the patterned rug beneath his feet. "I will never give it to you."

"Enough!" growled Feydir, his patience at an end. He snapped his fingers at Nankus. "Bring the boy!" After the captain had gone, he turned on Daryn again. "When I've done with Gaylon Reysson, he'll beg you to give me the weapon."

They were alone in the chamber. The duke's head was bowed, and Feydir watched the shadows thrown by the firelight shifting over the bookshelves, the tapestries. A sound in the hall made both men look expectantly at the open doorway. It was Lucien. He leaned heavily against the door frame a moment, then took two graceless steps into the room.

"Your Highness," Feydir said, but didn't rise from his seat.

"She's dead," Lucien said, his sibilants softly slurred. "The princess is dead."

The ambassador's fingers gripped the arms of the chair, and his face grew livid. "See what your meddling has cost us! Her father arrives tomorrow."

"He'll attend her funeral rather than her wedding," Lucien said callously. His eyes were on Daryn now.

"You're drunk." Feydir settled back in disgust.

"I am most definitely drunk," the king admitted. His loose-jointed steps took him in a wide circle around the duke. Daryn watched him without expression.

"Your presence here is not required," Feydir told his nephew firmly. "You're free to go and mourn in private."

"I am king!" Lucien barked. "I'll mourn where it pleases me!" His fingers fumbled at the hilt of his sword, and he drew it, the steel hissing as it cleared the scabbard.

"What are you doing?" Feydir demanded, coming to his feet. His Stone flared to life.

Lucien, oblivious, paused before Daryn. "It *is* the duke of Gosney," he said with wonder. "But so changed . . . Shall I finish what I began these many years past?" The blade flickered, and the point came to rest on the breast of Daryn's robes.

"Get back, you fool!" Feydir cried, his fingers going to the Stone.

There was no fear in the duke's eyes, only insolence and invitation. "Yes," Daryn said suddenly. "Fool!"

He wants to die, thought Lucien as he shoved the blade home. From the doorway came a wail of anguish, and from his uncle, a shout of rage. Lucien paid no attention. Daryn's life, pinned like a bright butterfly on the sword, quivered up the steel. It brought an ecstasy Lucien had never known. A brief moment of pain crossed the duke's face, then his knees gave way and he crumpled slowly. The life fled his body.

A memory flared in Lucien's mind as he became aware of the sound of mourning in the room. Gaylon had torn free of his guards and crouched beside the body, weeping. Reflexively Lucien drew the blade from Daryn's heart and turned it on the prince, but Nankus's gloved hand caught his wrist in an iron grip and wrenched the sword from his fingers.

Feydir, his face black with fury, clutched his Stone, ready to strike. Oddly Lucien began to laugh. Then the king reached down to put his thumb in the warm blood pooling on the carpet and with it drew a scarlet streak across his own forehead.

"You're mad!" his uncle raged.

"Mad enough that I know where Kingslayer is hidden." Lucien widened his blue eyes. He'd gotten Feydir's full attention now. "I saw Daryn the night I found the riddle in his chambers—"

"I've searched those rooms; I've searched the entire keep!"

"It's not *in* the keep, Uncle."

"Where? Where is my sword?"

Lucien laughed again. "Not so quickly! I'll bring it to you, but I want a thing in return."

Feydir's hand came away slowly from his pendant. "What?"

"Give me Gaylon, to do with as I please."

Feydir smiled wryly. "Your request is not unreasonable. *But*, know this, Nephew: if you fail to deliver Orym's Legacy, you are forfeit."

Those words brought a sober light to Lucien's eyes. "How so?"

"For Daryn's premature death, you'll lose something dear to you—a thing of my choosing."

Lucien swallowed, but he nodded. "Agreed." He snapped his fingers at one of the guards standing over Gaylon. "You! I'll want your help."

The fellow looked to Nankus, and his noseless captain, nodding slightly, gave his consent.

"I will have back my sword, Captain." Lucien put out his hand, and with reluctance the weapon was returned. The king swung the blade quickly in the prince's direction, grinning as his uncle tensed, but he only tapped the youth on a shoulder with the blade. Gaylon looked up, his face streaked with blood and tears.

"I'll come for you . . . soon," the king told him, hoping to see fear. The youth only looked bewildered. With a sigh,

Lucien departed on his search for Kingslayer, the lone guard in tow.

Gaylon struggled when he was dragged back from Daryn's body, and Nankus stilled the prince with a brutal kick. His thoughts racing, Feydir took his seat again and surveyed the scene. It was obvious from Gaylon's bloodied face that Nankus had been taking vindictive liberties. And Lucien! The ambassador decided Lucien would be forfeit in any case. Once Kingslayer was recovered, the ambassador would no longer need to hide behind a puppet king. Nankus would be severely reprimanded, but Lucien would die. Yes, his nephew had at last outlived his usefulness.

"Captain, you may take the prince to the dungeon," Feydir said at last. As Nankus moved to obey, he added, "You will not mistreat him further. Should Lucien fail, I'll need the boy with his wits about him. Is that clear?"

"Yes, Your Lordship," Nankus replied, but there was an angry edge to his voice.

"First, remove the body." The ambassador motioned to Daryn's corpse. "Take the rug, as well. It's soiled."

Seventeen

The dreams were sweet and vivid, but short, a seeming moment's respite before the pain returned. Soon her muscles would be strung tight, her stomach turned to stone. Ages passed while Jessmyn lay in that helpless, rigid agony, then suddenly, it would be gone and she would dream again. In those dreams she found Gaylon, sometimes the indulgent boy of ten, sometimes the young man with the lute beside the river.

Another spasm came and went, but this time, before the princess could fall into exhausted sleep, gentle fingers caressed her face. Someone called her name softly, and she opened her eyes on darkness, a filmy night through which a shadowy figure moved. A hand slipped beneath her neck and lifted her head from the pillows, then something warm and foul tasting poured into her mouth. Jessmyn choked on the first swallow, but the liquid flooding over her tongue brought relief from a terrible thirst of which she'd only been dimly aware. She gulped the rest eagerly and licked her lips, searching blindly for more. The cup was gone, but the voice that had called her name remained to whisper fierce encouragement when her body stiffened again and her teeth clenched.

She was given water afterward, cool and sweet, and she wept when the cup was taken from her.

"Hush, now, hush," came the voice. The fingers touched Jessmyn's face again, stroking, soothing. She slept, and it seemed this dream was longer, the next bout of pain of less duration. Insinuated throughout came that kindly voice, cooing, coaxing, caring.

* * * * *

The prince's last words with Daryn had been angry ones. He remembered the argument over his returning to the keep and all his foolish boasts, all the bitter things he'd said. He could never take back those words now. Daryn was gone, and the pain Gaylon felt inside was far worse than any of the physical punishment he'd been dealt.

Hot tears blinded the youth, and he stumbled, going to his knees on the step. Only the guard's grip on his arm kept him from falling all the long way down the narrow stairs. With vile curses, the man beat him verbally for his clumsiness; they dared not hurt him. No man had struck him since Feydir's command, but neither had they been gentle. He was jerked to his feet, forced to move on, downward into the bowels of the keep.

When Gaylon had lived in the keep as a child, the dungeons had been all but empty. Under Lucien's reign, they had become a labyrinth of misery and despair. Even now, in the dead of night, voices could be heard, some begging, others weeping, many only moaning quietly in dark corners. The stench was beyond description, death and corruption wafting from every passageway. A charnel house couldn't reek as did this place. Gaylon's senses were dulled with the loss of his Stone, but still the smells, the sounds assailed him.

They came at last into a cavernous chamber where the smoking torches on the far walls cast only a fitful light through the murk. Gaylon kept his eyes to the straw-littered floor under his feet, refusing to see the evil machinery that lined the room. Nankus had arrived before the prince and his guard and was already in earnest conversation with the master of the dungeon.

"He's not to be touched," Nankus related sourly, "but he'll have no food or water, or I'll have your head, Rum."

"Aye," the master acknowledged, an odd little man, deathly

pale and thin to emaciation. He grinned up into the captain's face. "Yer a most fortunate man, sir. Thirteen's come empty only this very night." He came to leer at Gaylon, prodding him with a stiff finger. "Had a bit a fun wid him already, I see."

"Watch your tongue, old man," Nankus growled. "The one in number four. Is he still there?"

"Wot's left of him," said Rum, chuckling. He turned to feed the fire in a great pit hollowed from the stone floor.

"Bring him," the captain said shortly to the guard, and Gaylon was shoved toward the mouth of one of the many corridors that led mazelike from the main chamber. They had walked only a short way when Nankus halted before a heavy oaken door. He pulled a rush light from the wall and tossed it into the cell through a small barred opening. From within there came a startled grunt. Nankus caught Gaylon by an elbow and slammed him up against the door, forcing his face to the bars.

"Look!" he commanded. "Do you recognize him? He was Dasser, your father's head councilman." The captain leaned close to murmur in the prince's ear. "It's amazing how much a man can endure, how much of his body can be cut and burned away and still he goes on living. Such torture is an art, and Rum's an artist. I can only hope you'll live to see him work." Gaylon mumbled under his breath, and Nankus pulled the boy around to better hear him. "What's that you say?"

"You're a pig, Nankus."

The captain raised a fist, then thought better of it. He turned suddenly and struck the guard a blow that sent him staggering. The soldier had been grinning behind his back. In his cell, the thing that had once been Dasser began a gleeful inhuman howling and was answered from all sides until the catacombs echoed with an insane screeching. The noise brought the master at a run.

"How you love to stir 'em up, damn yer eyes!" he cried at Nankus over the clamor. "The lad's in my charge now, so get out of my dungeon!" Then he struck a club against Dasser's door. "Shut up in there!"

The captain, smiling tightly, strode back down the tunnel with the guard at his heels.

* * * * *

The night had gone strange. Outside, the air was warm and wet without the slightest breeze to stir it. Lucien tilted back his head to look at the sky. The stars were obscured by sooty black clouds, so low he thought he could touch them by only reaching up a hand. Deep within those clouds fingers of blue lightning probed, but no thunder followed.

Sweat trickled in the hollow of Lucien's chest, soaking the front of his shirt. It beaded his face, and he wiped the moisture away impatiently, then signaled the guard to lead the way into the cairn. The whites of the soldier's eyes glinted in the torchlight, and he stank of fear. Superstitious idiot! Lucien thought. But the man's fear of the king was apparently greater than his fear of the night spirits for he only hesitated briefly before he carried himself and the torch through the portal.

Lucien gave the urn of ashes beside the door the barest glance as he entered. He disdained Wynnamyrian custom—the streak of Daryn's blood on his forehead was the only offering he would give the old bones in this burial mound. Girkin had said that somewhere within this cairn Daryn's mother, Edonna, lay. What better place to hide Kingslayer? It *was* here! He'd never felt so sure of anything.

The soldier paused on the stair. Lucien glanced one last time out into the night, then turned and began his descent into the tomb of the Dark Kings.

* * * * *

The child slept easily now. Misk rose from the edge of the bed and went to sit wearily at the open window. She tasted the air, thick with moisture, heavy with the scent of roses, and searched the dark with her inhuman vision. Sezran had come for Kingslayer, but the blade was still ensorcelled, hidden from him. Until someone woke the sword, the wizard could only guess at its location.

Her brother was somewhere in the night, waiting. This was his storm, ominous and black, held in check by his will alone.

Misk could feel his energy around her, building, growing, and soon it would be loosed. The thought terrified her. The game was drawing to an end, and she, for all her manipulation, for all her movement along the lines of time, couldn't call the victor. Sezran had been right about Gaylon. The prince was an unknown element. His instability might well be the ruin of them all. Would he take up Kingslayer, and if he did, how would he use it? But the boy could die before ever he had the chance. . . .

She heard the muted weeping near the bed and knew it was her own voice—rather, the voice of a Misk who'd come too late to save the child, who cried bitter tears over a dead princess.

"Nanny?" Jessmyn had awakened. "Why do you weep?"

Misk went quickly to the bed, fighting to dispel the image of that other self. Jessmyn blinked in confusion as she beheld two similar figures before her. Then there was only the one smiling down on her.

"Nanny?" she said again.

"Yes, my darling."

The child's eyelids began to flutter, and she sank back into sleep. Misk shook her gently.

"Jessmyn, you must wake now. Time grows short."

The girl roused. "I'm so tired," she murmured dreamily. "So very . . . tired."

"I know, sweet child. It's so much to ask of you. But my powers weaken. I'll not be able to remain with you much longer."

The princess opened her eyes and looked around her. "This is the king's chamber. . . . How did we come here, Nanny? Where's my lord?"

"Ask no questions, but listen well, Jessmyn. I shall try to be clear, but it's . . . difficult for me. Gaylon has come to claim his crown. Lucien has vowed his death, and even now the prince lies in the dungeons below us. They've taken his Stone and done him hurt. Daryn already lies dead by Lucien's hand, and you were left to die from the poison he had intended for Gaylon—"

"That can't be true!" cried Jessmyn, and her eyes glittered

angrily. "The king is kind. He's—"

"Hush!" Misk snapped. "Lucien is evil itself. You've been sheltered from that part of him. By Feydir's spell you were made to forget your love of Gaylon. Remember it now, for to you is given the task of saving him."

"No . . . I can't."

"Listen! He'll die if you don't help him, but *your* fate will be far worse. You must find his Stone and return it to him."

"Nanny, please! What you ask of me is impossible. I wouldn't know how to begin. I'm only . . ."

"A girl?" Misk demanded harshly, then her expression softened and there was pity on her narrow face. "My darling. My poor, poor dear. So much has been taken from you." She picked up Jessmyn's thin hands in her own. "There was a little girl once who stole her cousin's wooden sword and spent whole afternoons practicing with it. At only five, she mounted the king's horse by climbing barefoot up the animal's leg as if it were a tree."

Jessmyn looked at the little woman in wonder and smiled wistfully. "Remy was such a gentle horse, but what a scolding I received." The smile faded. "Somehow I lost that part of me."

"It was stolen, darling, but you've got to find it again, or all is lost." A mad light had come into the old woman's dark eyes. "My strength fails," she said with desperation. "And he comes! He makes his bid for the sword. Go quickly, child! I'll hold my brother as long as possible. Gaylon must take up the sword!" She began to diminish, as if she were rushing backward into the distance. "In Feydir's room, the Stone is there. Beware!" Misk cried, voice dwindling. "Do not touch it . . ." She was only a pinpoint of light, then even that winked out.

In disbelief, Jessmyn looked around her.

"How will I take it if I may not touch it?" she asked the empty room. "And what sword do you speak of? Where shall I find Gaylon?" Against her will, tears began to flow. "Nanny, please! I can't do this alone!"

* * * * *

Lucien stood back with the torch as the guard put his shoulder to the lid of the sarcophagus. The man threw his weight against it, and the lid gave slightly with a sound of grinding, stone on stone. The torch guttered suddenly, nearly going out, and both men froze, hardly daring to breath.

Whatever the weather outside, here in the cairn it was cold. Throûghout the search, Lucien had felt an eerie sense of unwelcome, but at last they'd come to an opening over which the Gosney coat of arms was carved. It had led them to this tiny chamber with a single stone coffin.

"Again," Lucien ordered as the light steadied. The soldier pushed once more, groaning under the strain. The lid gave way of a sudden, sliding aside, and for a moment it teetered on the far edge of the coffin before going all the way over to shatter with a resounding crash on the stone floor. The sweet odor of violets filled the winter chamber like a gust of spring wind.

"Milord!" the guard said breathlessly. "A sword!"

There, laid carefully alongside the small skeleton of a woman, was an ancient two-edged sword in a broad leather scabbard. Bits of colored cloth and desiccated flesh still clung to the bones in the coffin, long strands of black hair trailed from the skull. While the soldier's attention was still on the sword, Lucien drew his dagger silently and stepped closer, throwing the light of the torch into his victim's eyes. The king stabbed him, one neat thrust along the spine, then gave the blade a quarter turn to tear the heart.

The man gasped once and fell dead across the rim of the coffin. Lucien jerked the knife free and pushed the body out of his way. No one would report back to Nankus or his uncle. He took hold of the rusted sword and tried to lift it, but a skeletal hand was wrapped tightly around the hilt. Leaning forward, he pried at the fingers, but they seemed fused to the grip. An angry frustration surged through the king, and he propped the torch against the stone in order to grasp the weapon with both hands.

The torch fluttered madly, and as the shadows streamed around him, Lucien clearly heard a woman's voice say, "Kingslayer, avenge my son!" Then the bone fingers opened from the hilt. The king grabbed both weapon and torch and fled the cairn.

* * * * *

A great sense of urgency pulled at Jessmyn now, and though her muscles ached with every move, she kicked back the covers and slid to the floor. Her tears had been brief. If Gaylon's life depended on her, then she must do everything in her power to save him. A sudden dizziness swept over her. The princess leaned against the bed and realized that she was dressed only in a camisole and petticoats. Her gown and shoes were gone, nowhere to be found in the chamber.

The door to the passage was locked, and there were voices outside. Jessmyn put an ear to the wood. Soldiers, standing guard. But she knew of another way out, one that even led to the lowest levels of the keep; as children, she and Gaylon had explored the secret stairwell to the king's apartments. Clothing would have to come first, though.

Items were chosen from the king's own wardrobe, all of them far too large. Still, the cuffs of the shirt buttoned tight enough to free her hands, and the breeches were secured with a sash. Her feet swam in Lucien's shoes, and Jessmyn soon resigned herself to going on this venture barefoot. She tied back her hair with a thong—hardly neat but it kept the thick mass of curls from falling in her face. Her final act was to choose a small jeweled dirk in an embroidered sheath.

With the donning of the weapon, a strange confidence came over her. For the first time, her feeling of helplessness was dispelled. Now, along with the fear came a fierce excitement, an odd energy.

The key to the bolt-hole lay hidden in a niche behind the drape-shrouded wall. She unlocked the door and let herself into the stairwell. The way was pitch black, but a hand on the left wall and sensitive feet on the steps were enough to guide the princess. On the first landing, she felt for a depression in the stones and, finding the lever, released the door. It opened slowly, grinding across the flags.

Jessmyn ducked through the low opening into the bushes along the wall of the southwest wing, below Feydir's upper-story apartments. Though pebbles and sticks bruised her feet, she crept between the shrubs, searching for the proper windows. High above her, the wind sang in the treetops and strange blue lightning lit her way.

* * * * *

A wind came to buffet Lucien as he made his way back to the keep. It seemed the clouds did battle now. The lightning ran dazzling through them with thunder rolling violently behind. The sword sat heavy in his hands. It truly was Orym's Legacy. Even his untrained senses felt faintly the power that emanated from the weapon, and with each streak of lightning, Kingslayer seemed to twist in his fingers as if it meant to break free and answer some beckoning call.

He neared the bolt-hole entrance to his chambers. Around him, the wind howled, storming the castle walls, circling the keep in search of a weak point on which to concentrate its assault. Every chink, every loose stone whistled or wailed, producing a cacophony of sounds. The gusts whipped the king's hair about his face, tore at the sword and the torch, and he fought back a rising apprehension. The wind seemed alive.

The bolt-hole door stood open, and he paused within, uncertain, then took the stairs three at a time to his rooms. The upper door was also open, and Jessmyn was gone. He found the cup with the antidote empty on the table, and clutched it to him, torn between anger and relief. His love for her still brought anguish, but Kingslayer lay heavy in his hand. After extinguishing the torch in a washbasin, Lucien went to search Feydir's chambers. A servant had told him that his uncle had gone to his rooms before heading to the library. That would be the likeliest place for the ambassador to put the ring he'd taken from the prince. If Kingslayer would answer only to one who bore a Sorcerer's Stone, then Lucien would take Gaylon's. The irony in that pleased him.

* * * * *

An ancient grapevine grew espaliered on the wall below Feydir's balcony. Its gnarled vines would never have supported a man's weight, but they held Jessmyn's. Using toes as well as fingers, she climbed the wall to slide finally over the stone balustrade. The wind swept in gusts around her while she crouched panting, her limbs weak and quivering. A single candle lit the room that led out onto the balcony. The windows of the rooms on either side were dark. Jessmyn pried the tall glass windows open with the dirk, then moved inside silently for fear the gaunt ambassador slept in one of the darkened rooms.

Unlike his nephew's sumptuous chambers, Feydir's apartments appeared meagerly furnished. The princess had entered the main sitting room, which held only a desk, some straight chairs, and several small statues. No fire burned on the hearth. She searched the desk first, not entirely certain what she sought. The only Sorcerer's Stone she'd ever seen was Feydir's, and Gaylon had not been wearing a chain or pendant around his neck. The drawers of the desk were locked and seemed impervious to the dirk. Frustrated, she gouged at the wood. That sense of urgency came again, doubly strong. The Stone. Where could it be?

A sudden noise off to the right made her jump: the sound of metal on metal, a key inserted in the lock on the passageway door. In panic, she froze, then a glint of blue from the desktop caught her eye. There, in a small porcelain bowl, was a gold ring set with a coarse gray stone. The key turned in the lock with a click. She snatched up the ring without thinking, and as her bare fingers touched the Stone it flared a brilliant blue-white.

Fire and ice ran through her. In her mind came a jumble of images of Gaylon and surges of agony, desire, fear, hate. The door opened. Ignoring her inner turmoil, the princess jammed the ring onto her thumb and raced to the balcony. In her haste, she lost her footing and fell. The vines tore at her face and clothing, but Jessmyn struck the ground running.

She found the small opening in the wall behind the bushes

and slipped inside to stand a moment, gasping for air, shaking with fright. The Stone on her thumb pulsed with a soft blue light, matching the rapid beat of her heart.

With its pale light to show her the way, the girl took the stairs into the depths of the keep. They had been built for only one purpose—to grant the king escape should he ever need it. Another landing led out into the wine cellars. Here the air was heavy with the sour, vinegar smell of grape pressings. She went quickly past, led by a more ominous smell—the stink of death and sickness.

What Misk had asked her to do frightened Jessmyn, but Gaylon's Stone soon began to frighten her more. The Stone tolerated her closeness because it sensed the almost magical bond that had been formed long ago between the prince and princess. That tolerance had limits though. She could not use the Stone's powers and could only accept this tenuous link with it. How this information was imparted to her, Jessmyn didn't know, except her thoughts were not entirely her own now. Long forgotten memories came in bright flashes, of she and Gaylon as children. There were darker remembrances of death, blood, and fire at the lodge when King Reys had died—and later, on a snowy mountainside, of the prince performing silent murder with a small dirk much like the one she carried tonight. His rage and hatred were overpowering. Sickened by those thoughts, the princess continued to move downward.

The stair deposited Jessmyn in a huge chamber nearly twice the size of the great hall on the first floor of the keep. A fire glowed in a pit near the center of the room, silhouetting the man that sat before it. She knew she must somehow gain the other side, but a thread of doubt wound its way around her heart. There were tunnels leading away from the chamber in all directions, hundreds of cells along them. She had no idea where to begin her search for the prince.

"Rum!"

The shout boomed hollowly through the chamber. The man at the fire leaped agilely to his feet and watched a tall figure crossing the floor to him. The voice was Nankus's, and Jessmyn stepped swiftly back into the deeper shadows of the staircase, guarding the faint light of the Stone with her hand. The two men spoke for a time in low voices, then, together, they set off toward one of the passages.

Without hesitation, Jessmyn followed, crossing the floor at a crouching run, her bare feet making little sound on the stones. Her quarry had just rounded a curve in the tunnel as she entered. The princess slowed her pace and moved with caution now. In one hand, the dirk was bared, held ready in a small fist. Voices drifted back to her along the walls.

"Lord Feydir will do the questioning," Nankus said. "He's impatient of the king's return. You need only ply your trade, Rum."

"Ya needn't tell me my duty, Captain," the other man answered shortly. "We've worked together often enough, his lordship and me. He trusts my skills."

Beyond the curve, another tunnel cut across the one in which Jessmyn stood. The voices stilled, and she heard her feet shuffling in the straw. That brought her to a halt out of fear that the captain and Rum may have heard her steps as well. Undecided, she remained motionless, listening. Except for the crackle of the rush lights along the walls, the passageway was quiet. Without the two men's voices to guide her, the princess had no idea which direction to take.

Finally, the inaction grating on her, Jessmyn chose to go right. With her first step past the corner, a gloved hand shot out to grab the wrist that held the knife. She gasped, looking up into Nankus's scarred face. His surprise seemed no less than hers.

"By the Unholy One! What's this? Have I trapped a ghost?" The captain frowned. "The king reported you dead of poison, but you feel very much alive to me. Milady, this is most importunate. Why have you come here, and so oddly dressed?"

"Loose me!" she cried and tried to pull away. Her struggles only made Nankus laugh.

"I think not." He jerked the princess to him, his free arm catching her about the waist. She swung at him with her other hand, the fist doubled. The ring on her thumb caught him across the cheek, and the Stone touched bare flesh. It flared, blinding them both momentarily. Nankus shrieked in pain, and the stench of burned skin filled Jessmyn's nostrils. He'd lost his grip on her knife hand, and she struck, but his cuirass deflected the blade. The captain flailed in an attempt to trap her wrists, and desperate, the princess slashed again, aiming higher. This time, the dirk found his throat and sank deep. Staggering away, Nankus pressed his fingers to his neck, blood pumping freely between them.

"Milady," he gasped, then fell back against a wall and toppled to the straw with a dull clank of armor.

Blade ready, Jessmyn spun on the little man standing by a cell door.

"Please, milady!" he cried. "Put away the knife before you do yourself hurt."

"It's you I'll hurt," she answered grimly, "if you don't stand fast."

"I stand! See? Ol' Rum don't move." But his fear seemed mock. A sly gleam lit the coal-black eyes.

"Where is the prince?" she demanded.

"Why, right here, milady." Rum patted the door with a hand.

"Free him."

"With pleasure, milady." He drew an iron ring from his belt and worked the single key into the lock. The mechanism was rusty, complaining as it gave way. Rum pushed the door inward, smiling.

The commotion outside his cell seemed to have held no interest for Gaylon. He sat in a corner with his back to the wall, knees drawn up, his forehead resting on them. The light from the corridor fell across him, and he made no move. Wary of Rum, Jessmyn moved into the doorway.

"Gaylon?" she said softly.

The young man looked up finally, and the hopelessness on his bloodied, swollen face hurt her. Jessmyn almost went to him, but her distrust of Rum held her back.

"Bring him out," she ordered the little man. "Be gentle, I warn you."

"Of course, of course."

Mumbling still, Rum entered the small chamber. He caught Gaylon by an elbow and, pulling him upright, brought the prince to Jessmyn. Even in the cell, they'd left him cruelly bound. The princess used the dirk to cut the cords and saw that he'd rubbed his wrist raw trying to free himself. The young man stared at his hands a long moment, then raised his eyes to her face. His brow furrowed.

"Don't you know me, Gaylon?"

"Jessmyn," he said dully, but his uncertainty frightened her.

"I've brought your Stone." She slipped the ring from her thumb and held it out to him. At its master's touch, the Stone flared to life. The princess watched him place it on his finger and felt a strange emptiness. That was soon forgotten, though, for the light had come back to Gaylon's eyes.

With the princess's attention elsewhere, the master of the dungeons had slipped to Nankus's still form and quietly pulled the dead man's sword. Now he came at her and the prince with only his quick footsteps as warning. Gaylon whirled, flinging up his ringed hand, and blue fire erupted from the Stone. The heat drove Jessmyn back. She covered her face with her arms, and when she dared to look again, Rum was white ashes on the stones.

"Come!" said Gaylon, his voice harsh from the foul smoke. "Stay close behind me!"

The princess followed him down the passageway, out into the main chamber. Just beyond the mouth of the tunnel, Gaylon slid to a sudden halt and threw out an arm to catch her. Jessmyn followed his gaze. Across the great room, Feydir stood with dark-robed arms crossed before him, his Stone blue-white upon his breast. The eerie glow from the Stone underlit his cruel face, and at the sight a chill swept through Jessmyn.

"If we do battle," the gaunt man called out to them, "the princess will die. I wish her no hurt. Send her away, Gaylon Reysson."

"Go, Jessmyn," the prince said quietly, urgently. "Go as far from this place as you can."

"I won't leave you," she answered, fighting a quaver in her throat.

"Uncle!"

At the voice, Jessmyn peered across the chamber and found Lucien, pale-haired and handsome in the torchlight. He stood on the edge of the main stair, a two-edged sword in his hands. For a moment his eyes came to rest on Jessmyn, then he looked away.

Feydir glanced behind him, then turned back to Gaylon. "You are lost, Red Prince. Bring me the sword, Nephew!"

Lucien descended the stair and crossed the chamber, smiling, the ancient rusting sword held out to his uncle. But as Feydir reached take it, his nephew made a sudden grab for the gold chain at the wizard's throat. The king jerked the Stone free and leaped away to the center of the room.

"Lucien!" Feydir screamed, then the ambassador began to change. His stature grew shrunken and old, and he moved as if feeble. "Lucien," he repeated, this time with forced calm. "Think what you do, Nephew. The Stone will not answer to you. If you touch it, the power will kill you. Please! It's of no use to you. Give the Stone to me, give them both to me, and I'll make you a monarch over an entire world!"

"No! I'll destroy you." Lucien's voice trembled with excitement, then he shouted, "I'll destroy you *all*!" He wrapped the chain around the hilt of Kingslayer and pulled it taut, drawing the Stone toward the grip. "First you, dear uncle!"

Feydir took two faltering steps toward the king, but Lucien backed away. The Stone touched the Kingslayer's hilt, and sparks flashed across the point of contact, blue and green. A deep vibration began, and with a hum of power, Kingslayer awoke in Lucien's hand. He stared in wonder at the golden weapon, dazzled by the fiery gems caught in the black stone at the center of the hilt. Laughing, he watched as blue fire ran the edge of the blade, over the tip, and back to the hilt.

"Gaylon!" Feydir cried. "I implore you. Stop him. Use your Stone!"

But the prince stood frozen, as mesmerized by the sword as Lucien.

Feydir turned to run, and Lucien brought up the weapon, pointing the tip at the man. A flash of radiant energy discharged from the blade, striking Feydir full on. The ambassador flung his arms in the air and vanished with only a last shriek to mark his passing. A terrible heat washed over the onlookers, and around them, the room seemed to erupt. The stones heaved under Gaylon's feet, and he staggered against Jessmyn, fighting to stay upright. It seemed the entire castle shuddered with the force. Thunder rolled through the chamber, beating in waves against their ears, and a wall near one tunnel collapsed, great blocks of granite tumbling to the ground.

Gaylon caught the princess in his arms to steady her until the ground finally stilled. Dust drifted on the air and, except for muted whimpers coming from the tunnels, all was quiet. At the center of the floor Lucien stood silent, the sword in his hands humming lightly. Red light flickered up from the fire pit, staining the king's pale hair rufous. His eyes gleamed a murderous blue as he smiled, his gaze coming to rest on the prince.

"Run, Jessmyn!" Gaylon flung her back toward the mouth of the tunnel a short distance behind them.

"No!" cried Lucien. "Wait!"

The king's voice had changed. The princess halted as the fair man stepped around the pit. With the red flames of the fire behind him, his face altered. His smile seemed sweet, his eyes warm and sane.

"Jessmyn, please. I never wished you harm. The poison was an accident. Forgive me." His tone was persuasive, but they both heard the sly intent in Lucien's next words. "Come to me, dear heart."

"Don't listen to him, Jess!" Gaylon shouted.

Lucien turned his eyes on the tall youth, his face serene, and said gently, "Do you tire of life so soon, my Prince? Keep silent, and you may breath yet a while longer." He looked again at Jessmyn. "I have loved you so long, wanted you so long. Come to me now, and I'll let Gaylon live."

Her fear and hatred carefully hidden, the princess stared at the man. She would bargain, if only to gain a little time. "Do you swear to let the prince live?" she demanded and braved a step forward.

"No!" Gaylon screamed and struck at Lucien with his Stone. In a move too swift to follow, Kingslayer swept up to parry the blow. The golden blade flared, and the sword roared as it absorbed the energy, then slipped back into a contented rumbling.

Lucien laughed pleasantly. "You don't understand, do you, my Prince? You're helpless in this, just as helpless as you once were in the dreams my uncle sent you. Do you remember Jessmyn in them? How I touched her?" He moistened his lips with his tongue. "You'll watch again, now."

The king looked at the princess. "How long I've waited for you, offered my cheek for your chaste little kisses when it was more than I could bear to keep my hands from you. Now I know I'll never have your love . . . but I'll have everything else."

Jessmyn trembled as Lucien spoke. The man terrified her, but she would never again give up the power over her life that she had gained. Turning slightly to conceal her motions, the princess pulled the little dirk from its sheath and hid the blade behind her.

"You will not be sorry," the king told her. "My skills are great. I'll pleasure you with pain so exquisite you'll beg for more. Ask Marcel. She'll tell you. In time you'll do anything I ask. Make your choice, dear heart. Come to me willingly, and the prince may live."

With what courage she could gather, the princess stepped toward Lucien, knife ready. Gaylon must have seen a flicker of light on the blade as she moved past, for he rushed to stop her.

"No, Jess," he said desperately and caught her in strong arms. The dirk fell with a clatter to the stone flagging.

"How quaint," snarled Lucien, his eyes first on the knife, then on the prince and princess. "You may die together."

Kingslayer was raised once more, it's song growing strident. There was nowhere to run, so Gaylon threw himself forward the short distance across the floor. Lucien struck at his head with the sword, and the prince ducked under the blade. His hands closed over the pommel, dangerously near Feydir's Stone.

Hot energy surged through Gaylon—Orym's dark power combined with that from Feydir's Stone. The prince's own Stone flared blindingly bright, and Kingslayer's hum spiraled into an ear-shattering pitch. Lucien wrenched at the sword, at the same instant driving a knee hard into Gaylon's side. Agony shot through the youth, but still he hung doggedly on. They grappled on the edge of the fire pit, the sword between them throwing bright sparks in the charged air.

"Kingslayer!" Gaylon cried breathlessly. "Obey me!"

Through the pain and fear, the prince felt the sword answer, felt its confusion at the pull of two Stones. Eyes closed, Gaylon whispered fiercely, "I am heir of the Red Kings and your master. Destroy my enemy, Kingslayer!"

In the combatants' hands the weapon squalled suddenly. Blue fire arced toward the ceiling, then was sucked back again. Next, cobalt flame raced the edge of the blade and circled the tip. Both men watched, frozen.

The fire returned to the hilt, and this time didn't stop. As it flowed over their hands, Lucien screamed; horrid burning pain wrung a strangled shriek from Gaylon. The prince tried to open his fingers and found them welded to the grip. The flames crawled onto his wrists. In agony, Gaylon sought the power of his Stone, melded now with Kingslayer. The little Stone answered just long enough for him to loose his hands and tumble away. The fire snapped back to the hilt and leaped higher up Lucien's arms.

The king's face contorted into a mask of horror and pain. Swiftly the blue flames spread to his head and down his body and legs. He staggered away, his shrieks joined with Kingslayer's deadly song of power. The flesh melted from bone like wax, then dripped burning to the floor and was consumed. Lucien's anguished screams were echoed long after his end by the terrified wails of the prisoners trapped in their cells.

Her back to the wall, Jessmyn felt pain shoot through her hand and realized she had sunk her teeth into the flesh to bridle her own cries. Gaylon climbed wearily to his feet and came toward the princess. His hands were blistered and red, his eyes glazed. The clamor of the prisoners faded slowly to silence.

"Gaylon," came a gentle voice. Jessmyn looked up and found Nanny Arcana in her long flowing skirts only a pace from them. Gaylon's face contorted with grief, and he went to the tiny woman. Jessmyn stood alone now, watching them.

"Oh, Misk," the prince said brokenly. "Daryn's dead."

"I know, child." She took him by the arm and led him to Orym's Legacy. "The sword is yours."

"I don't want it," he muttered dully, staring down at Kingslayer. Lucien's fleshless fingers still gripped the hilt. Feydir's Stone had fallen aside, the gold chain melted and fused.

"You must have it all the same," Misk said. "You have your kingdom. Now, take up Kingslayer." She drew his blistered hand close to the pommel before releasing him, then stood back. An infinite sadness had filled the tiny woman's face.

Gaylon's fingers trembled only a short distance from the grip, and his face twisted in an agony of doubt.

"Take it," the old woman urged. "If not for your own sake, then for Daryn's. Kingslayer was to have been his, but he never came to know his full potential." She glanced around the dungeon. "You must hurry, Gaylon. My brother comes. He's heard Kingslayer's call, and I can no longer hold him back. Quickly! Take up the sword and destroy your enemies."

Tears spilled down Gaylon's cheeks. "My enemies are dead," he choked.

Another voice boomed in the broken chamber. "Take up my sword, and you'll have no end of enemies!"

A gust of moist, salty air swept through the ruined chamber and Jessmyn saw a small man in blue-black robes near the center of the floor. "Kingslayer is mine, and I will have it. Don't touch that sword!"

"No, Sezran!" Misk cried. She moved between Gaylon and the sorcerer.

"Stand away, Sister!"

The prince straightened, his sorrow gone. "Do as he says, Misk."

Fear stark on her face, the tiny woman stepped away.

"You've made my decision for me, old man," Gaylon called

to the wizard and reached for Kingslayer.

With a roar, Sezran clutched his Stone and raised the hand high. Blue lightning cracked and arced across the cold damp air. Gaylon dived clear, forced to abandon the sword. The floor erupted beneath his feet and stinging debris showered over them all. Straightening, the prince caught the wizard's next bolt with his ringed hand. His own Stone flared, and the youth flung the lightning back, doubled in size.

Jessmyn could see the fury in Gaylon's face, and it frightened her. All around came the stink of ozone and sulphur, and the ground rolled with such force under the magical blows that the princess fled back to the wall. Misk had taken refuge near the stair.

Sezran caught a flickering bolt from the air and fashioned it quickly into a great ball of fire. The blue glow was replaced by a white-hot incandescence, and he tossed the orb over his head. The small sun bobbed there momentarily before sliding behind him to drift lower. At his feet a Shadow crept across the straw-littered floor. The patch of darkness writhed and lengthened on its way to Gaylon.

The prince laughed. "Is that the best you can do? It seems the pupil must now instruct the teacher."

Blue light blazed from his ring. It swirled into a sphere and the color changed until above him, Gaylon's own white sun hovered, far bigger and brighter than Sezran's. Under the noonday glare, the wizard's Shadows withered and died. Sharply outlined, the prince's own long Shadow stalked the old man now.

Sezran shrieked with rage and began to whirl, his robes fluttering wildly. A wind roared in the chamber, an icy gale that flattened Gaylon's hair and forced him to squint against the blast. The storm spun toward him, and engulfed, he felt ice form instantly on his hands and face. His limbs grew stiff.

A brief fear swelled in the prince, and he called on his Stone. It answered, rebuilding the heat of his small sun, then drew the fireball into the storm. Ice melted, turned to steam that boiled away in hot clouds. Now the storm winds howled, but there was agony in that elemental voice. Gaylon, choking and scalded, fell to the floor. Fire and storm dissipated, and the prince found Sezran lying in the rubble only a pace away.

"Do you yield?" the little wizard panted. His black eyes glittered.

Gaylon managed a bitter laugh. "Do you?" He pushed himself upright and climbed slowly to his feet. "Whatever your claim, I am a Red King and heir to Kingslayer. The sword is mine."

"No," Sezran growled, but had no strength to rise.

The prince had already found the blade in the dust and debris. Misk came to stand beside him again, a smile on her thin lips.

"Take it," she said gently.

Jessmyn watched, and as Gaylon reached for the hilt, she was suddenly afraid. This was the legendary Kingslayer. Orym's Legacy had destroyed two kings—what might it do to Gaylon?

"No!" she cried and raced over the broken floor to stop him. Her hands closed on his wrist just as he gripped the sword, too late.

At the touch of the prince's ring, Kingslayer blazed once more into life, and the energy that surged through them both made Jessmyn cry out. A jumble of emotions slammed through her, incredible strength, and anger, then exultation. She fell back. Her hand tingled and ached as she watched him lift the weapon high.

The prince was no longer aware of her—of anything except what he held. Before Jessmyn's eyes, Gaylon was transformed, his red-bearded face suffused with joy and wonder, with power. He was truly a sorcerer king, the princess realized, heartsick.

"You fool!" wailed Sezran, finally on his feet.

"Hold your tongue, old man!" Gaylon snarled. He pointed Kingslayer at the wizard, and Sezran shrank back. "I *know* you now." The little mage flinched as if struck. Misk began to laugh, mirthlessly, but Gaylon went on, "I know you as thief and liar!"

Impotent fury flared onto Sezran's face. "How dare you,

you impudent upstart!"

"Beware how you speak to him, Brother," Misk said.

"Hush, little mother," Gaylon gently chided. There was both peace and passion in his eyes, but no hint of anger. "Listen, Sezran!" He struck the blade of the sword against the stones of the floor, and its song of power was terrible to hear. "Now that Kingslayer is mine, I shall take this world and everything in it. And when I'm done, the sword will lead me to other worlds. Even yours."

At these words, Misk bowed her head.

Sezran turned his fury on her now. "Woman! See what you've done? I told you he was too powerful, too erratic!"

"Hold your tongue!" Gaylon roared. Then smiling faintly, he looked at the tiny woman. "You have no need to fear me, good Misk. My life is only a moment next to yours, but because of you, mine will be long remembered. I'd never harm you." He looked up. "Or your brother."

The chamber grew strangely quiet, and now in the corners, other Misks moved restlessly, their sad murmuring drifting on the chill air. The one that stood before Gaylon looked at him with that same deep sadness Jessmyn had seen earlier.

"Once my brother took a stone that was not his—a black gem with the stars' fire caught in it," the woman murmured. "With its power, he brought us here, then used the gem to fashion a weapon, which he traded for a Sorcerer's Stone. Through Sezran's greed and selfishness, this world's destiny was long ago changed."

Misk's narrow face filled with regret. "I knew the risks of your taking up Kingslayer, but it had to be done. You are the only one capable of carrying your world into a new age. But mark me, Gaylon Reysson, the cost will be high. Sorrow and death will be your companions always.

"Perhaps it would have been better if the weapon had gone to Feydir," the tiny woman muttered. Her dark eyes stared into Gaylon's. "Evil as he was, he was at least shortsighted, unable to see beyond this one world. My brother may be right, I may have done a great wrong."

"No," Gaylon began, but Misk began to dwindle even as he

spoke, shrinking into some distant point until nothing remained. The prince's eyes glittered with fresh tears, but he turned a hardened face on the wizard. "You'll attend me here, old man, while I build my armies. You'll advise me."

"As you wish," Sezran said, oddly quiet, but there was a bitterness in his tone. "But beware, Red King. My curse on the weapon is strong. I need only wait. It *will* destroy you, and when it does, I shall be there to finally claim what is mine." His hand went to his Stone, and he was engulfed in a whirlwind that spun wildly across the floor, dissipating as it went until there was nothing left of the wind or the sorcerer.

Gaylon's eyes found Jessmyn, seeing her as if for the first time. His look terrified her, the triumph on his face, the intensity, the power. She spun and ran from him, dashed across the rubble-strewn ground.

"Jessmyn!"

She halted and turned, and with long, quick strides he was before her.

"Don't touch me," Jessmyn warned, her fear turning to anger.

Doubt replaced the look of triumph on the prince's face, and she was aware suddenly that she had power over him—the power that love provides. Her fear, even her anger disappeared then, only to be replaced by hope. It was clear to the princess that, in the long years of their separation, a darkness had come to fill Gaylon's soul; she had seen him mercilessly take his revenge upon Lucien, seen through the Stone his dark attack on Nankus's men. Yes, Jessmyn decided, a darkness has taken hold of Gaylon Reysson, and only I can help him overcome it.

The princess looked into his face, her heart pounding. Against Jessmyn's will, tears of sorrow flowed as Gaylon laid Kingslayer on the stones at her feet and brought gentle hands to her face. With blistered fingers, he drew back the honey-colored hair from her eyes and brushed the tears from her cheeks with his thumbs.

His touch was fever hot, and she closed her eyes, then felt his hands cup her ears. Slowly Gaylon tilted her head back, leaning close, his breath warm on her face. His lips brushed her eyelids, found her mouth and lingered there. She tasted the blood on them, felt the prickle of his mustache. His hands dropped to her shoulders, pulling her roughly against him, and she knew that hunger drove him. The kiss became demanding. This night, he had claimed his crown and his kingdom, and now he would claim one final thing. She couldn't stop him, and realized that she no longer wanted to.

Epilogue

❖

The news spread quickly, changing form and substance from place to place. Gaylon Reysson had returned from the dead to take his rightful seat on the throne of Wynnamyr. Some said that he was a gomeril, a puppet of an ancient, evil sorcerer called Sezran. Others said that he wielded a Sorcerer's Stone, that he carried Kingslayer, the fabled sword of power.

The white-haired men of the North whispered the news with fear. In the South, dark-eyed sailors took ship from the Inland Sea and carried the word to the nations all along the coast of the Western Sea and beyond. Not in a thousand years had one small country caused such a ripple in the pond of civilization—not since Orym, the Dark King, had first drawn Kingslayer and laid bloody waste to his neighbors.

For good or ill, another sorcerer king walked the world, and a millennium hadn't been long enough to cleanse the memory of the previous one. Mankind was terrified, and well they might have been.

Web of Futures

Jefferson P. Swycaffer

The tall man-shape with saucer eyes was covered from head to foot with dark, gleaming fur. It was definitely alien, while still being, in an odd way, earthly. Maddock O'Shaughnessy—born liar, tavern-goer, idle fisherman—felt himslf lifted up by the neck and held the way a man would display a rabbit. The next thing he knew, he was walking the strands of time in the house of webs. Incredibly, it was he who was picked to save men's lives, to collect their souls, and to roam the future. Available now.

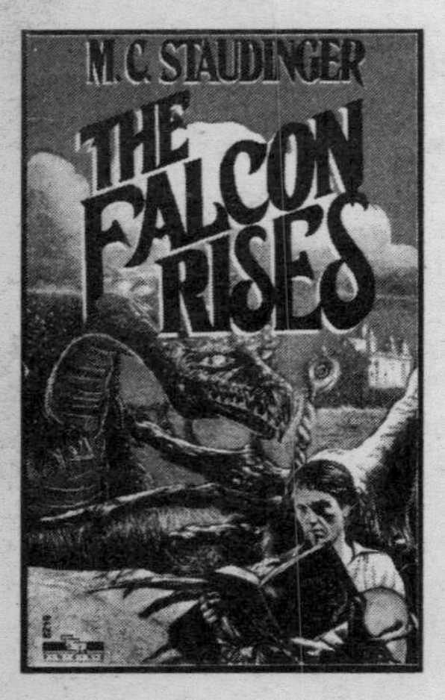

The Falcon Rises

Michael C. Staudinger

An overworked college professor is struck by lightning, and his energy pulse propels him into another plane. In this medieval fantasy world, he enlists the help of a falcon and some good dragons to fight the evil powers of the warlord Mordeth. On sale in June 1991.